The Redundant Wife

The Destruction and Resurrection of a Woman

KAY GREEN

Kay Green

THE REDUNDANT WIFE

Mum

My final promise to you was the launchpad for this book.
Thank you for teaching me how to be brave enough to dive
headfirst into my aspirations.

I love you xx

Prologue

The dreams didn't happen all the time.

My body silently stored up my needs and desires for as long as it could, and when it couldn't stand the frustration any longer, it released them while I was sleeping.

My dreams would take me to a man I didn't know, I never ever saw his face, just our mid fuck, naked flesh, my imaginary friend would be on top and inside me, the hips of our missionary position bodies moving in unison, I would be flooded with pleasure, right on the edge, two more thrusts and I would be on the glorious ride to an intense finish.

At precisely that point, on the verge of climax, my body quaking with the effort of getting myself to my ultimate goal, I would wake up with a jolt, deeply shocked by the intensity of the dream.

As a rule, I slept with my back to my husband, as he did me. Whenever I woke from these dreams, my vagina throbbing from the almost orgasm, I would turn over quickly to see if he had noticed my unusual movement, or if I had disturbed him in any way.

He would be oblivious, the same as he was when he was awake, to my yearning for sex.

The day after the dream I would be unsettled, the thought of my nighttime activities constantly on my mind. The realisation that I was having these mid-sleep fantasies because I wasn't getting the real thing kept hitting me time and again.

I was sad, I was lonely, and I was quite clearly horny.

Part One

The Destruction

1

Are you absolutely sure about this Rachel?

"Yes, Ivy I'm sure, we always knew this was going to happen, we've been discussing it for months."

Oh but Rach, it's such a long way down, look at all that water. The river's running really fast and see those rocks... Rach there's loads of rocks, they look dangerous. I'm a bit scared now we're here. I think we should turn around. No one knows we're here, so no one will ever know how close you came to doing it, your secret's safe.

I bend my body forward slightly so I can see beyond the toes of my grubby trainers that are slightly over the edge. She's right, it is one hell of a plunge, and if I'm honest, I'm a bit scared too, but the temptation to take the leap is becoming harder to resist by the second. Besides, I've planned this, I'm ready for it, I know it's the right thing to do. I don't want to quit now no matter how persuasive Ivy is. I lift my eyes from the sheer drop beneath me to look up at the cloudless sky; it is the most beautiful shade of blue I can ever remember seeing. The late afternoon sun is sharing its warmth with my shoulders and back, it is a glorious day, the perfect day to do this; if there ever was such a thing.

I glance down again and without warning, Ivy's fear invades me. My heart starts beating hard, the fear dries my mouth so quickly I can barely swallow. I look down at the water again, sparkling at me, taunting my bravery. I will my body to move but it refuses. In my panic I start to second guess myself, to rethink my long time plan: should I jump feet first or throw myself headfirst? Would one be quicker than the other, get it over with faster? Maybe Ivy is right, perhaps I should forget it and just carry on as if nothing had happened, act like I've never even been here, like the thought has never crossed my mind.

And then as quickly as it came the terror is replaced by a huge rush of relief, a sense of calm descends into the entirety of my being. I find my peace. I pull my shoulders back, take a deep breath through my nose as I shuffle my previously unwilling feet a tiny bit closer towards the point of no return. This is it. The right time.

Ivy's obstreperous voice brings me back again. *Do you ever wish things had been different? Maybe you should never have left that supermarket job you had straight after school?*

"For fuck's sake Ivy, I loved that job, it was you that insisted I'd never be truly happy filling shelves five and a half days a week, you insisted I look for more. You kick started my ambition!"

Yeah ok, fair cop. Well maybe you should have listened to your dad when he introduced you to that Trevor at the cricket club, he said he was a straight up guy, decent job, good prospects, that he'd look after you. You could have had 2.4 kids and a dog if you'd married him. We would never have ended up here if you'd taken that path.

"STOP re-writing history Ivy! We both agreed that there was no way I was going to latch myself to that life. Besides it was nearly 30 years ago, if I'd have married Trevor, I'd have grandchildren by now, I'd be doing the school run all over again, while my kids lived the life I'd always wanted. It would have been shit. Shut up now, I'm trying to concentrate."

What about that guy in Milan the other week with the sexy white teeth and incredible dress sense, no socks with his shoes, him? Maybe you should have gone back to his place when he asked you. He struck me as being a bit of a bad lad - the sex might have been amazing!

"I make it a habit of never having sex with men who can't remember my name!"

Can't argue with that.

I turn my focus back to my feet.

What about the guy in Geneva, let's have a chat about him then.

She stops me in my tracks there. The man in Switzerland had been a bit special. It's not every day a girl has sex on a fake fur rug on a balcony overlooking an iconic water fountain. God it was good sex too, his tongue was wide and long, and he'd dragged it slowly up my fizzy clit whilst I held myself as wide open as I could for him. Even now, under these circumstances, balancing precariously on a precipice, my vagina pulsed with joy.

Ok then, I'll give in. We can talk about Tim if you want. I know I've kept distracting you every time you've wanted to drag yourself back down heartache boulevard but if it'll stop you from doing this ridiculousness, *then we can talk about him for as long as you like. I won't even yawn or roll my eyes I promise. Deal? Just step away from the edge, turn round, walk back the way you came and let's go for a beer.*

"I don't want to talk about Tim. I can't go there again, it was too hard, I was so broken. I don't want to think about any of that anymore. I just want to jump."

Oh fuck, fuck, fuck, I love you Rachel, but are you sure I've got to come with you?

"Of course you do Ivy, you're my inner voice. Where I go, you go."

Shit. Well at least close your eyes for me please.

So I do. But not for long.

2

I used the time spent in this Friday afternoon traffic jam productively. I've familiarised myself with my brand new company car, I've worked out the state-of-the-art hands-free phone system, I've sussed out how to turn off the heated seats and I finally managed to get the bass on the stereo just right; I fiddled with the control buttons for ages - studiously ignoring Inner Voice Ivy who insisted I read the handbook – and now to celebrate, my gym-fit - and now much cooler - arse cheeks, were clenching in time to the beat of a Sister Sledge tune at a volume that was making my rear-view mirror shudder.

I was in a great mood. I'd had a very rewarding week at work, I sold medical surgical equipment, and I had done it, very successfully, for years; but yesterday I closed my biggest deal ever, the result of nearly a year's hard work. To mark my success I'd stopped at the wine merchants on my way home and bought three bottles of Veuve, they were chilling in the wine fridge now waiting for me. I was hoping to be halfway down the first bottle by the time my husband Tim got home from his business trip and my best friend Jude turned up so that the three of us could celebrate her 42nd birthday week-end.

****

When I finally got myself free from the traffic jam I drove the last part of the motorway journey home just a bit too fast, I could have used the fact that I needed to pee as an excuse, but in truth, I was indulging myself with the exhilaration the speed of my new car gave me, it excited me. I was excited, and not just for the evening's party and our 'oh I only do this on special occasions' cigarettes and Charlie, I'm excited about my life. I carried a perpetual sense of a thrill that Tim and my many years of hard work and dedication to our careers and each other had paid off, we lived in the house of our dreams, we had great friends, I had a job I loved that kept me in the style I have become very accustomed to, a shoe collection so big it had its own wardrobe and a husband I adored.

I believed had everything I had ever wanted either at, or very close to, my fingertips.

This evening was going to change all that though, it would create a chink, that over time would become a hole, that would eventually become a vortex of destruction: of me.

3

April 25th 2008

1.45 am (there or thereabouts)

Turgid, it's turgid. Seriously Rach you need to check out his cock!

I really didn't need Inner Voice Ivy to bring my attention to my husband's penis. Trust me when I tell you his rock-hard dick was impossible to miss, it was a significant feature of the horror I was currently living through; cornered by a beautiful young woman wearing Primark's finest, breast-enhancing underwear.

I had never seen my husband behave like this before; Tim was sitting upright in a chair designed for lounging, he had the look of a begging dog, he was definitely panting and he hadn't taken his eyes away from the lap dancer's magnificent cleavage for quite some time. He was mesmerised by her, while I was stuck between a rock - looking like a boring, up-tight middle-aged woman - and a hard place - surrendering to Tim's coercion to join in with his – obviously cock-led - wish for a couple's lap dance.

****

If I'm forced to be specific about when the night took a turn for the worse, I would have to say it was while Jude and I were on our age-old traditional double-up visit to a toilet cubicle, taking it in turns to snort a line of coke off a specially designed compact mirror (yes, I know it's ridiculous) and having a wee each. She was fresh-hit-high and more than a bit drunk when she casually suggested we drink up and move the party on to somewhere else, like the local lap dance bar. We had been best friends long enough for her to know, even before she suggested it, that my first reaction would be to refuse, but she knew today of all days, she had a huge advantage over me, and she was making the most of it.

As Jude was giving me her best insouciant stare waiting for the agreement she knew was hard for me but would come anyway, Ivy was shouting at me. *Do not give in to her, Rachel. She's not being fair to you. Who in their right mind wants to go to a place that offers sex for sale with their husband? You know you don't want to go, don't say yes to it, for fuck's sake!*

What was I supposed to do, though? Jude was recently single and, as usual when she'd had a breakup with a totally 'told you so' unsuitable man, she'd decided she finally wanted to 'have a go with a woman for a change' to explore her bisexual side, I figured she was presuming a lap dance bar would be the ideal place to start...

How could I refuse? It was her birthday after all. And there were long-established rules for birthdays.

4

April 1982

For Jude's 16th birthday, I had surprised her with a trip to the ice rink, I thought it would be a laugh, there were usually some fit lads to flirt with and the bar staff were pretty lackadaisical about checking your age before serving you a lager and lime. Unfortunately, she'd been anticipating getting dolled up and going to the local disco.

After that crushing disappointment we'd agreed - whoever's birthday it is gets to choose what we do to celebrate it, and the other is not allowed, under any circumstances, to say no to the suggestion, they just must go with the flow.

One year in our early 20's she'd made us go to the ballet – it was a phase she was going through at the time - the only thing that made it bearable was the spliff we'd had beforehand and the sight of all that male junk trapped in tight tights. She grew out of her cultural pretensions immediately after that and for her next birthday we went limbo dancing while shooting tequila. I was sick for days after.

There was a theme throughout Jude's celebrations, they usually involved drug use, too much alcohol and were generally bloody exhausting.

This one was about to be beyond anything we'd experienced before though.

5

April 2008

And now I found myself pinned with fear to a wipe-clean red vinyl chair, while a smiling marriage assassin in a nylon G string offered to take us both to a private cubicle so she could gyrate her arse cheeks, and by default her youthful vagina, over both mine and my husband's laps – and all for the introductory starter price of twenty five quid.

Of course, now we were in the club and I could have done with her help, there was no bloody sign of Jude. It was just me, the titty girl and Tim and I was starting to feel a bit left out, to be honest. She was not stupid this young woman, she was selling her wares, and it was obvious from the way his penis was happily bobbing up and down underneath his favourite going-out trousers that she'd already got Tim on her side. I was trying to get his attention by staring at his profile while he stared at the fake lace on the double D cup of desire. When I finally managed to speak there was an unmistakable pleading in my voice. "I don't want to do this. Please don't put me in this position Tim, I'm not comfortable with this situation at all, please stop this, let's go home." He eventually turned to look at me and our eyes connected, his eyes were brimming with lust for her and he was giving me the facial equivalent of a 'fuck you'. He wasn't ready to stop this, not even for me. It felt like he'd forgotten me, that I didn't figure in this man's

14

mind right then, because the image of her was burned into his retinas. It scared me shitless and made me furious at the same time.

He shook his head at me, a defiant refusal to put a halt to proceedings and I found I could barely breathe, I needed air. I stood up quickly and took myself across the club, through the wide selection of bare arse cheeks and high heels touting for business, to the exit. When I finally stepped outside the first thing I did was scrounge a cigarette from the bouncer on duty at the door. My hands were shaking so badly he had to hold the lighter for me.

He was chatty and comical and as I smoked I tried hard to go along with his banter, but I didn't hear much of what he was saying. I was too busy having an out-of-body experience, trying to work out what going on with Tim.

Inner voice Ivy came through to me loud and clear *More to the point Rachel what's he doing now? Cos he certainly hasn't come looking for you!*

I didn't need her to point out the obvious to me. I crushed the end of my borrowed smoke with the toe of my uncomfortable high heels, and headed back into the lioness's den, knowing with complete certainty that when I went back into the room he'd be gone.

And he was.

He was nowhere to be seen. He was in the cubicle with a young woman, dancing for him, just the two of them. Him and her.

And he'd left my handbag on the table, the fucking prick!

I left the club and went home.

6

By the time I got through the front door of my beloved home, I was so full of anger I didn't even sigh with relief when I kicked my shoes off. When I'd reached inside my bag to pay the fare for my ride home, I realised I had our party packet of cigarettes and the coke wrap; I took a little bit of satisfaction from that. I set myself up in the kitchen at the breakfast bar with a drink and lit a cigarette. I lifted the middle finger of my right hand in response to Ivy attempting to chime in something about not being allowed to smoke in the house.

****

I adored my husband there wasn't anything about him I didn't delight in. We met at a rave in the early 90s, we were stood next to each other at the bar. It was the heat radiating from his body that first grabbed my attention and when I turned to look fully at him, his white T-shirt was wet with sweat and sticking to his body. He was tall, a lot taller than me - I liked that - he was dark too, brown eyes, and the hairs on his arms and head were almost black, and slick with moisture. I took it as a very good sign that he'd obviously been having as much fun with the music as I had. He must have sensed me looking at him and when he turned his head and smiled at me, I was instantly fascinated by his face. He was gorgeous. He insisted on paying for my drinks and I led him by the hand to the place Jude and I had claimed as our own little piece of dance floor and the three of us bonded over an illegal pill with a cherry stamped on it, ciggies, and some very energetic dance moves. We'd been together ever since; we classed that as our first date.

We had a strong friendship and marriage, he was my soul mate, he would never do anything to hurt me. Which is why I was completely stunned by the events of the last hour or so. No matter which way I thought about it, I found it hard to comprehend the whole scenario with Tim and the titty-girl. His behaviour didn't seem real, none of it made any sense. It was just so out of character, like he'd been possessed by his evil twin.

Where do you suppose he is now, the fanny-hungry doppelgangor who's replaced your man – is he still at the club in that tiny room, getting his money's worth? Him and her, all alone the two of them, so private and intimate? Inner Voice Ivy wasn't going to let me live in denial for long.

A shudder of revulsion forced its way up my spine as I pushed back images of Tim with the lapdance girl. She'd danced for my husband, on my husband, she'd titillated him, turned him on. While I was in the back of a cab on my way home, she'd had her vagina hanging over my husband's cock.

Cheeky. Fucking. Bitch.

I needed to know what was going on. I retrieved my phone from the bottom of my handbag, and for a few happy seconds I imagined Tim had texted me to say he was sorry, and he was on his way home. But there was no message from him. I texted Jude to see if she knew where he was.

"Where are you?"

It took two songs from the iPod, one and a half ciggies and a tiny little snort up a filthy ten-pound note for her to answer. "Still in the club."

"Is Tim with you?"

She came back to me almost instantly this time, "Yeah babe, we're just having a beer and a chat."

About what? sneered Ivy. *The state of the economy? How movie stars shouldn't become presidents? What is there to discuss? Why isn't she here with you? Why isn't he here with you?* Inner Voice Ivy filled in the time between my text and Jude's reply.

"He says he doesn't understand why you didn't want to join in, or why you made such a big fuss over it all and stormed out. He says it was just a bit of fun." Another text followed: "Why did you walk out Rachel?"

WHAT THE FUCK? Cheeky bastard! I heard Ivy loud and clear but despite her fury doubt crept in to confuse me. Jude had always been straight with me, always on my side, and if she didn't see the wrong in what he'd done, paying a scantily clad woman to dance for him, then surely it must be me at fault. Maybe I was a boring middle-aged woman?

Ivy came immediately to my rescue.

Didn't do anything wrong? Just a bit of fun? What is wrong with her! He ridiculed and bullied you and then watched you walk away from a situation he knew you were scared of. Instead of following you like any decent human being should have done, to make sure you were ok, he let you walk away and then put himself directly into the firing line of that girl's tits. She's not right, he's not right, don't start second guessing yourself - you have every right to be furious.

I couldn't bring myself to text Jude back. I threw my phone back into my handbag and got another drink.

I sat for what seemed like hours, my head reeling. Another drink, another smoke, watching the clock, waiting for the sound of the key in the door, until eventually, finally, at last, I heard a taxi come up the drive. My head turned quickly to the hallway, and I saw car lights shine through the glass on the front door. I heard doors slam and then their loud voices as they headed toward the house.

They'd come home together, like we always did on any other night out, particularly the ones we didn't want to end. We would come back to ours for more fun; but this evening wasn't fun, at least not for me. I braced myself for the emotions I knew were on the way, my heart thudding in my chest as I tried to compose myself.

They came into the house together talking loudly to each other, both shored up with the confidence of each other's company, booze, and no doubt more Charlie. (Jude would have managed to score from someone at the club; she had a talent for that.)

There was a conceited arrogance radiating from Tim, it was clear to me that the lengthy chat they'd been having had given him a sense of self-righteous indignation. He gave me a dismissive look as he walked into the kitchen, Jude following behind him like his faithful little lapdog. At least I got a smile from her.

As soon as they stepped into the room they started talking at me and I was instantly faced with the onslaught of direct confrontation. Words came tumbling from each of them - excuses, reasons, justifications. They'd made their minds up between them that he was completely blameless, and I found myself on the back foot, guilty of being boring for not wanting to partake, foolish for blowing things out of proportion. There wasn't one word of apology from Tim, not one hint of a sorry. He showed no remorse at all.

As they talked, they were moving around the kitchen, both busy with a separate task. Part way through some bullshit about how he hadn't realised how upset I was, Tim actually held his hand up to pause the conversation while he asked Jude if she wanted beer or wine. She stopped her concentration on chopping out the contents of a newly acquired (told you!) bag of coke to tell him, 'Beer please,' and then continued her task, as he took up where he'd left off - blaming me for not making it clear enough that I objected to him going for a lap dance on his own.

I hadn't said a word yet. I was astounded by their behavior but transfixed by them both. I slowly swivelled my bar stool to turn towards them and continued to watch them in fascination, they were behaving so normally. I listened to them both; him justifying himself with every word that left his lips, and her chipping in every now and again supporting what he said. It was surreal, like they had been on a completely different night out to me.

Despite the temptation to say something to them, I sat silently and listened until my anger got so fierce and consuming that I nearly crushed my still-empty glass in my fingers; Tim hadn't asked me what I wanted to drink when he'd asked Jude.

I couldn't watch or hear another thing from either of them and for the first time since they came into the house, I made an obvious and aggressive movement. I stood up swiftly, and they both stopped speaking mid-sentence. I felt sure Jude had moved her body away from me a little bit, just to be on the safe side.

"I appreciate that you two have had time for a long chat over lots of beers and maybe a couple of extra lap dances while the wife's been out of the picture. And it's obvious that between you, you've built a story you are both so convinced with, you think I should forgive and forget the minute you explain it to me. But I'm here to tell you both, however, you paint it, this is an unacceptable situation."

I could feel my anger rushing to the surface, uncontrollable, I was shaking as I pointed my finger at the man I'd shared my bed with for over a decade. "You're a fucking idiot. You had no consideration for me this evening, you were thinking with your greedy, selfish cock! I have seen a side to you that I didn't even realise existed. I'm shocked and appalled by you." my chin wobbled a bit but there was no way I was going to let this anger be ruined by tears "I strongly suggest that you get out of my sight and when you wake up in the morning, full of shame and remorse, come back to me and we can talk again." I nodded my head in the direction of the hall, "You can go now! You're not the man I thought you were, but I'm hoping that when this beer wears off and you look back at the way you've treated me, you'll be mortified by your behaviour."

The look he gave me was full of insolence, he met my stare and held it steadily. I hardened myself for an eyeball battle and refused to look away. I could sense Jude watching us - she hated confrontation and whether she intended to or not she broke the staring deadlock by knocking her beer over. Tim turned to see what the noise was as Ivy spoke. *That was an aco bit of sticking up for yourself Rachel, up yours Tim, you wanker.*

Releasing my outrage left me feeling a bit calmer, more in control. I also had a fleeting sense of victory at my win of the eye-contact competition. But it would all have been non-existent if my crystal ball had been switched on because the events of this evening were just a tiny insight into things to come.

As Tim's newly revealed self-centered behaviour continues, it would take over the gentle, loving man I thought was my husband. There wouldn't be many more staring competitions for us because he'd avoid direct eye contact with me altogether. Instead, he would, from then on, have shifty eyes that rarely met mine because he was afraid that I would discover the secrets behind them.

7

No one was more surprised than me when he did as I'd demanded and left the room leaving me with Jude. Neither of us spoke until the sound of Tim's footsteps, on the continually creaky floorboards in our bedroom directly above us, stopped. She was still standing out of arms' reach, her eyes cast downwards looking at the pattern on the mosaic tiles on the floor. As she did that, I watched her. I knew she could feel the weight of my stare on her - but she didn't look up - she couldn't meet my eyes either.

I realised two things simultaneously - I'd made a great job of the kitchen renovation and Jude was letting me down. A lot.

Still not looking in my direction, she moved over to the wine fridge and pulled out the bottle of champagne she'd brought with her, one that we hadn't had a chance to drink earlier in the evening. She reached for a couple of flutes from the cupboard above her head and brought them to the table.

She set the glasses down gently and passed me the bottle to open. I took it without a word and worked my magic with the cork. As I felt it leave the bottle with a satisfying gentle pop, I looked over to her. We smiled a small knowing smile at each other, our eyes finally meeting.

We were both aware how much of a thrill I got from breaking open a bottle of decent bubbly. How, as we'd become more successful in our careers, more financially secure, champagne had become our essential item for a night worthy of celebration and whenever we indulged in a bottle, I was always the one to pop the cork, and I never spilt a drop. We always joked it was one of my superpowers.

The intimacy of the exchange broke the ice between us and in another familiar move, she lit a cigarette and handed it to me, and then fished another one out of the packet for herself. When that too was lit, she said softly, "He didn't mean any harm you know. He thought it was a bit of fun you could have together.

Disappointment hit me hard. "And what do you think? Do you really think it was just a bit of fun? Can you see the harm in it?"

She shrugged. "Not really, no."

While they'd sat together in that filthy club and talked, she'd taken his side. Should I try to convince her otherwise? Should I shout at her the same way I had him? Should I try to influence her thinking by insisting that my own feelings and thoughts were more important than Tim's? At that moment, without her support, I'm not even sure they were.

When I eventually spoke, my voice was quiet and full of the disappointment I was carrying with me. "Tell me what he said."

She shrugged again, giving herself a moment to gather her thoughts. "Like I said, he presumed you'd be up for it. That it would be a bit of a laugh."

Bullshit! Ivy's unequivocal declaration was accompanied by an exasperated blow of air that left my body quickly.

Jude pulled the mirror of pre-chopped lines towards her, snorted the fattest one among them, then slid it over to me. I couldn't face it; I pushed it out of the way. I was impatient with her stalling tactics. "Jude, just tell me will you. I'm heartbroken."

The line had done its job. It had shored her confidence back up again, making her freer with her words. More confident, and, to be honest, a bit more of a twat. It was almost as if he was speaking through her, as she explained his reasons and his thinking.

"He assumed that because you were willing to go to the club, because you'd agreed to it you'd also feel the same about taking part in whatever went on there."

Ivy's voice came into the conversation. *Are you going to let her carry on defending him Rachel? Really?*

"But, Jude, he forgot me. He left me, and my handbag, and went in that room with that girl to get his rocks off, just him, his hard on, and a complete stranger dancing for him in exchange for our hard-earned cash. It's the concealment of his pleasure that bothers me most. The out-of-sight nature of the situation; that he forgot me and went behind my back."

She took another swig of her drink. I could see the head shake of disagreement start up and as she put her glass down her shoulders were heading towards her ears in anticipation of a careless shrug. I was amazed she was being so stubborn about this, that she couldn't see my point of view. "He got carried away, that's all."

I threw my hands into the air in frustration, my anger starting to build again. "He was horrible to me Jude! He ridiculed me. I genuinely felt uncomfortable and threatened in there. I told him that, but he didn't care. His cock took over and his brain stopped working. My husband is always telling me it's his job to make sure I'm the happiest I can be, and that if I'm happy he's happy. Well, I wasn't very happy then, and he knew it, and he still went ahead. Self-centered prick."

I had to turn away from her, I couldn't stand to see her do that shrug again. I hoped that when the booze and drugs wore off a bit in the morning she'd come to her senses and be as pissed off with him as I was, because he had treated me appallingly.

Tim knew it too. He'd lobbied her during those hours in the club, because in the back of his head, he knew he was wrong.

He needed Jude on his side, to help dampen the flames of my argument. I'd every right to be bloody furious, and instead of admitting it, he'd stolen her from me in order to vindicate himself. His self-righteous indignation was intact. Not only had he disrespected me, he'd manipulated her too. He used her to get to me. And by all accounts, listening to her now, it has worked.

Jude started to tidy the kitchen. The tidying up thing was her unconscious signal that she was done for the day. Silently, I watched her fill the dishwasher, wipe down all the work-surfaces, empty the ashtray.

It was nearly 3.30 am, technically the day after her birthday, but I still wanted to be sure to let her know I hadn't forgotten why we'd gone out in the first place. My anger was spent. In a much more gentle tone I said, "Happy birthday darling, I hope some of it was good at least. Before you got in the middle of this marital cluster fuck. Did you have fun?"

She wiped the top of the breakfast bar where we'd been sat across from each other, dropped the cloth in the sink and picked up her shoes and handbag, to take them up to her room with her. "I've had better, and I've had worse. Do you know what though Rach? I decided maybe I'm happy being straight, that I didn't want to get a lap dance after all. The chicks working there looked a bit...... oh I don't know, I suppose they all looked a bit cheap."

Ivy shouted, *You stupid bitch, you're as narcissistic as he is!*

8

The sound of Jude in her room at the front of the house getting ready to settle down for the night and the not-so-gentle snores coming from mine and Tim's bedroom directly above my head created a huge wave of sadness and loneliness in me. They'd both left me on my own; in more ways than one.

I was profoundly dispirited by their attitude and exhausted from the amount of energy I'd wasted trying to get my point across.

I made a cup of tea and unearthed my secret stash of ciggies from the back of the pan cupboard. I needed to get away from the constriction of the house, from the sounds created by the two perpetrators of my misery. I stepped through the huge floor-to-ceiling glass doors into the back garden and sat on one of the wooden patio chairs, bracing myself for the feel of cold and damp on my bum cheeks.

The light that glowed softly from the kitchen behind me was the only thing that broke up the darkness and I felt the cool early April air start to cling to me. I'd only intended to take a deep breath of the freshness it offered, but almost as soon as I took the breath in, I started to cry the tears that had formed from my outrage and wretchedness. The emotion shook my body and the disbelief at the way the evening had turned out hit me all over again.

The memory of Tim's servile reaction to the girl in the club brought more sobs. As did the thought of the two people I trusted more than anyone else in the world repeatedly telling me that the lap dance incident was nothing to be concerned about, merely a moment of madness. They had tried to convince me it could even have been my own fault.

Sleep was a stranger to me that night, the same as it would be for many nights to come. In the end I would lose count of the number of times I would stay awake all night watching the sunrise through eyes full of tears, my puffy face and bloated eyelids telling their own story of my misery the following day.

I sometimes wonder if, in the early hours of that morning after the lap dance incident, I'd been able to see what was in store for me over the next few years what I would've done. If I'd known what the future had in store for me would I have left there and then, or would I have let my belief in my marriage persuade me to stand my ground and fight for it?

Because that's what happened, I did stay in our relationship and I fought hard for it, I was a stubborn, foolish woman and I almost lost myself for the sake of a man that wasn't even mine anymore.

9

By the time I heard the tread of footsteps upstairs again, I was halfway through an obligatory Saturday morning, middle-class TV cooking show, watching a bright-eyed TV Chef demonstrating how to create a flavoursome lamb tagine. I felt awful. I still hadn't slept, and just to add more misery upon misery my hangover was kicking in with a vengeance. My eyes were sore from crying and last night's makeup was now mostly under my chin and on my chest in little rivulets of dried-up tears. In short, I felt and looked like shit.

I knew from the impression of the sounds that it was Jude getting up. I could tell she's trying to tiptoe, to be quiet, so she didn't wake us. She didn't know I hadn't even gone to bed. I left the celebrity chef to carry on explaining about the origins of couscous to an empty room and moved into the kitchen. I stood by the kettle because I knew no matter how desperate she was to get out of the house, out of harm's way, there was no way she would leave the scene of the crime without coming into the kitchen. I'm not convinced she even knew how to start her car without at least one cup of coffee in her.

As she walked through the door, she did a little gasp. I'm not sure if it was in horror at my being in the kitchen, lying in wait for her, or at how bloody awful I looked. She didn't look very fresh herself in all honesty, but at least she'd taken last night's makeup off.

"Fuck's sake Rach you made me jump. What time did you get up?"

I pretended to check my wrist for my watch "Oh not that long ago. I think it was about 6.30 am. Yesterday."

She pointed towards me - not at me, but at the kettle "Well you must have loads of energy to put that on then and make a brew." Her familiarity was forced, not like her at all.

We spent the next few minutes with a very rare silence between us. I made myself busy with the mugs and coffee while she was doing some spurious rummaging in the bottom of her handbag to keep herself busy, keeping her eyes out of any danger of meeting mine.

While I was watching her not watch me, I realised how sore my eyes were from keeping them open so long and crying so much. It actually hurt to blink. My hangover was awful, and I needed to sleep, but there was no way I was letting her go without her looking at me directly and telling me she still thought Tim was in the right.

I dragged my weary self over to the breakfast bar and we sat in the same places we had been last night.

I finally gave in and rubbed my eyes; hard.

Jude finally broke the silence. "Fancy a line and a smoke?"

My bent head shot up and my face turned towards hers in shock. She smiled at me. Her eyes looked a bit watery; her bottom lip was a bit shaky. This turn of events was unprecedented, she rarely cried, and we hadn't had ciggies for breakfast since we officially 'gave up smoking' about 5 years ago; those days we only smoked when we drink - i.e. often. And we had never had a line of coke unless it was a special occasion and definitely not before the pubs opened.

She took a deep juddery breath in and spoke quickly "I took half a sleeping tablet when I went to bed. It did its trick. I passed out for a bit, so at least one of us got some sleep." She looked at me apologetically, "I woke up about half an hour ago, and it took me a few minutes to remember what had gone on last night. Seriously, Rachel, have you got any ciggies?"

I reached in the pocket of my dress, the one I had been wearing since yesterday evening and threw her my mostly empty packet. She lit one quickly. "The thing is, when I woke, I had the worst feeling of dread in me. I knew something was wrong, but I honestly couldn't think why I felt so bad. I had to concentrate really hard so I could remember what had happened last night. When it finally came to me, I was horrified at how I'd treated you. I am so sorry. I was such a fucking idiot." Her voice quivered and she took a huge gulp of her coffee to cover up any real show of emotion. Her eyes met mine over the rim of her cup and I could see them filling up a little bit.

I was relieved to say the least. Mostly because while she had been reversing her thoughts during her sleep and in her early waking moments, I had spent all night awake, torturing myself, asking myself if I'd been wrong to be so angry with him and in part, if I'm being totally honest, with her. "Thanks Jude, I needed to hear that."

"You were owed it babe, I'm sorry. His argument seemed so plausible last night. He was so sure that he was right, he managed to convince me too."

"Yeah well, I'll deal with his version of events when he eventually stirs himself. I'm probably better off not knowing the answer to this question, but I'm going to ask you anyway. Did he have more than one dance?" Even in my own head I sounded casual in my approach to the query, but as soon as I'd asked her my heart started to beat harder in my chest, I was so afraid of her reply.

She looked at me for a couple of seconds, and I could tell she was still uncomfortable telling a tale on him - even to me, "The girl that was coming on to you both earlier in the evening, the one with great tits and cheap undies?"

I nodded. "You mean the one that he went off with while I was still there?"

"Yeah her, well she came to sit with us a couple of times while we were talking, she was flirty and really suggestive with him. I reckon she knew she was on to a good thing. I think he'd done that over-tipping thing he does everywhere he goes. She came around another time while I was stood at the bar waiting to be served. I watched them have a chat, then she grabbed his hand, and they went off again."

She was about to carry on with the details, I knew that because I was about to insist on them, but at that precise moment we heard movement above our heads. It was coming from our - mine and Tim's - bedroom; Tim was awake and out of bed. Jude clammed up instantly. Both of us were looking at the kitchen ceiling trying to work out from the noise of his footsteps if he was coming in our direction. It sounded like he was.

Jude looked at me in panic. She looked trapped and scared.

"I think it's time for you to go and start your lovely birthday weekend mate. Have some fun for me, will you?"

She didn't even ask me if I was sure it was ok, to check if I really meant it, she just gulped the last of her brew down in one go, stole a cigarette out of the packet on the table and went to leave. She dropped a kiss on my cheek on the way past, "Good luck babe, I'm sorry again, remember you're in the right. Call me if you need me."

I followed her progress down the hall, her head turned as she flicked a worried look up the stairs, checking for Tim. I watched her bend over to scoop her bags that she had left by the door. She took her keys off the hook she always left them on, unlocked the door and was gone in record time. I almost wish I could tell you I heard her tyres squealing as she left the drive, just for extra dramatic effect, but I didn't. Instead as the front door closed behind her and silence fell on the house once again, I realised that Tim had stopped moving about upstairs.

He'd gone back to bed.

10

I realised I couldn't stay awake much longer. I was so sad, and so tired, I needed to give my eyes a rest, to close them and sleep. Preferably for the rest of the weekend.

I couldn't bear to take myself into the same space as Tim. There was no way I was getting into bed with him, so I used the bathroom in Jude's room. I finally took my makeup off and brushed my teeth, the combination of stale booze and every cigarette I'd smoked left a residue, a smell that told its own story of the last few hours. They'd left a bitter taste in my mouth. I had a hot shower, that felt so good. I didn't want to leave the enclosed space of the warm steamy glass box, but I did eventually. I dried myself as ineffectively as I always do and then fell into the bed Jude had left less than an hour ago. It was still slightly warm from her body. I could smell her perfume, but I could also smell her remnants of the night before, her own staleness.

I was desperate to go to sleep but as soon as my body started to relax my guard slipped and the tears came again. I didn't hold back this time, I didn't deny myself my hungover, sorrowful, angry release.

I lay with my head under the covers, feeling my breath add to the warmth already trapped inside 10 togs. The weight of the duvet acted as a silencer for the wail of anger and sadness that came to me as I remembered that Tim had been back to the girl for seconds.

I reckon I was almost done with the sobbing and the "you fucking bastard-ing." I don't think it would have been very long before I cried myself to sleep but the stillness that came between the sobs gave me the chance to hear the bedroom door open. I sensed Tim in the room with me. I was so stunned I didn't know what to do. I was desperate for him to get the message as quickly and efficiently as possible, that I was very fucking angry with him, but he'd caught me mid vulnerable. I sensed him come to the side of the bed I was curled into. I didn't feel him sit on the bed but when he spoke, I knew his face was directly next to mine, only the duvet separated us.

"Rachel?" his voice was quiet, gentle, "please stop crying..." He seemed to stop mid-sentence, like he was searching for another thing to say, as if he couldn't quite decide what came next. I kept my head under the covers. His voice was even quieter this time as he said, "I'm sorry."

There they were the words I had been waiting for. I expected to be delighted, but all they did was create more anger. I'd been sure all along he would say apologise to me - eventually. I'd been positive that he would be desperately regretful when he had stopped being a cocaine superhero. Because despite evidence to the contrary Tim is a genuinely nice man, and he loves me.

"Fuck off Tim." A nice original come back.

"Can we talk please?" he shook my duvet covered shoulder very lightly.

I pulled myself away from him violently. I sat up quickly, taking the covers with me to be sure that I maintained my dignity. Despite the fact he had invaded my space, and apologised, there was no way he was seeing my tits. "What? Talk? Why?"

I saw him then for the first time since I'd left the club when he had been panting like a thirsty dog in the mid-day sun. He looked a lot different now. He looked hungover and tired. He looked like a man who that knew he'd pushed his luck way too far. I almost felt some pity for him; I wanted to comfort him, to help him feel better, because that was my job, to support him when he was so upset. Reliably, Ivy slapped me back into reality. *Comfort him? Why would you do that? Stop being such a push over, let him suffer.*

"What, so you can feed me that total bollocks that you fed Jude? So you can try and find justification in your actions by blaming me?" Ivy urged me on. *That was a good one, you've got him on the ropes now, have another go!* I didn't need telling twice.

"The excuses you used last night with Jude are useless with me and you can apologise all you want but I won't accept it. You were a disrespectful prick."

"It was stupid. I was stupid, I was drunk, I was high; I thought we were both up for it."

"And?"

"I'm so sorry, so very sorry. It was a massive mistake; it won't happen again Rachel." His grey, hungover face with its hang-dog expression made me want to punch him. The softness and forgiveness that I'd been teetering on the edge of less than a minute earlier, were gone. At least for now.

"Fuck off Tim. I'm not interested in your bullshit or your apologies." He had the cheek to look affronted by my rejection of his attempt to get into my good books. I slid back down the bed and pulled the covers back over my head to let him know it wasn't working. That I was done talking.

"Can I get you anything babe? A cup of tea, something to eat? Anything at all?"

I didn't reply. I was seething with fury. I felt him get up from the floor beside me and cocked my ear out of the quilt so I could hear him as he closed the door behind him.

11

I put my head back under the covers, back into my safe, warm space. Inner Voice Ivy wasn't about to give me any of the peace I craved though. It wasn't as if putting my fingers in my ears would shut her up.

I shudder to think how much of a tip he pushed down the front of that dancer's 36DD bra; in fact, hang on, what if she'd taken her bra off? Do you suppose he saw her breasts? Did she undress for him? How aroused was he? Oh my god, what if she gave him a wank?

That sent my tears and anxiety into overdrive. I knew I would never swallow my pride enough to ask him if any of this were true, and I wasn't sure he would be honest with his answers even if I did. I stayed on the merry-go-round of thoughts and conversations with him in my head, talking to myself and Ivy under the covers, the pain of his carelessness lighting a fire of fury in my belly, then I fell back into crying as I imagined what had gone on with my husband and that casual marriage terrorist in peep-toe high heels. I spent hours torturing myself with a train of thought that kept coming, kept increasing my anguish, and producing more tears.

At some point during my self-inflicted mental agony I heard Tim come back into the room. I stilled myself and pretended to be asleep. I felt him touch my shoulder very gently; I ignored him. He did it again; I still ignored him. When I was convinced he'd left the room I lowered the duvet, I must confess the fresh air was nice, it was a bit smelly under those covers. As I freed myself further, I saw a familiar brown McDonalds bag sat on the bedside cabinet. As soon as my eyes saw it, my tummy realised how hungry it was. I might be still mad with him, but there was no need to cut my nose off to spite my face. The smell of the food was taunting me, and I couldn't resist the bag any longer.

A large Big Mac meal, with an extra cheeseburger and a large fizzy, ice cold drink. This man knows me so well. I ate the lot. I didn't even take the gherkins off. Eating calmed my spirits no end and within minutes of devouring my junk food I could feel myself sliding into sleep. No thoughts this time, even Ivy had clocked off for the day, and now it was time to rest, to find a bit of peace and quiet for my exhausted brain.

I slept until the next morning. I didn't even wake up for a pee.

* * * * * * * * * *

When I eventually opened my eyes, it took me a couple of seconds to realise where I was. As I started to come round from my sleep, I remembered why I was in Jude's bed. I tested myself to see how I felt about everything that had happened in the last 36 hours. It was the mental equivalent of probing the hole in a bad tooth with your tongue: I knew the action wasn't going to be without consequence, and that it would cause me some pain, but I had no idea how bad it was actually going to feel until I did it. I let my guard down slowly and allowed the emotions to come to me. I felt like most of my anger had gone - I found out much later that in fact it was only pretending to be gone. The truth of the matter was, it had just found a very clever hiding place, buried itself deep, and rested itself there for quite some time (despite Ivy's strenuous attempts to win-kle it out) – but for now, at least, I was relieved by its absence. I remembered the peace offering of junk food that Tim had left me. I couldn't see the empty bag or wrappers anywhere, so he must have collected them whilst I'd been out of it. I wondered how many times he'd been to check on me. I felt a little lilt of gentleness in my body. I imagined him coming in to make sure I was ok, to see if I'd woken up yet; looking after me. The thought caused a huge wave of sadness to cascade over me, and my bottom lip quivered again.

I didn't need to do any more crying, what I did need to do was check to see how bad I looked. I pulled my reluctant body out of its little nest and went straight to the en-suite bathroom. I didn't consult the mirror until after the best pee I'd had for a very long time, but once I did my reflection wasn't looking too pretty, my eyelids were swollen from the hours of crying, they were so bad my eyelashes were made invisible by the flesh. I wasn't sure it I was ready to confront Tim yet. I wasn't even sure if I was ready to leave the comfortable, if not a bit smelly, haven that I'd locked myself into nearly twenty four hours earlier. But I was hungry again, and I needed a cup of tea. I left the bathroom, duplicating Jude's tiptoe movements to be sure I was as quiet as possible. I didn't want to give Tim too much of a heads up that I was awake; if I was going to have to see him, at least I wanted to be in control of how it happened and not give him the chance to prepare himself to see me first.

I continued my light tread journey downstairs; I was astounded by how nervous I was. My heart was beating hard and I felt a bit shaky. Without casting my head left or right to check the other rooms on the ground floor I made my way to the back of the house, to the kitchen, towards the kettle. I flicked the switch, and as I did, I saw Tim sat outside on the decking. There had been no need for my efforts to be silent, he wasn't even within earshot of me, the patio door was closed. He was sat with his back to the house, facing the garden. His body was slumped forward, his elbows on his knees, and head dropped low held in place by his hands that seemed to be grasping his hair. His bent over body looked defeated and tired. My natural instinct to comfort the man I loved kicked in and I yearned to go to him, to run my hands across his broad shoulders, kiss the dip on the back of his neck, brush my hands through his dark brown constantly unruly hair; to do all the tiny things I knew would calm and relax him. To make it better.

However much Tim had hurt me with his carelessness, he was still my favourite person ever. I was his wife and incredibly proud of that status. We had a beautiful marriage, full of trust and friendship for each other. Yes, our sex life could be a bit hit and miss, but we'd been together for fifteen years. Surely no married couple that had been together as long as we had were still shagging like rabbits three or four nights a week? Or even once a month for that matter. That's normal though, isn't it? Everyone changes over the years, don't they? I stood at the other side of the doors from him. I was rooted to my spot watching him, silently observing him looking so vulnerable, feeling the love for him overtake my anger, and letting the thoughts of our lives together bring tenderness into me. As if he had sensed my presence he straightened up; his hair was stuck up either side of his head where his hands had just been. He turned towards me, and for the first time since the early hours of Saturday morning, I saw his face. The cocky, arrogant alter ego I'd sent to bed with disgusted words, was gone, and in its place was an unshaven, shambolic man with tears dripping off his nose.

12

I instantly pulled open the door to narrow the gap between us. He stood immediately, and as he walked towards me, I had a flash back from the club and anger flew up inside my body hard until it got stuck in the middle of my throat. It couldn't decide if it was going to produce a scream or a sob. He came into the house so quickly I had to step back to get out of his way. Suddenly I was in the middle of the room, caught between the longed-for kettle and the wine rack, which was looking equally tempting given the current circumstances. I pulled the fabric of Jude's dressing gown closer to my body to protect me from what was coming next, even though I had no conception of what it might be from either of us.

He moved closer as if to touch me, I stepped away from him quickly, he didn't want to be bringing those testicles too close to my knees at the present time, god only knew where they might've ended up. My swift avoidance of him confused him, he faltered with his arms half in the air the start of the hug he had been expecting (*fucking idiot*), he looked like someone had pressed the pause button on him doing a robot dance. It took him a few seconds to regain his composure.

"You're awake. How are you?" He was suspiciously lively, considering his outward appearance.

"I'm not really sure yet." I made my way to the kettle. He blocked my path. "No, no, sit down, I'll make you tea." His voice was shaky, he turned to look at me fully, and he looked awful. His olive complexion had a tinge of grey, the stubble he usually worked so hard to keep under control had been let free to escape from underneath his skin. My swollen eyes gave away my sadness, and his disheveled, overeager persona did the same.

We sat outside in the unseasonably warm weather. We drank our brew and we smoked our forbidden daytime cigarettes. He told me what he planned to cook us for dinner. It was all my favourite things, accompanied by wine – another of my favourite things. We were sat side by side; a deliberate move, so we didn't have to look directly at each other. We chose to ignore the damage the weekend had done to us both. Instead, with stiff voices full of politeness, we discussed our plans for the garden and got creative with our ideas for the landscaping project we were saving up for.

We had more tea, followed by a glass of wine and more cigarettes. We began to warm to each other again, our voices loosened. Eventually in the glow of red wine and on the verge of forgiveness, I popped the balloon that was holding the one question we both knew required an answer.

"Why did you do it Tim?" I turned to look at him, to see his eyes, so I could witness his honest reply. His face did not turn to meet mine; I was speaking to his profile.

"I don't know." His voice sounded full of regret, "I was fueled by booze and coke," the sound of a deep breath being drawn into his body, "and I thought you'd be up for it." He shrugged his shoulders. "I am deeply sorry though, I will do anything I can to make it up to you, and I promise it won't happen again. You deserve better."

I continued staring at the left-hand side of his unshaven face and waited for him to carry on talking, but he stood up and left me where I was. He went into the house and started clattering the pots and pans needed to make our meal, busying himself with cooking dinner.

I waited ages for him to come back to me so we could carry on the conversation. I wanted to ask him again why he had thought it was acceptable to go with a woman he didn't know and leave the woman he loved behind to deal with the fallout. I needed him to fully explain to me what had caused him to show me so much contempt; what had motivated him to start slicing through the fabric that weaved our lives together.

He didn't come back outside. And I was left second guessing him.

13

May 2008

The everyday ordinary slowly overtook the one-off extraordinary night that had rocked our marital boat.

Tim won a new contract at work, and with it came a promotion. It would mean he had to work away from home more often, but we agreed long before he even went for the interview that it was a sacrifice worth making. The day he was told he'd got the next step up, we went to our favourite restaurant for a two bottles of champagne celebration, just the pair of us. We were giddy at his triumph; this next step at work was a big one for him, for both of us really. We were an amazing team. Our belief and support of each other was the foundation of our success.

We'd both worked hard to become the best we could be for each other. We'd been together for a long time - the days, weeks, months, years, the mundane, the grind, the celebrations, the tears, the frustrations, the joy, the peace, the devotion. Layer upon layer of history had cemented our relationship.

Once upon a time we were Mr & Mrs Indestructible.

We both took our knocks at work; there were times when we struggled personally and professionally, and each time did, we automatically knew that the other would make it better. For me, hearing his voice, having him home, a hug or a kiss took all the bad stuff away. It made everything right in the world;

in our world. The door to our home firmly locked to anything outside, while we were locked into each other; warmth, protection, certainty. An unquestioning faith in each other and our lives together; in our future. We had it all, everything we had aspired to over the years.

And yet, I had a sixth sense I couldn't shake off. My intuition was telling me not to get too comfortable, that something wasn't quite right. I suspected that mischief was going on behind my back, but it would seem crazy to suddenly introduce my fears and bring the whole sorry lap dancing mess back into our lovely life. I knew I should find the strength to bring it up, Tim was my best friend, we talked all the time. About everything. I'd always thought there wasn't anything that could part us mentally and physically, not one person that would turn our heads and distract us from our intense focus on each other.

I was confused about why this subject was so hard to broach, I would practice constantly, and each time I got home from work I'd be determined that tonight would be the night I would find the guts to talk to Tim about my fears.

I was preparing myself this evening. with Ivy's help, of course, as I made the pasta sauce.

"How's your pasta darling?" I would begin. *Start normally, good plan,* critiqued Ivy.

"Lovely thank you." *He'll smile back unsuspectingly.*

"Not too hard for you?" *I don't know why you'd ask that one Rach, it's never right for him is it?*

"No, I like my pasta al-dente," *In that sarcastic tone and wry grin.*

"More wine?"

"Yes please," *Of course he does.*

And at this point I could ask him, "What is it you're up to behind my back that I can't quite fathom out?"

No that won't do.

Ok how about: -

"Tim, I'm a bit worried. As much as I try to bring things back to normal since our evening out at the lap dancing club, I am finding it difficult to look you properly in the eye. I'm finding it hard to believe that the man I saw that night isn't an intrinsic part of you, that you don't always wander round like a dog with two dicks looking for a way to satisfy yourself. When we've finished dinner, I would like to discuss this a bit further, explore the situation, are you up for that?"

Ivy approved. *Nice, do that, that's the best one yet. He'll never say no to that!*

I continued to practice the imaginary conversation in my head while I looked for the parmesan in the back of the fridge. When I found it I realised it had been out of date for a week, but I served it up anyway. By the time I sat down with him to eat, my several Ivy conversations had my stress levels high and my hands were shaking as I reach for my wine glass.

Ask him, ask him, ask him. Ivy was kicking my arse to be brave. *Do it now how we practiced it get it in the open.* I ignored her.

I just poured the wine, let him fill the dishwasher after dinner, berthed myself on the sofa and watched cerebral TV - you know, clever BBC 2 stuff where Jeremy Paxman gets to show off his excellent pronunciation in several foreign languages.

The smart woman in me knew that even if I were to broach the subject, I wouldn't get a straight answer. I also knew that bringing it up now when we were on a high, after Tim's new job and not inconsiderable pay rise, would make me look like a crazy woman and I definitely was not one of those. At least not yet.

So instead I buried my head in the sand, swept my worries under the carpet, pushed it to the back of my mind. All those metaphors, mixed as they were, that simply meant I was ignoring the intuition that nagged at me that something was wrong.

As I got myself settled that night, as I started to fall asleep, something jolted me awake. A rush of panic and anxiety. My even deeper than Ivy inner self was whispering at me not to get too comfy, to sleep with a gun under my pillow, because there was an intruder in my relationship and I might need to fire off a couple of rounds any time.

14

May 2008

The weekend had been a good one. I was still feeling the effects of an unexpected little party that had started in the gym, of all places.

I'd finished my usual Saturday morning personal training session and was having a sauna to ease my achy muscles when the door was open with gusto by a tall woman with a magnificent body in a red high leg, low fronted swimming costume, she actually took my breath away she was so sexy. I was still staring at the vision of this woman's breasts when her voice calling my name snapped my attention away from her cleavage to her face. It was my long-time, I-never-see-you-although-you-only-live-a-mile-down-the-road-from me, we-really-must-have-a-catch-up-soon, ex-colleague Naomi.

I had a real connection with Nai, I'd forgotten how much I liked her until we started to chat in the dry heat of the sauna, and then steam room. We had a shower in cubicles next to each other so we could carry on our catch up, then a coffee in the place next door to the gym, and then I asked her, "What are you doing today?"

"No plans, you?"

"Nothing much, Jude's coming round for lunch, do you fancy coming too?"

Twelve hours later Naomi and I were still together in the kitchen dancing to tunes on the iPod, while Tim chopped lines and Jude was in charge of tequila shots. Naomi eventually left our house in a cab at midnight (ish) and when I eventually went to bed in the early hours of Sunday morning leaving Jude and Tim to carry on partying, I still had the lanyard holding my gym pass round my neck.

Sunday was a complete write off for me, Jude left early to get home to her PC so she could carry on flirting outrageously with some guy she'd met on a dating site and Tim was going away on Monday lunchtime, so he was busy being a responsible adult, ironing his shirts, packing his suitcase for the week ahead; being organised. I'd stayed in bed with my hangover for company, drank tea and ate a bacon sandwich and had another little snooze. Tim woke me mid-afternoon.

I tried to tempt him back into bed for lazy Sunday afternoon sex, I pulled the covers off me so he could see my naked body, ran my hands over my breasts, I wet my fingers with my tongue and put my right hand between my legs. I was hoping my sexy showing off might get him going but in the process I'd pushed my own buttons and I was rapidly very horny; I was just getting into my best wanking stroke when he turned away from me. "Ah Rach come on you've been in bed all day, I've been busy, I'm starving, come on get up let's go and get some food"

I was a bit disappointed to say the least, in fact I was so shocked by his rebuff I didn't even finish myself off. I just got out of bed, all thoughts of lust disintegrated.

We went out for a very late Sunday lunch and shared a bottle of red. By the time we got home with a belly full of food I was feeling a bit more mellow, I had a long bath and an early night; and then the next thing I knew the alarm clock went off. It was Monday morning (again).

I worked on the road, I travelled a lot, not in the same way Tim did, mostly I came home each evening, but my car was my office, and the boot was my filing cabinet; I kept my whole work life there. I was still slightly hungover from our middle-class misdemeanours and I was rushing to say goodbye to my husband, get out of the house and on the motorway before the school traffic started. I was part way though my checking routine to make sure I had everything I needed for my day and as I opened the boot of the car I noticed my gym bag, in my rush to have fun on Saturday afternoon, I'd forgotten it was there. The contents included my still wet swimming costume (nowhere near as sexy as Naomi's by the way) the thought of the smell of the damp towel and my sweaty gym pants forced me to run back in to the house and put them in the washing machine, this unplanned activity threw a curve ball into my Monday morning routine, and consequently it all went horribly wrong.

****

It wasn't until I was accelerating down the slip road to join the motorway, still trying to catch my breath from the unexpected rush of the morning, and mentally running through the cluster fuck that was the start of my week that I realised the reason I had opened the boot of my car was to put my laptop bag in there. It was as I'd approached the slowly lifting boot lid I'd noticed my gym bag, and at the sight of it and the thought of the mildewy smell that would pervade the car if I didn't deal with it, I was so distracted I hadn't given anything else another thought. Groaning, I realised my laptop was still in the hallway, at home, and I was already on the motorway.

Ivy commented: *What a shit way to start a week.*

It seemed that way to me too; and that was before I got back home.

By the time I'd come off the slip road at the next exit of the motorway and doubled back on myself for the ridiculous return journey, the school rush I'd tried so hard to avoid was in full swing. It took me ages to get home and I was more than a bit stressed when I eventually pulled up the drive. I didn't turn my engine off, and I left the car door open so I could make a hasty getaway once I had retrieved the bag from its resting place by the door.

The room we use as our his 'n' hers home office was situated to the left of the front door; it was a good room, full of natural light from the skylight windows and my sales awards decorated the walls and shelves. With Tim working away so often he didn't use the office as much as I did, so when he needed to work from home he would squeeze his laptop onto the same desk our ancient PC sat on, which we'd had forever and a day. We had laptops by then, so we never used it, mostly because it was a pain in the arse, it took forever to boot up, and close down, and well, to respond to anything it was required to do really; it was a steam roller in a world of super cars. It was so old it seemed to have developed asthma, judging by the wheezing of the hard drive. The only reason we still kept it was because loads of our digital photos were downloaded to the mainframe, and I hadn't got round to transferring them yet.

I didn't want to startle Tim by my unexpected return, so I shouted to him as soon as I opened the door to the house, "Tim, it's only me! I had a complete brain freeze this morning, finding my gym bag in the back of my car totally threw me off. Bloody smelly swimming costume!" I put my head around the office door to smile, let him see my face, let me see his. "I realised as soon as I got on the motorway that I'd left my laptop here." I walked towards him, he didn't look too good, he looked a bit guilty in some way, and he seemed to have a sheen of sweat on his face. "Hey are you ok? You look odd?"

He was jittery and seemed anxious. I wondered if something to do with work had upset him, but everything looked the same as usual, his desk was full of papers his laptop screen displaying some spreadsheet or another. That's when I noticed our old boiler of a PC closing itself down, the blue screen and never-ending circle of doom that told us it was getting round to performing the latest command, but it was only doing so in its own time.

It struck me as strange that he was using it, why would he have done that on a Monday morning when he has his perfectly well-functioning, fully wireless work laptop in front of him?

Tim had shame weeping out of his pores, I just didn't understand why. There's no need to feel guilty about accessing the internet is there? Unless you have something to feel guilty for.

Told you, didn't I? shouted Inner Voice Ivy. He's up to something; AGAIN.

I was looking at my husband who was unable to look back at me, and the PC was still striving to close down. It didn't seem unreasonable at this time to point at the offending and offensive hardware on the desk and say, "Why have you got that on?"

It seemed like a perfectly reasonable question to me.

"Oh," said he, "I was looking for a gym close to the hotel I'm staying in this week." He was aiming for nonchalance, but his eyes looked shifty, they were moving from side to side, metronome style and he was still unable to meet my gaze.

I was still pointing at our geriatric PC. "Why would you use that?"

"Ahhhh, um I erm had this spreadsheet open and I didn't want to lose my work."

Now the deeper functions of spreadsheets are generally beyond me but, auto sum, filter columns and 'save' I can manage. I'm no Bill Gates but even I know I can save a page, minimise it and open a new tab or go to the great goddess Google and search for a gym. I know I don't need to crank the PC up; unless I've got something to hide. He knows that and so do I. And so does Ivy. *Bollocks, it's PORN, PORN! He was looking at porn.*

"Rach, have you left your car engine running?" A clever diversionary tactic there from Tim, "you'll be really late if you don't leave soon." He made shooing motions with his hands, which brought me back to reality and I turned to leave. I walked back to the door and this time I picked up the laptop bag that created this situation in the first place.

He followed me into the hall and rested there with his back against the wall, I turned to give him a kiss goodbye and, as always when I was in close proximity to my chosen life partner, I had a little pull of lust for him. I went in for a full snog, leaning my lower body into his, bringing our clothes covered genitals into close proximity of each other. Tim pulled away sharply leaving me still leaning my lower body slightly towards him. I recovered from the rebuff quickly though, and instead of a lovely deep, sexy kiss I accepted his chaste peck on the lips.

"Have a great week babe, see you on Friday afternoon when you get home." I was still looking up at him trying to tempt him into meeting my gaze; nothing. He was already turning away from me back towards the office as he replied, "You too, hope you're not too late for your calls today, see you at the end of the week. Love you."

"Love you too."

By the time I was back on the motorway I'd rationalised the situation and decided there was no way Tim was using our PC to access anything remotely pornographic. He'd been truthful with me when he told me he was looking for a gym, we didn't lie to each other, or hide things from each other, we weren't like that! Course then I started to feel bad about my subtle accusation, so I called him to apologise.

"I'm sorry I was arsey with you before babe."

"That's ok, don't think anything of it." He sounded distracted like he always did when I called him during working hours.

"I didn't mean to question you, I'm sorry." I realised I was a bit sorry, but there was also just a tiny bit of doubt running through me, and if I'm honest I was looking for Tim's reassurance to dampen it down a bit.

"It's forgotten, it's ok. Don't mention it again."

The sense of relief that everything was ok between us before he left home for the week completely overtook any respect for Ivy's advice to me. *Can you see what he's doing here, he's a clever bastard isn't he? Forgiving you for accusing him of something he's actually done; and he's made sure you don't bring the subject up again.*

But I refused to believe that he'd manipulate me like that, and I ignored Ivy again when she sighed and said, *You idiot, Rachel.*

15

I knew Jude would be busy at work all day and more than likely out of contact, but I tried to call her anyway. I left messages on both her mobiles and with her PA; we'd arranged to meet at the gym that evening so we could pretend to race each other on the treadmill, but I figured this morning's events had given me something else to sweat over and I needed her help. The message I left was simple; don't meet me at the gym, please come to the house instead.

My day came and went in a flurry of being late for every appointment I had, and I hate being late. I was distracted and busy, and I didn't have time to think about much else other than work. I immersed myself in my much-loved job and it wasn't until I arrived at the bottom of our street and ended my last business phone conversation of the day that this morning's events hit me again.

Fuck it, fuck it, fuck it. I was torn between declaring a marital state of emergency or sweeping all of my doubts away and going out for dinner with my best friend to discuss how stupid I was being suspecting Tim of anything at all.

As usual the house was beautifully lit when I got home, the lamps were timed to turn on as dusk fell, and the pools of light they created were a warm welcome. I loved that house, I loved the space, I loved the atmosphere, I loved what Tim and I had worked so hard to build. It was our dream come true. As I walked in, I dropped my bags and kicked off my shoes. The calm I usually felt when I walked into our home, the sense of belonging, was conspicuous by its absence.

As I walked past the door to the office, I could feel tension fill my body and my heart beat a bit faster. I knew what I was going to do, I really had no choice, the questions I'd been ignoring all day needed answers. I walked into the room of doom and turned on the PC. Rather than sit and watch it go through the laborious process of starting up I went straight to the beer fridge in the kitchen and pulled myself a couple of bottles out, I grabbed my packet of secret ciggies, a lighter and a bottle opener and by the time I was heading my way back down the hallway I was shaking and a bit breathless with the fear of confirming my suspicions.

I was worried that if I did the thing that I already knew I was going to do, I would have allowed something into my most precious place, something that didn't belong in the relationship I had with Tim; mistrust.

****

As was often the case, I hadn't heard from Jude all day. There was no reason why she would call me, it wasn't unusual for one of us to cry off going to the gym to do something much more exciting instead. Consequently, I hadn't had the chance to warn her that her evening was going to be less about meeting at mine for food and a laugh and more about us both becoming the Miss Marple of marital misdemeanours.

When she walked into the house, I was on my third beer and my second cigarette. She came straight into the office, straight to me, I'm not sure if it was the smell of smoke or the swearing that gave my location away. I was sat at the old PC, I had the internet browser open and I was furiously pressing keys to make it work, to encourage it to reveal the truth about my husband's website surfing that morning. I was pressing refresh, swearing, pressing another key and swearing again. I was on the edge of my seat, the less I found in the history of this computer the more I was convinced there was something to find.

"Rachel? What are you doing?" She was stood to my left behind my shoulder.

"I don't believe him. Gym my arse, he was up to something on this piece of crap, I haven't found it yet but now you're here, you can tell me how." I was still pressing keys.

"What are you talking about? Why are you smoking in the office? We don't smoke in the office now do we?" Jude looked a bit confused at the change in our normal rules.

I handed her the packet in response to her question and she lit one as I started to explain. "I left my gym bag in the car on Saturday when I was excited about Naomi being here and us all having a party. I found it this morning in the boot of my car, and in all the confusion I forgot my laptop bag, I had to come back for it."

"Bloody hell, how far had you got before your realised?"

I waved the question away as I turned the swivel chair and myself to face her, "That's not important Jude, when I got home Tim was behaving in a very strange way, he was using this..." I pointed behind at the monitor, "and I can't find out why, there's no history to show what he was doing, it's all been cleared out. Come and do it for me please, you know how, I know you do."

I stood up to give her the chair, the computer driver's seat. Jude looked at me and then the chair. Jude is much cleverer than me at the IT stuff, she should be, she runs a company full of IT tech heads.

"Let me get us a beer." She walked out of the room and into the kitchen. When she came back, she had a bottle in both hands. I took mine and threw my head back for a long swig as I stood up again, so Jude could take control.

"Are you sure?" she looked at me and I could see she was torn. She met my eye and sucked the air through her teeth, she gave me her most questioning stare.

"I'm not sure what he was doing, but I'm sure he was lying, and I am absolutely sure I want you to find out what he was looking at." I met her face on, our eye contact full of fear from both of us, but with added insistence from me. I nodded my consent to her, "Show me. Show me how to find out what he was doing."

And so we sat for quite some time, side by side, drinking beer and smoking cigarettes working on a cranky slow computer, I watched her navigate us around the obvious places to search in and to begin opening hidden internet doors into secrets we were never supposed to find. Until a final press of a back-slash key revealed it all before me, before us; the web addresses, the sites he'd used, all catalogued; dates, times, sexual preferences. All hidden so deep it would take a near expert to find it, buried by a clever man who knows what he's doing, covering his back, protecting himself.

Careful, insular, sneaky, lying, betraying behaviour.

16

Because she was still sat in front of the PC and officially still in the driving seat of our journey into the revelations of my husband's sexual proclivities, I watched the screen as Jude scrolled down the list of web addresses. There were many. The history of his wank festivities that he'd taken so much care to hide were there for us both to see.

Gotcha, you're not as clever as you think you are Tim.

There was nothing too scary about the porn he'd been using, it wasn't nasty or particularly unusual, it was run of the mill stuff, tits, fannys, cock-sucking, cum all over some random 56 DDD breasts, doggy style, threesomes, dominatrix, a bit of bondage. It didn't even make me blush; but it did make me angry.

I took over the mouse so I could choose which links I clicked so I could see the images. I looked again and again at the sites he'd looked at and saw the sights he'd seen. Jude was sat next to me the whole time her head swiveling backwards and forwards as she looked at the images slowly unfold onto the screen, and then she looked at me to see my reaction.

The anger rose up from my belly, I'm not exaggerating when I tell you I could actually feel it move up my body and into my throat in a gush. I started to laugh. I don't know why I do this, I'm a woman who is slow to anger and as a rule I have a lot of patience, but when I really lose my shit, I laugh.

I suppose laughter is one way to relieve the pressure a bit, let some steam off, but it didn't work this time because behind the super villain cackle I was incandescent with a rage that came in waves, big ones. The laughter built to a crescendo until I was ready to scream. I had never felt this fierce bubble in my body, an explosion waiting to erupt, I could feel the blood rushing through my veins. My hands were shaking as I scrabbled to get another cigarette out of the packet next to me. Jude gave me the same look as she had when she'd first come in and I was smoking in the porn room/home office. I challenged her expression.

"What is that face for Jude? We're both sat here looking at my husband's complete and utter betrayal of me and you'ro worried because I'm lighting up in the house?" I passed her the packet and the lighter.

"Well, when you put it like that." She shrugged her shoulders and lit her own smoke, and then turned her swivel chair towards me. I could see her trying to form the words to her next question, I knew my rage and laughter had scared her, I had scared myself a bit. "Go on J say it, whatever it is you have on your mind. I can tell you want to say something."

"I don't want to upset you anymore than you are, I've never seen you so angry Rach, help me understand it a bit, why are you so mad?" Her eyes were searching my face waiting to see how I was going to react to her question.

Is she thick or something? What a stupid question.

As much as I was tempted to repeat Ivy's words I tried hard to keep my voice as calm as I could. "You know what Jude, it's not the porn, babe, its exactly as I imagined his wank bank to look like, ordinary, normal, if you want to call it that. But things have been a bit slow in the sex department between me and Tim for a while. It's been ages since we've had un-complicated sex. I know we've been together for years and that things change, I know I'm in my 40's and I'm not as moist as I was in my 30's but once I realised that I did something about it! I went online to look for help and I found it; how long is it since I bought that lube and happy clit gel?"

Without thinking for too long she said, "Ages Rach, maybe even twelve months, I've almost finished my tin of that gel."

"Yeah well since we got it, I've used it every time we have had sex. I don't think it's been out of my bedside drawer more than twice, and you've shagged and got yourself off through the lot." As close as we were, I rarely discussed mine and Tim's sex life with Jude. I didn't discuss this stuff with anyone, mostly out of loyalty to him, the prick.

I didn't want anyone to think any less of Tim. I would be the last person to diminish anyone's opinion of him, I'd always been steadfast in my respect for him and our marriage. But the list of www dots on the screen in front of us kind of put an end to that for me, at least for the time being, and with her of all people it was time to come clean. The relief of finally opening up to her, for this shitstorm to finally be about me and not about Tim, made my anger turn into outrage.

"I have tried Jude, so many times, to ask him what the matter is, one night when we were off our tits on Es he dropped his barriers just far enough for us to talk about our lack of sex life. I asked him if he sorted himself out very often, and what he used to get himself off." The words were tumbling out of my mouth, like they had been waiting all this time to release themselves and were making sure they got out before I clammed up again.

"He told me that he didn't fantasise, he claimed not to wank, that he didn't really have sexual thoughts." She pulled her head back and looked at me in disbelief "Hey Jude, the best thing about all those lies is he was protecting himself even when we were taking whatever it is they put in those ten quid pills that makes you tell the truth!"

My voice had risen slightly with every point I made, Jude had moved herself away from me a bit, the passion and ferocity behind my words was forcing me to spit as I spoke. I lifted my arse from the chair I was sat in so I could get closer to the screen to point at the web addresses displayed on there as I said, "More lies! More ways to blatantly disrespect your wife. What the fuck is the matter with him?" She shook her head at me to let me know she had nothing to say. Instead she lit me a fag and handed it to me, lit herself one straight after.

The normality of the movement slowed my emotions down a bit, and I calmed myself slightly. "I've always been open about the things I like Jude, about the stuff that turns me on, I've been open to sharing our fantasies, act them out together, create new things to turn us on. I've tried to give myself time and time again. I've got three shelves of fuck me shoes upstairs in my wardrobe because I know he likes high heels, I dress up, I will try anything with him he wants, all he has to do is ask. I have willingly made myself vulnerable for the sake of our married life, for him, for us. I've even suggested we watch porn together"

Jude was still looking at me like a very scared rabbit in some very bright headlights. I didn't have the time to worry about her, I was busy being pissed off. I carried on explaining to her why I was mad with him. "And still, still he chose to lie, to protect himself rather than make an effort and build an understanding and trust, to try and sort out our sorry sex life. He wouldn't do that because he thought about himself over everything else. He lied and betrayed and disrespected me, the cunt."

17

The C word wasn't one we used very often in our social circle, it's not like we grabbed our coats and left the premises when someone said it, but we didn't litter our everyday conversation with it either, we saved it for extra special occasions, for when we really needed it. The sweary equivalent of our Sunday best.

Silently, Jude stood up from the chair in front of the PC and with a gesture offered me her seat. I took it eagerly. I scrolled the wheel on my mouse up and down, the screen in front of me moving in tandem with the action. I came across a site we had missed the first time we had been delving deep into Tim's sexual psyche, and I clicked on the link. It didn't take me long to work out that rather than watching other people have sex to get his rocks off, Tim had moved to another level in his search for a thrill that wasn't with me; it was a hook-up site. And although they didn't use the exact words, it was, on closer inspection, the internet superhighway equivalent of a pimp. My stress levels had reached peak performance again. "What the fuck is this?" I gestured towards the photos and information in front of me "Jude, he's looking at prostitute sites!" I was incredulous, "what is he up to?"

"You don't know that for sure Rachel, he might not have actually hired one of these girls." These were the first words she had spoken since our conversation about the lovely, fizzy clit cream, and she sounded like she was defending him.

The shock of the notion made me lose some of the lager down my nose, "Are you sticking up for him?"

"No, no, not at all babe, but just cos he's looked doesn't mean he's done anything about it does it? I go on Asos all the time and more often than not I don't buy anything. I'm just trying to shine some perspective into this that's all."

"What happens if you do see something you like though Jude, on Asos, or anywhere online for that matter, what do you do then?"

She shrugged, "I buy it."

"Exactly, you go online because you're searching for something, you're waiting to be tempted into parting with your hard earned by an item you simply can't resist!" The indignation I was feeling was causing my head to wobble from side to side, "it's just a matter of time, that's all. Maybe Tim found a suitable prozzie on here that was within his budget and conveniently in his geographical area, this site even has a postcode search facility!" Oh, I was shouting now, "He's looking for a hole to hire. Where am I supposed to get my perspective from now? Seriously let's not look for a silver lining in this cloud! Don't even think about defending him again!" I reached for my mobile, opened a text box and started to type.

"What you doing?"

I didn't reply to her question, I guessed she'd work it out soon enough. I was facing the monitor and I begin to type the www's displayed in front of me, each one in a separate text, one after another, after another. Type, send, type, send, type, send. Wherever he was, and let's get it right, I really had no idea; prior to discovering Tim's alter sex mad ego, I imagined he would be in a hotel restaurant right now, having a fully expensed dinner but suddenly my husband had become very unpredictable.

Whatever he was up to, I was sure of one thing, his bang-on-trend Nokia flip phone would be beep, beep, beeping the incessant call of the received text message. The one we don't ignore. The pull from whoever, from wherever, the 'I have something to say to you' message that is difficult to resist.

Jude was still watching me. "Are you sure you should be doing this Rachel?"

I didn't stop my mission in order to answer her, I multi-tasked; text, send, text, send. "Tell me the alternative; what, ignore it? Pretend I've not seen it? Act like nothing's happened? Like I've not discovered this Pandora's box full of tits? Who will that help? Not me that's for sure!"

"Maybe wait until he gets home, talk to him then, face to face?"

"If I don't do this now, I'll burst, there is no way I'm sitting on this one until Friday when he gets home. Not a chance. If I've got to face up to it then so does he." I was on the verge of shouting again.

I realised that watching your best friend bombard your other best friend with evidence of his extra marital misconduct is not very thrilling in terms of a spectator sport. "I know you have an early start tomorrow Jude, and you probably fancy another beer but you can't have one cos you've got to drive, so please don't feel like you have to hang around here, darling, for this. It's ok to go, really it is."

"Are you sure you're ok?" She was already gathering her bag and phone, looking on the desk for her car keys, "I will stay if you want me to?"

She didn't really mean it, she didn't want to stay, and if I was honest I needed her to leave. I needed to be on my own to come to terms with what I'd discovered, no one else was going to make this better for me. For the first time in the fifteen years that Tim and I had been together I was faced with the loneliness of knowing that I was on my own with a big problem, and he was the last person I could go to with it. In his need to satiate himself I'd been forgotten.

As she left the house, she looked back at me one more time. It was a loaded look; we knew, we both knew, this was a shit storm and it'd hit my life, it'd hit our lives. We understood that I was going to fight hard to get to the bottom of why Tim had lied to me, and we both knew that despite my anger I would willingly listen to his pitiful excuses. There were going to be questions asked, and demands for answers and explanations. The one thing neither of us knew is how he was going to talk his way out of this one, how he was going to react, what was going to come back from him.

When she had gone, I locked the front door, I got another beer and my ciggies and sat back on the bottom step in my beautiful home. I rocked backwards and forwards and lit another cigarette and waited for his reply to my texts. The smell of smoke permeated the atmosphere, it polluted the seventy-five pound a roll wallpaper, it wafted upstairs, to our thousand pound bed that we slept in but rarely had sex in; in fact, we'd had it for months, and now I came to think about it, I'm not sure we'd christened it yet.

I sat, I smoked, I drank, and I waited for the reply to my dozen or so messages.

It came about half an hour later. Two words.

"I'm sorry."

The second his text came through to me, I tried to call him. But he'd switched his phone off, it went straight to voicemail.

18

There's another C word that I never expected to use to describe my husband, and Ivy provided it the following morning when, despite trying to reach him on both his work and personal mobile and, for the first time ever, calling the hotel and asking the receptionist to put me through to his room, he didn't answer any of my calls.

The coward.

I'd eventually left my spot on the stairs just before 1am and gone to bed. As a tiny protest that meant nothing to anyone but me, I threw Tim's pillows across the room and parked myself straight down the middle of the very comfortable, but chaste mattress. I didn't breathe deeply so I could smell him on the sheets as I usually did, and notably I didn't cry either; I even managed to sleep.

After I'd made the unanswered phone calls, I got myself ready for my day as normal. With Tim working away so often, I was used to being on my own; I'd go so far to say, that more often than not, I actually enjoyed it, my own space. I was very much business as usual, only a much calmer version than normal.

My mascara went on my lashes like a dream, considering less than 12 hours beforehand I'd discovered my husband's brain was being unfaithful with a whole world of websites. I would, under usual circumstances have expected a few (floods of) tears, but there hadn't been any. I didn't really question it too hard; I had no time for tears or anger today, I had a full diary of back-to-back appointments and my first ever body combat class booked for half six. The rest could go fuck itself.

A text beeped part way through the morning and my stomach turned briefly thinking it might be Tim; but it was only Jude checking in. "Hope you're ok babe. You know where I am if you want me."

Inner Voice Ivy had been under orders to button her lip for the day but this one was too hard for her to resist.

Ask her if she's contacted Tim. I bet if she has, he's replied to her. Because she's not the wife.

I'd no idea if Jude would try to call him or not, I hoped not, I needed to be sure she was on my side for this event. I'd just had all trust for my husband wrecked and the last thing I needed was to lose my best friend too.

I let the issue go and without that to ruffle my feathers I was a self-contained, peaceful little soul all day.

The 6.30 class was so hard I was nearly sick. If I learned one thing from this day it was that I don't like body combat and I would never ever do it again. I went straight home after the class for a well-earned shower, a frozen fish pie warmed up in the oven and glass of chilled Chablis. I had an early night and slept like a log.

The same day followed a similar vein, apart from calling Tim. I didn't do that - I wasn't going to give him the satisfaction of not picking up again, the prick. Oh, and the class at the gym of course. I got another short text from Jude checking on me but I still wasn't in the mood to rehash what had happened on Monday night and I knew if I started speaking to her that would be exactly what we'd do. I texted her back to say I was ok and left it at that.

I was in a good place. I felt serene and focused on what I was doing. I didn't let anything phase me, and to put a crown on an already pretty good day, I finally closed a deal I'd been waiting for an answer on for weeks. Total calm pervaded my world. Well, okay, not total calm, I did do a little excited bum wiggling dance on my drive home when I relived the thrill of my sales success, but apart from that it was a level, even keel kind of day. I even stopped at the supermarket on my way home and bought myself a bottle of my favourite Champagne and a packet of cigarettes to celebrate the amount of extra noughts I knew was going to be on the end of my next commission cheque.

Once I got home I deliberately left my work and personal mobiles where they were in the bottom of my laptop bag and left that in the car. I was empowered by that defiance and within five minutes of getting home I was sat in the garden under my favourite tree with the bottle of bubbles in an ice bucket, the naughty ciggies and a joint I'd kept in case of emergencies.

It was a gorgeous evening, the birds were having a sing, there was a gentle breeze rustling the leaves above my head, I was in a little bubble of stoned inner peace. My brain was flitting from one lovely stoned thought to another.

Every so often Tim crossed my foggy brain and at one point I had an image of him shagging some skanky prostitute down a dark alley somewhere, her with her back against the wall and skirt up round her waist and him with his pants round his knees and his shirt tails flapping over his arse cheeks as he fucked her. I had visions of him getting a blow job from some random woman as he sat behind the steering wheel of his much-loved motor.

It was so hard to associate either of those acts with him; I kept shaking my head in denial and in an effort to get rid of the image of his cum face.

I wonder if his cum face is different if he's paying for sex? And even more importantly Rach I wonder if he can keep it up

*for quids? Maybe that's what you should do, start charging him!
Tell him you'll suck him off for a tenner.*

As I've mentioned before I don't share my concerns about my marriage issues with anyone and in the interest of total honesty I don't share them with Tim either, but I can't hide anything from Ivy because she lives in my head. In an effort to drown her voice out I put my headphones in, turned my music up loud and carried on drinking my self-indulgent bubbles.

It was dark and a bit chilly when I made my way back into the house, and by that time I'd finished half the packet of smokes, most of the spliff and all of the champagne.

The little stagger in my step gave me a bit of a clue that I was thoroughly pissed and more than a bit stoned and stepping into the kitchen brought on a massive attack of the munchies. I wandered round opening cupboards and the fridge, collecting things for a picnic in bed. By the time I was finished I had my hands full of chocolate, crisps, cherry tomatoes, fizzy water and a plate of chicken left over from Saturday night's dinner that probably should already be in the bin, what with it being Tuesday.

On my way upstairs, I walked past the place that used to be my office but was, I decided now, to be considered my husband's wank station; that caused me to giggle a bit until I remembered my mobile still in my bag, in the car. I did toy with the idea of looking for it and checking it for messages, but my muddled brain couldn't comprehend how I would do that without putting my delicious collection of food and drink down, so I didn't bother.

****

When the alarm woke me up the next morning, I was laying in the middle of the bed still propped up on my pillows, surrounded by half eaten food, empty crisp packets and half a mars bar melting under the covers with me. I concluded that I'd had an excellent night.

Even though I knew my day was going to be a busy one I didn't feel in a rush to do any of it. I felt so chilled and unperturbed that my usual Monday to Friday compulsion to perform at my peak seemed impossible to comprehend. I stayed in bed long after the alarm and luxuriated in the space the absence of Tim's pillows created. I had a starfish stretch across the mattress and rolled myself out of bed. Wearing my favourite dressing gown, I sauntered downstairs to make myself a cup of tea. It was only when I wandered past the door to the office that a tiny bit of reality crept into my morning.

I remembered my bag still trapped in the boot of my car while I'd been in my defiant 'up yours' mood, which, combined with my eagerness to crack open the bubbles and tear the cellophane off the pack of twenty the night before, I'd not thought about until I was on my way to bed.

I was tempted to leave it where it was, let the sleeping dog lie, but my good girl brain told me to be sensible. Once I'd retrieved my bag out of the car I emptied it out on my desk, the paperwork I had forgotten about when I got home last night was still there waiting to be dealt with. I knew I'd have business emails to take care of too, so I started the process of booting up my laptop. When I eventually found my phone it was completely dead, the black screen an indication of my neglect to charge it the night before. I made good my deliberate mistake and while I was waiting to get enough juice into it to fire it up again, I went to make myself a cup of tea to power myself up and get my champagne brain to function.

As I walked away from the office, I noticed a jittery, shaky feeling was making my heart pump a bit harder than usual, but I put that down to the midweek madness of bubbles and spliff. As I waited for the kettle to boil, another flutter of nerves moved from my chest up into my throat and I realised the sensation was more than a comedown from the booze and drugs; I was nervous.

The thought of my charging mobile pulled me back down the hallway into the office. I turned it on and while I was waiting for it to come to life, I found I had to steady my breathing a bit. Yesterday's calm felt like an illusion, I couldn't find any peace in me today.

As the screen came to life the icons lit up to tell me I had sixteen missed calls and four new text messages. Fuck, fuck, fuck. My heart was pounding hard in my chest now and I was struggling to breathe. With shaking fingers, I opened the call log; the first missed call had been at 6pm yesterday and the sixteenth was just before midnight, every one of them from Tim. Three of the missed text messages were from Jude asking me where I was, was I ok and would I give her a call please. She'd been trying to contact me on the hour from 8 o'clock. The last text message was from Tim sent just before he'd made the final call.

"Please, please pick up Rachel, I need to speak to you. I'm sorry I haven't been in touch before now. I can't stand this anymore. I'm finishing work tomorrow lunchtime the drive will take me a while, but I'll be home by 6 at the latest x"

19

I think I've already mentioned I'm not a thrower of things, so you can imagine how shocked I was to see my purple and black Nokia fly across the room. It had left my hand before I even had chance to think about it; it missed the wall and sailed straight through the door and into the hallway. I lost sight of it then, but I heard it clatter as it hit something and fell to the floor.

I've no idea where I had been storing the fury that came from me, but I went from 0 to 60 on the apoplexy scale in less than a second. The snarling, spitting explosion of swear words I thought I had left behind me on Monday night were back, and they were fierce.

"You cheeky, son of a bitch, how dare you! 'Please, please, please pick up' - how about Tuesday morning when I was calling you and you didn't answer!" My voice was somewhere between a shout and a scream. The gall of him deciding he wanted to speak to me and expecting me to pick up straight away, "Snap your fingers Tim, of course I'll pick up the phone darling, let's forget about the fact that you have ignored me for nearly three days, you coward!" While I was screaming at the husband-shaped imaginary person, I went into the hall to see what damage I'd done to my phone. It was laid in the centre of the floor still in one piece, solid as ever.

I knew it wasn't the phone's fault my husband was a dis-respectful bell end, nor was it responsible for the fact that my best mate had quite clearly contacted me on his behalf, but once it was in my hand I spent some of my anger shouting directly at it. "And you Jude, what is that all about? You and the bastard chatting behind my back, 'Ooooo Jude, I can't get in touch with Rachel, will you try for me?' Why didn't you just tell him no? Tell him to fuck off? Tell him not to bother because the last time you saw me I was rightfully angry and upset. Stop being on his side for fuck's sake!"

I thought I might call her and let her know how pissed off I was by her support of him, and not of me. I checked the clock to see what time it was so I could work out where she might be, and at that point I realised I only had forty five minutes to get to my first appointment; and in amongst all the other reasons why I was incapable of attending, I wasn't dressed yet and I was a sixty-minute drive away.

I made an executive decision, I called a halt to my hostilities and temporarily swallowed down my outrage at the two closest people in my life, I put on my best professional voice while I made several phone calls and cancelled my appointments for the day. There was no way I was going to be able to plaster a smile over the snarl I had on my face.

While I was still reasonably sane, I sorted out my paperwork and answered my emails, the flow of admin tasks soothing me a bit. It was the first time since Monday night I'd spent any length of time in that particular room and out of the corner of my eye I could see the spectre of the PC taunting me. There was no real reason for me to reacquaint myself with it, I knew the secrets that it held now, and I was sure Jude's clever IT investigation had unearthed all of Tim's feverish porn searches.

I knew it was stupid to rub my own nose in my husband's shit, but before I knew it, I was pushing the on button, knowing that by the time it had warmed itself up enough to work properly, my distracting tasks would be finished, and it would be ready to let me have another look at the images that had been delighting my spouse over the last few months.

Sat at one desk completing my work, I couldn't stop my head turning slightly to the left every so often to look at the other desk next to me, the closer the PC was to starting itself up, the fizzier my anger got; by the time the home screen appeared on the monitor I was boiling over with rage again.

I slammed my laptop lid closed and rolled my chair over towards the other X rated screen. It was the sex for hire site that I went to first; there were so many girls to choose from, pages and pages of them. The images were so raw; it seemed the girls had made a bit of effort to make themselves look attractive but on the whole, it felt grimy, as unkempt as the lap dance club had been. It might as well have been called www.streetcorner-shag.com because that's the impression it was giving. I was taken aback at the tawdriness of it all. Tim is a man who likes the good things in life; if there are two identical pairs of shoes in a shop, one half the price of the other, he will always, without fail, buy the more expensive one, he can't help himself.

The women in the photographs were dressed, if you could call it that, in similar underwear to the dancer who had obliged my husband with his slavering need to get his rocks off. There was a variety of women of all ages and all shapes and sizes, most were trying for sultry, suggestive faces, with bodies leaning backwards and legs wide open, a few had favoured leaning into the camera with their tits pushed together to create a deep cleavage and pouting lips; it was grubby. There was no description or biography with the images, there was no promise of the ride of your life, or even satisfaction guaranteed. Just the geographical area the woman worked in and a contact number she could be reached at. It was the www. equivalent of the cards that used to litter the walls of phone boxes.

The more I saw, the more my devastation grew, and my temper flared. I found myself wanting to punish Tim, to shame him. I wanted to see the expression on his face when he looked at the photographs of women who were offering him sex for money. I needed him to understand what it had meant to me when I'd found the hidden searches, and for him to see it from my shocked point of view. I started to click into the image of each girl and then send each photograph to the printer, it was a simple task carried out quickly and before long the printed paper was coming out thick and fast, one woman after another.

While the printer was working hard to keep up with the work I'd given it, I went on to search back through the other sites, the porn, to provide me with more hard copy shaming evidence. I copied and pasted each web address into a word document, as the list grew from a handful, to a few, to many, I started to shout again, demanding answers from someone who wasn't even there. The effort of it all made my body shake and then I started to cry.

The truth of the situation hit me like a wrecking ball. I wasn't trying to shame Tim with the websites at all, the images made no real difference, what I really wanted to do was shock him into seeing what those photos represented to me, about me and about our marriage. He was betraying both. He was lying and cheating, and as the evidence had continued to stack up against him, it also looked like he'd been sticking his dick into some random woman's fanny that had seen more pricks than a pub dartboard.

The thought of him committing to the physical act propelled me from my chair; it rolled a short distance from the desk and typically blocked the doorway. I kicked it out of my way and marched through the hallway and took the stairs two at a time up to our bedroom. I was still crying but my sobs weren't the 'boo hoo' kind, they were more of the 'fuck you' kind. These were very annoyed tears; they were a liquid representation of my outrage at being treated like an idiot. As I cried, I opened every drawer in the cupboard that held Tim's things, his T-shirt drawer being the biggest. I grabbed armfuls of his beautifully folded casual clothing and I carried them to the spare bedroom where I dumped them on the bed.

I went back into our room and repeated the process, another armful thrown on to the pile. Next, I did his sock drawer; the matching pairs were folded in together at the top so they didn't get separated, that didn't last long after I gathered them up with angry hands and took them to the same place as the T-shirts had gone. I threw them carelessly in the general direction of the other stuff.

I didn't even bother lifting his underwear out, I just pulled the whole drawer out of its casing, took it to the growing pile of jumbled up clothes, tipped it upside down and emptied the contents on top. I was still crying as I pushed his bedside cabinet from our room to his new boudoir; I left that in the middle of the room.

The his and hers bathroom cabinets that sat over the his and hers sinks made it easy to organise the removal of his things out of the en-suite attached to what was rapidly becoming my bedroom. I swept the entire contents of the three shelves into a towel, grabbed the corners and carried it back down the hall to what was now Tim's room; I threw the home-made towelling sack in the general direction of all his other belongings.

There was an immense feeling of satisfaction removing all trace of him from the sumptuous bedroom we had created for ourselves. This was my room now; Tim's room was the poor relation of the rest of the house.

The spare room was very neglected and badly in need of redecoration, and it never seemed to get as warm as the other rooms. The bed in there was one we had years ago and had never found very comfy. It was the room where we stored our suitcases, left over rolls of wallpaper, a tatty old chest of drawers I had kept promising to renovate, and the sit-ups cradle we'd bought from QVC full of enthusiasm and then only used twice.

Satisfied that the place looked like a bomb had dropped on it, I threw a two-finger salute at the room and its contents and closed the door behind me. I was still crying.

As I made my way back downstairs, and went straight outside to sit back under my favourite tree with what was left of last night's ciggies, my face was still wet from furious tears. It was only as I began to gather my self together and settle down from rushing around that I realised I had been fooling myself for the last couple of days.

I hadn't been calm at all; I'd been in the eye of the storm.

20

I felt restless, verging on a bit manic. The temptation to have a beer and finish off last night's spliff was massive, but I didn't want to go into battle impinged with any influence other than my own well-justified wrath. I was torn in two about the way I felt and physically I fluctuated between bunching my hands into tight fists of frustration and temper, and then shaking them out to try and get rid of the nerves that were making the ends of my fingers itch.

Every clock in the house was, in my opinion, running slow and by the time I'd finished the Wednesday night ciggies it was still at least three hours before the time Tim had told me to expect him. I went to the shop and bought lots more cigarettes (I think at this point I realised my declarations of being a non-smoker were just hyperbole). While I was out, I had a long walk around the local park and stopped off at the café by the pond for a coffee and yet another smoke.

Jude came into my thoughts and Ivy wasn't far behind.

What were her texts about last night? Had she tried to be your early warning system that that dickhead was trying to get in touch? With his 'boo hoo I'm sorry' nonsense? Or is she still batting for his team, was she trying to get you to answer him because he was distraught, and she wanted to help him?

I wasn't sure, and I wanted - needed - to talk to her, to ask her. The thought of her aiding and abetting the man who was tearing me in two hurt more that I could have imagined, but

I was worried that whatever her answer was I might misdirect my outrage at her. I wasn't sure how much of it I had in stock and I didn't want to waste any of it on anyone other than Tim who was driving home towards me.

****

As a rule, even after a short absence, when Tim was on his way home, I had an extra spring in my step. I was never consciously aware of the fact that I was running on eighty percent until he came home, and suddenly, I was full again, complete, totally happy. Today though my anticipation of seeing him had been poisoned. I couldn't settle so I paced around the house, looking for the best place to sit, planning the best vantage point, so I could see him as soon as we were in the same space, my heart was pumping with nerves and fear. It was a sunny afternoon, so I opted for sitting outside on the patio with my chair turned to face the house rather than the garden, the wide glass sliding doors pulled back, nothing to impede my view through the kitchen and down the long hallway to the front door.

By the time it got to 5.30 I caved in and hurriedly poured myself a glass of wine, then rushed back to my carefully thought-out spying spot. As soon as my bum touched the chair again, I was sure I heard his car engine and tried hard to listen closely to be sure, but the blood was pumping so hard around my body the only thing I could hear was the heavy beat of my heart.

My anxiety levels were high, I had a lump in my throat that was threatening to deliver the tears I'd promised myself I wouldn't shed in front of Tim. My hands were shaking as I lit yet another cigarette. I was only momentarily distracted from my guard duty but when I looked back towards the front door he was there.

He had three bags in his two hands and he dropped all of them at the bottom of the stairs and walked straight towards me. He looked so handsome. His jacket hugged his broad shoulders like a second skin, the matching trousers complemented his slim hips and clung to his thighs. These were the details I saw every time I studied him; he looked powerful and sexy. This was not a revelation to me. I had spent many happy hours learning the minutiae of this man who filled my world. I had hungry eyes; I absorbed every detail of him again now. His face needed a shave, but that made him look vulnerable, his dark eyebrows, that would meet in the middle if it wasn't for vanity and a razor, were pulled down into a frown. It wasn't his concentrating face; that frown was slightly different to this one, this one told me he was worried.

My body reacted to his presence immediately; he was home, at last. My first instinct was to be happy we were together again. He could make me stop hurting right now, all this angst and hatred could be mended because he was with me. Oh no wait, who do you go to when your go-to guy is gone? The reality of the situation hit me again.

We still hadn't spoken; I wasn't even sure I could. Several emotions clamoured to be the first impression he got of my state of mind, and I'd no idea which was going to win, nor did I have any control over it. He came straight towards me and the closer he got the more of a height advantage he had and I found myself looking up at him. He bent towards me for a kiss hello, and I drew myself back sharply, as far away from him as I could.

Ivy was in like a shot. *Headbutt him.*

I was so tempted I realised the winner of the emotions race was fury. I'd nothing else in me for him, I was repulsed by the idea of showing him anything that might be misconstrued as remotely gentle or kind. I stood up quickly and turned my back to him, a nonverbal "fuck you".

The forty or so pieces of paper I'd printed off earlier from the 'shags-r-us' websites were sitting on the kitchen worktop by the wine rack. At the time I was printing them off I hadn't had any fixed idea how I was going to use them, but coming face to face with him now, I realised I wanted to hurt this man. I wanted to embarrass him, I wanted to punish him and I wanted to watch him closely while I did it. I dropped my half-smoked cigarette on the floor and walked past him into the house straight to the incriminating evidence. I could feel his eyes following me.

"Rachel?" His voice was deep, he sounded sad.

"Sit down Tim, I have something for you." He moved towards the breakfast bar and sat in Jude's usual spot. I sat opposite him with the papers clutched to my chest. I handed them to him. The first one was a photograph of a woman who plied her trade in the same district of Bristol as Tim stayed when he was needed at head office. He looked at the image then looked up at me. His eyes didn't meet mine; they fell on my face but there was no eyeball contact between us. He looked scared. I nodded my head at the pile of paper in front of him, "Don't stop, there's lots more where that came from. Have a look through and let me know if you come across a familiar face." I watched him closely as he glanced at the photographs. I knew he wasn't really looking; he was just trying to appease me.

As he turned over the fifth page his eyes came over to my general direction, "Rachel, none of these women are familiar to me, I can promise you that. I can look at them forever and not see someone I know, I've never, ever used this site."

"Oh, but you have Tim, on several occasions; window-shopping, were you? There's lots of others you've been looking at too, haven't you?" I was trying my hardest to restrain myself from screaming at him, but it was there in my body. I could feel its ferocity forcing itself from my chest, my breath was shallow, "In fact," I reached over to his side of the table towards the stack of papers. The speed of my movement suggested violence and Tim moved his body away from me, took his hands from off the table and out of my way.

I took control of the pile of papers again and starting from the top I peeled each one away from the others and slid them to him like a casino dealer in a game of Blackjack. As I pushed them across the shiny surface, they were sliding quickly and falling off the other side of the table at different angles, most were littering the floor, but some landed in his lap, he sat with his head bowed not looking at what I was sending over to him, one after another after another.

"It's not just this site is it?" By this time, I'd got past the sexy girl shots and arrived at the pages with web addresses I'd copied and pasted. I held either side of this piece of paper in a tight grip, I shoved it directly under his nose into his line of sight, "What is this all about Tim? Why are you hiding this from me?" The scream came then, "Why are you lying to me, what are you doing behind my back?" His head shot up in shock at the sound of my impassioned plea delivered at the top of my vocal range, "Why are you bringing this deceit into our marriage?"

He stood up quickly, walked directly to the wide-open back door and slid it closed. I was flabbergasted at his action. "What the fuck Tim, you prick! You haven't shown any interest in having sex with me for months, you can sit in our office on a Monday morning with your dick in your hand having a sly wank, but god forbid the neighbours should hear me be upset at you!"

"It's not what you think Rachel, I promise you." He didn't sit back down again, instead he took the opportunity to move away from me. He crossed the kitchen in a move that meant we were no longer opposite each other. He leaned back slightly with his arse against the worktop. From the way he was standing all I could see was his profile, and it's very difficult, even for me with all my body language superpowers, to read someone's face when it's half hidden.

"How can it not be what I think Tim, what are you looking at this piss poor porn in secret for? And prostitutes for God's sake?" I was spewing out the words, I was back to spitting with rage, "How dare you disrespect me and our marriage by even thinking of shagging some skanky woman who sells sex for money! Why would you threaten us in this way?"

If there had been any defiance in his stance before, it left him now. I watched as his shoulders dropped and his head followed immediately after, his chin almost touching his chest. At last he was showing his shame.

I willed my voice to dial down a couple of notches. I had a huge lump in my throat, it was so big it hurt and I couldn't get the shouts past it. "It's not the porn Tim, I couldn't give a shit, if you want to use it every day. I don't mind that you want to get your rocks off in that way, but don't exclude me from it! Tell me, let me join in, it wouldn't be the first time would it?"

"No." He kept his head low and brought his hands the short distance to his face, he used the heel of his hands to wipe his eyes. "I'm sorry. Since you texted me on Monday night, I haven't been able to think of anything else. I know I've let you down, I'm so ashamed of myself. I don't know why I did it." He still didn't move to face me; he was looking at the floor. All I had to convince me his words were coming from a place of honesty and not cowardice was his voice, and that was full of emotion. I didn't take my eyes from him, searching for a clue to tell me his apology was a genuine one and not a get out of jail free card he was playing. I turned in my seat so I could look directly at him. I took in the sight of him stood before me. He was still wearing his suit jacket, his body leaning, and his long legs were crossed at the ankles. I could see the bottom of his right shoe and I could make out the trace of red lacquer the soles had when I bought them for his birthday last year, mostly gone now because they were his favourite shoes, and he wore them often.

In the split second my glance was at his feet, a tear landed on the toe of his beautiful leather brogue. My heart hurt; I hate to see him cry. My own tears were so close to the surface I couldn't speak, I knew the dam would burst if I did. My unintended silence must have panicked him into coming back into the conversation, "I can't discuss this anymore today Rachel, I haven't slept for days, I'm exhausted and sad. The drive was a nightmare, I have to rest, I have to sleep. I can't take anymore. I'm going to bed now." He pushed himself forward and with the motion he moved to go past me, back into the hall. He hadn't looked at me since I'd shown him the images of the women selling their holes for cash and it didn't seem like he was going to meet my gaze even now.

I was shattered at his early exit. To me it was another excuse not to be honest, to not face up to my questions, and the melt that had started when I'd seen the evidence of his tears stopped immediately. I didn't have a shout left in me, but I did have a hard edge to my voice, "Your things are in the spare room."

"Oh, Rachel no!" He spoke with a whimper, and what sounded like a genuine plead.

I had nothing left to say to him, instead I stood up myself and went back through the doors he had closed only a few minutes before. I left them open and sat back in my chair facing the house. I lit a cigarette, picked up my glass and watched him walk to the bottom of the stairs. As he gathered up the bags he'd dropped earlier, he looked up and along the length of the house directly at me. I turned my gaze away from him and by the time I looked back, he was gone.

Once he was out of my sight the blockage in my windpipe burst itself with a sob of mammoth proportions, my anger replaced by the devastation that truly afflicted me.

21

I'd spent so many years living in our Tim and Rachel, Rachel and Tim bubble of contentedness, my loyalty to him was carved in stone. As far as I was concerned, to say something against him to another soul was an act of faithlessness. I only had good things to say about my man and in the main, prior to the agony of lap dance and porn-gate, he deserved my devotion.

I'm not saying his unreasonable behaviour totally unzipped my patriotic resolve, but it had definitely punched a hole in it. Don't get me wrong, I would never stand at bus stops and chat to complete strangers about my husband and his recent appalling behaviour, nor would I speak to the numerous girlfriends I have in my social circle. There was only one person I would even consider going to with this unravelling of our tight bond, and that was Jude. Speaking to her was safe. She knew and respected Tim enough to see beyond his current failings, to the man he really was - solid, dependable, trustworthy.

In the end, I'd plucked up the courage to ask her if the missed calls from her, mingled in with the sixteen from Tim, were as a result of him asking her for help. And she'd admitted it was. She told me he'd been desperate and devastated and she wanted to help us both. I didn't tell her how hurt I felt that she hadn't taken my side because I didn't need another toe-to-toe with someone I loved.

Since the day he'd come home early from his business trip his hangdog persona pervaded the whole house. He was sulky, truculent and on the rare occasion I could find it in me to communicate with him at all, monosyllabic. Cheeky fucker, talk about turning the tables, anyone would have thought he'd caught me watching spit roast sex while having a sneaky wank, not the other way round. I was already bloody furious with him and finding it hard to see any reason to even like him, but this new layer of bullshit pushed me over the edge.

****

I genuinely didn't go out to open a can of worms the night I met Jude for dinner. We talked about work she told me a funny story about one of her team in the call centre and I told her about the latest invention in the world of medical devices that was shaping up to be a commission gravy train and was going to pay for me and Tim to go to the Maldives for a fortnight. At the mention of Tim's name, Jude's face went all quizzical, her eyebrows raised, and her lips pursed slightly. I instantly felt my hackles rise, "What?"

"You kicked him out of the bedroom, dumped all his stuff on the bed." She had the slightest catch of a laugh in her throat.

"I did yeah, and I am glad I did, what else was I supposed to do, greet him at the door with a subscription for Playboy and a box of Kleenex?" I was on the back foot instantly my voice raised to the challenge.

She laughed again. "No of course not, but you could have moved him into my room, at least the radiator works in there."

"Why would I do that? Why would I put him in your room? He's in the worst room in the house and that's the one he deserves, the doghouse! Besides it's suiting him to stay there, it makes him think he has another reason to sulk, the dick!"

The waitress came over and I ordered a bottle of red. While we were waiting for her to bring it to us I asked Jude if Tim had been in touch with her again. She admitted he had, but was quick to tell me it was just the once, and that she was equally concerned about us both.

Well don't be you disloyal bitch, be on her side. What is wrong with this woman?

Because I was the only one to be able to hear Ivy, Jude had carried on trying to tell me how sorry Tim was, that he admitted he'd got lazy.

"What the hell? Well you know more than I do about why his penis decided to go wandering down porn street! I'm so delighted he could find the words to discuss it with you, but not with me!"

"He's ashamed Rachel, he's upset and confused." The wine arrived. I didn't wait long to unscrew the top and slosh a decent amount into both glasses while she said "Do you think you might be reading a bit too much into this, babe?"

I hadn't meant to slam the bottle down quite as hard as I did but I was incredulous at her question.

"Are you really asking me that? At what point do you suggest I really lose my shit then? The months and months of wank-bank material he has been using not enough for you? How about we consider the fact that after he'd been online to use it, he covered his tracks so thoroughly that we were almost forensic investigators in our efforts to find it, that if I hadn't stumbled on him looking seedy and guilty last Monday I might never have found out." I took a mouthful of wine, it was horrible stuff. "Maybe, I would have read a bit less into it if I hadn't discovered he'd been looking through the prostitute equivalent of a Freemans catalogue, so not only is he playing with his own dick, he's paying someone else to do it too. I know how much you think of Tim babe, I really do. I understand it must be hard to be in the middle of us right now, but I need you to understand why I am so upset about this situation." She nodded at me to carry on. "I love Tim, Jude, very much. I don't need to tell you that, he's my world. I am incredibly proud him and of our marriage, but for the last couple of years our sex life has gone off the boil a bit." She started to say something, but I held my hand up to stop her, I suspected that if she interrupted me now I would lose my impetus and might not carry on. The betrayal of Tim during my confession felt like I was stripping a layer off him and taking something away from our marriage.

"Don't start trying to tell me that every couple who's been together for as long as us has a similar experience. I know that, I've read Cosmo too. But I'd hoped that we might be better than the average couple, that the quality of our lives, our friendship and the fact we've no kids to reduce our chances of a shag on the dining room table any time we fancied it, might keep us going. But it hasn't. We are such a cliché."

It wasn't just the quantity though, it was the quality of our sex life that had become less of a pleasure and more of a curse. I loved sex and I still have an intense lust for Tim, I thought he was gorgeous, but he rarely, if ever any more, made the first move. I can't remember the last time he came on to me. It was always me that initiated sex, and when I did it felt like he'd submitted to me, giving in because he couldn't put it off any longer. The tension was unbearable.

All I wanted was for him to remember me, for something to unlock in his head and take him back to the early days when we made love without any complications. I felt sure it must be my fault and I felt guilty and worried about the dark spot in our otherwise wonderful life. I told her all of this.

When I'd finished spilling my guts Jude was quick with her assurances "Tim adores you, he loves you to bits Rachel, you know that don't you? Don't lose sight of that. I even asked him about the hookers, and he swore to me, on his life, he has never paid for sex."

Why the bloody hell is he talking to her about this and not you?

"I know he loves me Jude, but his cock doesn't always get the message and our sex life feels like a mine field. Until this last week when I've found out what he's been up to behind my back, I've been terrified to even broach the subject with him because I think talking about it might make it even worse and I don't want to push him further away. But the fact is, once I have his attention the rush to finish the race between him coming and him losing his hard on is making me feel useless and unattractive. I'd like to think he's looking at porn to get himself turned on for me, but he's not, is he? He's taking the easy option. He's being lazy, having a sly wank instead of putting some effort in to respecting our relationship enough and getting our sex life back to where it was, where it should be. The thing that hurts me, that's making me so angry, is the fact he's being lazy at my expense. He's not considering me at all while he's doing what he's doing. And you know what the worst thing is Jude?" I met her gaze, her face looked fuzzy through the water I was trying to keep inside my eyes, "he knows it. He knows he's hurting me but he still does it." I drained my glass "and don't even get me started on the potential news he might be shagging streetwalkers."

It was after 10.30pm by the time I got home. As I pulled up the drive I noticed there was a dim light coming through a crack of the bloody awful curtains in Tim's new bedroom, and I assumed he was already in bed. To announce the fact that I was home I deliberately slammed the car door shut and without another glance up to the window I walked towards the house with my right hand raised above my head and my middle finger lifted in the finger "fuck-you" salute. I'd no idea if he'd seen it or not but it made me feel better and right now that was all that mattered.

22

June 2008

The weekend after the counter meal confessional with Jude, we had a long-standing invitation to a party. Trish and Matt, a couple we had known for the longest time, were celebrating their 25th wedding anniversary and had decided to mark the miracle of marital longevity by an informal evening renewing their vows and getting drunk.

The evening was lovely, the hotel had pulled out all the stops, the room was festooned with fairy lights, balloons and streamers; it looked gorgeous, and we were hanging out with a big group of our mates. Everyone was dancing, singing, laughing, and just generally having a blast. Apart from me. Despite the anticipation of the event and the new frock I bought myself, I found it hard to enjoy myself. I tried, I really did, but I just couldn't join the dots of the evening up. I wanted to be there fully but I couldn't, I felt angry and irritated by everyone. I was feeling a loneliness I'd never experienced before, a chasm of emptiness and a distance from everyone, like I was watching the party from behind a thick pane of glass. My mouth smiled a smile that didn't reach my eyes, and my eyes were busy observing the guests but not joining in the hilarity like I usually would.

When it came time for the renewing of the vows, we all gathered into the adjacent room where Matt and Trish were waiting for us. Matt looked happy and proud as he gazed at Trish; her delight with the re-commitment of their vows shone from her. They both lit up the room.

I had no desire to be close to Tim, I purposely hung back so that I was one of the last to enter the room and could keep myself away from him, so I could see, but not be seen. I resumed my position as the watcher. As my eyes scanned the room they fell on his face. He was in profile to me. His eyes weren't seeking mine; they were doing their own thing. What that thing was or what it had been for the months before I'd no idea. I realised there was a very real chance we'd lost each other.

The vows the happy couple had written were sweet and heartfelt. They stood close to each other with their hands clasped together, each adoringly absorbing the details of the other one's face as they willingly and wholeheartedly said "I do, I will, of course," all over again. A reaffirmation of their original intention to love, honour, respect and obey.

I heard Inner Voice Ivy start up her own running commentary.

I mean obey, really? In this day and age? What does obey actually mean? Why should she say it and not him? Why doesn't he step up to the mark, hold his hands up and admit that he needs to toe the line too, that he needs to say "yes dear" when she asks something of him, or expects something of him? It's bollocks really, Rach.

I felt the start of a snort of derision produced by the diatribe from my inner voice, I stopped it quickly and looked around to make sure no one close by had heard me.

I wonder why your marriage licence doesn't come up for renewal like your TV one does or your driving licence? It should really, once a year on the anniversary of the magical date that you tied the knot, there should be a review. Like the one you get at work; I might even create an appraisal form for it:

How has your performance been in the last twelve months?

Have you been honest and faithful in your mind and body?

What are the qualities you feel still qualify you for this role?

Are you happy in your current position?

What, if anything, would help you to be better at this particular role?

Is there anything else I as your spouse can do to support you in your efforts?

Please furnish me with your happiest and unhappiest memory of the last year.

Any other questions?

What questions would you ask Tim during this renewal process?

She'd made me smile with her diatribe, and I knew the answer to her question straight away, I wanted to ask him why he'd hurt me so much, why he preferred online sex to real life sex and why he couldn't even talk to me about it. What had I done wrong? What was I doing wrong? The truth of the matter was I only wanted to understand so I could try and be the type of woman he'd desire. I wanted to find a way to stop our lives from running between my fingers. To find a way to stop the flow of our lives from moving in opposite directions, but most of all I needed him to help me, guide me, tell me how to stop hating him.

The H word scared me, hating him scared me. While Ivy had been sharing her thoughts on the yearly marriage performance assessment I hadn't taken my eyes off Tim. I sharpened my focus on him now and watched him as he bent his head towards Jude stood next to him, looking all fabulous in her high waisted pants and crisp white shirt, the lucky bitch. He threw his head back and laughed. I realised then that whilst I'd been listening to my inner voice the happy couple had finished their declaration of continued commitment into the next 25 years and everyone was winding themselves back up for more beers and a boogie.

Needless to say, I wasn't really in the mood for the rest of the evening. Jude and Naomi were having a blast on the dance floor, and as a rule I'd be there with them but I didn't have it in me.

Tim, the master of illusion, had definitely been drinking for quite a while, his body was loose, his stride had a cocky swagger to it, he was protected amongst this crowd. Only three people in the room knew what a shambles our marriage was at the moment, and it seemed only one of us was conscious of it now. I was completely taken aback by Tim, who was in the middle of a group of six or seven of our mates, laughing like he didn't have a care in the world. I saw him walk towards me, full of 40% proof vodka confidence. He slid behind me, grabbed my waist with both his arms and pulled me towards him. His body was swaying in time to the music, he pulled me close and tight, my arse cheeks were resting against him. A public display of affection. The feel of his proximity made my body stiffen; I couldn't help but notice it didn't make his do the same. The pretence was the final straw for me, I needed to get out of there, away from the people, the fun, the vows, and the temptation to turn round and knee him in the bollocks. I prised his arms away from my waist and turned slightly to see his face. "I'm going home Tim."

He looked a bit puzzled, "Aren't you having fun?" I was flabbergasted he had to ask at all, hadn't he noticed my reluctance to join in, my absence amongst the group when Matt and Trish were getting re-married? "Not really no, my head's not in the right place for this tonight."

And if you'd heard the conversation I've just had with her you'd know why, you careless knobhead, said Ivy.

"You stay if you want but I need to go home now."

He stood back from me. I could see him weighing up his options, his eyes flicking around the room working out what he was going to miss if he came with me; whether or not it was worth the chance he would be deeper in the shit if he stayed. To be honest I couldn't care less if he came with me or not. "I'm calling a cab, stay if you want or come home with me, whatever you want to do."

He rushed to reassure me "No, no of course I'll come home with you. I'll get the taxi!"

The ride home was tense, we didn't speak a word to each other. There was none of the usual discussion about the night we'd just had. No chat about the dress or the food, no joy at being alone together so we could exchange our views and laugh at the evening and the time we'd had with the others. I couldn't do any of that because since Ivy had made me aware of its existence, I understood that I was full to the brim with sadness and frustration, and shockingly, hatred for this man; I couldn't stop it.

As we walked into the house, him slightly behind me, I had to clutch my fists hard to my body to stop me turning round and planting a bunch of fives right between his eyes, a really good one, with all the force of all the anger I'd been carrying round with me since PC porngate.

Witnessing his belligerent behaviour in the last week or so, and being subjected to him trying to make me feel guilty for being angry with him, had highlighted a characteristic in my husband of nearly fifteen years that I really didn't like at all. I'd always known he was an influential man, but I never expected he would try to manipulate me. I had a strong suspicion he was trying to find any excuse to blame me for everything that had been going on behind my back in the last few months.

Once we were in the house we automatically fell into our usual routine. Tim got me a beer and poured himself a glass of red whilst I found my seat outside and lit a cigarette, then he came to sit with me and did the same. We still hadn't said a word to each other. We sat in silence and drank. I looked over to him, to his familiar but unfamiliar face and the thoughts that had come to me while I was watching the wedding vows came back to me again.

I drew my breath in deeply giving an indication I was about to start speaking. Tim turned his head eagerly in my direction, he looked pleased that I was finally breaking the silence.

I hadn't planned this conversation. I was speaking without thinking about what I was going to say, because the words had been a secret even to me up until now, but as I said them my voice was almost a whisper.

"I watched those people this evening, I heard the words they said, saw the emotion, the love and the dedication that motivated them to renew their vows and I know in my heart of hearts I couldn't say those words to you now. I hate you. I hate you for making me feel like this. I don't know what to do about it all anymore I think we need help, I want us to go to counselling."

I hadn't taken my eyes from his face the whole time I was speaking, I watched the shock register in his expression as the words hit him harder than any punch I could have thrown.

23

The Relate office was based slap bang in the central business area, on a busy main road of shops, cafes and bars, with lots of passing traffic. It was a less than ideal location for a place where couples go to thrash out their differences, where they would try hard to understand the reasons why they were struggling to keep their relationship together. Something so personal and heartbreaking should be done in private, complete private, like a nice little cottage somewhere miles away from anywhere.

To his credit, once Tim had picked his jaw up from the floor, he agreed to us seeking outside help with the inside of our relationship, without any more coercion on my part. When I'd watched the blood drain from his face and his smile melting into an expression of abject horror it told me everything I needed to know. It confirmed my suspicion that he hadn't really, for one minute, considered what I'd been going through.

I didn't want to give either of us the chance to change our mind so I hadn't wasted any time booking the appointment with the counsellor. I got us the first available slot on Thursday evening for our initial 'interview'.

We were shown to a waiting room, a small place with chairs lining the four walls, forcing everyone waiting to be seen to sit across from each other in one way or another.

Tim and I sat side by side not saying anything to each other. I wasn't sure there was an appropriate conversation to have in a place like this; what would we talk about, the shopping list, last night's TV? There were posters all over the room, the most positive thing about them was that they covered up the bloody awful wallpaper. They gave information about domestic violence, rape, suicide rates, STD's; horrible stuff, hellish things some of us go through at some point in our lives, shattering ourselves and others around us. This was not a cheerful place, there wasn't much sign of redemption or hope in this room. If I was in charge, I would offer up posters showing success rates, something like:

"Out of the two hundred and fifty five couples we counselled last year, two hundred and forty nine are back living a normal happy life! We are so successful with our therapy that they have managed to get their relationship back on track. They are shagging like rabbits and communicating with each other like never before. We are happy to report that after counselling, the other six couples parted amicably and often have dinner parties together with their new partners and happy extended families!"

Our names being called made me jump to attention. The woman at the door smiled in a professional and friendly way, and we stood and walked towards her. In the past, our immediate reaction when walking anywhere is to feel for the other one's hand, both reaching out at the same time, and as a rule we found each other easily, such was the habit we had formed over the years. We didn't do that today; Tim stood to one side to let me pass him and I followed the woman who would be our guide through the shitstorm of our betrothal, up a staircase and along a corridor towards an open door. Tim was directly behind me. Not too long ago, I would have wiggled my arse at him in a suggestive way, waiting for him to respond by slapping it for me or pinching a cheek. Today my body was ramrod straight. I entered the room and walked towards the chairs that were sat side by side, the one opposite was clearly intended for her. Tim sat beside me; she closed the door.

Fucking hell, this is some grown up serious shit, you're doing here, Ivy cranked up. *You're sat with the man you've treasured for years, in a strange, sparse room, waiting to see how this dour looking woman with a blow wave is going help you find each other again. There's a maze of complications she's going have to navigate you through. I don't know who I feel sorriest for, her or you. Good luck Rachel because I'll tell you now, you're going to need it.*

Once she'd got over the initial niceties, our names and hers, Glenda ('but you can call me Glen') gave us a stern look and then a speech about physical violence, how it would not be tolerated, how, if there was any sign of it in our relationship at all, she would have to refuse to continue with our sessions, and if there was any physical abuse of each other, or her, while we were in our meeting our counselling would stop immediately.

It made me feel like a fake, like I was running to the teacher to tell on my husband for being a naughty boy, that our problems were insignificant compared to her other clients. Maybe my deep fears and desolation were an overreaction to Tim's behaviour. I began to doubt the validity of my need to be here at all; were our problems trivial? Were we ok because we weren't kicking the shit out of each other?

And then I remembered the couple of times I had been quite tempted to smash Tim's teeth down the back of this throat, that there had been at least one occasion where I had had to stop myself from reacting in a way that was totally against my nature. I realised that Glenda was probably witness to a great deal of unreasonable behaviour caused by passion, disappointment, disagreements and hatred in this drab room, that was only made marginally better at the moment because it was lit by the late evening summer sun.

Sat across from us as she was, it was easy to talk to both of us at the same time. I was impressed by the way when she asked what it was that had brought us here, she didn't look to either one of us for an answer. I turned to Tim to wait for him to start talking, he was resolutely silent, he looked at me and gave me the 'go on then' nod.

"I was hoping that Tim might have wanted to explain about our current situation, but I can do it if he can't. We've been experiencing some changes in our marriage over the last few months, maybe longer. We have changed, our lives have changed and our sex life has definitely suffered. I've recently discovered some behaviours of Tim's that have made me question everything about our lives together, they are disrespectful and sneaky. I don't want this to be a mudslinging blame-game, I want us to be able to find a way to get through this awful time without any long-lasting damage. I'm here because I want to save our marriage, get it back to where it was. I looked over at Tim as I said this, he still didn't say anything.

Glenda looked at him too. "And you Tim, do you want to save your marriage?"

Tim's expression was one of indignation, "Of course I do! Rachel said she wanted to come here and I agreed. I did it because I want to show her, I am willing to work hard on our relationship, to put all the other stuff behind us and move on." He gave a tiny bow with his head, a sharp movement, almost the nodding equivalent of saying "so there." Glenda seemed quite happy with that response. It had sounded like he genuinely wanted to open up and share the truth behind his wandering eye and mouse clicking fingers.

That presumption didn't last very long though because the next question she asked was, "And is there any drug use in your relationship?" Without hesitation or thought Tim said firmly, "No." I glanced at him confused. Maybe honesty was not going to be the best policy for him after all. I wasn't sure where we were going to go from here, he'd lied within the first ten minutes of our first session.

To my great shame I didn't correct him, I let it ride. I was desperate that this woman should like us enough to think we had a chance to make things right again, and admitting I was partial to the odd line of coke didn't seem the way to do that. I was worried she would judge us, think us unworthy of her attentions, tell us to leave. My desperation kept me quiet.

****

The initial fib seemed to set the tone for the rest of the sessions, and so the three of us sat in that room in the same positions every Thursday evening, week in week out, we talked and we talked, and still there were no conclusions. We wore polite with each other, and with her, but all we really did was skirt round the issues we had. And whilst we touched on some of the things that were fermenting into something noxious between us, we never got to the bottom of any of it. Our inability to be honest broke my heart. I knew there were things we both had to say, that we should have been compelled to say, but it became apparent we couldn't. For the longest time I was too scared to admit that we had problems in case it created problems! Go figure.

I'm not sure if Glenda suspected we were being sparse with the truth or assumed we were always so vocally inept.

As the weeks ran into each other, life carried on as per our 'new normal' - separate bedrooms and remaining polite with each other. The pull of our friendship was bubbling underneath the surface of my hostility, and sometimes I had to rely on my underlying anger and disappointment to reinforce my determination to keep my own space. I had to protect myself from falling back into our usual, comfortable state of play – I wasn't prepared to do that without some kind of insight as to why he'd disrespected me so easily. I learned to keep my defences high and I guarded my privacy hard. The rest of the house might have felt tainted by the atmosphere between us, but the time on my own whilst Tim was working away, and having my own bedroom, became my sanctuary.

One evening, after I'd finished my workout at the gym, instead of doing my usual thing and having a shower there, I went straight home for a hot bath. It was a day I was expecting Tim back from work, but not until later. Feeling nicely chilled with a slight ache in my body from the exertion of my weights session, I laid in the bath for a while with a glass of wine and some of my favourite music playing through the upstairs speakers. Once the water started to become tepid, I got out and wandered from my bathroom into the dressing room. I'd been wrapped in a towel but it felt damp and uncomfortable on my skin so I dropped it on the floor. I was completely naked, unconsciously moving about my own space. I opened my wardrobe doors and was stood admiring the magnificent array of 'going out' clothes, deciding what to wear for a night out with Naomi and Jude at the weekend. I sensed rather than heard movement behind me, and turned quickly to see what it was. It was Tim, home early. He was stood in the doorway, less than ten feet away from me, his tall body and broad shoulders seeming to fill most of the space in the frame. My heart sank and I immediately felt conscious of my nakedness. I grabbed the wet towel from the floor to cover myself up from his inspection. Once I was confident that I'd shielded my nudity I asked him to move out of my way and as he stood aside. I walked past him as quickly as possible. When I got into the safety of my own room my hands were shaking and my legs felt weak from the shock and shame of him seeing me. I had no idea how long he'd been watching me for, but I felt exposed, inadequate and vulnerable.

The following week at the start of the session with Glenda, she asked if anything of note had happened during the previous week. Ivy started shouting at me, she was jumping up and down with her fists clenched screaming at me to talk about it.

Tell her about the dressing room scenario! Tell her how you felt when he saw you naked, tell her and Tim how ashamed you were that you weren't one of those blonde, bouncy women with fake tits that he has been spending his fantasy life with! Stand up for yourself, please, please be brave!

But I didn't.

Instead when she turned her gaze to me, our eye contact held, she gave me a slight nod, and without any forethought I began to talk about our past; the words came straight from my heart. I spoke of our lives together, explained how I'd always thought of our marriage as a magical thing, that being married to Tim felt like the most perfect thing I'd ever done. How proud I was to be Mrs Tim Bradbury, how much I loved being his wife. How I carried him with me everywhere I went, my best friend, my soul mate. I couldn't keep the pride out of my voice when I talked about our synchronicity, finishing each other's sentences, the eye contact that said more than a thousand words; the alignment that made us hard to tell apart.

As I spoke, the last few weeks of keeping Tim at arm's length, trying to protect myself from my feelings for him melted away to nothing. I'd broken my own defences. I tried to dial the passion in my voice down a bit as I told her about how doing even the most mundane things with him made me full of contentment, how my love for him consumed me, how I knew deep in my soul that he was my life and he was all that mattered to me.

I talked unconsciously; I couldn't stop. Eventually I took a deep breath, and let my brain work out what, if anything, I was going to say next. Inner Voice Ivy was silent. Glen was leaning forward in her chair, her usually neutral body turned into the direction of mine, I could see Tim in my peripheral vision, he was leaning towards me too. "Everything I do, I do it for him, and for us, for our lives. I worship him, and up until recently I thought we worshipped each other. And yet it seems that still isn't enough for him, that I'm not enough for him, because every time he presses that fucking button to power up his porn PC he makes a mockery of me, of us and of everything I thought was true."

I was done, I had nothing else to say. I gave a shrug of my shoulders and I sat back in my chair. Glen hadn't taken her eyes off me the whole time I spoke. Her professionalism might have stopped her showing emotion but it couldn't stop her from feeling it. She gave me a weak but encouraging smile and it felt like the equivalent of a pat on the back and a vote of sympathy for my belief in my relationship. I reflected her smile back to her. As she pulled her gaze away from me and towards Tim, my head moved in the same direction as hers. I hadn't shed one tear the whole time I'd been speaking but Tim's eyes were brimming with them, and when he spoke his voice was thick, "I'm sorry Rachel."

I thought I heard Glenda squeak with delight, but I'm sure it was just my imagination.

24

Things changed between us after my Relate revelations. Tim's apology was more genuine than any I'd had from him before. I can't say we skipped out of the session hand in hand with blue birds flying round our heads and a rainbow unrolling under our feet, but we did leave with a palpable sense of relief; I certainly felt it. The easing of my obstinate self-protection and finding the courage to finally remind Tim how much we stood to lose was exceptionally cathartic. He snapped out of his sulk the same night, he seemed lighter too, his one-word answers were gone and his tone of voice shifted from a whine redolent of a tired toddler, to that of a grown man.

He spent the next few weeks making sure I had everything I needed. He was extremely attentive, pulling out all the stops to defrost me, and it was working. Instead of stiff lipped exchanges of need-to-know information we started having conversations. He made a big effort to amuse me, it felt good to laugh with him, I was transforming from ice queen, to just a bit frosty queen, to actually I'm quite a warm queen now. He was displaying an extreme amount of patience and because of that I continually checked to make sure I wasn't punishing him, that I still genuinely needed time to get over his fuckwittery.

Being aware that we were getting along better and there was a softening of hostilities between us Glenda's role changed and instead of being our truth-seeker she became our cheerleader, she said lots of lovely encouraging things to us, about us; she said she could see the love we had for each other, she suggested we should try slowing our lives down a bit, commenting that perhaps we should stop pushing ourselves too hard to achieve things, to enjoy the things we already had rather than look to how we were going to take ourselves to the next thing we thought we should have. It made sense, and we promised her and each other with earnest that we would try. Confident that we were coping with our recovery we reduced our counselling sessions to once a month to give us time to work out between us, like the grownups we were, how to repair our friendship and marriage. She told us that I was in the driving seat when it came to Tim coming back into our shared bedroom. I think we've already established the fact that I was a pushover where my husband was concerned, and despite my restraint, I constantly looked for the appropriate time to invite him back into our marital bed.

It came very unexpectedly, one Friday evening five or six weeks after our breakthrough session. We had been apart for most of the week, and instead of his absence being a blessing, I had realised I missed him. I was home earlier than usual that day, I was buzzing from a good week at work, the fact that I had two days off and, if I was honest, with the anticipation of seeing Tim. I watched the clock waiting for him to come home with eagerness rather than the sense of dread I'd had in the couple of months before. I hadn't cooked, I wasn't that far back into Mrs Bradbury's world, but I had got a takeaway menu out and restocked the wine and beer fridges.

When he eventually arrived home, I heard his car pull up the drive and a bubble of excitement flew up from my belly to my chest. He was home. My eager eyes watched for him, I sat in the kitchen facing the front door, it was all very reminiscent of his return home after I'd discovered the hidden wank bank, but this time as soon as he stepped over the threshold and his presence filled the house, I had to hold on to the breakfast bar to stop myself from running down the hall and climbing up his body. My clit pulsed. I was, without a doubt, fully thawed out, I wasn't just the warm queen, I was hot, right royally fucking hot.

I watched his face light up when he noticed me, his body language was fluid and open, he was buoyant; he even had a bounce in his step. Unusually he'd left his bags in the car, instead of the tangle of briefcases and suitcases, for once he'd just brought himself in, sending me a clear message that he had no time for mundanity, he was keen to get in the house, he wanted to see me. Me. Me. Me. Even from the distance between us I felt the warmth flow from him, the bones in my spine straightened and I felt myself sit to attention.

"Hi." I smiled my ten-point Richter scale grin.

He smiled back, he looked delicious, his eyes were shiny, "Hey you."

We sat in the kitchen all evening, at the breakfast bar/party table. We made an effort, we flirted, we drank and we smoked in the house without either one of us pulling the "we really shouldn't" face. It was fabulous.

I was right on the very edge of submitting to my yearning to have my husband back. I couldn't decide if I should suggest drugs or sex, or both. Fortunately, my need to pee saved me from leaping too soon. I used the bathroom and as I washed my hands, I caught sight of my reflection and met my own gaze. As I looked myself in the eye, Inner Voice Ivy came to my support:

Go to bed, leave him for now, please take some time to cool your jets. You need to be absolutely sure you trust him again, that he's definitely worth the next metric fuck tonne of heartache that's going to come your way. If you forgive him now and let him back in, the trap door will be closed and you'll be back in a very bad place.

The thought pulled me up short. I was half pissed and more than a little bit clit-led. I was quite tempted to tell her to mind her own business, but she'd never let me down before and there was nothing to suggest she was doing that now. Tim was sat with his back to me as I made my return journey to the kitchen. I started speaking as soon as I was confident he would hear me over the music, "I'm going to bed now!" His head turned sharply, there was a definite look of surprise on his face, maybe even disappointment. Instead of taking my seat opposite him I stood facing him, an arm's length away, "I've had a big week, I'm knackered." I smiled at him to let him know I wasn't being a bitch. "Oh...ok then," he smiled back, "have a good night's sleep."

He stood up and leaned towards me, he was coming in for a kiss, and the temptation to grab him and pull him towards me, to surrender myself right this very second was huge, but I heard Ivy's advice once more and moved my lips away from the danger zone of his. He ended up kissing my cheek. It was more than a bit awkward but I brushed it off, and made my way towards the stairs.

"Rachel, are you busy this weekend?" His question stopped me in my tracks, my body turned back towards his. "Not really, why?" His eyes met mine for the first time in months, probably the first time since the lap dance club. "I wondered if I could take you out for lunch?" I tried to keep the delight out of my voice, but I don't really know why I bothered because I couldn't wipe the grin off my face.

"That would be lovely, yes." I left him sat in the kitchen with a topped-up glass of red wine. When I finally got into the bed I had guarded so carefully for the last few weeks I knew it wouldn't be long before he was sleeping in it with me again, in the meantime I gave myself and Ivy a mental hug, a pat on the back and her last words of the day were, *Good job resisting him tonight Rach, you should be very proud of yourself.*

I fell asleep with a tiny fizz of excitement in my belly for lunch the next day and a massive fizz in my clit with the anticipation of riding my much-loved husband's cock in the not too distant future.

****

Jude texted me the following morning to invite me to an afternoon drinking session with her and Nai, and I turned her down with the perfect excuse of a date with my husband she texted back, 'About bloody time ;0) '.

I was beside myself with excitement while I was getting ready, I chose my outfit carefully, I could feel my vaginal muscles jumping with anticipatory joy while I was in the shower concentrating on making myself a kilo lighter trimming my bush and shaving my neglected hairy bits. By the time I was finished I was able to look at my reflection with pride, I knew for the first time for ages I looked lovely. I was proud of myself for the way I'd stuck to my guns and worked hard to save my marriage. This was my reward, the start of a new phase in my life; today I was going to get my husband back.

It was a fabulous afternoon; we went to my most favourite Italian. Tim had reserved us the best table on the mezzanine floor, we ate light, and at Tim's insistence after a couple of beers we splashed out and had a bottle of their best champagne. Our easy manner from the evening before carried on, we were flirty, the subjects we talked about were light and easy, there was no trace in our conversation of anything that had happened over the last year or so, no reference to Glenda, the Relate sessions, or Tim's wander down the online equivalent of the Red Light district. We played on each other's memories, laughing and teasing, remembering the good times, our plethora of holidays and weekends away, we spoke fondly of our early relationship when we lived in a tiny house and had been so skint, we both did three jobs. We celebrated, a lot.

We moved on from the restaurant to a bar close by, there were only a few other drinkers in the late afternoon and the music was mellow. We were sat side by side on high stools at a window seat, the second bottle of champagne of the day sat between us. As Tim refilled my glass, the melted ice water dripped from the bottom of the bottle onto my forearm and his left hand immediately moved to it and tenderly brushed the water away. It was the first time he had put his hands anywhere near my body for months. I looked down at his fingers, at his wedding ring sat where I had put it during a comical and tear-jerking ceremony in a packed registry office nearly sixteen years ago. The longevity of our relationship had been a massive source of pride for me and I felt it anew now. The sense of pride was swiftly followed by the longing for everything to be back to normal between us, to sweep the past few months of heartache under the carpet, and never lift the corner to inspect it again.

I was still staring at his hand, he had left it resting lightly on my arm, his thumb was stroking my wrist, my whole body shuddered with delight, the throb of sexual excitement pulsed deep inside me, a tiny explosion, almost an orgasm. The mood was broken by a sudden racket coming from the bar behind us, much hilarity and high-pitched friendly banter. I knew even before I turned round to look it was Jude and Naomi. I didn't want to see them, I didn't want them to see us, I didn't want anyone to break the spell. I met Tim's eyes, he said quietly, "Do you want to go and join them babe?" I shook my head, my eyes never leaving his. "Not really no, I'd rather go home and spend some more time with you, just us." He nodded his agreement, "How quickly can you finish that glass of bubbles?" I laughed quietly lifted the glass to my lips and downed it in one go, smacking my lips in a self-satisfied way, "That quickly. You?" He did the same, I snorted a laugh as he hiccupped, and we started to leave. He moved in front of me to shield me from view from our friends at the bar, his hand reached behind him feeling for mine, I put mine in his.

All was well in the world.

25

The intimacy I felt from the quality time we'd spent together made my spirit calm; a happy glow encompassed me. Bolstered up by this renewed feeling of security and encouraged by our pleasurable day, I decided it was time to throw myself at his mercy, the intimacy and familiarity of the gentle touch of his thumb on my wrist earlier made me crave more.

I needed to feel something sexual between us, I needed physical proof that my conviction and hope were justified. I wanted to be able to approach him in his mellow state and see desire in his eyes: for me. Before I could talk myself out of it, I left Tim in the kitchen with a beer and took mine with me upstairs, to the dressing room, to the shelves in my shoe wardrobe that held my fuck-me pairs. I chose quickly, and with as little thought as possible, stripped off my blouse and skinny jeans down to my beautiful white silk underwear. I didn't want to talk myself out of this, I needed it. I couldn't let my fractured self-esteem hold me back, so I didn't inspect myself too closely, instead I took another pull on my beer, shoring myself up with another mouthful of liquid confidence-booster and began my journey down the stairs. My heart was beating so hard in my chest I was convinced he'd be able to hear it from where he was, that it would give my game away. I was breathless, the nerves caused by the thought of Tim's possible rejection were in danger of outweighing my tsunami of desire.

I steeled myself against it, I wasn't going to be put off by this, I was a woman on a mission.

I forced myself into the kitchen. Tim had his back to me while he looked for a playlist on the iPod. He was leaning over at the waist; his Levi clad arse in all its glory was all the encouragement I needed to carry on. I wanted to say something saucy and sexy to get his attention, but as I formed the words I wanted to say, I stopped myself. I thought of another phrase to use, a better one, I stopped myself again speechless with fear. While I was dithering, he sensed me behind him and turned round, "Oh fuck Rachel, wow, you look gorgeous." His eyes roamed up and down my body, his expression seemed genuinely lustful.

This was exactly the response I was hoping for, the one that had motivated me in the first place, and my heart sang. I got my best sex kitten strut on and walked towards him, my cellulite and rounded stomach - that still had the indentation of the zip from my skinny jeans - were pushed to the back of my mind. As I approached him, I took a glance at his cock, how was it? Was it responding in the way it should? Was it joining in? I almost slurped with greed when I saw the denim stretched across his hard on. As I reached him, I pushed the full length of my body into his, I could feel his cock throb hard, I could feel my body respond and felt myself throb back, like genital Morse code. My body started to prepare me for him. We kissed, a deep, full on, promise of things to come. I loved the way this man kissed me; the instant our tongues met it set a wave of motion in me that started at my cunt and burned right into my heart. It melted me and made me want to be part of him, and him me.

My shoes helped reduce the difference in our size, I was the perfect height now. I ran my hands up behind him to feel the strength in his shoulders, then slowly let them slide down the muscles of his back and the ravine of his spine. My hands found his arse, and with force I pulled the lower half of his body closer to mine. I gasped with longing, I needed this so badly, to feel his desire for me, this confirmation that he still wanted me.

I released my hold on him slightly and moved myself towards the kitchen worktop, I pulled myself up onto the cool granite surface and into a sitting position, I pulled my knickers to one side, allowing us both easy access to my vagina. I wrapped my legs round his waist and pulled him towards me again.

I knew from experience that Tim liked to be led, I knew it would seal the deal for me if I was in control, but the act of being in charge scared me. He grabbed the outside of my thighs and brought himself even closer, and I felt a jolt of delight when I realised he was joining in. He pulled the buttons of his flies open in one movement and pulled his boxers away from his cock, tucked them under his balls, I'd never known him do that move before. He was harder than I'd seen him for a very long time, he thrust himself inside me, I was so wet he slid into me without any effort, hard and deep, I felt the tip of his penis hit my cervix, and then he was moving away from me again, my legs tightened around him so he couldn't move away too far. I left just enough room for my hand and as soon as I sent my fingers to join our genitals, with the first touch of my clit I came, my orgasm was deep and long, my moans were genuine but unusually for me quite quiet, I didn't want to startle him, to put him under pressure.

I watched his face as he heard my triumphant cries, I felt my muscles contract around his cock, they pulled him further into me, tiny shocks of pleasure still shooting through me with every thrust. I saw him realise it was his turn, and it occurred to me that he hadn't been holding back waiting for me, he'd been busy concentrating on getting himself there, trying hard to make himself come. The relief I felt when I saw his face full of concentration relax with the pleasure of his orgasm made me want to weep.

His body shook with the effort of his come, he vocalised his pleasure with a long guttural sound coming from the back of his throat, a dirty, satisfied, glorious sex sound. This time we were both breathless. He stayed inside me, his body leaning away slightly, he roughly pulled the cups of my bra under my breasts, he took his mouth to my nipples his tongue and teeth taking it in turns to tease me. Although his cock was losing its hardness the feel of him still inside me drove me crazy with lust for him, as he teased my rock hard nipples I slid my hand back to my pussy, I was sticky with a mixture of both our juices, Tim bit my nipples gently and within seconds I came again, harder than the last time, as I cried with pleasure he watched my face, dropped his gaze to watch my fingers as I finished my masturbation. He pulled my hand away from my clit and sucked every finger I had used to get myself off, he came to me and kissed me again, I could taste us both, mingled again. Just as we should be.

****

It wasn't until much later that evening after several hours tactile, loved-up touching, smoking, drinking, talking and laughing and enjoying the feeling of fullness the sex had left me with that Ivy whispered, *He's never done that dirty sexy thing with his flies before, and what about that bra pulling nipple biting thing, that's not a Tim move is it?* I rolled my eyes towards my forehead and said "Fuck off Ivy and leave me in peace."

26

The next time I saw Jude, for a midweek, 2-for-1 meal deal at yet another of our favourite pubs, she confessed she had actually seen Tim and I on that Saturday afternoon, but not until her and Naomi were already in the bar. I was happy that she'd been thoughtful enough to give us a swerve.

We discussed how wonderful our date had been although I didn't go into too much detail with Jude about what had happened on the kitchen worktop. I alluded to the fact that our 'dry spell' was over, but I didn't get into the full-on conversation: "Oh and then I got home and seduced my husband, fucked him senseless on the sparkly granite worksurface by the sink." "Did you really? Good for you, what did you wear?"

Because of my reticence to share the more intimate details of our sexy peace treaty, I didn't mention the new tricks my old dog had performed. I did think about them though - a lot. I vacillated between tiny electric shocks of delight followed by a deep shudder of desire at the memory, to a spine straightening jolt of fear and a slap of reality when Ivy kept on with her intense investigation into how Tim had learned to release his penis and tuck his undies under his bollocks in one swift move if it wasn't, as per my recent imaginings of him, from shagging a woman down a back alley for a stack of cash.

Jude and I didn't dwell too much on my marriage for a change, we had so much other news to share that evening. Jude had outdone herself at the weekend, not only had she managed to beat her personal best on the treadmill she'd done it with a hangover of mammoth proportions after her Saturday session with Naomi, which had included the two of them eating a full KFC family feast whilst booking a ten-day holiday to Sardinia together. I was torn between being delighted for them and almost wishing I was still pissed off with Tim so I could go too.

When I eventually got home, full of enough mushroom risotto to soak up the two large glasses of red I'd consumed, Tim was already in bed; our bed.

Whilst Jude had spent Sunday morning in the gym, on the treadmill, running 15k, despite being full of tequila and fried chicken coated with the Colonel's secret recipe, I'd invited my husband back into our room. Full of sexed up satiated love, my thinking was that perhaps the joy of us sharing the same mattress might induce him to finally get round to christening it. The items I had violently evacuated to the room with no working radiator several months beforehand were once again back in their place, the T shirts carefully folded (by Tim, not me obviously) nestled in colour sequence in their drawer, his Kindle and alarm clock were back on the bedside table and his pillows were placed carefully on his side of the bed; my sleeping down the middle of the mattress hiatus, both a blessing and a curse, was over. Now when I rolled over in my sleep instead of finding more lovely extra space, I found my lover's warm body and downy arse cheeks to spoon in to. It was Wednesday now, a full four days since Tim's semi turgid dick and my cum-hungry fingers had brought me to my second orgasm, and while the burn of the afterglow was still with me, it was wearing off a bit. I didn't want to appear greedy but to be honest I was ready for another go on my husband's penis.

My subtle attempts at seduction weren't going too well, I'd tried rock hard nipples against his back as I hugged him goodnight, stroking his bum cheeks, kissing his neck, having a cheeky reach round to his balls but his reaction was far from favourable and I quickly realised that Tim being back in our bedroom wasn't about us making love more often, it was a comfort thing, I'd basically gained nothing in the sex department but lost half the bed. I needed some big moves if I was going to pull this one off, if you'll excuse the pun.

****

Tim's birthday was only a couple of weeks away and it was our wedding anniversary a few weeks later. I thought we deserved a treat so as a surprise for his special day, and to take my mind off the fact that those two best mates of mine were jetting off on holiday together, I booked us a four night long weekend break in a log cabin in the middle of nowhere, with wood-burning fires, a super-king four poster bed, incredible views over the Peak District, and a hot tub guaranteed to have no one overlooking it at all. A shag palace. I spent a stupid amount of money on underwear, champagne, four E's, cocaine and food that was already prepared and only needed heating up.

As well as the complete indulgence of the weekend I decided I wanted to buy him a gift so special he would drop his jaw when he opened it. I had a picture in my mind of us lying in bed on the morning of his birthday, I would give him his present, and he would be so blown away by it that he would immediately throw it to one side, shimmy under the covers and give me mind blowing head as a display of his thanks. What, I pondered in the department store, might that be? "How about an iPhone? They're amazing, the best thing ever!" Suggested a sales assistant, "The Phone store's two floors down, next door to the shop that has those lovely smelly candles and body creams."

And so, I bought a mobile phone that the bright and well-trained salesperson promised me, had a 'mind-blowing array of technological advancement.' I was told with the earnest conviction of a newly trained sales pitch that 'it was a breakthrough communications device'. It was, as Joe on the genius bar pointed out as he joined in with his colleague's enthusiasm, 'opening up a whole new world of possibilities – it's like carrying the internet around in your pocket'. I bought it. After a little indulgent purchase of the most beautiful smelling body lotion in the shop next door, I went home; my credit card limit was a bit damaged but my reputation as a generous, it not a bit naïve, gift giver was maintained.

✳✳✳✳✳✳✳✳✳✳✳

The only thing I could say about the weekend away is, I'm glad it wasn't for my birthday, because if it had been, I would have been even more disappointed than I already was.

The log cabin was gorgeous, the rolling views of the countryside were magnificent, and the hot tub was, without doubt, exceptionally private. Tim was blown away with my choice of accommodation, and even more delighted when I surprised him with the size of the stash I'd brought. Neither of us needed much encouragement to indulge ourselves these days – it was fast-becoming one of our few shared hobbies. We drank most of the champagne, took all of the E's and more than half the coke. Tim crashed out and went to bed at 3am but I was wired and stayed up to watch the sunrise from the comfort of the hot tub whilst carrying on smoking, drinking and having the odd toot for good measure. There's no action without reaction and when I finally fell into bed at 8.30am, I had pruney, water-aged skin, I was dehydrated, I could smell the ciggies on my own breath and my hangover was kicking in.

There's nothing glamorous about drugs the day after. I felt like death warmed up when I eventually woke up late in the afternoon the same day. Every movement made me want to vomit. I was so hungover all I wanted to do was eat rubbish food and go back to bed, and that was exactly what I did. Tim, who despite his comparatively early night wasn't feeling much better, came with me and we slept from early evening until the next morning; his birthday.

The anticipation of giving him his gift woke me early. I showered away the final remnants of Friday night's blowout and used my new body lotion to try and replace the moisture that the hot tub had stolen from me. I wore my sexiest lace French knickers with one of his T shirts, tousled my hair surfer-chick style and hoped I looked sexy rather than cute. I woke him with a cup of his favourite coffee and his massively indulgent present on a tray.

The phone went down a storm with the birthday boy, his jaw did indeed drop, but rather than the shimmy under the sheets for the anticipated coitus, I got a "Wow Rach, this is amazing thank you," with a chaste kiss on the lips. And then I lost him for most of the day whilst he transferred all his numbers from his other phone, set up his ID, and buried his nose in the user manual; I mean for fuck's sake, who actually reads the instructions? I sat and watched him for a while, but one man and his mobile phone isn't really a spectator sport, so I went for a long, cobweb-clearing walk.

When I got back, Tim was still glued to his new toy, so I stripped naked in the bedroom and walked past him in all my bare-arsed glory, wiggled my bum at him as I passed, and I climbed into the hot tub with an ice-cold beer, the iPod on shuffle and a strategically placed jacuzzi jet. Tim came to join me about half an hour later, along with my other two great weaknesses, champagne and Charlie, and after a couple of glasses of the first and shored up with a nostril full of the second, I showed him my trick with the newly discovered hot tub clitoris activity centre. But rather than join in the fun, he watched me with an expression that implied embarrassment rather than eroticism; not quite what I'd been aiming for. Still, at least I had one orgasm that weekend.

When I woke up in our indulgent four poster bed the next morning, I was flooded with sadness that, despite my continued endeavours, we still hadn't connected with each other in a physical way. I needed to feel some enthu siasm from him, some validation he still desired me and was ready for us to return to a full married life, to help me trust him again by showing he desired me, and not some dark-haired skinny dominatrix from the websites he'd spent so much time exciting himself with.

In my desperation, I decided to take an even less subtle approach than getting myself off in the hot tub to attract his attention. I woke him gently with long unhurried fingertip strokes down the length of his back, it took a while to awaken him but when he finally did, I felt his body stiffen. To encourage him to relax back, I ran the palm of my hand along the shape of his side, my touch was light and an expression of the overwhelming love I had for him that I wanted him to experience. As I reached his waist and bum cheek, I pushed the length of my body into his and curled myself into him, warm naked skin touching warm naked skin. I tenderly kissed his shoulder, I slid my hand as far down his leg as I could reach, and then slowly moved it round to the front of his body, I could feel the hardness of the muscles in his thighs, my fingers ran along the outline of them until I reached the top.

These are my best tricks, they come from years and years of working out what turns my lover on. I've brought him to a frenzied orgasm many times with tenderness and teasing strokes. It had never failed me before and I was confident I was on to a winner now. As I slowly reached for his cock his body jerked away from me, he moved so far away he was almost hanging off the edge of the bed, he threw his body a hundred and eighty degrees to face me, his expression had a panic-stricken look that he was trying hard but failing miserably to hide. The timbre in his voice when he spoke was almost a plead, "Don't Rachel, please."

He threw the covers off himself and got up from the bed so quickly my hand was left mid stroke hanging in the space his body had left. He headed straight for the bathroom and as hard as he tried to shield himself from my vision I could see, that despite my best efforts, his dick was flaccid. I was devastated. I instantly felt like I was in the wrong.

I got up myself and followed him to the bathroom door; it was locked. "Tim, please open the door, I'm sorry, I shouldn't have put you under so much pressure, please come out and talk to me about it, what did I do wrong? Help me to understand?"

Eventually he opened the door. We were stood as face to face as we could be with the height difference and my bare feet. I was naked still; he was wearing a towel around his waist. He didn't look at me - not at my eyes, my face or my bare body - he looked around me rather than at me.

"I'm so sorry Tim, I just thought after the other weekend and everything..." The look of hurt on his face stopped me from speaking, I felt guilty, the shadow of blame laid across me. "Is there something wrong with you that we can go to the doctors for? Are you sick? Tell me how I can help - please." I moved to touch him, but he stepped away from me. "It's ok Rach, really, let's not talk about it anymore." He nodded his head indicating that he wanted me to get out of his way so he could go back into the bedroom, I stepped away for him, confused and ashamed.

There wasn't much chat over our breakfast, I was contrite and guilty and felt almost villainous for my wandering hands and he was back in his comfortable persona of the victim. We were each painted back into our corners. Throughout the day I apologised repeatedly; after one heartfelt expression of my sorrow for scaring him with my passion and desire, for needing some confirmation of his feelings for me in the form of a rock-hard cock, (although given the outcome I would have settled for a semi on), he smiled at me, a real smile that reached his eyes as well as his lips, it made my heart leap with joy. "Ok Rach, lets drop it now hey? But I'll tell you something, I'm telling Glenda of you when we see her next."

****

With an honesty he'd rarely used with Glenda during our next meeting he shared the barest details of the weekend with her. He alluded to my attempt to get him to join in the jiggy fun I'd had in mind, but he offered no explanation as to why he was so scared by my touch or the reason behind the vehemence of his escape from the bed. I didn't ask her to pursue his reasons any further because, to be frank, I thought I'd be on the naughty step for it. The relief and validation I felt when Glenda looked first at me and then Tim, saying, "Actually Tim, I must say Rachel is completely within her rights to express a desire for intimate relations with you, honesty is a healthy approach, how else will you both move forward, if it not by expressing your desires and having open conversation?"

I had to sit on my hands to stop myself punching the air with my delight at this turn of events.

Inner voice Ivy was blowing kisses at Glen and flicking the V's in Tim's general direction and gloating. *Take that you supercilious wanker. Time to say you're sorry, dick head.*

But he didn't, of course, and once we left the relate room, we never mentioned the incident again.

27

My sales territory was vast, consequently I spent a lot of time in my car, the daily grind of motorway driving giving me lots of downtime to do all manner of things. The first car I ever got with cruise control, while the car was keeping itself at a steady 80mph without any interference from me I went through a phase of motorway masturbation; in my defence, I only did it when the roads were quiet.

Now though, I stick to much safer forms of in-car entertainment: pelvic floor muscle exercises, squeezing my bum cheeks in time to tunes on the radio while alternately flexing my biceps, chatting to my mates on my hands free; and thinking. The thinking bit was becoming very tiring, Ivy and I had continual conversations about the same subject, Tim.

Ivy had a field day with Glenda's seal of approval of my urge to have sex with Tim, she spent days on end conversationally patting my back for *being brave enough to come on to him*, but in the next breath asked those hard questions only she can: *Why was he so scared in bed that morning? What was the panic on his face about and why was his cock soft when you did all his favourite stuff?*

I was exhausted trying to work out what was going on, so in the end I convinced us both to sweep the deeply dissatisfying weekend and Tim's terror at my sexual advances under the imaginary carpet with all the other stuff and leave it there.

Realising I was close to the end of my tether with it all, she agreed.

Even with the ceasefire called on my mental torture, I was more stressed than usual. I seemed to be so busy I barely had time to do everything I wanted during the week. Our weekends were the same and I didn't seem to be enjoying anything as much as I used to. Just to add another level of pressure, I'd been asked to take part in a new scheme at work and found myself with the responsibility of being a mentor to a newly recruited Uni graduate.

I wasn't looking forward to it at all, but when Laura bounded into my work life like a cross between an overenthusiastic puppy and a thoroughbred racehorse, her joie de vivre was as wonderful as it was irritating. But providing she sat still for long enough, there was no mistaking she was pure class. She stood taller than me (not too difficult to do), slim without being skinny, with bum-length, perfectly straight, shiny brown hair, big brown eyes and don't even get me started on her teeth; I don't believe I have never seen such perfect dentistry. All in all, she was a good kid, and despite her energetic insistence on stopping me from being 'such an old woman,' I discovered I had a big soft spot for her.

Which is why I let her return the mentor's favour and humoured her efforts to 'drag me out of the 90's and into the 21st century'. Since following her guidance I started using the expression 'get involved,' I was no longer allowed to use the word 'cool' and she even in sisted I change my brand of lip gloss because the one I was using was 'rank', apparently. The one change I was deeply resistant to was joining Facebook, but she talked about it almost evangelically and was constantly on at me to sign myself up to it. She wouldn't take no for an answer, and despite my instance that I had enough friends, that I didn't care about finding my long-lost school mates or want to play stupid games with complete strangers she eventually snapped and said "Oh for fuck sake Grandma, just open an account and see if you like it." With that type of motivational speech how could I refuse?

The following weekend I sat down with my laptop, and as with anything remotely resembling IT, I got Tim to help as I created my profile page. He seemed to find his way around the site easily and once the basics had been set up, he gave me an overview of how it worked, how to add friends and so on. I added Laura the nag, thinking how delighted she would be. As far as I was concerned, I'd done as I'd been told and my reputation with Laura as 'almost bang on trend' was reinstated, so that was it. "You know a lot about this Facebook thing, how have you managed to pick it up so quickly?" Tim was navigating his way around like a pro. "I've got my own page babe, I've had it for ages, it's great fun.

I could hear Ivy nearly choking in her effort to comment on this news. *He's what? Had it for how long? Why didn't he tell you?* As casually as possible I said, "You never mentioned it." He was concentrating and didn't move his eyes away from the screen. "I set it up a while ago, it was someone at work that was saying it could be handy for networking, I thought I'd give it a go. Check your page now, Rach." I took my suspicious eyes away from the side of his face and back to my own laptop, I had a friend request from Tim Bradbury, I accepted straight away. "I might as well add Jude and Naomi now I'm on here, they'll get a right bloody shock when they find out I've caved in, now we're all on here we can start throwing sheep at each other or whatever else it was that Laura was telling me about."

****

The snow started Monday afternoon as I was driving home from work and didn't stop until well after the 10 o'clock news had told me to expect blizzard conditions. I was snowed in. My car was so entrenched behind a deep drift I couldn't even see it never mind hope to get it off the drive. Not without a tiny bit of glee, I realised I was going to be stuck where I was for at least a couple of days. Tim was working away, so I was home alone, just me surrounded by the quality of light and silence that only snow can create.

The following morning, I logged onto my emails in a half-hearted attempt at pretending to work and caught up with a backlog of administration tasks that needed doing. By lunchtime I was twiddling my thumbs. A text from Laura begging me to have a look at her photos on Facebook from her Saturday night out provided me with just the distraction I needed. I hadn't paid Facebook any attention since I'd set up my profile a couple of weeks back, so I logged on to have a nosy. Once I was on the site it didn't take me long to figure out that anyone who was determined, bored or motivated enough could have a thorough delve into everything it had to offer. And so, I did. I had a look at Laura's photos, and once I'd estab lished that I might be an 'old woman' but she still had a lot to learn about how to really misbehave on a Saturday night, I went looking for the games she'd mentioned at some point during her more persuasive period. She'll do well in sales that girl.

I was delighted to find Scrabble. There's nothing like my most favourite word game to pass an hour or so and in the absence of Tim, my fiercest opponent, I thought I'd have a go on Facebook instead. I worked out how to start the game and nipped for a quick wee before I got involved. By the time I got back a few minutes later there was a message waiting for me "Hi, how are you? I'm a massive Scrabble fan too. Where are you playing from?" The unrequested contact felt like a massive invasion of my privacy, I had no idea how the other person had contacted me. I totally freaked and slammed the laptop shut.

Later that evening after a couple of beers, half a joint and a lovely giggly stoned chat with Jude about lots of things but nothing in particular, I sat inside my beautiful warm house looking out at the back garden lit by the moon beaming from a cloudless sky. I was smiling at the mad pattern my footprints had made that afternoon when I had a run around in the snow, now frozen into place by the sub-zero temperatures.

Definitely another day off tomorrow Rach, Ivy said gleefully and then, *I know you don't want to talk about this...* "Let's not then," I muttered. She carried on anyway.

The Facebook privacy thing, that's what's bothering me, I think a clever person with previous form for sneaky behaviour could have a whole lot of stuff going on with Facebook, and no one else need know about it. I knew she was right but I didn't want to have to face up to it *He never even told you he had a page thingy did he? Said he'd been on it for ages, didn't he? Who is he friends with on there? Go and check.*

I didn't need much more prompting, I logged back in to my account again and then went straight to Tim's page. I clicked on the tab with the title Friends and as I did I got a message telling me the account I had accessed was private and I wouldn't be able to see Tim Bradbury's friend list. *Well, fancy that*, Ivy said. *So to go back to my previous question who is he friends with on there? Why does he hide their names do you think? What's the big secret?*

I began to gasp for air and I realised I'd been holding my breath. I tried to be logical and sensible, to stay calm, but without warning, a whole box of anxiety fireworks exploded in my chest.

28

There might have been a few hours, sometimes even a couple of days, when the anxiety I carried was only a tiny flutter in the background of my life, and then other times it was a boom of a terror that shocked me to my core. I had no control over it, sometimes it crept up behind me when I was doing the most mundane task and let off a bomb deep in my chest.

My mind wouldn't stop, it was a whirr of so many conflicting emotions. Inner voice Ivy and I had had to lift the ban on not over-analysing Tim's behaviour. I wanted to trust him, to be sure he had both our best interests at heart and not just his. And despite there being no real evidence that he was 'doing something he shouldn't', my growing mistrust of him turned me into someone I didn't know - a suspicious, mistrustful woman - and I hated myself for it. I wasn't very keen on Ivy either.

I sometimes caught myself watching him when he was on his phone or laptop and I would literally bite my tongue to stop me from asking outright what he was up to. It seemed to me he had even taken to slanting his phone away from my direct line of sight when he was using it, I was sure I wasn't imagining it, he tried so hard to shield his pin number it was painful to watch. I was sat on the sofa one evening pretending to be engrossed with the TV but the corner of my eyes were busy observing him while he did the minutest twist of his body away from me.

He might was well just ask you to turn your back when he's doing it, his code's 6899, we both know that, it's the two years Man U won the champions league.

****

Tim and I carried on with our everyday lives, but the depth of our friendship had changed again. It felt like we were dancing round each other, we were certainly avoiding the issue of our non-existent sex life and I still found myself unable to talk to him about it. I was scared our marriage was slipping through my fingers whilst I just left my suspicions to fester. Days on end went by when I just got on with living, working, eating, drinking and sleeping, without the perpetual temptation to sneak a look at his variety of devices of deception or delve into his pockets and search his wallet.

But then came the fear; it was more subtle than the anxiety but just as invasive, it slithered up my spine, a lazy curl of dread unfolding its way slowly but surely into the back of my thoughts. It was a stubborn bastard and I absolutely could not shake it off. I wouldn't allow myself to sink so low though, I am not and never have been a jealous woman as a rule and I had a feeling that if I started behaving like one, I would lose even more of my self-respect and right then I hadn't got much more to lose. I was ashamed of myself for so many things, it was hard to prioritise them.

As usual I used that familiar old brush to sweep everything away, and it joined all the other things under what was fast becoming a very big lump in the carpet. And on I went, trying my hardest to carry on as normal, there were even some occasions when I realised I was actually enjoying myself, but they were rare days.

I really needed to speak to Jude but I hadn't had the chance to get her alone for any length of time; she was busier than usual at work and then there was the guy she met in Sardinia, he seemed to be taking up a big portion of her spare time.

Although she was playing it down, I could see there was a sparkle in her eye. She was trying to be cool (sorry Laura) but I witnessed her do a little dance, including a twirl, when he called her one day as we were leaving the gym; I'd never, ever seen her do that before.

It's funny how things work out though, this afternoon we met by chance in our favourite boutique and once we were together, we stayed that way. We called in the pub for a 'quick one' on the way home, of course one turned into two, and in the end we'd let Tim know where we were and he came to meet us. During the evening the pub filled up with a mixture of regulars, acquaintances and several of our drinking mates. We had a ball. At one-point Tim and I were dancing to Status Quo, we were laughing so hard it hurt my belly. There were at least a dozen of our friends joining in the unplanned gathering, we were all hanging out at the bar, drinking too fast, laughing hard and making up bawdy lyrics to whatever song was playing on the jukebox.

I was sitting on a stool with Tim standing next to me - we were together, close, like we used to be - his arm wrapped round my waist, and he squeezed my body to him and kissed me a couple of times. It turned into one of the best nights out I'd had for ages.

Unwilling to stop partying just because the pub was closing, Jude came home with us. We sat in our usual spots in the kitchen having another beer. Tim had gone into the lounge to watch the football, leaving us with the space, time and motivation to finally have a catch up. She was trying to be tight with her information about the man who had created the pirouette situation. "I don't want to spoil it, it's lovely and I think the reason it's lovely is because he's so far away from real life. I don't think it'll come to anything - the distance, his circumstances are enough to make me run for my life!" She rolled her eyes and sighed as if I'd twisted her arm, "He's got four kids under 12 that live with him and his ex-wife is a right bitch by all accounts. It's never going to work with us, but he's fucking gorgeous, seriously sexy, and from what I can tell, more than a bit wealthy. Please let's not analyse it because I worry if I admit what I really feel, I might fall for him hard. And I can't, it's too complicated." Her face was a mixture of expressions but mostly it was still an intense plead. "At least tell me his name Jude, unless you want me to keep calling him Mr Sardinia." She smiled her, face flooded with joy as she said "Comita".

Now we were in such close proximity of each other, without anyone else around, my need to speak to her overwhelmed me. Under the pretense of checking the status of his red wine glass, in case it needed filling, I put my head round the door to the lounge. The fire was on full blast, the tele was on the Sports channel and some irritating commentator was telling Tim about the way today's football results had affected the league tables, not that he was paying any attention because he was fast asleep.

Feeling secure in the knowledge that there was no way he was going to wake up, I went back to my spot across from Jude. My hands clasped in front of me I leaned my weight on my forearms and took myself closer to her, immediately she did the same; the body language of the confidant.

Being sat with my secret keeper unzipped me; even though I knew he was dead to the world I was worried that Tim might hear me, so my rushed words were quiet. "I'm scared Jude, in fact let's not call it that, I'm fucking terrified." Her head pulled back from me, her quizzical look could mean so many things, I didn't stop to question any of them, "I can't help it. I can't find it in me to trust him anymore. I can't ignore all the things my feely-feels are feeling - Inner voice Ivy is having a field day. I can't deny it anymore, I am completely and utterly convinced that he's up to something behind my back." The next expression on her face was undoubtable, it told me she thought I was overreacting. She leant away from me completely. "Rachel, fuck's sake babe, what do you think he's up to now? Are you sure you're not just twitchy because of the porn and stuff? Why would he be 'up to something' as you call it? He promised, you've been going to the counselling thing for ages, why would he go to all that trouble and then still carry on behind your back?"

I tried to let her appease me, I really did. I let her words wash over me, I wanted her to be right. I listened with a will to believe her that was nearly as strong as hers was to convince me that I'm wrong. "There's something, I don't know what it is, he spends all his time on that iPhone."

"That's my fault for introducing him to Angry Birds."

"Well it's turning me into an angry bird, why is he being so secretive?"

"Be careful what you're looking for Rachel, I'm sorry you're struggling, and I suppose it's only to be expected after everything, but please, please be careful that you don't pin things on him he's not doing." Her mobile started to ring, and her head shot towards her handbag, she looked from it to me and then back to it again. She dipped her hand into her bag and retrieved her phone, "It's Mr Sardinia, he said he would call if he could." I smiled an encouraging smile, "Answer, Jude."

"But you need to talk..."

"I'm ok, take Comita up to bed with you if you want." she didn't need any more encouragement. I watched her back retreat from me down the hallway, turn to take the stairs and I heard her say, "Hello gorgeous," in what she thought was her sexiest voice. It wasn't.

Thank fuck for that I thought she'd never leave!

"Bugger off Ivy, she's my best friend."

No, she's not, she's not listening anyway. I'm not even sure she's on your side, why can't you see that? Now stop wasting time and go and check that cocksucker's phone. I lit another ciggie. 'No, I bloody well won't, stop it.'

Well I think you should, enough of this 'I'm better than that' bollocks, all that's doing is making things worse, you're driving yourself mad with worry, at least if you check then you'll know for sure one way or another.

"I am not going to be that woman Ivy, I can't do it, I have to trust him." She snorted a sort of laugh. *Really Rachel? Do you? Why?* Suddenly, I pushed my smoke into the ashtray, full of determination and stood from my chair. "Actually, when you put it like that......."

To be sure I didn't talk myself out of it again, I left the kitchen and headed for the lounge straight away. I've no idea why, but for some reason I tiptoed down the hall desperate not to rouse him; I almost put my finger to my lips as I pushed the door wide enough for me to get through it.

When I stepped into the room, it was so uncomfortably hot from the fire it was stifling. As a rule, I'd look for the remote control and turn it down, and probably do the same with the volume on the TV, but the fewer chances I gave myself to disturb his unknowing, booze-filled semi-coma, the better. He was in his usual chair, his head had fallen back into the soft cushioning, exposing his long neck and his luscious Adam's apple. His shoulders were relaxed, one of his hands was resting in his lap the other, the one closest to me, was on the arm of the chair and his precious iPhone was sat next to it. He was fast asleep, snoring slightly - he looked comfy and peaceful - I could even mistake his look for innocence. I walked with exaggerated carefulness, close enough to him to reach his mobile without any chance of touching him, or creating any kind of draught in the stuffiness that engulfed the room. My pores sprang open, I felt myself start to sweat with a mixture of terror, guilt and gas fire heat. The thought of him waking right this very second and catching me in the act of stealing his phone made the adrenaline rush through my body. As I reached out for it my hands were shaking. I picked it up carefully and started backing out of the room as slowly as I had gone in. He slept on.

I topped up my glass with the heel of the bottle of red that had been left on the kitchen work top. I sat for a few moments at the table, in my spot, across from Jude's empty seat. Tim's phone was laid face up in front of me. I already knew what I was going to do; I hadn't gone to all that knee-trembling trouble to sit and just look at his phone. I was going to break into it, and at the same time break into the pool of trust and respect I've carried for my husband for many years. I was about to become the kind of woman that checked up on her man, I knew this with complete certainty, I was just building up the courage to do it.

As I lit another cigarette, I deliberately put the lighter down next to the phone and as my hand moved past I snatched it up. The screen came to life with my touch, there was no more dillydallying to be done, the hand that held the ciggie typed in the numbers 6899, Ivy was right about the number, the phone unlocked.

My eyes searched the icons quickly, the green SMS button was at the top left of the screen, there was no backing out now, I was committed. I rested my finger on it and as it opened, a list of names sprang into my vision; my eyes didn't have far to go before they met with an unfamiliar one, it was at the top of the inbox, the last text he'd received. A tsunami of adrenaline hit me so hard I lost my grip, and as it dropped out of my hand the phone clattered on the table. I held my breath, had I disturbed him? Was he awake? I could barely hear anything apart from my thudding heartbeat forcing the blood around my body.

I waited for a few seconds listening for movement from him, but there was nothing that I could tell. My quivering finger hit the screen directly on the name Melissa. This was the very second that I knew for sure, no matter how hard I'd tried to fool myself that it wasn't happening, it was here, the undeniable truth: he had someone else in his life, yet another secret. I opened the text messages before I could think about it again, the last one was sent at 8.21pm, part way through our evening with our friends; an evening of fun, a 'nothing else to do but this' kind of evening. An evening we sang daft lyrics to the tunes played on the juke box to each other, where his public displays of affection towards me shored up everyone's belief that ours was a tight, happy, enviable relationship, the one that people admired and strived to achieve. And the worst thing is he even had me fooled there for a while.

Received text 8.14pm: "Are you as mindlessly bored with your company this evening as I am?"

Reply sent at 8.15pm: "God yes, absolutely nothing here to keep me entertained, apart from you :-)"

Received text 8.16pm: It was an image, a photograph of a pair of socks side by side. Underneath Melissa had typed. "This is you and me, you're the one on the left and I'm always right." Reply sent at 8.21pm: "Ha I love that ;-) xxxx"

The intimacy of the conversation almost knocked me off my chair.

The phone was face up on the breakfast bar and still open on the text message page. I pulled it back closer to me to take another look at the messages from Melissa. My finger quivered as I touched the screen and start to scroll, text after text flowed into my vision, hundreds of them, and they went back weeks, many weeks. I didn't read the detail in them all particularly, I wasn't sure I could. Instead I looked at the dates they were sent and received, the days and the times. Every day of the week, all times of day and night. Times when we would have been together, times that I'd sat with him, watching TV with one eye and him texting with the other. All those occasions when I almost asked who he was texting, but not wanting to seem like I didn't trust him, or that I was nagging him. What an idiot I am.

Ivy's voice was by now screaming in my head. *Go and kick the lounge door off its fucking hinges! Storm into that boiling hot room and slap his face so hard he wakes up instantly. Then grab him by the front of his t-shirt and pull him just far enough out of his chair so you're at the same height then head-butt him so hard his teeth fall out and his eyeballs explode, and then drop him into a heap on the floor. Give his bollocks a kick so hard they end up in his diaphragm! Then rub the palms of your hands together for a job well done, leave him out for the count and walk out of the front door, into the night, never to return.*

I did wonder for a moment if I should listen to Inner Voice Ivy's advice and do exactly as she suggested. It was tempting, because this fresh iPhone evidence told me he was essentially a deceitful bastard, only this time he'd upgraded his disrespect from being an online peeping Tom to real life, flesh and blood, other women, or at least one other woman; and she was called Melissa.

29

There was nothing quiet about my entry into the room this time, I did as Ivy had told me and kicked the door open. It flew back into the room with such force it hit the arm of the sofa and rebounded back towards me. I kicked it out of my way again and stepped into the room. The brief flurry of noise and activity hadn't made a blind bit of difference to Tim's sleeping state, he was blissfully unaware of my infidelity-finding mission. His repose gave me chance to study him for the first time in a long while. I seized the opportunity and squatted on the floor in front of him, looking at his face - restful, peaceful, comatose - unaware of me sat there watching him with hatred, anger, terrible hurt and utter confusion coursing through my body.

He looked like him, still. The contours of his face were the same as they had been for ever, since I'd first set my eyes on them. Sometimes during those years his face had been a bit fuller than others, sometimes it had been too gaunt. It definitely looked older now, but it was the face of my husband, my partner, the man I called 'the love of my life', the man that I'd built myself around. My love.

In a seamless, nimble move I used the power in my gym-trained legs to push myself up to a stand, I drew my right arm back behind me as far as it could go and launched his mobile phone at his head.

Naturally, I missed him. I'm a bloody awful shot, always have been. It flew past him, but only just. I reckon it was within a millimetre of his ear. It bounced off the back of the soft, buck-hide cushion supporting his head, rebounded and landed in his lap, right on his balls. If only I'd thought of pitching it there in the first place. He stirred. He did the double-blink of a person who has just received a very rude awakening and looked at me, confused and dazed. He sat up fully and wiped his mouth with the back of his hand.

I had no patience to stand and watch him come round, I was boiling over with contempt and anger, and more importantly I needed a drink. I turned on my heel and left the room. Once I was in the kitchen, I grabbed a beer out of the fridge. I deliberately stood with my back to the kitchen door so he wouldn't see my face when he came in. I heard him shuffle to the upright position and, as he walked into the kitchen, I could see his reflection in the kitchen window. His hair stuck out at the back from hours of leaning in one place, his hands were rubbing his face in an effort to erase the final bits of sleep from his eyes. He didn't touch me as he walked past me, instead he came and stood directly opposite me and looked at me askance, his face the picture of bewildered innocence. Well of course it was - he had no idea he needed to look any different at that point.

"You woke me? Are you ok?" His voice was mixture of concern and irritation. When I replied, my voice was full of harshness, "Not really no. I'm not ok, I'm far from ok."

He hadn't picked up on the tone of my voice. He thought there was something the matter with me that he could help me with, rather than him being the cause of my consternation. He was recently woken, half-pissed, probably a bit hungover and definitely very groggy, "Rachel, are you ok? You seem odd."

"No Tim no, I'm not ok. I'm scared, I'm really scared." As I turned to face him, I could see the concern in his face; he still didn't realise. I had a coil of anger building in me, it was so big it was giving me a pain in my chest. I could feel tears spring to my eyes and I tried desperately to stop them from falling. I didn't want him to witness any weakness in me because these weren't tears of sorrow, these were much fiercer, even the way they ran down my cheeks was different; they fell as a torrent of violent anger.

I tried repeatedly to brush the tears away. I realised it was a futile effort. I couldn't stop them. I couldn't get them off my cheeks, there were too many of them. They were coming too fast, mixed with the snot that bubbled out of my nostrils. Slimy, wet emotion.

He still had some concern in his tone but now it was tinged with the definite sound of unease, and he came close to me again, our bodies almost touching, "Tell me, what's wrong?"

In my rush to get a drink, I'd left his phone in the other room and, for once, he didn't seem to have it attached to him. I needed to retrieve it. First, I had to move his proximity to me, and rather than spare him a word, I spread my fingers on my right hand as wide as I could, and I dug each digit into his chest as I pushed him out of my way. The force of it rocked him backwards and I used the space to walk past him, away from him, so all he could see was my back. I left him there, nonplussed, and went back into the lounge. My tears were slowing down, my face was still damp but my eyes were clear at least and I could see his phone on the floor where it must have dropped from his lap as he stood to come and find me. I bent down and swept it up in one forceful movement, my fingers immediately stabbing his pin-code to unlock the device. This time I wasn't terrified of what I was going to find when I opened it; I already knew what secrets it held.

Tim had followed me into the room, he was right behind me; I could feel him. I didn't waste any more time. I turned to face him, I held the phone up to display the intimate conversation between him and a woman called Melissa. The index finger of my right-hand pointed to the image of the socks. It was only a split second before I brought my face to his face. The only thing between me and the headbutt Ivy suggested I give him earlier was my hand holding his phone. It was close enough for him to see it. He could see her name against the text messages - he knew I knew. I took the evidence from in between us so I could get closer still, I stood on my tip-toes so we were as close to eye-to-eye as I could get. My voice was quiet, calm and very, very scary. I actually scared myself.

"Want to tell me what this is all about?"

It took the briefest of moments for him to register that he was trapped in his own tangled web. I watched his eyes move rapidly from side to side, like he was looking for an escape route. The prudent thing for him to have done, of course, would have been to apologise. We were still stood toe to tip-toe. His mouth moved as if he was about to say something, but nothing came out, his eyes held mine in a defiant challenging way.

The cheeky bastards trying to stare you out. How fucking dare he? Don't look away, do not look away.

With or without Ivy's encouragement, there was no way I was going to look away first, so while he waited for me to submit, I became more determined. I took his eye contact, and I stood my ground.

"What the fuck is going on Tim? What trouble have you brought to us now?" He dropped his eyes to the small space between us, he shook his head, "It's nothing Rachel, it's just a friendship." There was no victory in my winning the stare competition. I lowered myself from the balls of my feet, so despite his bowed head the difference in our height meant I could seek his eye contact again. My heart was breaking with his inability to tell me anything, anything at all, never mind the truth.

"Do you think I'm stupid? If it was nothing Tim, just a friendship then you would've told me, wouldn't you? But you haven't. Instead, for weeks and weeks, you've been communicating with her in secret. I've seen the number of texts that have passed between you, they've been at all times of day and night, you've even been sat in the same room as me and been texting her - how am I supposed to process that? Even in the pub tonight, while I thought we were having a brilliant time, you've texted this woman! She's sent you pictures of a pair of socks; you must see how intimate all of this is, Tim?"

When I threw my arms up in the air with exasperation, he flinched. He quickly disguised it; he shrugged his shoulders in the same careless way Jude does when she's got something to hide. "She's just someone I met on Facebook." He closed his lips again and pushed them tightly together, as if to indicate that was all the explanation I was going to get. "And?" I nodded my head in encouragement for him to carry on. "There's nothing to say, Rach, there's nothing going on. We played the same card game on there for a while, we got chatting while we played, we got on, that's it." If he shrugs his shoulders like that again I'm going to knee him in the bollocks. "But it's not it is it? That isn't all that happened. It can't be because you ended up swapping phone numbers. What made you decide to move your chats from the games room into the living room. Our. Fucking. Living room. Why have you brought her into our lives?"

He stammered a bit. "She's with someone, and obviously so am I..." He gestured towards me, just to clarify that I was, in fact, the person he considered himself to be with. "She's got kids. She's unhappy."

"What point are you trying to make Tim?"

"I'm sorry."

The top popped off my quiet - it exploded into loud. "Too bloody late, too many pathetic excuses have come from you before this apology finally dripped from your lips. I don't believe you, you disingenuous, lying bastard." I pushed him away from me with the entire length of my forearm, and went back

into the kitchen, a fresh beer first and a cigarette second. I'd
no sooner lit it than he came and stood in the doorway, "I'm
shattered Rachel, I can't talk about this now."

"On the contrary, Tim, you can talk about this now. You've
pulled that 'I'm shattered' one with me before. When the going
gets tough, the tough go to bed? You might not have anything
to say to me, but I do to you. Sit down." I gestured to the
chair. He sighed heavily as he did it, but he sat down and took
a cigarette out of the packet, he lit it and tossed the lighter
carelessly across the table. I ignored his churlishness and took
the seat opposite him; my body was ramrod straight.

"Now, please answer me this: how stupid do you think I
am to believe that a casual acquaintance from a virtual world,
where the two of you have a laugh and play games, means
nothing. How can that be if you now have each other's mobile
numbers? Why would you do that if not to take the relationship forward, to move it to another level?"

He smoked but didn't speak. I carried on "If you and the
unhappily married mother are just friends, then what's wrong
with keeping it where it was? On Facebook, at arm's length? If
there's nothing in it, nothing else you want from it then why
let her into your life any further?" His mobile was next to me,
I lifted it with one hand and waved it in the air and off I went
again, "It's like an open invitation for deeper, easier communi-
cation, at any time of day or night, whatever else you're up to,
she or you, are just a predictive text away from each other; and
that's too close for my comfort."

I sat back to show him I'd stopped talking, but he continued to look at me in silence. In my pause came a strong wave
of disbelief at myself, at my stupidity and my stubbornness
that kept me fighting with him, for him. It was causing me so
much anguish. Everything I'd just said made sense to me. As
the words had left me, their truth hit me hard and made his
lies even worse than they'd been before. I dropped his phone,

copying the careless gesture he'd made with the lighter, and slid it away from us both.

You've left a question out, Rach. Inner voice Ivy prompted me; it was such an obvious one now that she'd mentioned it, I couldn't believe I hadn't already asked it. "Have you met her?" The answer to this question scared me so much. "No! No, of course not." His voice had an insistent, shocked quality to it.

"Why should I believe you, though? How am I supposed to trust you?" The sadness began to engulf me, I could feel it getting busy creating tears and I knew it wouldn't be long before they started to fall. "Why have you done this, Tim? Can't you see how dangerous this is, to you, to us? Maybe she's looking for a plan B, did that ever occur to you? Someone to move on to so she can leave her husband." His hair was still stuck up from his chair sleep, he ran both his hands through it now from the top of his head to the back; it flattened a bit. "I don't think that's it at all babe, she's sad and a bit lonely I think, she needed to talk to someone."

The banks burst then, the sob came first and the tears followed quickly after. He dropped his gaze to the tabletop, he put his hands back into his hair to support the weight of his head as it dropped forward. "Tell me what it is I'm doing wrong Tim? What am I doing to push you so far away that you are so secretive about your friendship with another woman? Please help me to understand, please tell me."

It's not you, you silly cow, stop that! It's him! He's a two-faced lying wanker! Please, please stop blaming yourself. Ivy's pleading tone was nearly as emphatic as mine.

"There's nothing wrong Rachel, I promise you. Melissa and me are friends, that's all." My stomach lurched at the sound of her name coming from him. It made her even more solid. I imagined him thinking about her. The way he'd said her name to me just then must be how it sounds to him when he thinks about her. The weight of his betrayal crushed me. The very idea of another woman occupying his thoughts, taking them away from me, broke me into tiny pieces. I gave up. My head leaned forward until my forehead rested on the breakfast bar, my body folded into itself, my hands heavy in my lap while my shoulders jerked with every heart-wrenching gasp.

"What do you want me to do?" His voice came across the table to me. He hadn't moved to comfort me, yet he wanted me to tell him how to make it better for me.

Drop dead!

"I want you to stop destroying me Tim. I need you to explain to me why I deserve what you are doing to me and to our marriage."

"It's nothing Rachel, I promise you, nothing at all. I really do need to go to bed, why don't you come with me?"

I lifted my head, so he could hear what I was about to say clearly. Because my head had been leaning forward, I could feel there was a bubble of snot joining in with the tears. I tried to get rid of it with the back of my hand, I felt it spread across my face, snot and tears, the broken woman's mix of bodily fluids. "I want you to end your friendship with her, and we need to see Glenda this week." The catch in the back of my throat was so deep it shook my shoulders.

He stood up from his chair. "I promise I'll sort it, and yes, if you want to see Glenda then I'm ok with that too." He raised his eyebrows to his hairline in a 'now can I go?' gesture. I waved him away with my right hand.

It was only when I got up to get another beer, I realised at some point during our conversation he'd retrieved his phone from next to me, and when he'd gone to bed, he'd taken it with him.

30

Seeing Glenda on Saturday morning, instead of our usual, monthly Thursday evening, felt weird. She looked a bit different, looser and freer somehow. She was dressed more casually than usual, wearing jeans and what I suspected was a River Island shirt from a couple of years ago. This was the first appointment she had spare when I'd called the Relate office two minutes after they'd opened on Monday morning. Saturday had felt like a lifetime away then, but I accepted it gratefully. As always, the days flew by, and here we were sat in the same seats, in the same room, only at a different time. It had been three weeks since our last meeting and seeing her now made me realise I'd come to trust Glenda over the months she'd counselled us; I'd even grown to like her, in a strange way.

Alongside my anger and frustration at this latest turn of events created by my errant husband, I was also full of confidence for the meeting. I knew without a doubt that this morning she would be on Team-Rachel, and Team-Tim was due a right arse-kicking.

There was another thing I was certain about: I was going to get my money's worth in the next hour. All the things I wanted to say while we were in the privacy of our own home but couldn't for fear of pushing Tim even fur ther away with my confrontation, were going to be said here in this room; and Glenda would mediate. She was going to help me make him see that his behaviour was ludicrous, that 'only friendship' was bullshit, and once again he'd put our marriage in harm's way.

As a couple we found ourselves in jeopardy and he had caused it; again.

Inner Voice Ivy had been practising with me, rehearsing me, for this meeting all week, I was fucking invincible.

The usual niceties at the start of the meeting were absent today, Glenda didn't even ask how we were, she went straight in the deep end.

"I'm sorry to see you both sat here today. There have obviously been some exceptional circumstances that have necessitated an extra meeting, would you like to tell me what has happened?" She did her usual non-preferential eye thing, including us both in her vision but not favouring either of us. There was no way I was waiting for anyone to give me permission to speak first, this was my show, I was in charge. I didn't give a shit who I upset because I had an awful lot to get off my chest and I was going to do it today. I took a big breath and off I went.

"Last weekend I discovered text messages on Tim's phone from another woman." I held my hands up in a gesture of supplication, "I know I shouldn't have checked - I should have respected his privacy - but I had a feeling something was going on and I needed to know for sure." Glenda looked at Tim in a questioning way, he gave a slight nod of his head. It seemed she was going to ask him something, but there was no way I was letting anyone else get a word in yet, so I ploughed straight back into my soliloquy. "Tim has been playing a card game on Facebook with a woman called Melissa -" the hate I felt for this woman was even loaded into the way I said her name. "Apparently, they got chatting while they were playing. They got along well and eventually exchanged mobile numbers. Since then they've been texting each other, from what I can gather, every day, backwards and forwards. A lot. The messages I saw last Saturday night were part of a conversation between them about how bored they were with their current company. My husband -" I pointed both of my forefingers to Tim, "told Melissa -" I spat the name out again, "that she was the only thing keeping him entertained! We were in the pub with friends at the time having one of the best nights out we've had in ages! We were dancing to Status Quo for fuck sake! Anyway, in her response Melissa sent him of a photo of a very cute pair of socks with, 'This is you and me, you're the one on the left and I'm always right' written underneath it. The familiarity of it was more intimate than if she had sent him a photo of her tits!"

I paused for breath. As I started to speak again my words were slightly louder than before and I gestured with my index finger. "Now, Tim claims there's nothing in this friendship, that Melissa is an unhappily married woman and mother of two, and he claims he's there for her because she needs a friend. Quite frankly Glenda, I'm calling this total and utter bullshit."

Glenda turned her attention towards Tim once again. I was trying to see if her facial expression was showing any disappointment in him; I couldn't tell - she would have made a great poker player. On I went, indignation pushing every word out of me. "Tim promised me that he would break all contact with her, that he would end their friendship. It's been nearly a week since I discovered the messages, and he still hasn't seen fit to let me know whether or not he's done as he promised. He's left me guessing and too scared to ask him!"

Glenda held up her hand to stop my flow, I skidded to a verbal halt. "And have you, Tim? Have you cut contact with her?" He had the cheek to look outraged by the question. "Of course I have! I said I would. I've even taken her number out of my phone, and I've closed my Facebook account. It's just not worth the hassle." He sniffed as if disgusted at the sacrifices he'd had to make and folded all his limbs. It was a very affected action that under normal circumstances I would have considered hilarious, but today was different, and I saw an opportunity in front of me. Whilst I was feeling brave and supported by Glenda, I asked him, "How did she take it?" He turned his head towards me, his arms and legs still crossed tightly, animosity was burning in his eyes, like I'd taken away his favourite toy. "She said she didn't understand why we had to stop being friends. I told her that you'd found out about her and you thought it was inappropriate for us to stay in touch." I made a noise that was somewhere between a tut and a sigh. It was full of disgust. "What the fuck, Tim?"

Glenda began to talk over me, metaphorically stepping in between us. "Why did you say that Tim? Why did you end it that way?" He looked surprised that she'd questioned his motives. "Well, erm, because that's why I did it I suppose." Glenda started to speak again but I got there first, "I'll tell you why he did it that way Glenda; because my husband is so worried that if he takes responsibility for cutting ties with this woman it'll make him look bad. He's more concerned with what others think about him than he is about showing me any respect at all. He's a weak man, he'll go down every path of least resistance there is as long as he doesn't have to take the blame for anything!" The force behind my words almost had me out of my seat, "He kept telling me there was nothing in it, that she was just a friend, and to some extent I believe that's true. I'm well aware of his need to have others think well of him, that he's a great guy... he would rather compromise me by becoming her friend than tell her no off his own back. And he's lied constantly since I found out about her. All he has given me are weak, feeble untruths. I've asked him - no actually scrap that - I've *begged* him to explain to me what it is that I am doing to him that's so bad it makes him seek out the company of another woman."

I paused for a few seconds, the truth in what I'd just said hit me hard and I had to give myself time to get over the fresh bout of hurt my words had unlocked for me. I cast my eyes over to the other two in the room, Tim looked disheveled, Glenda was listening carefully to me and I was encouraged to carry on. "If this thing with her was just a friendship Glenda, then why is he going behind my back? Why doesn't he trust me enough to tell me? Why has he kept it a secret? We both turned to look at him, I watched him pale and shrink back into his seat a bit. I had him; he was trapped. Glenda was about to throw my final punch for me. She was going to ask the question I needed an answer to more than anything else. Her voice was as calm as mine was crazy. Her tone gentle, she leaned forward to him as though her kindness and proximity would pull down the last of his bullshit façade, "Can you answer that question Tim? Are you able to help Melissa understand why you are keeping this other woman a secret from her?"

My head snapped back from his face to hers, at the same time as hers came to face me. I saw her swallow hard and the colour instantly rise from the collar of her 'dress down' checked shirt, it flooded her face while I said "Rachel, Glenda - *my* name is Rachel."

31

Everything went into slow motion for me whilst Glenda continued to blush. I was pinned to my seat, completely stunned.

Meanwhile, Tim had been so busy trying to find a plausible explanation, as to why he'd blamed me when ending his 'friendship' with the aforementioned Melissa, he hadn't picked up on it straight away. However, Tim is not a stupid man. Careless - yes, disrespectful, arrogant, and verging on becoming a serial abuser - he was all of those things, but he was not daft; unfortunately. He soon picked up on the general despondency in the room, on my total and utter deflation, and Glenda's mortification at her mistake that would cause her nightmares for years to come – I hope. As he processed the events there was an exhalation of air from him that can only be called a sigh of relief.

That LUCKY bastard - he's managed to get away with it again! WHAT THE FUCK? Give my girl a break someone, holy SHIT! You useless bitch, Glenda, you had him, you had him! Inner voice Ivy was screaming again, she was apoplectic with rage and I was inclined to agree whole heartedly with her, Glenda was a useless bitch.

I didn't see much point in carrying on with the conversation we were having, it seemed I was the only one invested in the process. Even my counsellor couldn't be arsed to get my name right. I sat on my hands quickly and let Glenda try and get back on track, but between her stammering and Tim's undisguised relief there wasn't much point, my momentum had been stolen by another person that was treating me carelessly.

I'm not a malicious woman but I sincerely hope Glenda wakes up in a cold sweat at least once a week for the rest of her life after what she did to me that Saturday morning.

****

Jude and I had arranged to meet up for a midweek dinner, which was becoming less of a regular thing these days. I was lining myself up to tell her the whole sorry story and mentally rubbing my hands together in anticipation of the punchline. I hadn't told her anything about the whole farce yet. I'd saved it especially so I could see her face when I relived the slow-motion moments after my counsellor had called me by my husband's new 'friend's' name, and I was forced to remind her that my name was Rachel.

I still felt the horror and deep sadness of the betrayal by the woman I had been relying on to help me get my world back into shape. And I needed to share it with Jude. I needed her to feel my devastation, so she could share the load with me, make it a trouble halved.

I was at the pub before her, I sat at our usual table, ordered us a bottle of red and poured myself a glass. I spent the next ten minutes drinking and turning my head every time someone walked through the door, watching for her. Ahh there she was, at last. She lit up the whole place when she walked in; there was a shiny, delighted quality about her I'd never seen before. *She's in love. She's never really been there before, but she is now.* Ivy was right a lot in those days, she was getting good at this shit.

Jude was one of the coolest women I know but she wasn't cool today, she was glowing. She looked warm and whole and happy. The thing that occurred to me as I watched her skip her way through the otherwise dreary pub towards me, was that her news was much more important than mine. And it was.

Jude's news was, in fact, earth shattering.

When a conversation starts with, "I don't know how to tell you this but…" it has a tendency to get an alarm bell ringing. I was already in a fragile state, I didn't think there was much further down for me to go. And then she told me she'd resigned her partnership from her lifelong career, had an offer on her apartment from someone at work, and she was packing up and moving to Sardinia to be with Comita and his four kids.

****

It was the day after her revelation and I was on the way to a meeting to close the deal of my life, it was going to be the biggest sale I've ever made. It would win me awards and cement my reputation as being the creme de la creme in my field. I was wearing my best suit, my new shoes and my lucky knickers.

I was less than a mile away sitting at the traffic lights waiting for them to change to green. One of the benefits of my job and the miles I had to travel was the quality of my company car, it was top of the range, classy and very powerful. I loved it. For some reason a lot of men were fascinated by it and when I was sat at traffic lights they had a tendency to pull up beside me and peer into the car to see who was driving such a status symbol. I often gave them a nice smile. I was a middle-aged woman with no discernible edge to me and they seemed to see this as an invitation to race me, stupid fuckers. I knew exactly what they were going to do and I was always ready for them, they never, ever won.

At least they didn't until today. As I was waiting for the lights to change I was so preoccupied with the sadness and shock at Jude's news that I didn't even see the lights change and the souped up Vauxhall Corsa shot past me so fast it made me jump. The overtaking boys were hanging out of the windows, jeering and flicking the V's at me and I didn't even respond.

My deal fell through because I missed a buying signal and pushed for the sale too hard long after it was necessary. Laura was aghast at my wrong-footed performance, I'd never missed a buying signal before.

I was beginning to think there might be something wrong with me.

****

The sale on Jude's place went so smoothly that six weeks after she'd broken the news of her emigration, she was technically homeless. She'd only worked half of her three months' notice and wasn't due to leave until the first week in May, so Tim and I agreed she would come and live with us. The day we finalised our plans for the move I was so giddy at the thought of being with my best friend for all that time, I was like a kid on Christmas Eve.

The week before Jude came to stay, before Tim had a definite excuse not to come for a ride on me. I thought I should have another crack at ending our dreary sex life drought. I'd been having the strange dreams for some time: the one where I was fucking a faceless man and almost achieving orgasm. They were so realistic I realised I had to finally listen to my poor, horny body begging for sex.

One evening, after a lovely day out together, spending money, having a laugh and an unusually romantic meal at our favourite restaurant, I gathered my courage. It was now or never.

I left Tim sat in the lounge going through our massive vinyl record collection, looking for an album we'd been talking about that afternoon. He seemed content enough with the task. He'd been fairly sparse with his phone use all day - I was sure Angry Birds must be missing him - but the less he used it, the more relaxed I felt. It was a welcome respite from the nagging unease about his fidelity.

To my shame, I'd tried to get into his phone a couple of weeks after the whole Melissa escapade; I wanted to make sure the contact between them was really ended. Of course, he'd changed his pin number, sneaky bastard, that put even more pressure on me; not only had I let myself down by checking up on him again, he hadn't trusted me not to. What a vicious circle that was!

Whilst he was busy with his non-cellular entertainment, I left him to it so I could execute my fiendish plan to get some erotic attention from my husband. I crept around the dressing room, opening drawers and cupboards as quietly as possible whilst I chose my sexiest basque and stockings. My heart pounded, adrenaline coursed through my body, when I tried to fasten my stockings up, I found my hands were shaking - they seemed to do that a lot back then. But it wasn't excitement getting me in this state, it was fear. Even as I was making the effort to make myself irresistible, I knew I had a 50/50 chance of success. Once Tim saw me, he would either respond with delight at my seduction, or he would look like a cornered animal, full of panic and fear.

Not that far in the past, I would have dressed up in my take-me-now best, had a quick look at myself in the full-length mirror - just to make sure I looked ok and check everything was in its place - then I'd blow myself a kiss and off I'd go, for a bit of grown-up fun with the person I preferred to play with more than anyone else.

That evening was different though. When I looked in the mirror, I didn't see anything sexy about the way I looked. I didn't like what I saw at all. I hated how my thighs hung over the top of the stockings, had they always done that? The basque didn't quite reach the knickers I was wearing, and there was way too much flesh poking out at odd angles and overhanging the tops of the lace pants to be sexy. Who did I think I was, dressing up in this gear? I looked awful. I looked like a desperate middle-aged woman, my declining body no competition for the perky tits and bald vaginas Tim had been spending his time wanking over.

My self-esteem was shattered. Ivy tried her hardest to tell me I was lovely, that I was sexy and beautiful, and that Tim should thank his lucky stars every day that I even considered sharing myself with him. But I didn't believe her. I stood in front of the mirror and cried. I watched my face crumple into tears of sadness and anger at my weakness. I didn't just talk myself out of my mission, I actually scorned myself for being so stupid. I ripped the sexy stuff off my body and pushed it to the back of the cupboard. Instead of outrageously dirty girl satin, I put my sweatpants and baggy t-shirt on, covered myself up, dried my tears and went back downstairs to the perpetrator of my complete misery. I felt utterly humiliated by my cowardice.

****

My mood lifted considerably with the arrival of my rambunctious best friend though. For a few blissful weeks she and I were together, that was all that mattered to me. Despite the fact I knew there was an end-date to our time - and it was coming round quickly - I enjoyed every day we had together. For a little while there, I was happier than I had been for a very long time. Jude was nervous and excited about her new start and we talked endlessly about it. I encouraged her every way I knew how, to go balls-deep into her new adventure.

I was genuinely delighted that she'd found a man she loved so much she was prepared to pack up her whole life, live in another country and, more astoundingly, take on four children in order to be with him.

But when she'd finally gone, I was consumed by desolation.

32

Part way through Jude's stay, Tim mentioned at dinner one evening that he was thinking of taking up golf.

How bloody predictable; a bored middle-aged man taking up golf. Might as well tell the old girl you've got a new hobby while she's having fun with her best mate, hey Tim you sly bastard?' Inner Voice Ivy didn't waste any time having a lot to say about that.

I told him I thought it was a great idea. I was genuinely happy for him to start another hobby. I liked the fact he would have other things to do, apart from work too hard and play with his dick the minute my back was turned.

Tim's absorption with his new game, and all the - very expensive - equipment that came with it, suited me; it gave me weekend time to myself. I started to try and fill the gaping hole that Jude had left and catch up with some of my other friends. I made more of an effort with them and stopped making excuses not to go to places. I said yes to invitations from the other lovely people I had in my life. Naomi and I started to do more together, we were each other's island in the stream of missing Jude.

Even now my stupid devotion to Tiger Woods (as Ivy had started calling him), meant there was a lot going on with me that I couldn't share with anyone really. I was without a close confidant. My most trusted friend was gone, she was living in a villa overlooking the vineyard Mr Sardinia owned, having the time of her life - she hadn't even complained about the kids yet. We talked often, but without the understanding of the minutiae in each other's lives it was never as intimate as before. It was hard to have to explain things to her now, when before her move she would have understood what I was talking about immediately.

Everything felt to be slipping through my fingers, I had no control over anything in my life. We didn't go back to counselling after Glenda had betrayed me so completely. Tim had taken the opportunity to prise me away from our regular Thursday sessions and spent the money behind the bar at the golf club instead. Despite my best efforts and good intentions, I was lonely, I felt lost. I was in abject misery and I was trying my hardest to fight it.

I noticed that I'd started to get really angry very quickly; things that I would normally brush off began to get under my skin and stay there. I was permanently frustrated by every-thing; on the verge of tears, all the time. I was forgetful and clumsy. There were times when I had to sit in my car and psych myself up before I went to see my clients. I started to dread going to work. The most damaging thing was, I permanently criticised myself. My internal dialogue was destroying my own self with a steady stream of insults. "You fucking idiot." "Get a grip woman." "Chill out you silly bitch, what's wrong with you?" "Oh my God, I'm driving myself mad." "I will not cry." Inner Voice Ivy fought against my self-deprecation, every time I criticised myself, she was straight on to it, reminding me not to be hard on myself. But the self-abuse kept coming, and in the end even she found it hard to resist the insults I'd created, handcrafted especially for me.

How on earth was I ever supposed to take care of myself when I was my own worst enemy? As the days and weeks went on, it got worse. I was locked into a miserable place there was no escape from. I didn't know where the feelings were coming from, but I knew that everything was making it worse. However, with each thing that happened, I simply kept going. I kept my head down and carried on working hard. I carried on trying to make everything right again, to be all that I could be for Tim, to stem the flow of love that was leaving my marriage; I thought I was superwoman. It turned out I wasn't.

I couldn't sleep. I had bad dreams that left me waking up in a sweat, the anxiety I'd been feeling for months as I was falling asleep – the nagging doubt that all was not well in my world – started to reveal itself as I slept. I would wake up early every morning with my heart pounding, a feeling of dread and fear coursing through my body. I lost all motivation for anything at all. I didn't want to eat healthy anymore, I wanted to eat junk, anything to help me feel a bit happier and bit more satisfied – it didn't work. I knew exercise would give me a bit of a boost, but the gym was the last place I wanted to be. I'd make excuse after excuse to not go.

The time we spent with our friends did nothing to lift my mood, everyone pissed me off in some way or another – not their fault at all, it was just where my head was at – all I wanted to do was stay home and watch TV; not that I could concentrate on much but at least it took my mind away from the bad place it had gone to.

I was angry and snappy, and well, a bitch to live with. If I could have got away from myself, I would have done.

It was the post that finally broke me, a Saturday morning delivery of junk mail and our credit card statement. I was closest to the door so I went to pick it up from the floor. Tim was getting himself ready to go to for a round of golf, he was in my general vicinity and we started to talk about the credit card bill. It wasn't an argument about money, we don't argue about anything - we should - but we don't - it was just a reasonable conversation between us.

Suddenly out of nowhere I started to get angry, I could feel it rush to meet me, I tried to swallow it down but it consumed me. The frustration that came with the rage made me cry; it took me to my knees. As I dropped myself down my torso doubled over my legs, my forehead rested on the floor. I was trying to stop the rise of the shout I had building in me. I threw the post to one side and with my free hands I started banging the floor. My tears were fast and seemingly endless: I thought my head was going to explode. Tim stopped fiddling about with the covers on his clubs and took a seat on the bottom stair, about six feet away from me.

His voice broke through my anguish, "Why are you so angry all the time Rachel?"

I couldn't catch my breath to speak to him, but Ivy had a few things she needed to get off her chest.

Because you are a lying, cheating, betraying, bastard! Your selfish, self-centred arrogance, and refusal to admit the problems you are causing in your marriage is ripping her guts out on a daily basis. How is she supposed to trust you? She suspects you of all manner of things and most days she's struggling to find any love for you at all. She hates you, I fucking hate you and the worst thing is she hates herself for feeling that way. She's lost, scared and desperate!

I unfolded myself and tried to get some of my composure back. "I don't know why I am, I'm just angry. I feel it all the time, I can't shake it off." I sat up, rested my bum on my heels, and through the final sobs of the bout of tears a thought came to me, and as it did, I spoke the words out loud. "I need to go to the doctors. I need some help. I think I may be depressed."

33

September 2009 – May 2010

In recent years Tim might have been *(was)* a classic example of a complete arsehole, but throughout the time I was going to the doctors to get the help and medication I needed, he was exceptionally supportive. Maybe it was because I was too burned-out and weary to pursue any sexual satisfaction from him, he dropped his guard. He was comfortable with me as an emotional invalid. Whilst I worked through the side-effects that came with filling my sad brain with the chemicals that would balance it out a bit, he was wholly sympathetic. He took care of the things I just couldn't be bothered with, which was almost everything. He didn't pressure me to get well or to 'buck up' or 'snap out of it', he let me talk when I needed to but didn't question me endlessly about how I was feeling.

Even with the aid of an understanding GP, it took months to get my medication right. One type gave me the worst nightmares I'd ever had - dreams of pain, and loss of my loved ones would leave me screaming in my sleep - they were awful. Another prescription made me feel so sick I had to constantly swallow down the bile my body produced. It came over me in waves, and despite the reassurances from the information leaflet – which I rarely read as a rule – that these symptoms would be a temporary thing, it never stopped. Eventually though, I found my serotonin buddy.

As much as I hated myself - even more - for it, I eventually 'gave in' and took time off work. My boss was surprisingly understanding; he said he'd seen a change in me over the last few months. Laura was devastated I was leaving her to her own devices, but I knew she'd be fine. She'd been taught by the best, whilst I was still the best.

Once all the practicalities had been taken care of, I hid myself away from almost everything and hoped I would soon start to feel a bit better. I dreaded any visitors to the house. An unexpected knock on the door could throw me into a panic and the first time I heard the window cleaner's ladders on the side of the house, I skulked from room to room so he couldn't see me through the window he was cleaning.

I sat at home doing nothing. The only time I left the house was for three hours every Friday when the cleaner came. I couldn't face her, or bear for anyone outside of my tight circle of support to know what I was going through. I even made up stories about how work had been when anyone asked.

I'd spend mornings unable to get out of bed. I'd sleep and wake and drop back off again, fitful dozing that brought vivid images of horrible situations. When I eventually did get up, I'd sit and watch shite on the TV for hours on end. It didn't matter what it was because I wasn't really paying any attention, my thoughts were like the long continuous beep of a life support machine that's just been unplugged. A lot of noisy nothingness.

Eventually, time, patience and the right tablets started to help and I got a bit of my old self back. I began to get up earlier, I resolved to make the most of my time off work, to take an interest in things again. I did the ironing, I gave the house a deep clean, and instead of driving my car to the park on Friday afternoons to sit and stare into space until it was safe to go home, I braved the supermarket. I began to feel brighter. I found the courage to confide in a couple of my most trusted friends that

I was off work, and discovered they were more than willing to meet for lunch or an afternoon shopping. I began to appreciate the much needed break, to see it as the rest I was quite clearly well overdue. Instead of punishing myself I started to treat myself instead, and the websites that offer deals on mid-week trips to a spa for indulgence and relaxation made a fortune out of me. I eventually forced myself to go to the golf club and back to the pub with Tim and meet our drinking mates.

As delicate as I was, the deepening of my friendship with Naomi was a huge help. I still hadn't talked to her about Tim's part in the devastation of my spirit. I wasn't sure I could take myself back there again, to start to feel the pain I was medicating myself against. So, I kept it tightly wound, hidden deep inside me. A close friend from many years ago, who'd moved to New York for work, came back into my life; she'd been asked to head up a project in the UK and had come home for a while. Petra was an amazing woman with a penchant for not giving a shit about what anyone thought of her, and we spent a lot of time together. She was good for me; I needed her self-confidence and spark in my life, to remind me there was another way, another me besides the one I was right now.

These women were saving my life. A couple of my colleagues, Laura included, texted me often to see how I was and if I needed anything. I realised there were still a lot of people who loved me, that Tim's behaviour and the absence of Jude's constant company didn't mean I was lost after all.

I'd had little room in my life for any thoughts other than getting myself well. I tried to be a good wife and friend, and I like to think I managed it in the main. The whole time I was trying to fight my way out of the fog, I left my worries about Tim alone. The medication masked a lot of my emotions and fears, and I was able to forget the things that had caused me to need to take it in the first place. It bolstered me up and gave me my spark back, and I was so grateful for that I stopped questioning what was going on behind my back. I dropped my suspicions, and Tim's kindness while I was ill helped me to see him in a different light. Once again, I began to consider him as a man that was on my side. And as I started to lose the anger and anxiety, I began to fall in love with him again.

I felt safe for the first time in a long time.

34

May 2010

My confidence in my confidence grew, especially when I got back to work and settled in quickly, like I'd never been away. I was happy in a kind of comfortably numb way.

I was carrying a bit more weight than usual, but I knew that was a result of taking the medication. It wasn't an issue for me, why did it matter? My self-esteem was coming back, and I was madly in love with my husband again. He was everything I needed him to be – apart from a fuck buddy, but to be honest the tablets dampened my craving for sex, so I overlooked that slight technical hitch. My bubble was a joyous place full of softness and gentle care.

As part of my return to work I'd been given shorter hours and only worked a four-day week. No one was more surprised than me when I decided that my life shouldn't be all about my career; not everything revolved around being the best all the time. The shift in my mind set during my careful recovery had ingrained itself, and now I was getting back into the flow of life I didn't see the point in working as hard as I had in the past. With Tim's agree ment I decided to work part-time and started to have every Friday off.

I met with my GP and we put a plan in place to start reducing my medication. I was sure my brain could cope with a controlled reduction, and as much as I'd come to terms with the help I'd needed for my poorly mind, the last thing I wanted was to become dependent on anti-depressants. I wanted my life to be my anti-depressant, not a small packet of pills with the days of the week on them.

****

One day towards the end of May I lost my mobile phone, I searched for days but in the end, I had to admit, it was gone for good.

I was mourning its loss over dinner one evening and worried it might take ages to get a new one from head office, when Tim remembered he had a spare mobile, the one he'd had before I bought him his shiny new iPhone.

I was delighted and grateful and as he handed it to me he said, "There's loads of text messages on that phone you know? The ones we used to send each other when we were playing that game, guessing lyrics to songs from stupid clues we'd made up. They made me laugh so much I couldn't bear to delete them! There are a couple of lovely ones from you too, they're all saved in a folder." He smiled at me. The way his bottom eyelashes rested on his cheeks when he was revealing a full-on grin made my heart soar. I adored this man.

I didn't think about the saved texts until Friday morning whilst I was waiting to go into my Zumba class. I was early, and the 9am spinning class was still going on. I had time on my hands so I sat on the comfy seats by the window, feeling the warmth of the sun on my back. I thought it might be nice to have a look through some happy memories. I wanted to see what he'd saved, the things that made him laugh. I was ridiculously touched that he'd kept them, and if I am honest about my reasons, I also wanted to read them to try and remember the more innocent times, before our mini marriage crisis. I was smiling as I opened the phone and went straight to the saved items file. I didn't come across any examples of texts from me, mostly because I didn't get that far down the list. The first saved texts were from a 4-digit number without a name against it. I'd no idea why it looked like that, the times they'd been sent were still on display, most of them were during the middle of the night.

What the fuck is this? Ivy enquired very quickly. My logical brain was quick on the defence: "It's nothing, it can't be, why would he have lent me the phone if he had something on it to hide?" That made perfect sense to the bits of my brain that believed my own feeble excuses. Despite my protestations that it couldn't possibly be anything untoward I felt a bit sick.

Open them, do it now!

I opened the first one, it had been sent at 3.30am: "You naughty boy, how dare you! Go and stand in the corner and hang your head in shame. And don't you dare play with your dick!"

There were a lot of them, all sent in the early hours of the morning. Dozens sent on different dates Tim's replies weren't saved, there were only texts sent to him by the unknown 4-digits. As I scrolled through and read each one, I began to feel the all too familiar sickness in my stomach, the acid from the bile of stress was burning my throat.

"You are so dirty... how much pain do you like?"

"Can you feel my nails digging into your skin while I squeeze your balls?"

"I want that rock hard cock inside me now!"

"You cum right now, or I will have to smack your arse so hard you will see stars!"

He's an idiot, is he trying to get caught? Is he doing this on purpose, so you catch him? He's a lying bastard! Ivy had lots of questions to ask, and they were all very valid - but they were going to have to wait for a while. My immediate issue was, what the fuck was I going to do right now, this minute? My impulse to go home and confront him was huge, but I wasn't sure I was strong enough to face that. I wanted him to know

I'd seen the messages though, there was no way I was keeping this discovery to myself. After another couple of minutes of startled thought, I copied the words from one of the texts and pasted them onto a new message. I sent the one about the feel of her fingernails squeezing his balls, and as I was imagining that shocker making its way across the ether, arriving as a beep of an incoming message, I sent a second, supplementary one. "My darling, I have just come across these messages on your old phone, I think we need to talk."

Shouting didn't work, screaming didn't work, crying didn't work. Maybe a reasonable, understanding conversation between two adults might be the thing that would finally get me the answers I was so desperate to hear.

I didn't receive a reply.

I couldn't find it in me to go home. I didn't know what to do for the best. As I sat outside the Zumba studio my faculties were starting to come back a bit. I looked back to the phone, at the texts, there were two left from the thread that I hadn't read yet. The first one was an enquiry from Ms 4-digit: "Why are you ashamed?"

For some reason the question left me deeply saddened. I imagined Tim, a long way from home, sat in a hotel room somewhere and feeling lonely and confused by his needs. My heart went out to him for the guilt he must feel about them. I was trying to understand, to put myself in his place, to find some empathy for his situation - rather than fury at the one he was forcing on me.

Until Ivy broke my train of thought: *Shame you can't see the reply to that one! "Why are you ashamed?" I hope it said, "Well I'm ashamed because I can't fuck my wife! I can't get it up for her. So instead of trying to work out a way to make it better between us, instead of committing myself to try and make it all better, I take the lazy bastard's option and get my kicks in other ways. I have been going behind her back for years now with this porn thing, I promise her I'll stop but I don't, instead I find new, sneakier ways to get my rocks off! I've moved it up a bit these days and gone from free images on the internet to paying a quid a text from people like you. I pay you to send me thrilling, dirty texts so I can get over the guilt and get the blood flowing to my penis. I know this hurts her and I know deep in my heart that I'm ruining something that means a lot to me, but I'm a selfish twat and I can't stop! I bet that wasn't his reply, was it, Rach, because he doesn't give a fuck!*

Whilst Ivy was busy trying to talk some sense into me, the fully coordinated, very lovely Zumba instructor was already setting up her music to start dancing and the other regular members of my Friday morning class were filing into the room. One of them caught my eye and smiled, it was too late to back out now. I'd sat for long enough it was time to either make my excuses and leave or go in the room with the others.

I did the class. I followed the music and busted out the moves in the wrong direction like I did every week. I didn't enjoy it. How could I with all that shit rushing through my brain? I was trying hard to concentrate on a salsa beat, but Ivy had something she needed to discuss with me, and it wouldn't wait.

How does that sexting thing work, anyway? How the hell anyone can text a reply with one hand while getting themselves off with the other is beyond me. I mean, for one thing how the hell do you hold the phone and type if you have five digits and the palm of your hand round your cock? Do you prop your phone up on the pillow? Do you rest it on your knee? Do you keep the messages in your head and remember them later while you get yourself off? It seems like a very un-thrilling way to get a thrill to me. And don't even get me started on how much bleeding money he's spending. As she paused for breath, the next routine that came on was one of my favourites and for a while I managed to put all my energy into the class.

It was only at the point where we slowed down and lay on the floor to do sit-ups in time to some funky tune that the full extent of what I'd found on Tim's phone hit me. The tears came and I had to gulp to stop the sob that fought its way up from my chest. Here I was, yet again, full of misery and confusion. I was angry and sad and so bloody disappointed in him. How was I going to find the strength to deal with it all? Mentally it had already taken me to the bottom and I didn't think I had much more to give. How much stronger would I have to be to even begin to make it right?

Ivy had a suggestion. *Maybe no matter how hard you fight for it, your marriage is on its vinegar stroke.*

When the class was finally over I went straight to my gym bag in the corner of the room, and with eager dread checked the phone to see if he'd deigned to get back to me to say "sorry" or "I can explain", or even, "yes darling I really need to speak to you about this, you are my best friend and I need to share this problem I have with you." There was no reply.

I drove home with wobbly legs, adrenalin rushing through me. I had no idea how to approach Tim this time but I knew I needed to see him, when I got home I stuck my head around the office door, he had his head down concentrating on something on his laptop, he looked completely unconcerned, when he eventually lifted his head to see me he didn't smile, he actually looked a bit bored when he said, "That must have been an awful way to find out what I'd been up to."

There was a turn up for the books - empathy! Ivy didn't agree with my assessment of the situation, *That's not empathy, that's him trying to get out of a row. Oi, Tim, you prick, you are without a doubt, the master of the understatement - an awful way to find out - fuck me! How else was she going to find out? Were you going to tell her? Were you going to sit her down at some point and confess? Of course you weren't! You were hoping she'd never find out. Again.*

Ivy's slant on his apology threw me off a bit so instead of saying anything in reply to him, I smiled a gentle smile; I tried for an expression of kindness and openness rather than my usual 'Yeah ok, ya wanker' one, that I'd perfected over the years.

I clung to the hope that the full effect of the compassionate words in my text earlier, and the fact that I hadn't kicked the office door down and entered in a sweary, screaming way, might help him see I was striving for a change in my attitude to the approach of the latest unveiling of his self-stimulating orgasm techniques. I was hoping it might encourage him to consider an honest discussion, rather than sulking and feeling hard done by. I pulled the door closed with forced gentleness and I left him to it.

****

I stood in the shower for ages, long after my body was clean, letting the water soothe the boogie aches in my muscles. The contents of the paid-for masturbation masterpieces kept replaying themselves in my head. I tried hard to shut out the imagery of him pulling himself off while he was thinking of a strange woman beating him or grabbing his balls with long pointed fingernails. I was trying to comprehend why he'd saved the texts in the first place. Was Ivy right? Did he want to get caught? Was it a cry for help? Did he save them so he could get himself off again? Getting his money's worth - like a buy-one erection, get another one free bargain.

I was standing in the warm, misty, sweet smelling wet-room drying myself off when the door opened with such force the steam bellowed madly around the room with the disturbance of it and brought an instant chill. Tim had come in; he was stood at the doorway. In a panic I grabbed the towel close to me, covered my body up quickly, once again I felt ashamed of it. Ashamed of its inability to keep him interested, ashamed of myself for being so unsexy and undesirable, for making him have to do all the things he was doing to feel remotely turned on. However, when he did turn to face me, he didn't even try for a sneaky look at my body, his gaze was fixed at a point slightly above my eyes.

I was a bit shocked at his rudeness, and at his sudden entrance. I had no time to compose myself. I knew there was very little I could do to hide my hurt and anger from him, but I adjusted my expression as much as I could to include some kindness and understanding. I was about to ask him if he wanted us to spend some time together later, I was about to issue an invitation to have a chat, so he could talk to me, to help me understand. One look at his face made me realise he hadn't taken me up on my empathetic approach. He didn't look like he was up for much discussion, instead of seeing apology and shame in him, I recognised aggression and fury.

He took a step towards me, came close so he could talk to me quietly. I pulled my head back slightly so I could still see his face, and for the first time in our lives together I felt physically threatened by him. He brought his index finger towards my forehead and pointed it sharply while he hissed, "It's not easy living with you and your fucking depression you know."

He turned on his heel and left the bathroom.

35

It took me a few days to even begin to come to terms with Tim's dismissive reaction to my finding the texts. There really was no comeback from his comment. Of course it hadn't been easy living with me - my depression had been all-consuming and, well, it was depressing. It had been a battle I'd faced and fought hard, and I'd done it with his support and encouragement. It stood to reason that he would be affected by worry and loneliness throughout it, as I had been; I hadn't been there for either of us, had I?

I tried to talk to Jude about what was going on, we Skyped as often as possible. She was doing well over there in her new home. She had a glorious tan and shiny health that comes from getting an immense amount of sunshiny Vitamin D, regular sex and a Mediterranean diet.

The day of the Zumba class, with the bollock-grabbing text messages, and the storming out of the steamy bathroom escapade, I'd called her. I was desperate to hear her voice and share my gut-wrenching story. I tried for a video chat first but didn't get through. I messaged her to get her attention and then when she called me back on Skype, she was dripping water from their swimming pool that was still in view behind her. It was full of happy, boisterous kids, throwing themselves around and having a whale of a time. I tried to tell her what was going on, my words garbled and rushed in the panic of getting them out as fast as I could before one of the kids needed her attention and she had to go. She was looking at the screen squinting in an effort to get rid of the glare from the sun and kept trying to find the right quality of shade, then in her efforts walked too far away from her Wi-Fi signal and we got cut off. She called me back straight away but once we'd finished wandering round her decking and patio and eventually found the ideal lighting and internet signal under the arches of her pergola, one of the kids shouted her to come quick, Fabrizio was holding his sister's head under the water. There was no way I was going to be able to retain her attention whilst one of her soon-to-be adopted sons was committing sororicide, she ran off to sort it out and I hung up at the other end.

****

My optimism for the future of my mental health sank like a stone and I went with it, fast. Within a week of him making it clear that any further discoveries of misdemeanors on his part were entirely my fault, I was back in the waiting room of my doctor's surgery, my arse stuck to the brown plastic seating in the waiting area; waiting. When I told her I was not coping well she immediately wrote me a new prescription and I was back on the higher dose of medication again, the one I'd worked so hard to reduce.

****

We carried on as usual, working hard and playing hard. Tim's new golf club crowd became a regular part of our social life too, and it seemed we rarely had a weekend at home, just the two of us. As much fun as our Saturday night shenanigans were, the aftershock on Sunday morning when we eventually came round from our stupor was never pleasant. Our Sunday morning habit of waking up chilled and fresh saw a dramatic change. Facing the start of the day with a massive hangover and ciggie breath is not sexy. We damaged ourselves so much over the weekend it took us until mid-week the week after to get over it – just in time to start again; we became the victims of our own excess.

At one time, a very long time ago, we would have luxuriated in the thought of nothing to do all day apart from whatever we chose to. We would have woken up in our own time and had a cuddle, naked skin on skin, chatted and flirted with each other, had a laugh, a gentle loving stroke causing goose pimples and a sexually charged shudder. Maybe a little kiss, leading to a bigger kiss, this was when we used to have sex. This was when we had time and headspace for each other. Oddly enough, over the years I began to think this was a bit predictable and not very exciting, but the alternative? Well, the alternative was shit, quite frankly.

On the 1st September 2010 even before I opened my eyes, Inner Voice Ivy said, *It's been two years since the fuck in the kitchen Rachel - two years, 24 months, count them 1,2,3,4,5,6,7,8,9,10,11,12,13,14,15,16,17,18,19,20,21,22,23,24. That's two birthdays each, two wedding anniversaries, two Christmases, four trips to the dentist, and how many holidays and weekends away have you been on in those one hundred and four weeks without any intimacy? Loads, that's how many.*

The anxiety shot through me again, the terror in my tummy forcing me to hold myself for a while to try and calm down a bit, to catch my breath whilst asking myself the age-old question. What the hell was I going to do?

****

And then there was another birthday for me. Another special occasion to add to the count - three birthdays since penetrative sex, which was really what I wanted as my present, but instead Tim bought me a gift of mind-blowing extravagance.

He'd always been a considerate and thoughtful gift buyer, he might have been a rubbish husband for the last few years but he couldn't be faulted for the present he gave me for my 45th birthday. I was nearly sick with excitement when I opened the shoe box with pale blue tissue paper inside it, but no shoes, to discover an email confirmation of our booking for the 2nd January 2011. Fourteen nights in a 5-star luxury villa on an exclusive resort in Barbados. Admittedly it was a golf resort, but the spa treatments looked very bloody special and cocktail hour was all day. It was exactly what we both needed, a break from everything and everyone, just the two of us so we could remember who we were together, get our marriage mojo back.

We went out for dinner that evening, we splashed out on a bottle of my favourite bubbly and sat across from each other chatting with giddy excitement about the trip. I was utterly thrilled and swept away by it. *Guilt gifting* Ivy happened to mention to me while I was putting on my make-up getting ready to go out. I spoke out-loud to my reflection, "Fuck off Ivy, leave me alone and let me enjoy this."

＊＊＊＊＊＊＊＊＊＊＊

Before I knew it, it was December, and it was time to get the Christmas decorations out of the loft again. Three fuckless festive seasons.

I ignored the shagless tally and concentrated on my excitement instead, I'm a big fan of Christmas and I also had a holiday of a lifetime to look forward to in the not too distant future. However, everything was overshadowed by the issue of how I was going to approach Tim about us having sex on our holidays. I assumed he was trying his best to get our marriage back on track; why, I asked Ivy, had he gone to all the trouble and expense if not?

I hoped with all my heart that was the case, but I also knew there was no way I could go on holiday and not know what to expect. It troubled me; a lot. I could feel the tension begin ramp up inside me on a daily basis, the thrill of the anticipation quickly being taken over by an ever-increasing sense of dread. My depression and the weight gain side effects of the medication caused me to hate the body I'd once been so proud of. Lap dancers, porn stars, facebook gamers and whores all contributed to my increasing shame. My confidence had taken so many hard knocks that my self-esteem was nonexistent.

I came to the conclusion that I would have to say something before we went. If I didn't I would drive myself a bit mad - and I was already taking tablets for that. I had to know what to expect, to know what he expected. As usual Inner Voice Ivy and I created hundreds of differ ent scenarios, where I would finally open myself up to him, what I would say, how I would say it, and how he would react.

As it was, in my panic, I became impatient and that made me clumsy and the much-planned words left my lips at the most inconvenient time. We were in the kitchen cooking dinner - this was my first stupid mistake. I knew he couldn't concentrate on anything else when he was cooking, even the simplest of questions threw him into a flap, never mind the query equivalent of a nuclear explosion I was about to drop on him.

We were stood side by side, he was making the pasta sauce and I was throwing a salad together; we were both busy with our designated tasks. Without warning the scary words were on my lips, I tried to stop them, I took a big slug of wine to delay myself but before I knew it they were out there, rushed, frightened sentences that were nothing like I'd practiced.

"Tim?" He had his head bent over the pan stirring, "Mmmm?"

"We need to talk darling." I was at the top of a very high conversational roller coaster, there was no way I could stop now, I plunged onwards, "we need to talk about our sex life."

Shiiiiiittttt I'd actually said it!

"It's been more than two years since we've had any kind of intimacy. So much stuff has gone on between us in that time." I felt his whole-body tense, heard him take a breath in but none out. I wasn't going to be put off, I was committed now. "I know we've had some tough times and I'm proud that we have got as far as we have, but I'm worried, I'm sad and I'm lonely, and I think you are too." He let go of the breath but not in a gentle easy way, it was part snort, part sigh. Undeterred I turned my body to face him, he resolutely stayed where he was, "I love you so much and I miss you. I don't want us to go on this incredible trip without us discussing what we're going to do about being with each other, about sex."

He finally turned to face me, our proximity and his height forcing me to look up at him. When I did, there was the awfully familiar look of panic on his face. "I know we do babe, but I.. I... I can't talk about it now. It's not the right time. I need to think about it first. I need to work out what to say about it all." He had so much fear on his face it destroyed me to see it. "Would it be ok with you if we agree to talk about it tomorrow? You've obviously been stewing over this for some time, but this conversation has kind of come from nowhere for me."

Come from nowhere? Why... where the fuck have you been for the last twenty seven months?

I ignored Ivy's valuable contribution to the conversation. Confrontational tactics were not needed now. I wanted to make him feel safe. I was desperate to find a solution, I was prepared to be patient and listen to his views.

A massive sense of discomfort pervaded the rest of the evening, there didn't feel to be much space to move in our house because of all the elephants in the rooms. Especially the enormous one in our bedroom. I made my excuses and went to bed early.

I didn't get much sleep; if I'm honest I spent most of the night wondering how we were going to unpack the years of compacted disrespect, lies, fears and my continual submission all in one evening. Even a fully trained counsellor couldn't get us to be truthful with each other with her laser beam of professionalism shining on us. I never really stood a chance.

Can't blame a girl for trying though.

The following evening was beyond awkward. Even with the addition of an expensive bottle of Rioja, our conversation was stilted. Tim was especially jittery, he tried to hide it but I could see his hands were shaking when he lit a cigarette – the days of us only smoking when we drank were a thing of the past, I tried to pretend I wasn't really back on twenty a day but that was just another lie I was telling myself. My ability for self-delusion was immense.

I was determined not to balls up the start of the conversation again, but I waited for ages for him to take the lead and in the end I just wanted to get it out of the way, and I ploughed straight in and asked him if we were going to have sex on holiday.

I don't know who was more shocked, me, him or Ivy because even she didn't realise I was going to go about it in such an indelicate way. The look on Tim's face was a picture, but the directness of my question meant he had no option but to answer me.

And then he delivered the blow I definitely hadn't seen coming, he told me he thought he was bordering on his own bout of depression, he said he'd been so deeply confused by everything that had gone on in the last couple of years or so he was struggling to find interest in anything remotely sexual. He looked so sad and stressed I moved over to him to comfort him, I hugged him to me as he explained how he'd lost all his carnal mojo, how the guilt and shame that had come from me finding his online wank bank and naughty boy texts had been crippling him. He said he hadn't been able to get an erection for months. I believed him.

He told me he was sure that it would come back with time but that he needed the space of the holiday to reconnect with himself, and with me and did I mind very much if we agreed that there would be no mention of us making love while we were away?

I was desperate to prove to him how willing I was to make things right between us so I agreed to yet another fuckless holiday – to a peace treaty between our genitalia. He seemed so relieved and grateful I almost ended the conversation there until Ivy's insistent voice came through loud and clear. *Don't let him pull one over on you Rach, do you really believe him?*

I did. I had to. How could I not? He looked completely shattered after his revelation, I was fighting depression myself, the thought of my husband feeling even a fraction of my mental illness filled me with horror.

Ok then ask him if he's using porn to try and get his prick hard, ask him if he's still using hookers and sextext workers to try and kick start his poorly performing libido.

I knew she was right, if I didn't take this opportunity to ask him the question now the doubt would fester in my mind. I moved away from him slightly so I could see his face. "I'm sorry darling, but I have to ask you if you're still using porn or………. anything?" If you are I won't be upset or angry I promise, I just need to know, please, Tim, don't lie to me again, just be honest with me."

He took hold of my shoulders and held me away from him, for the first time since I could remember his eye contact was intensely focused on mine

"No, absolutely not, I promise you faithfully all that's behind me. I've no idea where my head was when I was doing that, I've seen how deeply it hurt you, I can't do that to you again. I won't do that to you again. Hand on heart, it's all over."

I didn't listen to Ivy as she sucked the air in between her teeth and shouted at me that he was lying, that it was all bullshit.

I should have done, but I didn't.

36

May 2011

Barbados was wonderful. When I left home 2 January 2011 in a taxi, at an hour of the morning that's only acceptable to be awake if there are drugs or airports involved, I was travelling with a stranger, an enemy, a man I'd hated more than I'd loved since the lap-dance incident in 2008.

I travelled home with my best friend, the love of my life... I was whole, complete, with the man of my dreams. I'd renewed the courage of my convictions that Tim was the man for me, that my life was meant to be spent with him. The surfeit of sacrifices of my own self I'd made were worth it, it had been the right thing to do. The prize for the belief I'd given my marriage was the husband I came home with. A new, more loving and trustworthy version of Tim R I Bradbury.

The day before we left for our trip we'd agreed that if we were going to get the most out of our holiday, we would unplug ourselves from real life completely; no internet, no Facebook, no emails - we even left our mobiles at home. I put mine in a safe place in the drawer of my bedside cabinet next to my sexuality; that was an other item that was definitely surplus to requirements for this holiday.

The absence of those distractions gave us a huge sense of freedom; unadulterated time for each other. Tim didn't even play golf, we just hung out together. Fourteen days and nights spent in each other's company was the greatest reminder of how much we liked each other, how well we got along when we weren't constantly at loggerheads. It created an emphatic surety of why we had committed ourselves to each other all those years ago. We rediscovered each other.

There were a few times while we'd been in the presence of other guests, when I'd been a bit uncomfortable about Tim's instigation of public displays of affection, because I knew there was no truth in them. The kisses and touching only served to remind me what I was missing. Inner voice Ivy was at the beach party with me on one particular occasion and dropped the comment he was being a *cruel, deceitful wanker, playing up to the audience*; I'd tried to leave her at home too, in the same place as my mobile and my lust, but she refused to stay put. In fairness to her she was quiet most of the time we were away, the only other time she had anything to say was the day Tim surprised me with a beautifully wrapped gift. He'd bought me a one-piece swimming costume, and as I pulled it from the tissue paper to get a closer look, he gave the slightest nod towards my tummy as he said, "I got it for you just in case you were feeling a bit self-conscious in your bikinis." I actually hadn't been until then.

The next day I gave the cossie a try, but it was way too warm to imprison my body in all that tight, clingy, suck-your-belly-in fabric.

Don't take any notice of that dickhead, put your bikini back on, you look fucking glorious! said Ivy. So, I did.

Despite the couple of minuscule bumps in the road, by the time we arrived home I was full to the brim with hope for our future. I was utterly convinced the past was firmly in the past, and now we were rested and ready and best mates again, we'd reached the next level in our relationship - the one where we could start to work out how to reinstate our physical love life.

But that was months ago now. My beautiful tan had faded long before the extra weight gain from cocktails and high-living had shifted off me (it still hadn't, not really. I just kidded myself it had). On my omnipresent shagless months count, we were now at thirty two. The words, "I promise you we'll sort it out, whatever it takes," had been forgotten by Tim. He fell back into our routine and carried on regardless without sorting anything out at all. For a while I'd lived in my rose-tinted, happy, post-holiday bubble, content that my hatred for him had been replaced with a resurgence of love.

Until one night when my sex dreams came back, and the penetrative penis most definitely wasn't Tim's, and it wasn't his orgasm face I was watching as I sat on top of him riding him with enthusiastic delight; but it was someone I vaguely knew.

When I woke up, I was horrified at my nocturnal unfaithfulness, shocked at the face I'd seen. I had no idea why this man had played a part in my bedtime fantasy, I'd only ever met him once through work, I'd never given him a second thought since. I was so close to orgasm with my uninvited dream lover, my vagina throbbed with tiny aftershocks. Sadly I'd become so stuck inside my sexless state, I didn't even finish the job off. In all the months of enforced abstinence, I hadn't even had a wank. My sex-toy box was dusty – hell-fire my *own* box was dusty! But my fuck-thirsty brain was continually reminding me of my needs. I had to start taking control again, I was even considering looking for a sex therapist – a genuine, qualified one, not one that stood on street corners.

****

And then there came a time when I needed to find a receipt for the proof of purchase for the dishwasher that had stopped working. I hunted high and low for it, I went through every place I could think of to find it, with no joy at all. Tim was away all week and I'd kept forgetting to ask him where it might be so in the end, I resorted to looking through our credit card statements. There were so many of them, my cards, his cards, joint cards, it was going to be a thankless task.

I was part way down the pile of paperwork when I came across some odd looking payments on Tim's credit card he used for his business expenses. I don't involve myself with his work stuff as a rule and my first thought was that maybe he'd been paying for Wi-Fi while he was staying in hotels, but with a growing sense of apprehension it started to occur to me that these charges looked a bit suspicious. The name of the payee didn't mean anything to me, it was a code or something.

He's not spent all that money on frigging Wi-Fi, that's for sure - you know why those charges look suspicious Rachel, because they are. Check them, see what they're for.

I can't ignore Ivy at times like this, her words worked like an injection of adrenaline. My legs instantly turned to jelly and I had to support myself as I moved away from the filing cabinet, the familiar rush of dread filled me so quickly I was in danger of hyperventilating. My work laptop was behind me on my desk, and as I dropped into the chair in front of it my whole body was trembling, the statement was still in my hand, shaking. I went straight to Google – the mistress of all knowledge, she would give me the answers I was looking for, I was sure of it – I typed in the puzzling name of the beneficiary. How obliging of the internet to reveal Tim's hand in such a prompt and efficient way. The search engine showed me the message that it had produced: - About 291,000,000 results (0.91 seconds).

The information provided so rapidly told me everything I needed to know; I was about to embark on another ride on the cock-led roundabout of lies and disrespect.

There should really have been a photo of Tim at the top of the page, face-on to the camera, holding a prison number underneath him, and a stamp across saying "GUILTY."

It was alarming how much information you could find on something that, up until five minutes before, I had been completely ignorant of. There was ream after ream of text about the contents of the website the credit card charge corresponded to – although no sign of the website itself. One of the first www.'s that came up was Mumsnet. I clicked the link and opened the page. I read dire warning after dire warning all along the same lines, giving one very clear message: if you've discovered your partner spending money with this company, it means he's cheating. Long stories from other women who had been in exactly the same situation as me. Poor, disillusioned, betrayed wives and girlfriends who deserved better, but ended up with a man with a weakness for expensive, secretive, sexual thrills.

There were tales of internet pornography abuse, highlighting the fact that this website Tim was using was a straightforward way to go about hiring prostitutes. It also acted as an intermediate to arrange telephone calls at £1.50 a minute and a huge range of options of how to get the blood flowing to your bored, eager penis. Basically, the website was an online pimp, balls deep into the sex industry; a one-stop shop for sperm removal.

There was lots of support and sympathy for the women on there. There were lots of comments telling me and all the others who had used the thread, that if our men were doing this behind our backs, we needed to reassess our commitment to them. For the first time for a long time I felt vindicated in my anger and hurt. Jude's continual insistence that Tim's penchant for pornography was just a normal bloke thing, and Tim's accusations of everything being my fault, had beaten my self-belief to a pulp. All this time I'd been thinking I was in the wrong; but I wasn't.

I went back to the filing cabinet and got out more of Tim's statements, there were two years' worth of them. I looked at each month and there were debits there for the same company, there hadn't been one single month that he hadn't spent money on the site at least three times.

I let my eyes give me the message he should have done when I'd asked him a direct but gentle question about his porn usage, when his words, "I've seen how much it hurts you," left his lips. He'd reached new depths this time, he'd looked me in the eye and lied, he'd betrayed me to my face, the thought of it made me want to weep. What had I done wrong? I almost fell back into the trap of looking for a way to take responsibility for his actions, to take the blame. Ivy spoke to me harshly and urgently.

He had the chance to confide in you. You offered him the opportunity to tell you, without recrimination, about his desire for something other than you, and he'd refused to take it. It's. Not. Your. Fault.

I knew she was right. I needed him to know I'd unearthed his continued deception so badly it was almost an itch. I'd no desire to hear his voice, so, enthused by Ivy's words, I started to compose an email to him. I made a list of the dates that the charges had shown up on his statements, I went back through all the months, even the ones he'd assured me he wasn't using porn, when he'd promised me it was over, once I'd done that and put a final tally of his erotic expenditure (£980), I then asked him the questions I needed answers to.

What kind of woman to you think I am?

What do you really think of me?

Do you think I'm stupid?

What's stopped you from coming to me and asking me for help?

If you want to use this stuff, why don't you invite me to join in with your thrills?

What have I actually done to deserve this treatment from you?

What is it about our relationship that makes you need to look for something else?

Am I a bad woman?

Do you even love me anymore?

Do I deserve to be treated with such contempt and disrespect?

As I pressed send Ivy said

Now send him another and ask him when he's moving out!

37

I couldn't stand still. I wandered round the house and into the garden I vacillated between angry, frustrated, jubilant, victorious, and then back to desperate. Most of all I felt trapped. The trail of my footsteps led me upstairs and into the dressing room. I slid open my wardrobe doors and looked at my clothes, I opened my drawers full of underwear and jewellery, I poked through the baskets on my dressing table overspilling with expensive, supposedly age-busting creams: ironically, I'd probably spent more on those than Tim had on the pimping website, in the hope that the next one would turn back the clock for me and make me desirable again. All that money I'd wasted in the hope that this next cream would be the one to stop me being a middle aged, undesirable woman whose husband had become a pornographic artful dodger. What was the use of it all?

A wave of sadness shook me so hard my legs seemed to stop working, I gave in and laid on the floor feeling the depth and softness of the cream carpet support my body. I watched the tiny dust particles float in the afternoon sunlight beaming through the window, I could hear my work phone ringing downstairs in the office. I shut out the noise whilst I looked at the carefully chosen photographs and artwork adorning the walls of the dressing room. My personal mobile started to ring; I ignored it. I looked at the colours of the clothes in the pile of ironing sat waiting to be done. I was calm, I didn't cry, I simply looked at my life in this room.

I realised it was time to leave it.

My phone rang again. I went back down the stairs to it and looked at the number of missed calls and texts, every one of them from Tim. "I'm sorry." "We need to talk." "Where are you?" "I'm free now if you want to call me." "Are you there?" "Rachel call me, I need to speak to you." "Please don't leave me hanging like this."

Self-centred, arrogant, selfish bastard. Now he wants to talk. He doesn't remember the times he's left me waiting for days to hear his explanations, he forgets about the messages and calls I've made, desperate to speak to him, only to give in again - let him excuse himself - hating him but wanting him to make it all feel right again for me. I pressed reply to his last message and typed quickly.

"Fuck off."

My decision was made, I was leaving. I went back online and started to search for somewhere to stay. Anywhere, away from here. I knew there were three or four friends I could go to, but I didn't want to involve anyone else. As ridiculous as it was, I still wasn't ready to tell on Tim. I didn't need anyone else's opinion or help, I needed to be alone for a while - somewhere no one knew me; somewhere I could breathe and think.

After an hour or so searching, I found a sea-front cottage on the outskirts of a small seaside town I'd always loved as a kid. It gave me everything I needed, remote enough for my needs, but within driving distance to my patch so I could still work. It looked comfortable and cosy. I booked it for a week.

As I was finalising my payment my phone rang again. I ignored it. The house phone rang, I ignored that too. The answer phone kicked in and Tim's voice filled the room. "Please Rachel, I can explain. I need to explain, please pick up the phone." I looked at the shiny black handset resting on the holder where his voice was coming from and flipped it the bird. I walked out of the office leaving his pleading voice behind me and started to pack. I threw a random jumble of items in a suitcase, I collected my things from the bathroom and when I turned to check that I'd got everything I needed I had a huge sense of satisfaction from seeing the shower and the vanity unit in its semi-bare state. No 'his n hers' now, no hers at all; just his. Fuck him. I was calm and determined, I knew absolutely I was doing the right thing.

As I was methodically packing my work things into my briefcase, I came across a pile of 'post it' notes. I'd used them in the past when I'd been going away anywhere, to leave Tim messages: in the pockets of his clothes, in the fridge, hiding them in the cereal packet, under his pillow. 'I love you' messages, ones that said hello or good morning, ones that I knew he would find through the days I wasn't going to be with him. I'd done it to make him smile. I picked up a pen and wrote one now. As I gathered the last of my things and put them in the car, I went to the kitchen and left the note on the breakfast bar. I was going to leave it under a bottle of wine, but it was the last one left in the house so in the end I decided to take it with me.

The kitchen was clean and tidy, the pink square of paper stood out on the grey granite worktop, I'd written in black ink.

Water the plants. You cunt.

I turned my phone off as I left the house.

* * * * * * * * * *

The further away from home I drove, the better I felt. I called at a supermarket and bought enough food and wine to last a few days and headed towards the coast. Late afternoon was turning into early evening when my sat nav advised me to turn right. I found myself on a narrow country lane with huge hedges either side of me - it felt like another world. I buzzed my window down to feel the fresh air on my face - I took a huge breath in. I could smell seaweed.

When I arrived at my destination, I realised how lucky I'd been to find the cottage; the surroundings were beautiful. The key had been left in the door for me and as I let myself in, it had a tranquil, comfortable feeling, everything about it invited me to be calm. I unpacked much more carefully than I'd packed, I familiarised myself with my new, albeit temporary home, then poured myself a glass of red from the bottle I'd requisitioned from the top of the post-it note.

I went to sit outside on the raised patio that faced the sea, breathing deeply, relishing the feeling of relief sinking into me. When I felt ready, I picked up my phone and turned it on again, there was a cacophony of racket informing me of incoming texts, missed calls and voicemail messages that had been left. I knew they were from Tim. I didn't read or listen to any of them; I deleted them all. I gazed out at the view that was changing from sunset to twilight and composed my reply in my head. Once I'd decided what I was going to say, I typed it carefully and sent it.

"I have no desire to hear your pathetic excuses anymore. I'm done. I hate you with a passion. I'm not at home and I won't be there when you get back tomorrow."

His reply came quickly. "Can we speak?"

"No." I'd barely sent the words when his reply beeped back at me,

"Where are you?"

I was undecided about what to do next, whether or not to even answer. I refilled my glass, lit another ciggie and then typed, "None of your business." Again, a rapid reply from Tim, "Are you safe?" I admired my surroundings once again, there was a field full of grazing sheep to the left of me and rolling hills to the right. From where I sat, I couldn't see much of the beach, but I could hear the waves as they broke onto the sand.

The sea was my horizon, the lamps lit inside my new living room shone through the patio door and cast an orange glow that embraced me where I sat; for the first time for as long as I could recollect, I did feel safe. I replied, "Yes. Don't contact me again until you hear from me."

****

I fell in love with my little haven full of Rachelness. The weight of the world I'd been carrying on my shoulders dissipated a bit more every day, I felt lighter; I felt free. Taking myself away from the damage Tim seemed intent on inflicting gave me an overwhelming sense of peace. I didn't want it to end. I knew I needed to be away for longer than a week, so with my fingers crossed I contacted the owners to see if I could extend my stay. I negotiated a deal on the rent for a month and when I put the phone down there was a competition in my body between the smile of joy and the sigh of contentment.

The same day, whilst I was exploring in the local village, I spotted a flyer in the window of the local post office advertising push bikes to rent. It sounded like more fun than the gym to me, so while I was on a negotiating roll, I made a cheeky offer on one for the whole time I was going be there. The guy at the cycle shop stuck an extra fiver on my price and then accepted. My ride was bright red with huge wheels and a basket on the front. I adored it.

I hadn't told Jude the details of the next episode of 'Rachel Bradbury - Sex Deviant Super Sleuth' until the day after my move. When I told her I'd finally had enough and packed my bags, she was very supportive of my decision to get away from Tim for a while. We kept in touch every day after that, it felt a bit like old times and her encouragement to enjoy my retreat from my fucked-up life seemed to free me even further. I guessed she'd be in touch with Tim too, to make sure he was ok, but I never asked her how he was, because quite frankly I found it hard to care. She was the only person apart from him (and probably our cleaner) who knew I wasn't at home, and the only person who knew exactly where I was, was me. The sense of liberation that came with my secret made me almost euphoric, and for the first time for as long as I could remember, I was proud of myself.

Contentment infused me and I made a point of finishing work early so I could get back to the view of the sea. I had a smile on my face every time I made the right turn down the hedge-lined lane towards home. Once I was there, I'd get on the bike and cycle down the tiny coastal path to a caravan park nearby, I'd have a couple of beers and sit outside enjoying the sun whilst I listened to the kids play in the swimming pool or the music from the inside of the bar. Over the weeks I became a regular, they drew me a pint as soon as they saw me come in to the bar. They never questioned me about the reason for my continual presence, they just said hello, served me ice cold lager and took my money; it was perfect for me.

One evening, as I was riding back, I passed two furtive-looking teenage lads sat with their legs dangling over the sea wall. There was the unmistakable whiff of weed surrounding them. I stopped my bike and turned round, and as I cycled back to them, I asked, "Have you two got a spliff?" The one furthest away from me, the smaller one of the two tried to hide the joint by the side of his leg. They both looked a bit scared, but the bigger one nodded guiltily. "Hand it over then." I got off my bike and joined them. We sat for a while watching the waves, getting high, having a laugh. When I eventually got back on my ride, it was nearly dark, I was very stoned, a bit unsteady and wobbled rather than cycled the rest of the way home.

As I cooked my dinner that evening, Inner Voice Ivy and I were having a giggly little chit chat when all of a sudden Tim came into my consciousness. It must have been the spliff because for the first time in a while I didn't immediately banish the thought of him with a dismissive shake of my head or a mental flick of my two fingers, instead I allowed him to stay there for a while, to give myself the chance to check in with my feelings about him now I had some distance from his toxicity.

My dope-soaked, mellow thoughts drifted through my mind, and I realised it might be coming close to the time for me to speak to him. My mood was as serene as it had been for as long as I could remember, and although I didn't really want to break the spell, I knew that I would have to eventually, so why not now? It had been more than a week since I'd left the house and the thought of how long I'd left it to contact him again kick-started my guilt. I began to wonder if I'd been a bit selfish not getting in touch with him before now.

Stop that bullshit immediately! You're not staying away to punish him, are you? No, you're not! You're doing this because you have to. For the first time in a long time, you're looking after yourself - do NOT feel guilty for that. In fact, fuck him, don't go back, ever.

As persuasive as Ivy was, my mind was made up and before she could talk me out of it anymore, I found my phone and sent him a text. I just said 'Hello,' and left it at that. His reply came back within seconds, "Rachel, it's so good to hear from you, thank you for getting in touch. I've been worried about you. Are you ok?"

Oh shit! I hadn't thought much beyond my first text to him, and now he'd replied I realised I didn't want to talk to him at all. I didn't want to get involved in a conversation. "I'm doing great thank you." Again, there was an immediate answer, "Can we talk?" Even my little haze from the spliff couldn't stop the panic I felt at the thought of having to actually speak to him. I was only just coming round to thinking about him as anything other than a betraying wanker. "No, I'm not ready yet, I was just checking in that's all. I'll be in touch again when I'm ready to talk." Another instant reply, "Ok, take care of yourself please, I love you xxxx"

Ivy was just winding herself up for a full onslaught related to the declaration of love when my phone beeped again. "I thought I'd let you know I've got an appointment with Glenda tomorrow." What was I supposed to say to that? Well done? Congratulations? I'm proud of you? About fucking time? I had no idea how to reply; so, I didn't.

I was relieved that he was making an effort finally and I hoped at least he would be able to be honest with Glenda this time while I wasn't there.

Never mind all that. I hope when he gets there, thingy-bob the counsellor's memory for names is better than the last time you saw her – Melissa. Ivy's comment brought my stoned mind away from the spiral into forlornness and back to my previous happy place. I laughed out loud.

<h1 style="text-align:center">38</h1>

I'd half expected to be curious about Tim's session with Glenda, but no matter how hard I tried to find it, there was nothing in me that actually gave a shit about how it had gone. It was another five days before I felt even remotely ready to contact him again. I wasn't completely convinced it was time for me to talk to him even then, but I wanted to be as fair as I could bring myself to be. As I expected I got an instantaneous reply to my, "Hi, how are you?" I resisted the temptation to think the same as Ivy - that the reason Tim was always so quick to reply to my text messages was because he already had his phone in his hand looking at images of prostitutes, deciding which one he would order next.

Whatever he was up to, he certainly didn't waste much time with idle chat, he came straight to the point. "I really need to see you Rachel. I know you aren't interested in my excuses, and I don't blame you, but PLEASE can we get together soon?"

The guilt came to me again, and this time I knew that if I didn't see him, then it would be because I was punishing him. I needed to be sure I was better than that. Taking care of myself was one thing, but doing it at the expense of him was another – that would just turn me into him.

We arranged to meet on Saturday morning. Saturday felt like a zombie walking towards me (I'm terrified of zombies) - no matter how slowly it shuffled towards me, I knew it was on its way and there was nothing I could do to stop it. By the time I was having my Friday evening caravan park lager, the last vestige of my inner peace dissipated and was replaced by stomach churning inner turmoil.

The whole time I'd been at the cottage, the weather had been glorious, each morning I'd woken up to sunshine and a cool, salty breeze through my open window. The morning Tim was due it rained heavily, the clouds were so low and dense it was hard to tell where they ended and the sea began. My mood was flat; depressed despite my medication, I could feel myself start to crumble again. I was on the verge of contacting him to tell him not to bother coming but I stopped myself at the last minute. I resigned myself to his visit and waited to hear his car engine come down the lane towards me. I was on my third cup of tea and sixth or seventh cigarette when I eventually heard it. The thought of him being just around the corner from me caused a rush of adrenaline that made my whole body tremble. As I stood up from my sheltered, outside seat to go and meet him, I found my legs wouldn't hold me up, there was intense pain but no strength in them at all. I tried to stand a couple of times but I couldn't so I had to sit where I was and watch him walk over to me.

He headed directly into my personal space; his presence overwhelmed me - he was coming in for a hug. I managed to stand and swerved my body away from him, I was almost embarrassed by my newly found instinct to protect myself from him, so to cover my reticence for the tactile greeting, I invited him inside the cottage and pointed to the large comfy sofa and directed him to sit. Finding the strenght returning slowly to my legs, I perched myself on the edge of the lounger opposite him. He looked shattered, his skin was grey, he had black rings under his eyes. He'd had a shave but he'd missed a bit; he looked helpless.

I felt trapped, I wanted to run screaming to the caravan park but I made myself busy instead and made a cup of tea for us both. In my glorious cottage by the sea, the kitchen was an extension of the lounge, so whilst I went about my task, we were technically still together but without the intensity of my having to look at his weary, porn-worn face. I was self-conscious of how my body must look to him. I had my back to him so I couldn't see where he was looking, but I imagined he would be watching me. As I reached for the mugs from the cupboard for some reason my fingers wouldn't bend, I knew what I needed them to do, they just wouldn't do it. I had to concentrate my efforts hard and squeeze them together to make them work so I could hold the cup handles.

As I placed his drink in front of him, I gave him the best smile I could summon under the circumstances and quickly moved away from him, back to the safety of my chair. The shooting pains in my legs had come back, spasm after spasm shot through my thigh muscles. I had to try hard to keep my face straight against the pain.

We still hadn't said a word to each other. He'd smiled gently at me as I gave him the tea, then continued to look around him at the place I'd been without him for so long. Whilst I waited for the pains in my legs to subside, I watched him take in the sight of the signs of me, Rachel Bradbury nee Stone, making myself at home, in a new home. I had flowers in a vase and handpicked purple lilac in a milk jug. I'd bought a DVD box set of a programme I'd always wanted to see but never got round to, it was sat by the TV, its presence making it clear that I'd been comfortable and relaxed enough to enjoy my escapism. I followed his gaze and realised that this was my place - somewhere I felt content to be alone in. We continued to sit wordlessly for a while, until he stopped taking in the evidence of my life without him, his gaze met mine and as he looked at me again, he began to weep. Then he started to talk.

"I met with Glenda last week and on her suggestion, I've started to see someone else, an expert in my type of addiction.

When you told me you were leaving me, it hit me hard." He swallowed and shook his head, struggling for words. "As soon as I got home and you weren't there, I realised that you really meant it, that you had left me. For the first time since this all began, I fully appreciated what I've been doing to you, to us. I thought long and hard about why I've been behaving the way I have, and I understand now that what started as a bit of titivation, has begun to consume me." His tears came faster, he started to sob. "Glenda realised that I needed more help than she could give me. She called the counsellor during our session together and he agreed to see me straight away as an emergency patient. I've seen him twice already."

I was trying hard to pay attention, but my thigh muscles were twitching and that distracted me a bit, it felt like I was watching him through the glass of a fish bowl. He didn't notice my distance he had a lot to get off his chest.

"The new counsellor, Alistair, asked me lots of questions about my early childhood and teenage years; the idea is to uncover the reasons for my addiction." His voice was loaded with sincerity. "It's given me a lot to think about and work through. I have to understand why I'm doing this before I can begin to help myself get over it." His chin wobbled and he started to cry again. I listened to his words through my brain fog and watched him cry. I didn't comment.

"I'm so ashamed and angry with myself for my behaviour. The porn was only ever to pass time whilst I was away from home but before I knew it, I was carried away by it and as much as I wanted to stop it, I couldn't." He was trying to get a grip on his tears, swallowing hard and breathing deeply. "I've been so lonely while you've been away Rachel, and so desperate to see you. I've found it hard to cope with all the emotions the counselling has stirred up inside me, and not knowing where you were. Understanding that I have pushed you so far away from me that you didn't want me to know, well it's destroyed me to be honest."

His breath caught on his words and this time his grief finally reached me. Without any further thought I went to him. For the first time in weeks I reached to touch him and he moved towards me. His head came into the crook of my neck and I stroked his hair as he sobbed, his noisy tears were matched with my unstoppable silent ones; they rolled down my face until the front of my shirt was damp with the mashed-up moisture of both our heartache.

I eventually felt him start to calm down. His sobs were further apart, he lifted his head away from my shoulder and as soon as I felt released from him, I stood again and removed my-self from the magnitude of emotion. As he tried to compose himself further, I looked at his face, the one I'd loved for so many years, the one I'd watched break into a grin as he saw me, the one I watched concentrate as he read, the one I'd watched sleep on the pillow next to mine; the face I'd adored. I realised I didn't adore it anymore.

39

He lifted his head from his misery, the tears on his face were starting to dry but his eyes were still full of emotion. He noticed me looking at him and tried to turn the corners of his mouth up ever so slightly. "The thing with my treatment is, the intimate details must remain between me and Alistair. As my counsellor, he has advised me not to divulge the details of our sessions or of the work I am going to be doing on myself... he says this journey must be mine and I shouldn't take on anyone else's influence or thoughts. So, I won't be able to talk about why I came to be where I am, or how I am working to change it."

"I understand that, Tim. Thank you for admitting that you have a problem and for going to see someone."

Finally, Rach. You forgot to say finally.

"I'll support you in any way I can. If you need me at all you just have to call or text me to let me know." I saw him blink a couple of times, his head drew back and his neatly waxed eyebrows nearly met up in the middle again with the depth of the quizzical frown he pulled, I could almost see the huge question mark hanging over his head. I figured now was as good a time as any to let him know my news - "I'm not coming home."

He tried but failed to hide his agitation.

"But, why not? Didn't I just tell you I was trying to get well again? I am making a big effort to understand why I have turned to porn, what more do you want me to do, Rachel?"

I kept my voice as calm as I could, trying my hardest not to give Ivy free reign on my reply "I can't give you my side of the story again, Tim. You know as well as I do that the porn isn't really the issue for me. I've tried so often to make you understand what your behaviour has done to me. I've pleaded with you to stop, and it's fallen on deaf ears. As your wife, my first instinct is to support you and to help you get through this, and I will as much as I can, but it'll have to be from a distance. I've no gentleness in my soul for you, I've nothing left to give you, and until you're on the road to recovery I can't live with you again."

He was battling hard but there was a touch of irritability in his voice he couldn't hide, "Well, how long do you think it's going to take?"

Cheeky cu-

I refused to be influenced by his mood. I stayed as calm as I could, "I don't know. I never, ever thought I would see this day, I never thought you would hurt me as much as you have. I loved you so much, but I've given you all I've got for now. I'm not going to make hollow promises, I'm sorry."

I inadvertently (or maybe not) looked outside to check the weather, Tim saw the glance and took it as his invitation to leave. He stood quickly and sighed as he walked to the door with his back to me, I noticed the slump in his shoulders, he looked as broken as I felt. He didn't come in for a hug or a kiss this time, he just let himself out of the house and set off across the courtyard, he didn't turn back to me, he didn't say goodbye.

I leaned on the door frame of my cottage and watched him get back into his car. As he started the engine, we acknowledged each other with a formal wave, almost a salute, and I followed his progress as he reversed out of the yard and drove away.

Finally on my own again, I sat back on the sheltered bench and lit the cigarette I'd been thinking about for a while. The emotional numbness was slowly overtaken by an immense pain in my heart. I started to replay the visit and think about what he'd said, his thoughts, his reasons, his turmoil, him wanting me home. As I was mulling it all over, it suddenly occurred to me with shock and surprise that I said out loud, "He never once asked me how I was!". Inevitably, Ivy joined in. *No, and not once during the whole pity-fucking-me conversation did he say he was sorry.*

She was right; he hadn't apologised once.

****

In my semi-indignant, partially outraged, totally devastated state I called Jude and started to tell her what had happened, but I caught the memory of the image of his back, as he walked away from me, and felt myself unfold. His unconscious display of helplessness, combined with the things I'd told him I couldn't feel, and how I'd rejected him - the misery of it all came at me in a torrent; it was agony. Every emotion I'd denied whilst we'd been in the same room burst out of me and now it was my turn to weep.

"I never, ever thought we would be this couple Jude, I can't get my head around where we are, what we've just said to each other. I can't believe I can't love him. I know it's there, but I can't reach it." I couldn't speak anymore, all I could do was cry, and all she could do was listen. I could hear her life in the background of our call. "Go Jude, I can hear you've got things going on there."

"Nah, I'm not going anywhere babe, they can manage without me for a bit." And so we stayed together for a couple of hours at least. I lay on the sofa that Tim had recently left, the phone was propped up on a cushion so Jude and I could talk whilst I curled into the fetal position, she made comforting shushing noises and I cried. The words I managed to speak through the thickness of the sadness in my throat were all about my devastation at the potential end to my marriage and friendship with Tim, and every time I thought I was done with the tears, I found some more and started to sob again.

I must have cried myself to sleep because it was dark by the time a deep chill woke me. My mobile was still next to my head. I was confused by the fact that I'd lost the day and my body was stiff, I tried to check the time on my phone but it was dead. I didn't bother to investigate any further, I pulled my achy-self off the settee, went for a wee and then fell into my bed and straight back to sleep.

* * * * * * * * * * *

When I woke the next morning, the sunshine was back. My eyes were sore from the tears I'd shed but otherwise the after-effects of Tim's non-apology visit seemed to have dissipated a lot faster than I ever thought was possible. Maybe it was the sunshine, maybe I'd cried it all out, but considering the depths of my despair the day before I felt buoyant today. I liked the feeling, so I made a deliberate decision not to think too deeply about any of it.

I went out for breakfast and read a couple of newspapers, I shopped and bought myself all the stuff I loved to eat and then I went on a massive bike ride. I spoke to Jude briefly to let her know I was doing ok, neither of us touched on the agonies of the day before. I was about to ask her if she'd spoken to Tim but before the words came out, I stopped myself; I decided ignorance was bliss. I was brimming over with bouncy energy, I felt full of life, and oddly enough, whilst I was stood up out of my seat trying to pedal my bike up a hill that had always defeated me before, I concluded that the strongest emotion I was feeling was hope. The woman who'd been curled up on the sofa unable to speak for sadness the day before had gone, and I'd replaced her with a much more light-hearted version; I even managed the hill without having to get off my bike and push.

To celebrate my metamorphosis, I stopped at the caravan site on my way back from my ride for a couple of early afternoon beers. When the guy behind the bar saw me walk in, he looked at the clock to check the time; he still didn't comment though. As I left the park, my little dope-smoking mates were walking towards their usual spot on the sea wall and without any discussion the three of us settled ourselves with a shared spliff and we passed a happy hour or so laughing so hard we had to hold onto our bellies whilst we thought of as many slang words we knew for vagina, breasts and the police. I was getting back on my bike when Rick, the taller of the two, handed me a pre-rolled spliff. "Here Rach, have this on us, it's been an ace afternoon thanks!" I couldn't wipe the grin off my face the whole ride home.

A gentle, happy beer and weed buzz and bellyaching from laughter kept me chirpy for the rest of the afternoon. I indulged myself with a soak in the bath, and as I lay there surrounded by soothing warm water and bubbles, the smell of my dinner cooking I realised I was singing to myself. I couldn't remember the last time I'd heard myself sing anything at all. I ate and watched six episodes of the DVD, back-to-back, and then I slept. Like a log.

****

I had a brilliant week at work, too. I was completely focused, and after one target-busting appointment, Laura and I got back in my car and she looked at me sideways on, "What the hell is different about you, Rach? You were bloody brilliant in there. I can't put my finger on what's going on, but you seem much more like your old self. Have you changed your meds?"

I laughed, "No babe, just having a good day that's all. Besides it's Thursday, I'm finishing for the weekend and the sun's shining, what's not to be happy about?" She looked unconvinced but got busy turning Radio 2 off in favour of Radio 1, and I changed the conversation.

She was right though, I was different, my confidence was high, I felt worthy again. Tim finally admitting he had a problem had helped me tremendously, it took some of the blame away from me. His better-late-than-never realisation that he needed help had released a lot of my torment and self-accusation: if it wasn't entirely my fault our marriage was completely fucked up then there was no reason to hate myself any more was there? It was slowly starting to sink in that maybe, if Tim worked hard at his counselling and I stayed away until I was sure I could trust him again, maybe, and it was just a maybe, there might be hope for my relationship with the love of my life after all.

The only fly in my ointment was my stay in the cottage was due to end next week, and I knew with all my heart there was no way I was going back to live with Tim yet; I wasn't ready for that.

I was driving towards the coast after my afternoon with Laura when Naomi called. I almost didn't take the call, but I'd been putting off speaking to her for over a week. She sounded delighted when I answered, and wanted to know if I fancied a beer at hers on my way home from work. As soon as I heard her voice, I realised I'd missed spending time with her and now was the time to tell her where I was, to finally come clean with my friend about what I'd been going through. I gave her the briefest synopsis of where I was and why; I could hear the shock in her voice as she started to ask incredulous questions, all of them were too hard to discuss over the phone, and instead of trying, I invited her to come to the seaside for the weekend for an in-depth, all-questions-answered conversation or two. She didn't waste any time accepting the invitation and within a couple of hours she was stood on my doorstep with a bottle of tequila and an overnight bag.

We sat up most of the night; it was like old times. I love Naomi, even Inner Voice Ivy loves Naomi and she's almost impossible to please. We sat outside on the tiny patio facing the sea and I described the last few years of my life in all its gory glory. She gasped in all the right places, her indignation on my behalf at Tim's misdemeanors was almost comical. She was outraged at Glenda's Melissa misnomer and cheered and applauded when I told her about the post it note I'd left for Tim reminding him to water the plants.

It was so wonderful to be in her company and equally wonderful to know that Jude hadn't once betrayed my confidence; Naomi genuinely had no idea what had been going on. Her take on my situation was simple, Tim had behaved appallingly, his pornography use and flagrant disregard for our marriage was criminal and was I really sure I should be going back to him at all? "I will go back, Nai, I've invested too much in our lives together to give up now. I know it's hard to understand, because I struggle to comprehend it too, but I love him, I can't imagine me or my life without him. You know something I thought of the other day? Since before we got married, he's always told me I make him want to be a better man. I've watched him grow up whilst we've been together, and before all of this crazy shit came along, he was a wonderful man - the best version of him I could ever have imagined. Despite everything, I still believe in him and I believe he can overcome this. When he does, we can move on with our lives together."

The more I spoke the more sense the words meant to me; I genuinely did feel all of those things. "But, the thought of going back now scares me, I'm not ready, he needs to prove to me it's me he wants. I've no idea how long that's going to take." She looked around us and gestured towards the beach, "Well you can't stay here forever can you darling?" I shook my head. "Do you have plans in place?" I shook my head again. "Come and live with me. God knows, I'm fed up of rattling around that big house on my own. Flick's bedroom's free, she's moved out again and you'll never see Max cos I never do; he's 19 and not bothered about spending any time with me."

We were sat side by side, she leaned over to me and gave me a nudge with her elbow, "Oh go on, say yes, remember Flick's bathroom has a jacuzzi bath, you'll technically be doing me a favour - it'll stop her thinking she can come back whenever she feels like it, a win-win situation if ever I saw one!" I turned to look at her and she winked, "It'll be fun, you can stay as long as you want." I was starting to catch her enthusiasm for the idea. I grinned and unconsciously nodded my head. "Is that a yes then?" Her voice was hopeful "If you're absolutely sure. I don't know how long I might stay."

"Of course I'm sure, now hurry up and say yes then we can have another tequila to celebrate!" How could I refuse! "I'll cut the lime, shall I?" Naomi and Ivy squealed with glee at exactly the same time.

40

June 2011

The one thing I hadn't considered when Naomi and I were making our excitable plans, was that moving in with her would reduce my proximity to Tim down to about two miles. It only really dawned on me as I approached the turning I usually used as a shortcut to our marital home; I was bringing myself back into very familiar ground, or as Ivy said: *Duck Rach, and run for cover - we're back in enemy territory!*

I hadn't considered any of the practicalities of keeping my distance from Tim when we'd be living so close to each other physically, but still emotionally apart. The complications it brought made my heart beat so hard it was almost thumping itself out of my chest. I felt a bit faint. Was I doing the right thing being so close to home? Should I just turn round and move back into my little cottage, or maybe live in a caravan on the park for a while? Anywhere that wasn't here. I felt shaky and a bit breathless, my senses were on high alert looking for any sign of my husband in the neighbourhood. By the time I'd covered the next couple of miles I was a gibbering wreck.

Nai had very thoughtfully left me enough room to pull my car around the back of her house - no one would ever know I was here; I was undiscoverable again. I calmed down a bit. As I parked up, she threw open the back door and with a screech of delight came running to meet me, her arms held out wide for a hug. The physical contact and strength of her embrace calmed me a bit more. Max came out too, and although his greeting was a lot less exuberant, he did carry my bags to my room; which, when I saw it again, I had to admit was pretty bloody special. Flick was a young woman with expensive tastes and an indulgent mum; I was going to be very comfortable here.

Nai and Max left me to unpack, but I didn't touch my things at all. Instead, for a while, I sat on the bottom of the very large bed and looked at my surroundings. There was no doubt I was lucky to be in such a beautiful home. But whilst I'd been at the cottage, it'd been easy to pretend I was taking a little break from my life - a holiday - a retreat from the realities of my marital shitstorm; but now the honest truth hit me like a ton of bricks. I was a lodger. Admittedly I was with a friend, but never the less I wasn't in my home. I was a married woman separated from my husband because he'd treated me badly, he'd neglected me, abused my trust and made me question my love for him; he'd turned my life upside down. And this was me, sitting on the edge of yet another strange bed I would sleep in whilst I carried on learning how to cope with the after-shock of it all.

I'd left my glorious cottage by the sea, my lovely red ride with the basket on the front, my boys on the wall and the ice-cold lager at the caravan park. I was going to miss them. I was going to miss the woman I was whilst I was hidden in my bolt hole. In my new 'home' I felt like a stranger, even to myself. I'd no idea who I was again now, how would I fit in to this life, living with a friend until things improved, until I felt ready to go back to Tim? Ivy had suggested to me that *maybe the best way to cope with this whole situation is to consider yourself as being on a trial separation. That way you're not really in a holding pattern waiting for the prince of porn to miraculously become someone you can trust again, are you? You're not waiting to go back to him, you're seeing how you like life without him.*

But 'trial' and 'separation' sounded like very scary words indeed and neither of them appealed to me in the slightest.

I was in the process of trying to motivate my sorry arse off the bed and start settling in when there was a knock on the door, followed by Naomi's voice at the other side asking could she come in? When I told her yes, she came into the room with a bottle of my most favourite champagne and two glasses, she gave me the bottle to open and in a familiar ritual I eased the cork. As it came away in my hand, we looked at each other, like I had with Jude all those years ago, after the first revelation of Tim's preference for cash-up-front sex, only this time there was an uncomplicated connection of friendship; her loyalty was to me, she wasn't torn between the two of us like Jude, this woman was definitely on my side and I knew she understood how I was feeling. "Hurry up and pour the bubbles Rachel, we've got a party to have! There's another bottle in the fridge, and just in case that doesn't say 'welcome home' loud enough, I've got some amazing Charlie in my knicker drawer!"

****

I hadn't told Tim I was moving into Naomi's. Preparing to tear myself away from the cottage was already as much as I could cope with at the time, and now being so close to our 'normal' lives was verging on claustrophobic. It felt like a huge step closer to me moving home and everything that implied; forgiveness, reconciliation, letting him get away with it. I wasn't ready to expose myself to the danger of a chance meeting, and I didn't feel like leaving the house, so I spent the first four days ensconced in my new abode, establishing myself through a haze of class-A Class As, alcohol, takeaways, sleep and learning how to feel safe where I was now.

Intermittently, over the weekend, Naomi and I discussed and unpicked every event during the years since the lap dance club incident, right up to the credit card statements. She was gentle with her questions and sparse with her opinions.

I described my marriage, the glorious and the truly bloody awful. I fluctuated between remembering the deep love I'd felt for Tim and the hate of equal measure that had overtaken me so often during the years of him misappropriating our sex life.

The scant geographical distance between us now and my confessional conversation kept Tim in the forefront of my mind, and as Naomi and I talked, I felt the urge to contact him, at times with outrage to tell him to fuck off and then at other times to tell him how much I loved him. Very wisely, Naomi had suggested I give her my phone when I was drunk and she'd give it me back when I was sober.

Throughout the extended weekend, we found ourselves in the most intense discussions. The pain of the memories was excruciating at times, and then two minutes later she would be telling me about one of her exploits and we would have to hold our bellies while we laughed.

To my delight we found an equal imagination in each other, and we built stories around stories. In the end, the things that had been so painful for me to even contemplate were suddenly out in the open, all the drama was removed from them and replaced by comical renditions of the same situation. It was the best welcome home I'd ever had. The sharing of my most intimate secrets seemed to seal a deal for her and me, and her reactions and total support strengthened our friendship even further.

By late Sunday afternoon as we sat in the garden, I was starting to think about how my Monday morning would look (besides being hungover). I had the sense of a new reality looming,and I thought I might as well come out of my bubble sooner rather than later and text Tim to tell him where I was. As if she'd sensed the change in me, wordlessly, Naomi handed me my mobile, and before I could talk myself out of it, I texted him hello.

He took at least half an hour to answer and when he did, he was apologetic. He'd been playing golf, he said. I told him where I was and that my plans were to stay here for a while. I almost apologised for not being ready to come home yet, but I stopped myself at the last moment. The subtext of my text, that I would be staying here until I was ready to go back to him, couldn't have been much clearer. I wondered if he felt the same way I did, now he knew where I was - that us living in the same postcode again felt like we were a step closer to being together in the same house. I didn't have to wonder for long, he told me he was delighted I was going to be so near now, and if I wanted him to call round and say hello anytime, to let him know.

As if, said Ivy, who had been conspicuous by her absence most of the weekend.

He must have had second thoughts about the likelihood of me inviting him round to my Tim-free sanctuary because straight after he'd sent the message his next one came quickly, and it was a bit more reserved. He said he would wait to hear from me again, and if I wanted to, he would love to take me out for a drink or a meal one evening soon.

Maybe it was the start of my hangover from the weekend's debauchery or simply the thought of being with him, but I felt myself retch slightly at his suggestion of going out for a drink.

41

Naomi and I fell into a steady, easy-going routine. She worked even more hours than me, so on the evenings when we were going to be home together, I got into the habit of cooking us dinner. I treasured her companionship, her attitude was a gust of fresh air through my stale Tim destroyed psyche. She'd recently decided to stop dating because, "I'm so over it all, I'm utterly jaded by boring men with massive egos." Instead of wasting time searching for unsuitable cock, she concentrated on her amazing social life and was often out with friends. Her contentment and fulfillment didn't escape me, mostly because Ivy was constantly dropping hints about how happy I could be if I was on my own, how Nai was a shining example of single womanhood, and it was all there for me if I just walked away from the agony of being married to an unfaithful man.

And still, I remained stubbornly, ridiculously loyal to Tim and our marriage, it kept me tight-lipped about my situation, and the only other person I brought into my tiny, trusted circle of confidants, was Petra. As soon as she found out I was 'Tim free', as she christened it, she too threw the doors of her home open to me. She invited me to almost everything she was doing, and I said yes to a lot of it. To my delight, my own social life expanded. I met new people - people who had no idea who I was with no preconceptions about my life. I was accepted for who I was, not Mrs B or Tim's wife or Rachel Bradbury. I was simply Rachel. Being with other people again brought back a spark in me that I'd been missing for such a long time.

The freedom was intoxicating.

I'd been with Nai and Max for 3 weeks before I met up with Tim. We'd kept in touch by text during that time - friendly, lighthearted banter - familiar jokes we'd adopted into our lives over the years. During one exchange he'd suggested we go out for a meal. I felt like I might be ready to see him, but I didn't want to commit myself to being trapped in his company, just in case it got too much for me. Instead of food, I suggested we went to a bar we'd never been to before, where no one knew us.

I was sick with nerves all day before we met. I considered what I was going to wear carefully but as I dressed, I found myself picking holes in my outfit and the way it fitted me. The confidence I'd begun to carry everywhere else drained from me, and by the time I had to leave I'd been in five different outfits, showing each one to Naomi for her approval. After the fifth one she said, "You look fucking gorgeous Rachel, but then you look fabulous in all of them. Please stop worrying, try and relax and enjoy yourself." I promised her I'd try, but by the time the taxi came I was hot and sweaty from pulling clothes on and off my body. I was worried my tits would bulge out over the top of my bra, and my mascara had refused to go on like it usually did and was clumped on my eyelashes; I was stressed and near to tears.

Tim on the other hand looked bloody gorgeous. He was already stood outside the bar waiting for me, wearing a new shirt and his (and my) favourite jeans. There was no sign of the grey-skinned, sobbing man who'd come to meet me at the cottage; he even had a tan, "from playing golf," he said, and opened his shirt at the neck so I could see where the tan line ended at his collar bone and the pale skin of his body started. I could see he'd trimmed his dark chest hair and when I caught a glimpse of his well-defined pecs it struck me again what a handsome, sexy man he was.

We kept our conversation light and fun, there was no mention of our home, or our lives together. He told me a couple of stories about the gang we hang round with at the pub, he told me how his golf swing was coming along, we both talked about our work, and I told him about my spliff-sharing boys, my bike rides and the beer at the caravan park.

As I stood at the bar buying our second drinks I had the feeling that Tim was watching me but when I looked at his reflection in the long mirror behind the bar his head was down, he was on his phone. He didn't put it down again until I took my seat next to him, he gave me one of his 100 watt smiles melting me into forgiveness for his rudeness and when he told me I looked nice in my outfit I was grateful for the compliment. I was about to gush my thank you but was stopped dead by the way he looked me up and down, as if searching for something else positive to say. "It's very flattering."

The back-handedness of the compliment knocked all the wind out of my sails and kick-started Ivy at the same time.

What did he just say? Very flattering, who are you, his granny? He might as well have told you it might fit better in a bigger size, cheeky prick.

She was right, I felt myself blush, I didn't want to be there anymore. I felt uncomfortable, I couldn't get back into the groove of our sprightly chat again. Part way down the glass of wine I'd just bought, I said I thought it was time I went home - I had a big day at work the next day and needed to be fresh for it. He seemed surprised. "Oh...ok, I was thinking we could have gone on somewhere else after this one, but if you need to get back then fair enough."

When I picked up my glass and drained it, he followed my lead and did the same. "Are we ok to share a cab at least? We're going in the same direction." He looked at me intently, and suddenly I wasn't sure he'd meant to insult me. Maybe he was being on his best behaviour and didn't want to be too personal, maybe the comment had come from a place of respect rather than anything else.

Bollocks.

We walked side by side to the taxi rank, a walk we've done many times. I put my hands into the pockets of my dress just so we were both sure there was no chance of us touching or holding hands as we walked. When we got in the car, we sat side by side in the back, the lump in the middle of the seat creating a natural barrier. We fell silent, and as we approached Naomi's house Tim leaned in towards me so he could speak quietly, "Thank you for this evening Rachel, it was so lovely to see you. Can we do it again soon please?" The breath from his whisper caught the side of my neck, and despite my disappointment and embarrassment at his reaction to my chosen outfit, I felt my body respond to the erotic sensation. I didn't look at him, I made myself busy with the seatbelt and as soon as the cab stopped, I opened the door and leapt out, away from him. "Thank you too, it was good to see you." I smiled as much as I could. He lifted his gaze to meet me. "Same time next week? Different venue maybe? Or earlier than next week if you want, you let me know."

I hadn't expected that. "Next week will be fine, I don't want to rush things." I was conscious that bending over to speak to him through the open car door was causing my breasts to slip out of the cups of the stupid bra I'd worn. I was desperate to get away.

I didn't wait for his response, I closed the door quickly and was back in the house before the taxi pulled away. Naomi came to meet me in the hallway, her eager expression holding hope that I'd had fun on my first date with my husband. "Well, how did it go?" I could feel my tears start to well up. "It was ok, until he told me I looked nice, that my dress was 'flattering'." I looked at her, still utterly bemused by his comment. Her reaction took me completely by surprise - she threw her head back and howled with laughter! She laughed until it became contagious, and in the end, I had no choice but to join in with her.

****

In my panic to excuse myself from our evening together I'd told Tim a bit of a fib, I didn't have a big day at work at all, it was my usual kind of day, apart from my last appointment with one of my all-time favourite customers who was due to retire in the next month or so.

Instead of meeting him in his office he'd invited me "to somewhere delightful for a glass of something with bubbles in it" to say goodbye. He was already at the swanky hotel bar when I arrived, sat facing the door, obviously watching for me. It was the first time in the ten years we'd worked together that he'd been punctual for anything we had arranged. I sat across from him, and as we settled down to drink our champagne, I was teasing him gently about it. We were laughing and flirting a little bit, talking about how much he was looking forward to his retirement and how brilliant the work of his replacement was, when he looked over my head and nodded a greeting. I instantly figured there was someone behind me, Roger looked back at me, "I hope you don't mind a third sharing our champers, but I invited my successor to join us; I thought this was the perfect time for you two to meet, break the ice as it were, so you won't have to go through the rigmarole of getting to know each other during business hours." He gestured to me as he said, "AJ this is Rachel, the equipment salesperson I've been telling you so much about."

AJ came to the left of me and into my peripheral vision. I stood up and held out my hand to shake his as I said hello. When he finally stood directly in front of me, I had a jolt of recognition, I was face to face with the guy from my sex dream. "Ahhh, so you're the famous Rachel!" He didn't take his eyes from my face while he said, "Thank you Roger, Rachel and I have already been introduced, at some black-tie function or another, I'm right aren't I? We've met once before haven't we?"

Yes you most certainly have AJ, the last time she saw you she was sat on your cock, riding you really, really fucking hard.

Sometimes, I'm profoundly glad I'm the only one that can hear Ivy.

42

I couldn't take my eyes away from his, he had me locked into his gaze. The grip of his handshake was firm; I like a firm handshake. Suddenly I had a vivid memory of my dream, I was straddled over his naked body looking down between my legs, watching him holding the base of his cock, using his right hand to guide himself into me. The memory of the dream was so intense I could almost feel the pressure of the first thrust of his penis as he penetrated me.

At that precise moment he squeezed my hand slightly, the extra pressure causing a shockwave up my arm, the sensation sending tiny shots of pinball pleasure through my body, my nipples tingling and hardening instantly. The lust wrapped itself round my spine, it was all I could do not to shake myself. The blood had rushed to my clit, it instantly pulsed with want, the fingers of my right hand unconsciously tightened at the same time in response to the pleasurable sensations, my vagina was alive with effervescent heat.

I had to break away from him, but his grip was strong. Hoping he might take the hint and release me, I tore my eyes away from his and flicked them downward towards our joined hands, they were clamped tightly together just above waist height. He was dressed to the left, I knew that because his massive erection was straining against the fabric of his suit pants. I wanted to jump onto his body, wrap my legs round his waist and feel his cock through the fabric of his trousers and my knickers, a teasing, sensual semi-penetration, the thought of it made my clit beat again.

Roger cleared his throat gently, and the rest of the world snapped back into focus. To his credit he sounded amused. "Well to think I was worried it might take the two of you a little time to warm to each other."

I pulled my eyes away from AJ's hard-on and extricated my hand from his grip. I turned and sat quickly in my seat, crossing my legs tightly and pulling my pelvic floor muscles tight in an attempt at making sure my insides didn't melt into a horny puddle. Roger leant forward and pushed my knee with his fingertips, "Well I never, Mrs Bradbury, there was me thinking you were Impervious to the charms of anyone other than your husband."

I didn't know what to say, the blood left my lower body in a reverse rush back towards my face and settled itself from the base of my neck to the roots of my hair; I haven't blushed like that since I was fourteen, there was nothing I could do or say to change what Roger had just had been privy too. I looked towards AJ who was currently taking a seat less than an arm's length away from me, within touching distance. He didn't look very composed either. His eyes met mine again and we started to laugh, it was a mutually amazed, "what the fuck just went on there?" burst of hilarity. Roger joined in immediately and the tension left the three of us.

Someone had refreshed my drink; I grabbed it and tipped my head back so I could get more of the contents of the glass into me as quickly as possible. I felt bubbles burst across the roof of my mouth and tongue, while the rest created tiny explosions as they slid down my throat - when did everything start feeling so sensuous? I marvelled. It felt so hedonistic it was almost post coital.

I gave myself a mental slap across the face and brought myself back to reality. I could see Roger and AJ were now both displaying comfortable, relaxed postures, AJ was reclined slightly, his erection had subsided a bit, but as I was looking at his cock, it throbbed again and my clit responded immediately.

"Please will you excuse me?" I started to unwrap my legs so I could stand, both men stood up before me, each of them offering me a hand, I took them both. My skin seemed to melt even with the briefest touch of AJ's. I smiled at them in turn, "Thank you, I just need to pee, then I'll be back."

This time when I walked away, no one picked up their phone to distract themselves. I knew for certain there were two pairs of eyes following my walk to the door.

I didn't think I really needed a pee, I just needed to get away to straighten my head a bit. I sat in a cubicle anyway, there was no toilet lid to rest my bum on, probably taken off to stop nouveau riche druggies snorting expensive chemicals off it. Instead I sat fully clothed on the seat, in a bit of a daze, a flashback of AJ's fingers tight around my hand, the fantasy of looking down at his body underneath mine, my thighs spread wide across him, the tip of his cock touching my most delicate skin – once again it was so real I was convinced I could feel it.

Without any more thought I dragged the front of my dress up to my waist with one hand while the other slid itself under the waistband of my knickers straight to my cunt. I was wet through. My fingers slid inside me like a warm knife through butter, the folds of my vagina wrapped round them greedily as I pushed them inside me. The back of my thumb touched my clitoris, the nerves were white hot; the combination of sensations forced my hips up with greed and the pressure of my body movement and fingers joined forces; I came instantly. My body folded over itself in an effort to contain the explosion of the orgasm but it was bigger than that, I couldn't restrain it, my head snapped backward as a long deep grunt forced itself from my throat. I closed the tops of my thighs around my hand, the beat of my cum muscles throbbed against it. I was temporarily paralysed with pleasure, gasping, breathless, my fingers soaked with my silky bodily fluid.

I luxuriated in the aftermath, until I got my breath back a bit. When I eventually dared, I drew my hand away from myself, another deep pulse of lust took me by surprise and forced me to gasp again.

When I could move again, I rearranged my clothes and with unsteady legs I left my masturbation chamber. Thankfully I was the only one in the room. I washed my hands and as I did, I leaned over into the mirror to study my flushed face. I met my own eyes, and for the first time in a long time I saw the shine of sexuality in my reflection. I smiled at myself and winked.

As I walked back to my seat, Roger and AJ both stood again. I tried to keep my smile between the two of them and tried even harder not to let myself get sucked back into the vortex of AJ's face and eyes; I wasn't sure my body could stand another shock like the last one.

Roger was the first to speak, "We were thinking we might go out for dinner, Rachel, would you care to join us?"

Nah Rog, thanks a lot, she can't do that, she's going to book herself into this hotel, take AJ upstairs with her and fuck his brains out for the next week or so.

"That would be lovely but I have a big drive home, and I know me, if I start on more champagne I won't want to stop; I'll end up staying for the weekend!" I smiled at them both, "I'm sorry to be so boring."

I started to collect my things, my hands were still a bit shaky from the sex I'd just had with myself. I was right, it was time to leave. I didn't want to change my mind. I knew it wouldn't take much to persuade me to stay, but I had no idea if I could handle the wantonness of my body and enthusiastic encouragement from Ivy, whilst holding a reasonable conversation and trying to eat at the same time. The potential sensual overload was too risky.

I leant over and gave Roger a kiss on his cheek, I really was very fond of him, "I will miss our chats, sir, it has been a pleasure to deal with you over the last few years, please be sure you have as much fun as is humanly possible with all your free time." I kissed him again.

"Young lady, you are a delight, I promise I will misbehave as much as my wife will allow. Now, it's my turn to pee, as you so eloquently put it, so I will leave you in the capable hands of AJ, he will walk you to your car."

There didn't seem to be much room for discussion, and as Roger headed off towards the toilets, AJ and I walked out of the hotel into the warmth of the early evening sun. We didn't touch.

My car was close by, I nodded to it, "I'm just here, I'm fine, thank you, don't wait too long to finish off that champagne otherwise all the bubbles will be gone." I turned to face him again and there it was, the magnet that pulled me to him. My back arched bringing my lower body closer to his. He took a step towards me, I watched his lips as he said, "Rachel, I have absolutely no idea what this is, but I must tell you I've never felt sexual attraction like this."

I wanted to kiss him, to feel his lips, to feel his tongue meeting mine. "Roger tells me you are a happily married woman and unlike me you aren't free to pursue the possibilities of our cupidity. Out of respect for you, I won't invite you to, but I will say this - if ever, ever you find yourself in a position to take a lover, please come to me immediately." My breath was ragged with longing, his words had only served to strengthen my desire, I smiled to him, "Thank you for your respect AJ, I appreciate it more than you can imagine. I'm not free to be with you, but it doesn't stop me wanting to be; a lot."

We both smiled. I needed to get away, before I changed my mind. I moved to get into my car and he stayed where he was, pushing his hands in to his pockets. I could see he was hard again. He watched me closely as I absorbed the sight of him, I wanted to feel his cock inside me so badly. "Drive safely Rachel, and no doubt I'll see you soon in a much more official capacity."

"Have a lovely evening, and make sure Roger pays for the champagne, it was his treat!"

He was still standing in the same spot as I drove away, his hands still in his pockets until he raised one to return my wave goodbye.

I could feel Ivy on her way to have a chat.

What the fuck are you doing woman? You are free! Turn round, take him to bed, have filthy, glorious sex with him in as many places as you can. I told you, you should consider yourself on a trial separation. Please give into your lust, your fidelity is wasted on Tim.

✳✳✳✳✳✳✳✳✳✳

Halfway home I passed a shopping mall. I pulled in and went to everyone's favourite lingerie shop and spent a reasonable amount of money on a vibrator that looked about the same size as AJ's erection. My toilet wank had been the first time I had touched myself for pleasure in years, it was time to change that. It was time to start reclaiming my sensuality and I'd just bought my new battery operated fuck buddy to prove it.

<h1 style="text-align:center">43</h1>

September 2011

I didn't see Naomi for ages after the purchase of my new Double A lover, which happened to be the same shape and size as my imaginary lover. By the time she came home from her long weekend, I was busting to tell her what had happened. I'd kept it to myself for long enough and it was a story that needed sharing so badly it was burning a hole in my psyche's pocket. It did occur to me at one point to call Jude and share the horny anecdote, but since my stint in the cottage, she'd finally stopped defending Tim's behaviour and I'd started to feel like I'd got her undiluted support back. Ivy warned me against revealing the details of my W.C wank to her; I know Ivy didn't trust Jude, she thought she might find a way to use my desirous feelings toward AJ to excuse Tim once again, so I let her convince me to stay quiet about it.

When Nai eventually walked through the door she was buzzing with her own celebratory energy. I was so excited to see her - I'd missed her. I was like a puppy; I followed her round the house from room to room as she unpacked and filled the washing machine, I even sat on the toilet while she had a shower. I was so excited to tell her what happened with AJ and my subsequent purchase. I also needed to tell her about using the vibrator in the bath and Max and the boys thinking there was something wrong with the water pipes because of the racket it made - but that could wait!

She had plenty of her own stuff about her trip away to tell me so I waited until she'd finished sharing her gossip. As she stepped out of the shower she finally said, "So what have you been up to?" I was so glad to finally spill the beans I went off like a verbal rocket. As I told my tale in great detail, she stopped drying herself and sat on the edge of the bath to listen. She was wrapped in a damp towel, water dripping from her hair onto her shoulders, and the more I told her, the closer in to me she leaned eager, to hear the next bit.

When I told her about getting myself off in the toilets, she laughed so hard she nearly fell backwards into the tub.

****

For a few weeks everything slipped into a strange normality, considering I was living two miles down the road from my marital home. I was sleeping well in Flick's massive bed and instead of going to the gym and risking seeing Tim unexpectedly, I started using Naomi's pushbike and going for a long ride instead, the fresh air and exercise kept my spirits up. I was more than happy with Nai's companionship and a bit of a party with Petra every now and again.

Tim and I had been on a couple more evenings out together. There was still no sexual connotation in our dates - we didn't touch, and we hadn't kissed yet – nevertheless, in between seeing him, I found myself thinking about him more and more. I realised I was starting to soften a bit towards him. Now, instead of anger and hatred, the thought of him brought a smile to my lips. I began to recall the better times we'd had together, pre-porn discoveries, when I'd lived in blissful ignorance without the cloud of mistrust that had hung over our lives for so many of our recent years together. We began to text each other every day and our conversations were friendly and funny; we were both making an effort to make it right between us.

My life, in the most curious way, was better than it had been for years. I felt confident that I was on top of my depression and the next time I saw my GP we discussed reducing my medication. I was on a roll, I felt great, my confidence was high.

****

During the summer months whilst we'd been living apart, our party central house had been unusually quiet and Tim and I had been turning a lot of invitations down. I was sure there had been some speculation as to why we'd absented ourselves so often but as far as I was aware, the only people who knew about our living arrangements were the ones I'd chosen to tell. We were trying hard to keep our separation a secret. It felt to me like we were working together for a change, we were protecting each other and our marriage from the gossips in our social circles who could be brutal in their critical analysis of other people's lives. There was nothing they liked better than salacious news and I knew with complete surety, Tim and my marital troubles would create a sense of delight amongst all of those who had always looked at us with envious eyes. I didn't want anyone to know there was paper covering the cracks in our relationship or to see the amount of heartache I'd swept under that imaginary carpet of mine.

However, there was one party we couldn't refuse: Tina, one of my longest-serving friends, was turning fifty and she'd been planning this event for over a year. It was formal black tie, champagne on arrival, canapes and a six-piece band kind of do. This was a party we were obliged to attend, there was no getting out of it.

I'd gone to town with the preparation for the event; I had been to the hairdressers, the nail salon, and bought new strappy high heels. I wore a deep green silk dress that was cut so cleverly it made my medication weight gain become an hourglass figure. Even I thought I looked hot, and it takes a lot for me to see beyond my critical spectacles when I'm looking at my reflection.

I was having a cheeky beer and a ciggie whilst I was waiting for Tim, when he texted to say he was having trouble getting a taxi, there were none free. He was worried we would be rudely late for Tina's party and so he'd decided to drive. He asked, if he left his car would I take him to collect it tomorrow?

Tina is a stickler for timekeeping and the last thing I wanted was to upset her by being fashionably late, so I understood why Tim looked so stressed when he practically screeched to a stop outside Naomi's. I got in the car as elegantly as I could with my heels and sexy frock, and he glanced at me with some impatience, eager to set off again. He hadn't mentioned my appearance but he was concentrating on the road so I forgave him for that. I smelled amazing though, my body was layered with the fragrance of bath milk, body lotion and perfume, and as far as I remembered, you didn't need your sense of smell to operate a motor engine. I pulled myself back from the brink of my contemptuous thoughts and decided to wait until things were calmer before I fished for a compliment.

Once we were out of the car, I got to see Tim in all his black-tie glory. He looked stunning - polished and sophisticated, his suit draped across his body and hung off him exactly as it should. As he walked in front of me into the hotel it was all I could do to stop myself from running my hands down his back to feel the shape of him that his jacket accentuated so well. I was proud of him and proud of us as we walked into the party, he held out his right hand for mine and I instantly joined him with my left; we were attached to each other, united, a couple - it felt right.

We were greeted with great enthusiasm by almost everyone. Alison, an outsider to our inner circle who I'd known would be itching for gossip managed to corner me in the toilets, she wasted no time and asked me very pointedly, with a faint, greedy gossip-glint in her eye, why I hadn't been around much during the summer? I was saved by Tina bowling through the door with a Tampax in one hand and a bottle of champagne in the other. Thankfully, in the melee that followed, I successfully dodged the question. I left her hanging and went back to the party.

I left Tim standing at the bar with his cronies and made my way through the room. Everyone was looking slick in their finest clothes, and with the excited atmosphere, there was much delighted hugging, kissing and general hilarity to be involved with. Every so often I searched out Tim, and each time I did, he was watching me. It felt fantastic to be so comfortable in myself, to feel so fabulous and to have him see me at my best for a change, instead of my usual personas of crying-Rachel or furious-Rachel, or completely-disappeared-Rachel. When I eventually went back to join him, he bent down so he could talk quietly into my ear, "You look stunning this evening, I'm so proud to be your husband."

I was thrilled.

There were times during the evening when his PDA's were shameful under the circumstances, and gave me a faint twitch of discomfort. I knew he was playing to his audience, and I was sure that, to the unknowing onlooker, we were exactly as they expected us to be: a loving, well-matched couple who, to all intents and purposes, had it all. I had to remind myself that no one knew there was anything wrong between us, so the connotations of his playful kisses and caresses were that of a loving husband appreciating his wife. I relaxed into them a bit more, and eventually I was enjoying the attention and flushed with warmth for him.

By the time the band had done their second set we were happily drunk. Tim had his arm round my waist, he manoeuvred me to face him and I lifted my eyes to his and smiled at him. He bent his head to kiss me, and when I felt his tongue part my pursed lips there was the familiar rush of lust that shot through me, I released myself into the kiss and what was left of my hard edges melted completely. Tim ran his hands down my back and grabbed my arse as I ran mine around his waist and into his jacket. The feel of the muscles in his back was making the ends of my fingers tingle with the want to feel his naked skin. He kissed me harder, I returned his passion. I'd missed him, I'd missed us doing this, it had been so long since we'd been so physically close. I was enjoying the heat he'd created in me. He used my bum cheeks to pull me closer to him, locking us in a tight embrace.

44

Why isn't he hard? What's up with his cock? Ask him if he's ok - let him know you've noticed the absence of his penis in these proceedings. There's not even a semi showing itself!

It was hard to concentrate on returning Tim's kisses with Ivy hollering at me. I pulled myself away from him, I smiled again, "You look wonderful tonight Tim, you are a very handsome man. I've missed you."

Nooooo don't let him get away with it, for fuck sake woman, ask him why his dick's floppy!

But I couldn't ask. I didn't want to ruin the first bit of affection we'd shared since goodness knows when by asking for more proof of his desire for me, preferably in the form of a rock-hard cock. He'd been drinking, it was probably that. Still, I didn't go back into his arms, I got busy talking to the birthday girl instead and distracted Ivy by trying to decide if Tina had had her tits done since I'd seen her last.

By the time the party was over there was a queue of cabs outside waiting to take us home. I got in the taxi first and before there could be any conversations about 'going back for coffee' or a night cap. I gave the driver Naomi's address making it clear to us all that this was his first drop off and that Tim and his flaccid knob would be going home alone.

"Thank you for a wonderful evening, Rachel." He took hold of my hand again and intertwined his fingers with mine. His hands were soft, his long fingers moved side to side in a gently hypnotic stroke, I was lulled into forgiveness by his touch and by the time we arrived at my home I was back in his thrall.

I kissed him goodnight as I got out of the car and stood at the edge of the kerb and watched it take him away from me.

****

I picked him up the following day to take him to his car. It felt strange turning into the street and pulling up outside the house, I wasn't sure what to do - let myself in? Knock on the door? So, I stayed where I was and beeped my horn instead to let him know I was outside. He came out straight away. "You could have come in you know." He got in the car and instantly pushed the passenger seat back to give him more leg room, such a familiar sight. "I wasn't sure to be honest, its technically not my home at the moment is it? It's yours." I was concentrating on the road but out of the corner of my eye I saw his head turn to me in shock, "Of course it's your home Rachel, it's our home! You can come whenever you want, it's always open to you."

Ask him, ask him about the counselling, do it now while he's being so open and nice, take the chance. Ivy's prompt rang loud and clear, it was time, plus if I did it when I was driving, I wouldn't have to watch his face for clues of deceit.

I went in for the kill. I tried to keep my voice light and casual. "How are your counselling sessions going Tim?" I sensed his body stiffen slightly. "I mean, I know you can't discuss the details of them, I appreciate that, and I'm so proud of you for taking control of your erm.. what did you call it?"

"An addiction Rachel, it was an addiction." His words were sent to me sharply but the use of the past tense wasn't lost on me. We drove in silence for a while and the hotel came in to view. "What are you doing after this?" His voice was back to normal, he'd clearly climbed off his high horse. I shrugged my shoulders.

"No plans really, what did you have in mind?"

"Why don't we go home and have a couple of beers in the back garden." Now he'd suggested it I couldn't think of anything I'd rather do. "Ok, let's do that."

It had been months since I'd set foot over the threshold, and when I did the house welcomed me like an old friend. Here it was; my home, the place I had worked hard to make beautiful. I'd carefully chosen every item it held and worked on every aspect of it. My eyes took in the framed photographs on the staircase. He'd had to pass these every day we'd been apart, he'd had to live with the evidence of happier times right under his nose. It must have been tough to have those constant reminders while I was gone, especially for the first few weeks when I'd found it hard to even speak to him. I felt a twitch of guilt swiftly followed by heart-wrenching sympathy and thoughts of owing him an apology. I moved smilingly towards him, not waiting to hear what Ivy had to say about *that*.

He led me into the kitchen, I was still taking in the sights of my familiar, beloved home when he nodded towards the fridge. "Get the beers in then." When I opened it there were a couple of ready meals in there, a protein shake and whole shelf full of bottles of lager. As I grabbed us one each, he went without being asked to the utensil drawer to get out the opener. It was something we'd done so many times before, moved around this kitchen together, neither of us getting in the way of the other because we'd been doing it for so long; we knew how the other moved and what their next action would be. This was an intimate room. A place that we had acted out our togetherness, one where we'd worked as a team to get a job done, like we had most of our lives together.

Yes, and the last time you had sex was on that worktop over there, can you remember how many years ago that was? Since your husband felt like making love to you? Its nearly three fucking years Rachel, in fact, no, my mistake, three fuckLESS years.

When is that situation going to change? When can we set the calendar back to zero on our shagless months' count?

I gritted my teeth. Hard "Shut the fuck up Ivy, I like it here, it's my home, it feels beautiful - it is beautiful, look at it!"

Course it's beautiful - you spent a fortune making it that way. All the time you were making plans for the garden and buying the hall carpet he was spending your hard earned on whores and online titty pictures. Slam your brakes on, don't fall for it yet!

It's really hard to put your fingers in your ears to shut out unwanted advice when the voice giving it is in your head, but I did the next best thing and distracted myself by wandering around the garden, humming softly to myself. After all the months away settling myself into strange places and new lives, I'd refused to think of this as home, I'd refused to miss it, and now I was seeing it with fresh eyes, I realised it was mine, my home and it was my safest place in the world.

Tim was sat at the end of the garden in the shade, lighting a ciggie. I went to join him and we sat and smoked. Some of what Inner Voice Ivy had said must have stuck with me because before I had chance to back out, I threw myself into a conversation I knew we had to have.

"Earlier, when we were discussing your counselling sessions, you talked about your addiction in the past tense." I held my breath waiting for his response. "Yes, I did, I've finished my sessions now. I've worked through my issues. I understand why I did what I did and how to stop myself in the future if I become tempted by it again." He took a deep shuddering breath, I was surprised to see he was close to tears. "I'm so deeply ashamed of myself and sorry for my behaviour. You deserve better than the way I've treated you the last few years. I got myself wrapped up into something I couldn't get out of, but that's over now, I'm done. I promise."

He was turned towards me and I searched his face for any sign of falsehood but there was none. I let his words become music to my ears. "I love you, Tim."

Ivy was apoplectic. *WHAT THE FUCK? Where did that come from? Shut up now before you go any further!*

His face lit up at my words. "Oh Rachel, I love you too, I miss you so much, please come home."

Nope, that's not happening. Thanks for asking but it's too soon. How about, when you've rugby tackled her to the bed and fucked her all ways up, THEN she'll consider coming home. You've some serious work to do first mate.

"If I am to consider moving back in with you Tim, you have to promise me that this whole episode is over. I'm not threatened by the fact it was porn you were addicted to, but I am devastated about your careless destruction of me, and our lives together. Can you promise me that it's over?"

"Yes, yes, I can, I do, hand on my heart, it's done." The plead in his voice was unmistakable, "I know what I've put you through and I promise you it will never happen again. Coming so close to losing you has shown me you are what I want. You are all I want."

No, no, no. Please don't fall for it Rachel, you're not ready, you haven't given yourself enough time to work out what you truly want for YOU.

I couldn't listen to Ivy's pleading any longer, I needed to be home, I wanted to be with Tim. I loved him, and if he was promising me he'd changed then that was enough for me. I ignored her, pushed her away.

"You must promise me Tim that you'll never, ever do this to me again. You nearly killed me with the constant deception and disrespect, I can't come back unless you give me your word you're done with the lies and the porn. I need your word that if you struggle with it again or go back to using it in any way that you'll be honest and tell me, that it will be something we face together. No more secrets."

I was so pleased to have been able to express myself so clearly. He came back instantly, "I promise you. I'm done. And if I do feel like I'm going to fall off the wagon I assure you I'll let you know as soon as I'm tempted." His face was still turned to mine and I could see the longing in his eyes.

I wanted to trust him so badly.

I loved this man with all my heart, and I had to believe that our time apart had resulted in us both knowing what we wanted, and that was each other.

Ivy wasn't quite done yet.

Ok, you've got him in honesty mode now, whilst he's there, ask him about sex, when are you going to have sex again?

"When I come home Tim, please can we start making love again? I miss you so much, I need to have that intimacy with you, I miss it so badly. And let's get it right babe, we do have good sex." I smiled to show him I was trying hard to be gentle with his newly restructured sex drive. He sounded almost hurt. "Why is sex so important to you Rachel? Why have you brought this up now?"

"Because to my mind Tim, it's the key to all of this, and I need to know you love me in every way there is to love me."

He smiled this time, a mixture of relief and kindness, "Ok."

He stood up and walked towards the house, to the fridge to get us another beer, leaving me sat where I was with the ciggies and my increasingly frustrated imaginary friend.

Bullshit, what kind of answer was that?

45

Ivy

You see that woman who was wanking in a toilet? The woman who rides a red bike with a basket on the front and sits with boys on walls and gets stoned and has a laugh. The woman who has friends that surround her with love when she needs them. That's the real Rachel, the authentic one.

She's not a woman who should be compromised by another's actions; she's better than that. But she's not listening to me anymore.

Tim was a good man once but he's not now; he can't remember how to be. He's not going to stop the lies, or the porn, and he knows it. He's a slave to his vanity and he'll find any way he can to validate himself; he'd wank himself off to the talking clock if it told him he was a naughty boy. Deep down he's ashamed of his behaviour but he can't admit it, even to himself. I don't know how much that top secret 'treatment' cost him, but it was a waste of money, he still can't look himself in the eye because he's hasn't taken any responsibility for his actions.

Rachel believes that the love she has for Tim is a reciprocal love. She thinks he's worthy of her: He's not. He's asked her to come home because it's good for him to have her around. While she's there he doesn't have to delve too deeply into his weakness because none of this is his fault, its hers. In his mind it's all her fault.

She, on the other hand, believes she can make it better, be his redeemer. She just needs to do this next bit properly, approach him in the right way, be gentle, be patient, and then she'll make it all perfect between them. She won't. He'll continue to look through her, to lie and cheat because he's so wrapped up in his own self he's lost sight of Rachel completely. And the scary thing is, she's in danger of losing sight of Rachel too. But she's not listening to me now. She doesn't want to hear it.

I'm afraid for her; I have no idea how to stop him from damaging her again, and try as I might, I can't stop her from giving him the power to. I don't know what else to do, I've tried everything, I've pulled out all the stops, I've got nothing else to give; I'm exhausted.

I'm fucked.

She's fucked.

We are fucked.

46

October 2011

Telling Naomi I was leaving was harder than I imagined it would be. As delighted as I was to be rejoining Tim in our home, the thought of leaving my lovely life with her and Max gave me a deep sense of loss. She was happy for me, as was Jude when I told her. Neither of them questioned my next step, they both supported my decision to go back to my husband; mostly, I think, because they always knew I would.

When I told Petra over a glass of wine, she was reticent with her opinion, well her verbal one anyway. Facially she made no secret of the fact she thought I was making a mistake, but she hugged me all the same and told me good luck. I pulled away from the embrace to take another look at her expression, her mouth turned down and her shoulders lifted in an unspoken condemnation of my planned reconciliation. "I'll always be here for you girl, please don't hide anything from me again."

I promised her I wouldn't, I had no intention of there being any secrets in my life; ever again.

****

I moved back into the house the following Friday. Tim had been working away most of the week, and I'd planned to be unpacked and settled in by the time he got back later that day. I was thrilled by the prospect of starting our lives over again. I had lots of romantic notions of us being back together, that our time apart would have served to be the making of us as a couple, the final confirmation that we really were joined 'till death do us part'.

I used my time alone to wander round the house, I spent ages in each room letting my eyes re-familiarise themselves with the details of my life here, my history, my past, and now my future. When I made my way into the office, the porn PC had gone. Its absence sent a torrent of relief through me. The almost-obsolete, chronically slow piece of hardware had represented the end of the innocent love that had filled my life and the start of my discoveries of furtive behaviour, sneaky wanks, cheating and deception, and the eventual loss of my previously wonderful husband. Its unrequested removal was a sign to me from Tim that it was all over, and the threat it represented to my contentment was gone too. I loved him for his consideration and for eradicating it from our lives.

With an even deeper sense of commitment, I made my way upstairs. I remembered how empty the place had looked when I'd left it all those months ago.

I went into our bedroom and made my way round to my side of the bed. There was a tinge of sadness in me that my days of starfish sleeping in the middle of Flick's mattress were over and sleeping with Tim meant I'd only have half the bed again. I waited for Ivy to supply me with something vaguely hilarious about waking up with an insistent semi in the small of my back, but she was quiet again today. I laid down to see how the bed felt after all this time. The fresh smelling sheets were my favourite ones, another indication of the care Tim had taken to welcome me home. I turned myself to face his pillows, a cool was breeze coming through the window we always left slightly open, and I closed my eyes and lay still. My attention moved to the sounds of the house, its familiar clicks and creaks.

I must have drifted off to sleep. I was a bit discombobulated when I woke up and couldn't work out where I was for a few seconds. It was the sight of the bedding that eventually brought me back to reality, whilst the need to pee motivated me to wake up fully. I got up from the bed but when I did my legs didn't seem to have any strength in them. I had a split second to wonder what was going on until they folded underneath me and before I knew it, I was on my knees. The carpet had softened my fall so I wasn't hurt, but I was confused by the collapse. I waited a little while for my body to respond to my brain signals, then grabbed the side of the bed and pulled myself up to standing. My legs seemed to have recovered mostly, I gave them a shake out as I walked to the bathroom.

****

We didn't get much of a chance to celebrate being back together that evening. Tim got stuck in Friday traffic and didn't get home until after 9pm. He was exhausted. I'd been having a solo homecoming party, so I was a bit drunk. We ate a takeaway pizza and crashed into bed without so much as a welcome home cuddle in the hallway, never mind sex. Still, there was plenty of time, wasn't there? We had the rest of our lives together.

It was the next morning before I even thought to mention to Tim about the falling to the floor incident. We were laid in bed, he was on his back with his arms behind his head, I was laid facing him with my leg thrown over the tops of his thighs. The dips in-between his bicep and triceps muscles were screaming at me to run my tongue along them, but I was resisting the temptation. My whole body was taut waiting for him to touch me, my vagina was millimetres away from the skin on his thigh, the heat of him was irresistible, drawing me to him like a moth to a flame. I wanted to attach myself to him, to feel his skin against my clit, actually I wanted to feel his tongue against my clit, but thigh skin would do for starters.

Although she'd been strangely silent the last few days, I could almost hear Ivy telling me that the smell of desperation is not attractive, and I did listen to her sometimes, so I decided to stop behaving like a mangy dog desperate for a fuck and wait for Tim to make the first move. Resolved with my decision, I tried to withdraw my leg away from his body, but it took a lot more effort than I imagined it should. It felt heavy and unresponsive. I managed eventually, but, in the same way as the day before, when I prised myself away from him and then tried to stand up, I fell again. This time though I was more ready for it. I put my hands out to soften my fall, so instead of landing on my knees I ended up in a kind of naked downward dog, plank position that was neither flattering or comfortable. Tim sat up to look at me, his face a picture of bewilderment, "Are you ok? What was that?"

"I have no idea Tim, it happened yesterday too. I think maybe I've been laid in one position for too long and my legs have gone dead. That's all it is."

As I was talking, he came round the bed and helped me up, his face full of concern. Once I was back on my feet, I felt ok - other than a little bit embarrassed that the first time he saw me in all my naked glory was in a deeply unsexy way.

****

We had a lovely day. We went out for brunch and when we got home we spent the rest of the afternoon in the back garden, listening to music, drinking and enjoying each other's company. We prepared dinner together, laughing and joking around with each other. I was supposed to be making the pasta but when I tried to lift the pan from the hob to drain off the water my fingers had no strength in them. I wasn't able to make my brain and body connect with each other again. I knew what I wanted my body to do, it just wouldn't do it. I looked at Tim in bemusement, he came to help me with the pan and in partial shock I sat at the breakfast bar, confused and a bit worried about what had happened. I recovered quickly again though and I insisted we carry on with our plans for dinner.

By the time we had finished eating I was overcome with an incredible weariness; I had an early night.

The next day was a bit worse. I had to slow down my usual energetic self quite considerably. I was careful when I moved anywhere or did anything and instead of taking my body for granted, I had to wait for a while to be sure it was listening to my brain and they were working together. I was baffled and a bit scared. Tim was a massive support, concerned and attentive. I didn't have to lift a finger to do anything all day. It was nice to be cared for, but I was deeply disappointed with this next intrusion into our weekend and my proper homecoming.

We decided between us that maybe this was a 48-hour bug or something, and that I'd shake it off soon enough. I had another early night and expected to feel much brighter the next day.

I didn't, not at all.

<h1 style="text-align:center">47</h1>

Over the next few weeks my health continued to deterio-
rate, my legs worked sometimes but not others, the stiffness
that had started in my fingers extended itself into most of
my limbs, the pain pulsed between a constant dull ache and
red hot pokers setting fire to the inside of my body. Bi-weekly
appointments with the doctor, who was continually searching
for a diagnosis, would result in a trip to the hospital for blood
tests, another sick note and stronger painkillers. My anti-
depressants were moved up a notch, I was on higher doses
than I had ever been. I was so full of medication that in the
end I had no idea what was causing me to feel the way I did.
The illness or the intended cure.

Naomi came to see me often; she brought me lots of
presents - books and DVD's. Petra rang and texted constantly,
she came to collect me every so often to gently encourage me
to get dressed and then take me out somewhere, away from
the four walls I loved so much but which had now become a
luxurious prison. Laura took over my territory and clients and
rang me most days to tell me what was happening, ask my
advice or to pass on the good wishes from the supporting cast
of characters that made up the contents of what I was quickly
coming to consider my previous life.

Jude had no idea what to do for me; at one point she
suggested coming over to stay with me for a week or so and
that brought my spirits up for a while, but in the end, she was

needed at home to care for one of the kids who had mumps and couldn't come. She invited me there, but I couldn't face the thought of the journey.

I had some good days, and the second my energy levels perked up a bit I would seize the day, make the most of it and do things with Tim. We would go out for a meal together, or a night out at the pub. I enjoyed myself at the time, but the next day I'd be shattered, and it would take me days to get over it. Our wider social circle who hadn't been privy to our time apart were now startlingly aware that I was poorly, on those rare evenings out I didn't need to have eyes in the back of my head to know I was being watched constantly, pitied and gossiped about. At the pub one evening, Alison – yes of course it had to be her – told me over a glass of wine, that she'd recently over-heard a conversation about my health and was shocked to hear I had struggled with depression. "Who would have thought?" she mused to my face, "That someone as go-getting and strong as you would be inflicted with depression. You're the last person I would expect to be down in the dumps." If anyone in that social circle had heard her, they would hear only concern. I heard a barely-suppressed glee. If only I had the energy to smack her in her supercilious face. And where the fuck was Ivy and her smart arse comments when you needed her?

My birthday came and went. Tim made a fuss about it – gave me flowers, champagne and a handbag I'd lusted after for years. I tried to bring plenty of energy to the party, but it was hard to come by that day and instead of giddy, ecstatic delight, I didn't really care. I felt so guilty that he was making so much effort and all I wanted to do was sit down, or for preference, lie down. I hated to be vulnerable and out of control, but his protection and kindness was a comfort, and I was grateful for it.

There were times when I was so depleted of any life force at all, I would sit with my hands resting in my lap and I wouldn't move for hours. During those times of immobility, I even started to be afraid to blink, the process seemed complicated beyond measure - it took ages - like it was performed in super-slow motion, I was scared to let the lids of my eyes close for too long in case when they touched, they would seal so tightly I'd be powerless to open them, that I would fall asleep and perhaps never wake up again.

I was like an overwound, windup toy; my spring was bust, exhausted, broken.

All the time I was trapped at home, everyone else's world carried on turning. Tim's life didn't grind to a torturous halt at the same time as mine did, he still had to go work. He spent a lot of time working away from home, and even though it meant more time alone, I actively encouraged him to carry on as usual. At least one of us should be having some fun.

The 'P' word hadn't come into conversation the whole time I'd been home, although of course, we did have other things to distract us from Tim's transgressions. It did cross my mind to wonder if, in the absence of a fully operative wife, he might still be looking for his thrills elsewhere, but the thoughts were more often than not overtaken by the drone of weariness, or on a really bad day, the sheer effort required to keep my head upright.

I trusted that he wasn't delighting himself with videos of women pleasuring themselves with power tools, but from what I could gather he had distracted himself quite well with other, less torrid hobbies whilst I'd been away from home. He'd started playing squash and was in a league with the local club. When he wasn't working away, he'd spend his Monday evenings there. I was glad he was doing something active, some-thing he quite clearly enjoyed. There was a good social side to it too and he was often out late after his match. Every other week there was an extra practice game on another evening; he played with someone he'd met through the club and thought could help him improve his game.

When he was at home with me, he still seemed to be a bit too attached to his phone but again what could I say about that? "Hey, see me over here? Your wife, the one who left you on your own for months on end. I'm back now, please cease all extra-curricular activities immediately and pay attention to me just in case I can stay awake long enough to be entertaining."

I weighed up my options carefully, and as poor as the humour was, considering my current health circumstances, I realised I didn't really have a leg to stand on. So, I encouraged him to carry on doing the things he enjoyed, whatever they were. When I noticed his attraction to his mobile hadn't abated a great deal, I spent a few days watching him carefully as he logged in to his phone in his habitual secretive manner, until I worked out from his finger movements that his pin code was 1823. This in formation wasn't intended for everyday use, but it might come in handy one day, you never knew.

I still had no idea where Ivy was though.

48

December 2011

There were lots of horrifying medical prognoses discussed during my many GP appointments, but over time all of them were ruled out one after another until there was nothing left to test my blood for.

Eventually, a couple of weeks before Christmas, it was agreed I should have an MRI scan on my brain and spine. The introduction of that suggestion into the investigation into my ill health brought with it an onslaught of even more horrifying possibilities.

I elected to wait until the festive season was over before I went for the scan. Whatever the result was I wanted to get the most out of my favourite time of year. Together, Tim and I festooned the house with tinsel, fat jolly Santas, reindeers, snowmen and pop-up brightly-lit trees.

On one absolutely lovely Sunday afternoon in mid-December, we put on our favourite tunes, smoked a spliff and drank whatever we wanted, when we wanted it, and decorated our biggest tree; the one we'd had since the year we got married. When it was folded up in its box, bare of adornment, it looked as old as it was, but once we decked it with the decorations we'd lovingly col lected over the last couple of decades, it was glorious. There were so many baubles and trinkets to hang from its branches and each one had a story that went with it. I touched every one of them, studied the detail of them closely while we reminisced. The punk rocker Santa we'd bought at an indie festival in 1999, the tiny pair of blue and white ceramic clogs joined together with a red ribbon someone once gave us in a bar in Amsterdam in response to Tim's massive tip. A grotesque wooden goth - one I'd bought that Tim hated and I loved. We had our usual laughing bicker about him hiding it at the back of the tree, out of sight. We shared a wonderfully happy time together.

Later in the afternoon, as I sat on the sofa and rested, watching him fight with the tangle of fairy lights, our conversational memories turned to thoughts of our future. It was our 20th wedding anniversary in 2012. We had a lot to look forward to - to make plans for. We talked about what we should do to mark the achievement. I suggested we both take a couple of months off work and travel, as far away as possible, Australia for preference, a destination I had dreamed of since I was a little girl. Tim wanted a massive party and two weeks in the Maldives. Either way we had given each other something to look forward to, a promise of a future together and that made me happier than anything else I could think of.

Our Christmas was an incredibly quiet one for us. Customarily we would have partied hard from the evening we finished work for the holidays right through to the day before we had to go back. Nothing was normal at the moment though. We stayed home on Christmas Eve and ventured out on Christmas Day for a couple of beers in the pub at lunchtime with Nai. Whilst we were there, Jude called us so we could wish each other Merry Christmas. We followed that with a late lunch in the same hotel we'd celebrated Tina's fiftieth and then home for a big sleep for me and some alone time for Tim to entertain himself however he may see fit. I had hoped that maybe my Christmas present might be a long, tender session of love making - I was poorly but I wasn't dead. We were on year four of fuckless festive seasons, and in between the pains, the worry, the fatigue and the lack of any interest shown by the man I shared my bed with, I wasn't feeling too horny, but I was sure I could have summoned up enough energy to treat my husband to one of my mind-bending blow jobs if he'd given me half a chance. But he didn't. And I was too scared to offer.

We'd been invited VIP to an event on New Year's Eve. In the days leading up to it, I made a real effort to conserve my energy to make sure I was fresh for the occasion and would be suitably fit to celebrate. I took most of the day slowly, preparing myself for our night out. A lot of my clothes were a bit tight, what with the extra medication, the lack of exercise, comfort eating and drinking, but I had just the dress for that - a pale pink ankle length chiffon with an adjustable cummerbund to cinch in what was left of my waist. I concentrated hard with my make-up, stuck a lot of very sparkly things on various parts of my body, added a pair of my favourite high heels, and when I finally presented myself to Tim, I looked amazing, even if I do say so myself. He gave a low whistle when I came into the kitchen, one I was compelled to return. He was wearing a dark grey suit that fitted him perfectly with a white shirt, open just far enough for me to see the start of the trimmed hairs on his chest. He looked gorgeous. Almost edible.

The VIP treatment was very special. The meal we had was lovely and the wine was free. By the time we'd finished eating and the show was about to start the ache in my legs had turned to shooting pains I couldn't control or ignore. Reluctantly I took my shoes off and Tim found me a chair, so I put my legs up, to rest them for a while. The opening act was a dance troupe; ten girls in bright red, glittery, low-cut leotards with feathers attached to their arses. They looked spectacular, full of energy and life. I let my eyes leave the sight of their beautiful dancing forms to take a sneaky look at my husband and how he was reacting to so much live, nubile flesh in front of his face. He was mesmerised, but then when I looked round the table of ten, so were the others. I searched the side of his neck for his pulse, was he palpitating at the sight of youthful arse cheeks? I checked out the penis situation, were those chicks creating any blood rush to his bell end? My check for evidence of a kick start to his otherwise invisible sex drive came back as inconclusive. I stopped my paranoid search and settled down to enjoy myself for a change.

The singer that followed was fabulous, the comedian was very funny, and the final Abba tribute act pushed everyone's giddy muscles and got most of the room up on the dance floor. Usually, I'd be up there with the rest of them, busting out my favourite moves, a split between 80's bopping, 90's hip hop and a piss take of Saturday Night Fever. Not tonight, though. Instead, Tim and I sat together watching everyone else. My feet were still up on a chair; I felt like an old lady.

I was so tired, my body ached. I was running on empty but the change of atmosphere in the room told me it was nearly midnight, not long now before I could go home and lie down. Tim had been busy on his phone for a while, but he put it back in his pocket and turned to me with a smile. He stood and held out his hand to help me do the same. In honour of the occasion, I found my shoes and put them back on again. We stood facing each other as the familiar peals from Big Ben began. The whole room was shouting out the count from ten backwards in perfect unison. Tim joined in whilst I watched his face. He turned his head a couple of times to look at the celebrations in the rest of the room; his profile was so beautiful. Then he turned back to me to carry on the count I wasn't even taking part in. When the final gong struck, I felt the floor shake with the collective jubilation of the other guests. I watched as Tim turned to me and brought me into his embrace.

The kiss he gave me was intended to see the old year out and the new one in, but in the first flush of 2012 I started to cry; uncontrollably.

He drew me into his arms and held me tighter to him, his hug encompassed me as he held me at the waist and grabbed my bum, drawing me into his entire body. He'd given my grief a home and I released my whole being into it. He held me so steadfastly. I was so sure of his presence during the delirious cheer of "Happy New Year!" that I was afraid his strength would crush me, that he would squeeze the insubstantial shadow of my former self so hard I would evaporate into thin air like dust. I had no idea where the passion or the tears had come from, but they came. Until then I hadn't realised I still had the ability for such profound sorrow, how could I be so capable of this anguish when my whole being was empty of anything of at all?

The rest of the room was busy with their own thing. They were lining up at the bar for last orders, the strings of newly exploded party poppers were scattered around the room, strangers were hugging each other, full of expectation for the year 2012, as they said goodbye to 2011. I disintegrated into wave after wave of emotion; loss, relief, hatred and anger and hope. There was no celebration for me. As far as I could bear to look into the future and as far back into the past I went, all I could see was fear.

I missed Naomi, I missed Jude, I missed me, and where the hell had Ivy gone? Because I missed her most of all.

49

January 2012

For a time during the middle of our married years, Tim and I had a tradition when we packed away the Christmas decorations. We would each write a list of the things we wanted to achieve during the following year, we would read each other's, and then put them in an envelope and store them away in the same box as our much-loved tatty tree. I loved doing it, it was a laugh, something to aim for and an unspoken reassurance that we would be together the following year to read them again. I wasn't quite sure when we decided to stop doing it, but I remember it had been Tim who'd called a halt to it all, he'd said he was bored of it. I was a bit disappointed at the time, it had been fun opening the envelopes each December and congratulating ourselves for achieving our early January ambitions, or shrugging our shoulders at the ones we hadn't managed to carry through.

It was only ever a bit of fun and I'd enjoyed it. As I was packing the tree away this year I did wonder if his dreams for our personal growth had ceased at the same time as he'd fallen by the marital sex wayside. Maybe he hadn't wanted to put pen to paper to list the things he'd wanted to achieve for himself during the year because it meant he'd have to share himself with me; his thoughts, his desires. Maybe his plans for the years were a lot more complicated than mine, which were mostly to weight train so hard I got Madonna's muscly arms and to be able to do an entire Zumba class facing the same direction as the others in the dance studio.

Maybe it wasn't his list he didn't want to me to read, maybe it was mine he didn't want to see; the level of importance of improving my sense of direction while dancing had changed considerably over the years, now my list would include a fully working bullshit detector for when my husband spoke to me, and anything that resembled a sex life.

January 2009

My ambitions for this year are; Have sex with my husband p.s just once will do I don't want to appear greedy

January 2010

Ditto last year

January 2011

Sex, if not penetrative I'll settle for oral.

****

The Saturday of the second weekend in January, the one after we'd taken the Christmas decorations down and packed them away, saw another tradition. We always met our favourite drinking mates as soon as the pubs opened and did a massive pub crawl. The day had become so popular it was almost legendary, and we looked forward to it as much as we did Christmas. There was no way I was going to make it this year. Even if I had enough energy to contemplate it, there was no way my body could have cashed the cheque my stubborn self was trying to write. Besides, my MRI scan was a few days later and the last thing I needed was for the radiologist to send back a report that talked about cocaine boulders up my nose and my brain showing signs of an early Peroni pickling process.

I insisted that Tim still went, though. The morning of the full-on Saturday session I sat in the dressing room and watched him get ready with a mixture of envy, because I wanted to go too, irritation as he fussed with the collar of his shirt, and terror because Tim's good-boy guard had started to slip, and he was heading back into furtive, almost conspiratorial behaviour. He was hiding something from me, and I didn't need Inner Voice Ivy to tell me I was teetering on the edge of an abyss, a dark place I'd been to many times before.

He eventually left the house in a flurry, and as he closed the door behind him, peace descended. I went straight into the lounge, got myself comfortable, covered myself with a blanket and found a movie channel. I was exhausted, shattered and sad. I was fed up with missing out on things and bored with living trapped inside my uncooperative body. I yearned for life to be back to normal, but it had been so long since I'd had a normal life, even the prospect of that wasn't much of a consolation.

Normal had been vile for a long time. I'd been so wrapped up with my pain and decrepitude recently I'd lost the last vestige of my own self, and there hadn't been much left of me to lose. I had nothing. I couldn't even find a way to validate myself to Tim anymore. I wasn't successful at my job because I wasn't going to work, I couldn't stand in the tree pose for longer than anyone else I knew because I didn't go to yoga anymore, I had no stories to tell him about how successful I was because I didn't do anything, and if I couldn't tell him about the way others admired me for my achievements then how was I to prove I was worthy of him? I couldn't, there was nothing left of me. I was a husk.

I was midway through my fourth film when I heard him come home, just after 9.30pm. I could tell he was drunk and trying to be quiet by the racket he was making. I stayed where I was until the sound of the door being pushed across the carpet and the smell of booze announced his arrival in the lounge. He leaned over to give me a kiss and to my delight he kissed my face in different places, after each one he said "I love you".

I was almost expecting Inner Voice Ivy to answer him back in her smarty pants way, but no matter how much prompting she'd had recently she was resolute in her silence. Instead, I said "Did you have fun?" I watched him sway a little bit as he stood up from his very unusual private display of affection. "Was ace, we had fun. We missed you though. Everyone sends their love. Alison even sang your favourite karaoke song and dedicated it to you."

I rolled my eyes, "Course she did, the silly bitch."

Eventually, after a fair bit of prompting from me, he staggered out of my peaceful space and made his way upstairs. I listened to the sounds above me of a heavily drunken man getting ready for bed and once I heard him settle, then so did I, to the point of falling asleep on the couch again.

I woke in the early hours of the morning and, trying hard not to wake myself too much, I made my way to bed. The bedroom resembled a crime scene. Tim's clothes were strewn all over the floor, a map of his trajectory as he'd undressed. He was laid on his back in a deep sleep, his phone was still locked into the grip of his left hand. I turned off the bedside lights and squeezed myself into the bit of space he'd actually left me. I was desperate to stay in my semi sleepy state and started to get myself comfortable. As I did, he stirred slightly and his phone slid from his hand landing softly in between us.

I wanted to leave it where it was. I *could* have left it where it was, I should have turned over and slipped into a deep, exhausted sleep. But that piece of cellular hardware with the half-eaten apple on the back of it taunted me. Tim was dead to the world, there was no way he would wake up, maybe this could be an appropriate time to check his phone. Just have a little cruise through to see if my feelings of mistrust were warranted, I needed to know how many faces he was wearing, or, gosh, who knew, if there was nothing untoward to find I could officially add paranoia to the long list of ailments currently affecting me. That would be fun.

I was wide awake now. I could almost feel the phone tapping me to get my attention - what had he actually been trying to look at whilst he had his beer goggles on? The football scores? Facebook? Porn?

Convinced I was doing the right thing I opened his phone. I tapped in the well-rehearsed four-digit numbers. The screen burst into life, and I was instantly looking at a video that must have been playing when he'd slipped into his alcohol induced semi-coma. I couldn't work out what I was seeing at first, it looked very amateurish and there was no sound at all. I sincerely hoped he wasn't paying twenty quid a burst for this shaky camera work.

However bad it was, I was fascinated by it. I was drawn to the images until finally, realisation dawned on me: it was a couple shagging on the back seat of a car. They were being filmed through a side window, hot breath in an enclosed space was fogging the glass with condensation, someone inside the car had obligingly wiped some of the moisture away, allowing the person filming from outside a clearer view, there were rivulets of the displaced water lazily making their random way away from the space that had been created.

The fear of Tim waking up suddenly and catching me intruding into his phone, coupled with a freezing shock, was making my hands shake. The film I was watching represented more betrayal - the disrespectful bastard - despite his promises he was spending money on porn again.

As the person taking care of the filming moved in closer to the action, I saw a woman on her hands and knees, her face was turned slightly to the camera, she was blonde, her big tits were swinging pendulously in metronome slavery to the thrusts of the guy fucking her from behind. He was hunched over her. I could make out the shape of his arched back and the top of his head, I presumed he was watching himself as he penetrated her again and again and again. They were totally wrapped up in what they were doing.

I was deeply shocked by the amount of eroticism that was sat so nonchalantly on my husband's phone, I knew it was the last thing he'd seen before he'd slipped into his drunken sleep less than five minutes after telling me he loved me, over and over.

I couldn't bring myself to stop the video, the rawness of the sex I was seeing was the thing of my wet dreams. I would have willingly watched this porn with Tim if only he'd asked.

The woman was being fucked doggy style so hard her whole body was shaking, her lover was so intent with his connection with her, so involved in the passion he was expressing he had grabbed her by her hair and snapped her head back, the movement changing the shape her body slightly. I could imagine his cock fitting into her in a different way, the heat of the moment was so fucking dirty I felt myself come alive again. I was fascinated, my clit responding to the images, the voyeurism making my pulse so strong the skin on my neck bounced.

Having her hair pulled back brought the blonde woman face to face with the camera, it gave the impression she was looking directly at me, a filthy, knowing grin spread across her face followed by a wink of her left eye then the rictus of orgasm overtook her face and body. Her lover raised the top half of his body above hers; he was hanging out of the back of her as they came in unison; together in their pleasure.

They both looked directly at the camera now.

The camera that was filming them having sex from the outside of my husband's car.

50

It had been a while since I'd seen Tim's cum face, but that was definitely my husband being filmed while he was balls deep into some skanky blonde with saggy tits, no two ways about it.

My vision blurred and my ears started ringing; I was going to be sick. I got myself out of bed as quickly as I could, but as soon as I made my way to the bathroom my legs went from under me. I fell on my knees in a not too dissimilar a position to the slapper my husband had been shagging; there was no pleasure for me though. I retched several times my back arching with the effort until I puked onto the carpet.

Here I was, naked on my bedroom floor, unable to stand for reasons I still didn't understand. My hands were covered in my own vomit, I'd just witnessed my husband taking part in exhibitionist sex whilst being filmed on his own phone. I pushed myself up to kneeling, bile still rising in my throat to join the pieces of sick in my mouth. I started to cry. I was lost, I was scared, I was humiliated by the utter contempt the film represented. I was fucked.

There was a wail building in my body. I needed to be away from Tim before I let it go, I still couldn't stand, so I dropped back onto all fours again and crawled over the pile of vomit into the bathroom in front of me. The under-floor heating had turned off and the tiles were cold. I grabbed a bath sheet from the towel rail and buried my face into its folds as I let the explosion of emotions leave me in a long, agonised scream. The towel muffled the noise but not enough to be sure that if I did it again, I wouldn't wake the sleeping man in the next room. I stuffed the corner of the fabric in my mouth for a few minutes and rocked my body to stop myself letting go of the torment again. I needed to get away from him.

I used the side of the bath to help me stand, my determination to get up from the floor was turbo powered by adrenaline. Once I had my balance, I grabbed my dressing gown from the back of the door and on my way past the bed I picked up his phone again. I couldn't bear to look at the prone form of my drunk husband, so content and oblivious in his sleep. With shaking legs and a drum beat pulse I made my way downstairs to the kitchen.

I hadn't had a drink since New Years Eve, and it had been months since my last cigarette. Both were on the menu now though. I opened a bottle of red and found my secret stash of smokes. The whole time I was on my mission, I was shaking my head in complete disbelief and sobbing at the same time. I sat at the breakfast bar opposite the wall of glass doors over-looking the garden.

The dark outside meant all I could see was the reflection of myself. I could still taste the sick in my mouth, it was mixed with tiny strands of cotton from the screaming towel and now the familiar disgusting taste of cigarette smoke mingled with it. I watched myself moving. I was too far away to see minute details of myself, but I could see me, my reflection was sat across from me. I looked at my counterpart in the window-pane, drinking wine and smoking cigarettes, a woman who had vomited on her bedroom floor with shock and horror after watching her husband fucking a blonde woman on the back seat of his car. I was a woman who had yielded to a man who didn't deserve her more times than she could count. And the worst thing about it all was, I sat there with no idea what to do. I wasn't packing my bags, or sitting on top of a pillow that was smothering Tim's many faces, I was still searching for the reason why.

The nicotine complemented the wine perfectly, they combined into a heady mixture that got me drunk very quickly, and with the drunk came the rage. There was a roar in my body that needed to be expelled and there was only one place I was going to be when it did. I sat for a while longer stewing in my own fury juices, my legs and feet jiggling with anxiety, anger and impatience. After my third glass of red and sixth ciggie I released myself from the chair and flew up the stairs.

Tim was still on his back in exactly the same position he'd been in when I'd left over an hour ago. I kneeled on to the bed beside him. He didn't stir. I braced myself and then threw my right leg over his body and arms, he was trapped between my thighs. I landed my arse as heavily as I could onto his stomach. The air left his body in an ooooomph, and his eyes flew open at the same time. "Rachel? What the fuck's going on?"

I squeezed his body tightly with my inner thighs, as I bent my body over him. I put my face into his and breathed on him hard, deliberately making sure he would be able to smell the wine, cigarette, and vomit combination. "I could ask you the same thing, you twat!" My voice was low. He tried to pull his head away from me but there was nowhere for him to go. I should have been jubilant at the look of panic on his face, but I was concentrating hard to keep his wriggly body under my command. I grabbed the top of his hair and pulled his head up. "Ouch for fuck's sake Rachel that hurts!"

I let go and threw his head back onto the mattress, then I let the roar have its own way. "Hurts? Hurts? Fucking hurts? You're lucky I'm not holding a pillow over your face. You seem to like a bit of rough Tim, how about I get you on your hands and knees and I spank your arse for you?"

I felt behind me and grabbed his cock and balls. I applied enough pressure to feel his testicles move in the palm of my hand. I applied more pressure, "Let's see if I can get that limp dick of yours hard by squeezing your balls so tight they pop in my hand!"

His eyes were like saucers, he whimpered and shook his head from side to side. "Would you like me to get your film crew round? Maybe that'll help get the blood flowing to your useless penis, what do you think?" I was still leaning into him. "Dogging, lap dancers, whores, porn. Tim, is this what you've been doing all along? I'm not surprised you don't want to touch me; you've dehumanised yourself with this putrid way of life! Where are you? Where have you gone?"

He looked terrified now, his eyes flicked to his phone laying next our wrestling bodies, he must know I'd seen the video. The fear in him made me even angrier. The insides of my thighs were killing me, that made me mad too, I lifted my bum up from his stomach and he tried to move but I sat down again with more force than the last time. My anger was so fierce I wanted to rip his ears off the side of his head, pull his hair out by the roots; I actually wanted to kill him. I've never shouted louder. "Why Tim? Why are you doing this to me? What the fuck have I done to deserve this from you? What is wrong with me that you have to treat me so fucking appallingly?" My anger turned in on myself, I was beating my chest with my fists, there were tears mingled with snot and spit all over my face, I wiped them down with the sleeve of my robe. A sob came into my throat, my thighs were aching, I had pins and needles in my left foot and my whole self deflated back into its previously exhausted state. I fell away from his body onto my side, facing him. I curled myself into a ball and gave in to the grief that decimated me once again.

I heard him take a deep breath, he held out his hand towards me, "Please give me my phone back." Like a naughty child I handed it to him.

"You asked me a lot of questions Rachel, I have some answers for you. I don't think you are going to like a lot of them, but I will get back to you with them at some point tomorrow." Phone in hand he turned his back to me and within seconds was snoring again. I uncurled myself and still sobbing went back to my two friends downstairs: red wine and cigarettes.

I spent hours sat in the kitchen, drinking, smoking, and talking to myself; sadness, shame and fury fighting for emotional pole position. I banged my fist on the top of the table, I smacked my forehead and I paced, but nothing helped. By the time it was coming light I was a pissed up, disheveled crazy woman, rocking backwards and forwards.

I had to do something, I had to get away. It was too early for Naomi to be up on Sunday, but I had a key, I decided to go there, to my safe place. I went back upstairs and got dressed, I'd no idea what was going to happen when Tim finally woke up. I had no idea what was going to happen ever again. I packed a couple of things into a bag and before I went downstairs again, I put my head round the bedroom door. Tim was still fast asleep. The hand he had taken his phone off me with, was now tucked under the pillow, shielding it from view. How could he sleep? Didn't he have any conscience at all? The smell of stale vomit was overpowering. I stepped inside the room ready to clean it up and then thought better of it; let him do it.

I had another glass of wine and another cig whilst I got my medication together.

It was just after 9.30am, twelve hours since Tim had kissed my face and told me that he loved me, and now he couldn't bring himself to stay awake for long enough to answer my questions about why he continued to betray me.

51

I wasn't familiar with the taxi driver that came to collect me, he was chatty though. I was slumped in the back seat, with my second bottle of red wine sloshing about in my handbag. We drove past a barefoot woman walking in the same direction as we were travelling; she was wearing very few clothes for mid-January and carrying her high heel shoes in her hand. He nodded towards her. "Walk of shame, check her out!" I snorted at the very thought, just because I was riding in the back of a cab fully dressed didn't make me any less shameful; I was the woman who stole her husband's phone to see if she could catch him in some serious misbehaviour, and when she had, she'd almost had a wank whilst unwittingly watching him dogging.

I'll take her shame and raise it with mine.

My misery scale was at 98% which meant I had the other 2% of my grief-sodden brain left to stand back and wonder why, as I pulled up outside her place, Naomi was turning in to her drive at the same time. The gym wasn't open yet, she never, ever ate a dirty takeaway breakfast - why was she out of the house at this time on a Sunday? Whatever her reasons were, as soon as she saw me almost fall out of the cab, she rushed towards me her face shrouded in concern. She came to me to help me stand fully and took my bag from me. Without a word she guided me into the house and into the kitchen.

I fished the wine and my cigarettes out of my bag. "Rachel? Wine? Now?"

I shrugged my shoulders at her carelessly and for extra defiance I took a slug out of the bottle and started to walk to the back door towards the garden so I could have a smoke. She came to get me and steered me towards the table, she lit me a cigarette and handed me a glass. I was crying a bit, rocking backwards and forwards a lot. I started to gabble my story out.

Nai held her hand up to me to stop me. "Jude, we need Jude for this, she might know something we don't." She found her phone and called her; she answered straight away. Nai had her phone on loudspeaker. "Naomi? What's wrong, is Rachel ok?" The panic in Jude's voice was clear, I hiccupped loudly as Naomi replied. "She's here, she's pissed, she's not looking too great." I heard Jude sigh.

"What's happened this time?"

I told them. I told them about the pissed-up kisses, about the phone making me check it, about the video, the doggy-style passionate sex I watched, the unknown busty blonde on her knees in receipt of a rock-hard dick that belonged to Tim. I've told them lots of tales before - delightful, funny tales. I've had them hanging from my every word waiting for the conclusion of my story only for us all to fall about laughing at the end of it. Not today though. Naomi was providing the facial clues to the fact that I was justified with my devastation while the peace and quiet on the other end of the phone indicated that Jude had moved away from the distractions that were usually the background noise of her life.

They both gasped when I told them about the acts of violence I'd committed whilst I was begging Tim to tell me what I'd done to deserve such cruelty, and when I got to the point of Tim demanding I give him back his phone, then turning over to go back to sleep, they both expressed their disbelief at exactly the same time. "He did what?" from Jude, and, "bastard" from

Nai. By the time I'd finished telling them the whole sex in public, falling, puking, screaming, drinking, violent, sorry story, I'd finished the last of the red wine and was in the process of looking for something else to drink when my text alert beeped on my phone.

It was a three-word message from Tim: "Check your email."

The fear climbed up my body so quickly I couldn't swallow, my stomach was churning. It seemed like the three of us were holding our breath as I opened my emails. I was so filled with terror I couldn't bear to read it myself, I passed my phone to Naomi and with my free hands opened a beer I'd found in her fridge and lit another cigarette. With a low sad voice Naomi said "There's an attachment, shall I open it?" I nodded and watched her click the screen to open document. When it presented itself, she took a deep breath and started to read it out loud.

Despite her voice being full of compassion it couldn't dull the brutality of the message it delivered. With clarity and tenderness, she read out the words Tim had written as he finally ended our nineteen year marriage: via Email

Rachel

When I asked you to come home, I was convinced that our time apart had given us the chance to reassess what it was we wanted from each other. I was sure we could find a way to make it work for us again, but we don't seem to have had much of a chance to do that do we?

Your being poorly since you came home hasn't helped us to achieve the things I'd expected we would, but despite that I have still clung to my love for you and the hope that that things will turn around and everything would fall into place for us again, but they haven't.

I understand that what I have to say now will come as a shock to you, particularly as it's only a couple of weeks since we were making plans to celebrate our 20th wedding anniversary, but your actions last night have finally convinced me that it is time to be honest with you.

I have to tell you that I love you very much and I'm sure I always will, but I can't see a way forward for us anymore. I no longer have any desire for you, and I don't think it's fair on either of us that we carry on with our pretense. I realise that this admission will mean the end of our marriage, that there will be no going back after today.

I am very sad that we have to go our separate ways now, but I'm sure given time we will both find happiness again.

Please take good care of yourself.

Tim

All the time she was reciting his words Nai never took her eyes from the screen, she faithfully read every one as he'd written them. I could hear Tim's voice coming from the text, the cadence in the sentences were exactly as he spoke. I've probably heard him saying the same words thousands of times; just never in that particular, marriage-ending order.

There was a sound in the room, a bellow of pure anguish, it took me a second to understand it was coming from me. I felt myself start to heave and ran to the toilet to be sick. Red wine, cigarettes and catastrophic news gave my body plenty to get rid of, I was back on my knees hanging over the toilet bowl, crying and puking, the truth of Tim's words hitting me over and over. He'd just ended our marriage. It was done. Another wail escaped from deep down in my guts, I thought the intensity of the pain was going to split me in two.

When I was confident my vomiting was over, and my need for more wine and a smoke overtook me, I picked myself up off the bathroom floor and went back into the kitchen. Nai was looking at me with concern but there was something else in her face that I couldn't fathom. "Babe, you need to sit down." I warily sat back in my chair, what else could he inflict on me? Naomi nodded to the table. "There's a glass of water there for you, a fresh beer and a wine, have whichever you want."

Jude joined in. "There's another email come in from him. There's another attachment on it, Rach."

I was confused. I looked at Naomi's mobile laid on the table, to the source of Jude's voice and then at my friend sat in front of me as she passed me my phone. I gave it her straight back "What? What attachment? I can't read this, I can hardly see, what is it?"

"It's a spreadsheet Rachel, it's a breakdown of yours and Tim's collective debt and your joint wealth. He's documented it all clearly and explained the breakdown of it. He's asked you to let him know if you agree to the final figure he's proposed as your share. He's suggested you open a new bank account in your name as soon as possible and let him have the details so he can transfer the money over to you as he liquidises your assets."

I spluttered out the wine in disbelief. "What? He's done what?" I stood as I shouted, "what the fuck? My share? What does that mean?"

I knew what it meant; it meant my marriage was over. Naomi tried to hold out my phone to me so I could see the screen, like seeing it in black and white would make it more acceptable. "I'm sorry to say this Rachel," she said quietly, "but this is not the work of a couple of hours; it's a complicated document. This is a considered, careful calculation. Jude and I have just had a chat whilst you've been gone, and we think he's been planning this for a while."

I knew she was right; he had been planning this. He didn't care. He hadn't given a shit about me for a long time. He'd lost sight of me, treated me with brutality; his actions had annihilated me once again.

Fear was my first emotion; the force of it shot through me so rapidly I stood up from my seat and started to shout "Who am I though? Who am I without him? Who am I if I'm not his wife?"

Naomi came to me, she sat me down and wrapped her arms around me. She didn't say a word, neither did Jude. I repeated the same questions more to myself than to my companions. "But how will I live without him? Who am I? I've no idea how I'm going to survive, how will I ever get through it? I don't think I can do this."

Naomi pushed me away from her so she could see me, as Jude spoke with urgency. "You will get through this Rachel, don't ever think you won't." Nai followed her lead as she held my face in her hands, her eye contact holding mine. "You will get through this, you are so much more than Tim's wife, I wish you could see yourself like we do. I'm not saying it's going to be easy, but you can do it; and you will."

I saw the kindness and love shining from my friend in front of me, the warmth and softness of the palms of her hands on my cheeks slowed my heartbeat a little. I shuddered on my inbreath, "How though Nai? How Jude? How will I do it?"

Before the other two could respond, a familiar, much missed and long absent voice, spoke to me softly.

With dignity. Dignity will get us through this, my darling.

Part Two

The Resurrection

1

I woke with a start, the second my eyes opened my brain stood to attention. I didn't have wait for reality to kick in - I didn't need to, I knew my reality right here, right now; I was back in Flick's bed.

I'd no idea what time it was, but it was very dark both outside and in. I reached my arm over to the bedside table, my fingers walking and patting its surface trying to find the pills Naomi had put there for me when she'd put me to bed. I couldn't find them. As I touched the lamp it flickered into a gentle glow, but even with the help of the light there was no sign of the sleeping tablets; I was convinced there should be another two somewhere.

I'd objected like a stroppy toddler the day before when she'd eventually taken my booze off me and made me eat food I didn't want. I'd sat for a long time staring into space, catatonic with shock. When I eventually came round, I paced the house trying to find somewhere that felt safe. I wailed a couple more times and cried a lot but eventually, by early evening, exhaustion had stopped my sobs and I gave in to her care and took a Valium. She'd insisted I have an early night. I couldn't think of anything worse than turning off the light and ending the day, I had no idea how I was supposed to be able sleep when I'd just been sawn in half.

Naomi had sat on the side of my bed tucking me in, calming me down with her words and more prescription medication.

When she gave me the tablets she said, "I know you think you'll never get over this Rachel, I know better than anyone how much faith and love you've put into your marriage, I watched you do it. I can't say I know how you feel right now because I've never walked a mile in your shoes, but I've had my own trip down this path you're on - several times - and it's devastating. I hate to sound like Gloria Gaynor but you will survive it, I promise you."

She gave me the pills and handed me a glass of water. "Take these two now and you'll sleep for a while. When you wake up in the middle of the night - which you will - there are two more within arm's reach, take those and they'll see you through to morning."

But they hadn't. It was the middle of the night, I was wide awake, and now I came to think about it, I'd taken my emergency back-up pills ages ago. Panic overtook me - what was I supposed to do now? There was no way I was prepared for the onslaught of agony I knew was waiting for me if I was awake for long but there were no more drugs to take, no more numbing potion, no more sleep to block it out.

There was no more alcohol to drink my pain away either because although I didn't know what time it was, I knew it was Monday and even I didn't drink pre-dawn on Mondays unless I was at an airport.

I needed to move myself, to do something to fend off the viciousness of the emotions that were there, lurking around in the shadows of my general vicinity. I knew they were waiting to pounce. Waiting for me to be sober or awake long enough so they could hit me again. I didn't want to give them the chance. As I got out of bed I prepared myself for my legs failing me, but they held me up just fine. I made my way downstairs to the kitchen where the big clock on the wall told me it was 4am - those sleeping tablets were shit.

While I waited for the kettle to boil I thought about the email Tim had sent me. Not the first one - I couldn't look at that one yet - I wasn't sure I would ever be ready to read those words with my own two eyes. Instead, I used the spreadsheet as a diversionary tactic. I hadn't wanted to study it closely yesterday, but Nai had made sure I'd seen the notes he'd written by the final figure advising me to open a bank account in my own name – the bastard - and suggesting that he stay in the house and cover the costs until it was sold – trying to assuage his guilt.

As it had been pointed out to me yesterday - in between vomits - these were all very unequivocal decisions for a hung-over man to have made in such a short space of time. I sat at the huge dining table I'd been at for yesterday's relationship-ending revelations. Naomi had thoughtfully printed the spreadsheet for me. Now I was up close and personal to it I realised she was right; its compilation had involved a lot of rigorous work. As far as I could see he'd taken every aspect of our finances into consideration, it was extremely detailed. It was very definite too; a numerical equivalent of his marriage-ending words.

I forced myself to stay as numb as I could while I made myself tea and then called the bank. The guy at the call centre doing the graveyard shift answered in a chirpy voice. He started to take me through the usual questions to prove my identity. Saying my surname was my first challenge; it struck me it technically wasn't mine anymore, was it? It was Tim's. I'd shared it with him for nearly twenty years, but by the looks of the calculations on the paper in front of me we didn't share things anymore, we separated them, like he'd separated us.

The helpline guy was lovely, he seemed to pick up on my badly disguised distress and when he asked me how he could help me my voice quivered a bit at the enormity of the significance of my pre-dawn call. I was making my first admission, even to myself, that from now on I was on my own. He was gentle with me; he even waited patiently as I struggled to think of a password that didn't involve any relevance to my previous life. That was a hard one.

Once the formalities were over with, the nice call centre guy wished me all the best for the future and we said our goodbyes. I sat back and looked at my surroundings, the narrow focus I'd had while I was sorting out my single woman's bank account had melted away, and it felt like my peripheral vision had suddenly come to life and brought with it the realisation that this was my new world, this was my future. Living here wasn't a temporary thing anymore, I wasn't staying while I was waiting for my husband to come to his senses because to all intents and purposes, I didn't have a husband. Now I was just Rachel, a middle-class, middle-aged woman who would soon be referring to Tim as 'my Ex' and heading to the divorce lawyer. I was such a fucking cliché. I shook my head in shock.

I'd spent the last 25 years entwining my life with Tim's - our memories, family, friends, pets, homes, money, heart and soul - the things that made me who I was. If I didn't have them anymore, then what did I have? Where did I fit in?

I was a woman who'd surrendered everything she had to a man who didn't really want her. I'd given so much of myself to him, I'd left myself empty handed. I had a shattered mind that was controlled by chemicals, a body that failed me regularly and I was single and homeless.

The intensity of the loss crashed into me again, an onslaught of physical pain that came into my heart and belly so furiously it knocked the wind out of me. I gasped and clutched the front of my body trying to stop it from exploding open and leaving my viscera all over Naomi's kitchen cupboard doors.

Ivy came to me, her voice emphatic, impossible to ignore even through the convulsions of misery.

Right, you've got a decision to make now, Rachel You have a choice; the end of your marriage can either be the death of you or it can be the making of you - which one do you want it to be?

I partially unfolded myself with indignation. "Well, it's not going to kill me, that's for sure."

Excellent, now we've established that, might I suggest you have another look at that spreadsheet. There are quite a few noughts on the end of that final figure.

I released my body a little bit more so I could stretch my hand out and pull the document back towards me.

That's a lot of coin for a homeless, single woman, with no commitments whatsoever. Instead of asking yourself who you are now you're not Tim's wife anymore, I reckon you should be asking yourself - what do you want to do next?

2

It was Monday lunchtime by the time I felt strong enough to break the news of my separation to my nearest and dearest. I had to finally admit to them all that the last few years of my life were not as they had appeared.

I discovered I'd been totally brilliant at pretending everything was well in my inner world to the outside-world because my news caused a great deal of shock and consternation. There were many questions from my family, and I had no idea how to start answering them. What was I supposed to say to my folks? "Well dad I think I realised that my marriage might be in trouble around the time I discovered Tim was watching spit-roast sex on the information superhighway. No, mum, the information superhighway's not really a road, and nope, the type of roast I'm referring to definitely isn't something that you get at a carvery."

It was all too raw, and too shameful and so ridiculous that I didn't know where to start explaining, so instead I said that Tim had decided he no longer wanted to be with me and refused to be drawn into deeper discussions. Between sobbing heavily and apologising for being such a failure at being married, it was about as much I could manage.

I knew I would only have to contact a couple of my most reliable friends and ask them to spread the news for me. I was as scant with them on the details of our separation as I was with my parents and siblings, but even so the shock of my news was causing confusion and consternation. I gave each of them the go ahead to tell who they liked without compunction, the sooner people knew Tim and I were no longer together, the better as far as I was concerned, like ripping a plaster off a hairy arm; best done as fast as possible to reduce the risk of prolonged agony.

In the spirit of the spreadsheet separation tactics Tim had used so callously I deliberately avoided contacting anyone associated with the pub and the golf club; as far as I was concerned, they were Tim's friends now, he could tell them. I needed people I could trust to support me, and I didn't want to get embroiled in the malicious delight I knew some of them would take from the news of our separation. I was sure Alison - and probably several others - would be more than happy to lend him a shoulder to cry on. I could smell her schadenfreude from where I was, and I certainly didn't want to hear her fake sympathy or let her anywhere near my wounded psyche.

I felt like I was free-falling, every experience had an other-worldly quality to it. I had no grasp on reality because I didn't know what that was anymore. I had no other experience to draw from to understand how to behave, or how to be - or who to be. Naomi advised me to distract myself as much as I could, and I'd taken her advice conscientiously; her kitchen cupboards were immaculate.

The day after I'd started the wildfire that would carry my news near and far, I finally gathered up enough courage to text Tim with my new bank details. It was the first contact we'd had since Separation Sunday. I decided I wouldn't ask him how he was, so I just sent my sort code and account number to him. He replied quickly. "Thank you, I'll send you your share of the money as it comes through. I hope you're somewhere safe." I started to text my reply until Ivy interrupted me.

Don't think about texting him back unless it's to say, fuck off knob head.

So, I didn't. Instead, I cleaned every bathroom in the house and replied to the many other sympathetic and helpful text messages that came through from people who liked having me in their life. I swerved all questions apart from the ones that included the words 'fancy a drink', 'catch up', or 'coming over to stay for the weekend'. I replied to all of those in the positive.

Ivy had taken to calling Tim arch-enemy number one, the bastard, the arsehole, and several other names with the word head immediately after them. A week after we'd separated, dickhead contacted me again to tell me he was going to be working away until the following Friday so if I needed to collect anything from the house this would be the optimum time.

Did he really use the word 'optimum' in a text? The pretentious wanker!

I hadn't been able to eat, sleep or even think about anything apart from cleaning Nai's house and the devastation caused by the end of my marriage, but it seemed like he was carrying on as if nothing had happened! He hadn't even needed to take time off work to acquaint himself with his new ex-husband status.

Because he's been rehearsing for the role for a long time Rachel, the heartless shit!

3

When I was a kid, maybe four or five years old, I unwittingly turned myself upside down in my bed while I'd been sleeping. This was back in the days of flannelette sheets, blankets, and eiderdowns. My mum, always keen to make sure we were safe and warm, used to tuck all the layers of our bedding tightly under the mattress.

My tiny bedroom always had a cool flow of air which came through the window I insisted stayed open, no matter what the weather. My curtains didn't quite meet in the middle even when they were closed, which meant I could always see some sort of light from outside. It was how I liked it.

This particular occasion, when I opened my eyes, I was in the pitch black. The air around me was warm and damp and felt hard to come by. I couldn't fathom out where I was or why I was there. I reached above my head expecting to find the top of the sheet so I could pull it down over my sweaty, breathless face but instead of the freedom and fresh air I expected I was met with resistance, I tried to push myself out of both the of sides of the bed and still found no way out, only tightly swaddled fabric.

My panic was in full force and my breath was shallow. In my child's mind I was convinced I was running out of air, and I was going to suffocate. In a frenzy of arms and legs and a scream of absolute terror, deadened by the thick covers and heavy eiderdown, I fought hard against my restraints. I whirled my legs and arms as hard as I could and rotated my body around the bed. Sheer determination, fear and physical strength eventually got me out of my entrapment. When I got my head out from under the covers, the relief was so strong I cried at the same time as filling my lungs with the fresh air I'd been deprived of for what felt like an eternity.

The sheer terror of those few minutes has never left me. I've never been able to forget it because it left me with a massive fear of enclosed spaces, spaces such as an MRI scanner. Which is where I was, right now.

I'd been told to expect to be inside the miniscule, yet extraordinarily lengthy tube for at least forty-five minutes. During that time, I couldn't move or speak, and was advised, if it was at all possible, not to open my eyes. When I did – because I couldn't resist the temptation – I realised why they didn't want me to see where I was. The top of the tube was less than 6 inches from my nose. Claustrophobia hit me so hard I wanted to fight my way out, I was five years old trapped under the blankets again; my body tingled with anxiety.

Shhhhh, calm yourself. Close your eyes again - take some deep breaths. The racket the machine's making sounds a bit like a Chemical Brothers' track, doesn't it? It's almost like you're off your head on something highly illegal that cost less than a tenner and you're dancing like no one's watching, and even if they are you don't really care.

She was right about the noise "I always used to do every-thing like no one was watching, now I worry about what people think about me all the time. Why do I do that?"

I don't know why you do it, but I do know it's hard work. It's soul destroying trying to prove your worth to other people. If you spend too long looking at yourself through someone else's eyes, you'll never really know who you are, will you? You'll be too busy trying to make other people love and respect you to even think about loving or respecting yourself. Where's the sense in that?

"We're talking about Tim, aren't we?"

Of course we are. We always end up talking about that knobhead, but we don't need to worry about him now, do we? Thankfully. Now we need to start working out how to get over the damage fighting for a life with him has done to you. You've battled so hard to try and make it right, forgiven him so many times and in the end all that's happened is you've forgotten all about you. And guess what? So did he. What kind of man ends a marriage days before his wife's due to go for a test that might reveal a crippling illness? What does that say about the human being you've wrapped your life around? He's an awful man, he's destroyed you piece by precious piece, and now you've reached rock bottom, he's wiped his hands of you.

"Well when you put it like that..."

Allowed full rein, Ivy was waxing eloquent.

That's the only way to put it, it's the truth. He didn't love you like you loved him, it's time to face up to that. But the most important thing to realise right now is that you didn't drive him towards porn and prostitutes, he took himself there. That's his weakness, not yours. While we're here and we've got nothing better to do, let's have a little delve into all that stuff you know but don't want to admit to yourself, shall we?

"What stuff? All I really know is that my heart's broken in pieces and I'm scared to death of what's going to come next."

Come on Rachel, it's time to stop excusing him for his fuckwittery. All that bollocks in the letter he wrote, about not desiring you anymore, what's that all about? He hasn't even tried to get it up for you for years and years, he's been too busy wasting his erections on solo hand jobs and hookers. And he's blaming you for his behaviour so he doesn't have to accept any responsibility for himself. You've become his excuse. All that bullshit about love and hope, there isn't any truth in that, he's been trying to get rid of you for years, he's just been too much of a coward to say it.

"What? No! Now come on, I'm not sure that's right...is it?"

It's the truth. He's stood back and watched you crumble. He's allowed you to diminish yourself for the sake of him. The harder you tried to keep it all together, the more he pushed you away. He could have shredded those credit card bills, he could have deleted those texts from that Melissa chick all those years ago. He didn't even need to watch that dogging video, he was so drunk he fell asleep watching himself have sex for fuck's sake. Maybe he did it on purpose so you'd discover what he's been up to all this time and then you would be the one to crack and end your marriage. That way he could still fool himself that none of it was his fault. If you were at work, you'd call it constructive dismissal. Am I right?

"What? All this time, what makes you think he'd be so devious and cruel?"

Because whatever else he said in that letter, he never once said he was sorry. He never apologised for his behaviour. Or what he's done to you.

The shock that came from the realisation that Tim, the love of my life, the complete focus of all my energies, had ended our marriage without apology stunned me so much I had no option but to lay still. I sank into a paralysis of deep disbelief. The fact I hadn't even noticed a lack of remorse from him as he'd ended our relationship brought it home to me how browbeaten I'd become by his behaviour; I finally admitted to myself I was in a bad place.

I didn't come round again until I heard the guy behind the glass wall tell me he was done, and he was about to move me out of the tube.

4

The revelations from my MRI chat with Ivy astonished me. I wasn't sure I was able to face most of it - it was lot to take in - but its essence had filled me with a bit more resolve than I'd had before.

Bolstered up with indignation I decided to take Tim's advice about him working away as a good time (*optimum, Rach, optimum*) to collect a few things from the house, but I decided if I was going back there at all, it wouldn't be for a few things. No, it would be all my things.

Petra and Naomi insisted they came with me, and despite my bluster I was glad of their company and help. My dignity mantra brought with it a determination that this next foray into ending my life as Tim's wife would not damage me any more than I already was. I promised myself I would be methodical and clinical with the task in hand and get it done as fast as possible. I didn't do too badly sticking at it either, I don't know where the strength came from, but I didn't let myself down. I went through the house from top to bottom and only packed what belonged to me. I didn't take a single piece of furniture, ornament, or memento of my life there; nothing.

It took three trips in a van Petra had managed to borrow from someone to move my possessions; that was all. Not much to show really for over forty-five years on this planet. As she and Nai left with the final load, I chose to stay behind. I wandered around the house, and said goodbye to all the rooms, a reverse action of the familiarisation trip I'd made only a few weeks beforehand when I'd been full of anticipation for mine and Tim's reconciliation.

I was physically exhausted from the effort of packing and mentally shattered by my self-imposed emotional block. When I got to the kitchen I sat at my usual seat and looked out at the garden. The lush greenery of the summer was hibernating from the January weather; it looked lifeless and miserable, its beauty diminished by its current environment. There wasn't much difference between us.

I opened a beer, lit a cigarette and rang Jude. She answered on the first ring. "Hey babe, where are you?" Her voice was soft.

"I'm in the kitchen, Jude, sat opposite your chair, drinking a beer and smoking."

"Hang on a minute then." I heard some activity on the other end of the phone - the opening and closing of the fridge and then the sound of her lighting her own cigarette.

"Jude! I thought you'd stopped smoking cos of the kids."

"Ahh, only sometimes when it suits me. I'm hiding in the pool house; the little buggers will never think to look for me here." We both chuckled. It felt nice to share a joke with her and good to release something from my congested emotional self. But once I'd popped the top off my imprisoned feelings, the giggly release was closely followed by the deepest sadness I'd ever felt; I inhaled trying to make it go away until I heard Jude start to cry, and then I let it go.

"It hurts, Jude."

"I know Rachel, I'm sorry you're in so much pain." We cried a bit more. "It's time now though, you know that don't you? It's time to let go of it all, to find a way to look forward and not back."

Her words melted the last of my bravado. I cried a bit harder. "I don't know how."

"Yes, you do. Remember who you are. There's so much more to you than you give yourself credit for - you're an amazing woman - let yourself see that. Please."

Well I frigging never, that's the first thing she's said for years that I actually agree with! Yay, go Jude - welcome to Team Rachel - about time you turned up!

"We've had so many happy times in this house - there's so much to leave behind me." The grief came again, big, fat juicy tears splashing on the tabletop. "What do I do with all these memories? All the ones I've been building and collecting with him, the ones we'd planned to share again and again so we could chuckle over them when we were old and sat on a sun lounger somewhere on the Costa Del Sol, getting drunk on cocktails and working on our melanomas. Where do I put those?"

She sighed and did a tiny sob at the same time. "I can't give you the answer to that one Rach, but you'll work out where to keep those memories. One thing's for sure though, knowing you, by the time you want them again you'll have forgotten where you left them!"

I laughed so hard I snorted beer bubbles down my nose and then I started to laugh a bit harder. It was as forceful as the tears had been, and it was as cathartic. Hearing her laugh with me, the two of us sharing something funny, something that was beyond my life with Tim, our own brand-new intimacy, gave me a split-second of a thrill.

While I was enjoying the lightness in me Jude said suddenly, "Come and stay with us for a couple of weeks Rachel, get on a plane as soon as you can. Comitas would love to meet you, I'd love to see you, and it'll do you good to get away."

Another thrill shot into instantaneous excitement. "Are you serious?"

"Course I am! Get your doctor's thingy out of the way and come over. Bring me some fruit gums, I haven't had any for ages. I'll even pay for your flight, how's about that for a plan?"

"I'll be there as soon as I can. And thanks for the offer but I'm ok for cash – some of my marital redundancy money will have come through by then."

She cheered and laughed. "That's my girl, I knew you were in there somewhere! You're going to be just fine. It'll take time and it's not going to be easy, but you will come out the other side of this."

Her words shored me up again. "I can, Jude, and you know what, I'm going to be the best I can be. I promise you this much, from now on I'm going to hold my head high. I'm going to be sure that whatever I do, I can always look myself in the eye and smile at me. And when it gets tough, I'll put my shoulders back, take some deep breaths and face it head on."

A swell of confidence filled my body. I breathed deeply through my nose to appreciate it all the more - my out-breath was full of relief and hope. It felt amazing.

Ivy gave a deep, delighted roar.

Go on girl, that's the way to tackle this! Get your self-respect back - believe in yourself. You've got nothing to lose and everything to gain. You're going to be so happy. I promise.

Jude and I talked for a while longer, making plans for my visit, both of us caught up with the thought of being together for the first time in a very long time. When we eventually said goodbye, my mood was lifted. I couldn't remember the last time I'd laughed with such gusto, nor could I recall the last time I had felt so light-hearted or excited.

While I'd been wrapped up in my future plans, I'd dipped my hand back into the fridge and helped myself to the last bottle of Tim's beer. Strange that I was already thinking that way, his and mine. Tim's or Rachel's. Not Tim's and Rachel's. I was just drunk enough to be egged on by Ivy when she said.

He's got that big box of two-pound coins upstairs under the bed, he's been saving them for ages, there must be loads by now - technically half of that money's yours. Go and get your share!

Without the need for any more persuasion, I went back upstairs into the bedroom, laid on my belly and reached under the bed to search for the container full of coins. My fingers touched something else first though. Not the hard edges of the coin-keeping box I'd expected, instead my fingertips told me it was soft fabric. As I reached for it, I realised what it must be. I dragged it into my view; it was the blue velvet bag that held our wedding photo album. I grabbed it and started to unfasten the rope on the top. Ivy shouted.

Stop that! What use is looking at that going to be? Don't torture yourself, put it back.

I didn't listen to her. I pulled the cream leather-bound book out of the bag and with some effort threw it on the top of the bed. Then I went back to my search for the box. When I found it, I took what looked like roughly half of the jingle and stashed my share in the big blue pouch that had held the wedding photos. I wasn't sure what to do with album, I knew for sure I didn't want it, so I left it where it was; sat in the middle of his single man's king-size wank nest. Let him decide what to do with it.

As I left the bedroom, I rang Naomi. When she answered, her voice was solicitous. "Are you ok, darling? Petra's still here helping me unload, do you want us to come and get you from the house?"

"Nah, fuck that, let's go to the pub and get drunk. Tim's paying!"

I was so busy organising which bar we would meet at, that I left the house and closed the door behind me without so much as a backward glance. I got to the bottom of the street and realised my handbag was so full of coins, it was too heavy to carry too far. I hailed a cab, and by the time Nai and Petra turned up at the bar, I'd bought us a bottle of fizz and was halfway through my first glass.

5

Naomi, Petra and I spent most of my under-the-bed cash-stash, we managed four bottles of champagne between the three of us that evening. It was a delightful way to get drunk after a traumatic couple of days officially leaving my life behind me.

At one point during our second bottle, a bit pissed and feeling excited for the future I'd raised my glass to Nai and I proposed a toast to the two of us being single at the same time, for the first time since we'd known each other. I was about to launch into champagne-fuelled plans for holidays and weekends away until something about the expression on her face alerted me to the fact that she may have something to tell us. I stopped mid-sentence and raised my eyebrows at her, encouraging her to speak.

She broke into an instant smile "The thing is Rach, I don't think I am single anymore. I've been seeing someone for a little while and I'm beginning to think it might be becoming a bit more serious than I'd first thought."

Petra and I looked at her and then at each other, our flabbergasted expressions were matching. "What? Why didn't you tell me?"

"Ahhh well, you were a bit busy - what with getting separated, having your brain scanned, moving house and all that. I didn't want to give you anything else to think about."

Petra was shaking her head in disbelief. "I thought you were off men after Richard? Less than three months ago you said they were all shallow wankers who made cock-led decisions."

"Oh, yes, I stand by that," stated Naomi, nodding emphatically with just the hint of a cheeky smirk.

"So, what's changed?"

Nai looked at Petra, in response to her comment she grinned broadly. "The sex of my lover."

I don't think I've been so surprised about a relationship status since mine had changed the month before.

* * * * * * * * * * *

I was sat in the same bar again, it felt like a good place to be, although I wasn't drinking such extravagant alcohol this evening. I'd ordered a bottle of lager from the girl behind the bar who smiled and told me she remembered me because "not many people buy four bottles of champagne in one night and even if they did, they defo don't pay for it with £2 coins."

Once I'd got my drink, I sat in an oversized comfy chair tucked in the corner of the room. I was on my own, and for the first time in days, I was able to sit still.

I wouldn't say my energy levels were back to normal by any stretch of the imagination, but since I'd moved in with Naomi some of my natural vigour seemed to be coming back. I wondered if maybe it was heartbreak adrenaline that was giving me so much impetus because from the second my eyes opened from any sleep I man aged to get (not a lot), I threw myself out of bed and got on with something constructive. Naomi's house was not a small affair, but because of my hyperactivity over the last couple of weeks, I was running out of things to clean and organise.

My days involved long periods of frantic physical activity, and then I would suddenly stop doing whatever it was I was in the middle of. The strangest thing was I didn't even know the stop had happened until I came back to reality, and when I did I was always surprised to find myself frozen in stillness with no idea how long I'd been that way.

One time, I was standing on a ladder mid-clean of the top of a kitchen cupboard, and when I came back from my trance my hand had been in a bucket of water so long the skin on my fingers were like raisins. Another time I was on the stairs with the vacuum cleaner hose in my hand, this time when I became conscious of my surroundings again the first thing that hit me was a pungent burning smell coming from the overheated motor that had been running too long.

Immediately after my repeated reveries, the emotions I was trying so hard to ignore by being a domestic goddess, made their presence felt with violent and intense waves of pain in my heart and chest, swiftly followed by an anguished wail that came from deep inside me. It was a noise I'd never heard myself make before and it took me hours to get over the shock and desolation it left behind.

The last time it had happened was the day before yesterday, when I'd been pushing the white wash into the tumble dryer. This time when I came round from my fugue, I was distracted from my usual peal of pain by the sight of my left hand resting on the drum of the dryer. The sunlight had caught the facets in the five large diamonds of the eternity ring Tim had bought me for my 30th birthday. I'd been lovingly fascinated by its sparkle since I got it, but today its lustrous presence on my finger taunted me. There were three rings on the third finger of my left hand, all of them the outdated signs of my commitment to a life that no longer existed.

Why are you still wearing them then?

I un-squatted my legs, sat on the floor and rested my back against the wall of the utility room. I held my left hand up in front of my face as Ivy carried on talking to me.

Take them off, Rachel. Take them all off.

I knew she was right. It was time to stop wearing them. I started by sliding my engagement ring off my finger. I pulled my eternity ring over my knuckle quickly afterwards. I reached out to do the same with my wedding ring, but I couldn't bring myself to do it; the bareness of my finger scared me.

Removing the two rings had left two noticeable hollows below my knuckle, the dips in the skin that had been created by them being in place for so many years. Witnessing the nakedness and the indentations was too much reality for me to take in one go, I left my gold band where it was. I put the diamond rings in my purse and a couple of days later when I was passing the jewellers we'd bought them from, Ivy encouraged me to call in and see how much they would give me for them.

The guy behind the counter was lovely but told me they had enough 'pre-loved' stock and they wouldn't buy them back. That's when I realised, no matter how much the rings cost when they were all sparkly and tempting in the shop window, diamond eternity rings are worth fuck all on the second-hand market. The dreams they represent are only precious to the people that share them. Once you try to sell those hopes back, their value is reduced considerably. My value had been reduced considerably. I was an unwanted piece of marital flotsam and jetsam - an ex-wife. As I left the shop reality hit me so hard, I had to stop walking so I could get my breath back. I rested my forehead on the huge display window and cried with such abandon a stranger came to me and asked me if she could do anything to help. The look of concern on her face overwhelmed me but I couldn't catch my breath enough between sobs to tell her why I was so upset. I gave her a soggy-faced sad smile and a shake of my head to convey my lack of ability to talk and walked away, still weeping.

I told Naomi the story that evening over a glass of wine and a spliff. "The thing is, Nai, I feel like a bit of a drama queen being so grief stricken about the end of my marriage, but I can't help it. When the pain of losing Tim comes back to me it bends me double. I'm so ashamed of it; my tears, my marriage, my inability to make it work out right. I know I shouldn't be but I am."

Naomi passed me the joint back just as Ivy spoke.

It'd be easier if he was dead.

I'm usually very careful to filter my Ivy thoughts - in the main they're wildly inappropriate and generally not fit for human consumption - but on this occasion I instantly repeated her words and followed it with, "because if he was, my grief would be 100% justifiable and have zero percent shame attached to it."

I'd meant to say this profundity in all seriousness but when I looked at Naomi she was giggling. "That's a classic Rachel line!" She laughed a bit more until I couldn't help but join in. We sat on the sofa opposite each other holding our tummies and trying to catch our breath.Eventually she said, "Rach, in a few weeks or months or whenever you start to come out of the other side of this grief, you'll realise you're glad he's not dead. A divorced woman is forgiven for going a bit wild - no one will bat an eyelid when you realise this is the time of your life and start having enormous amounts of fun. A widowed woman is expected to have much more decorum. If you want to look on the bright side of the situation, at least the bastard didn't die while you were in the process of learning to hate him - now that would have been a complete travesty. For you, not him."

At the time she'd said it, the laughter and weed had stopped me from objecting to her comment about me learning to hate him. In the short space of time, we'd been apart, I'd managed to lose a lot of my previous negative emotions, and now I couldn't remember what it had felt like to hate Tim. I adored him, I loved our life, he'd been my whole reason for being who I was.

But the conversation with Nai had taken place before my appointment with the Neurologist and now, an hour or so since getting the results of my MRI scan, I was revising my entire back catalogue of thoughts concerning my love for my husband.

****

The consultant had confirmed the results of my scan in a professionally calm voice. She assured me emphatically that physically I was as healthy as any normal woman of my age.

My relief was huge. After she'd given me the medical results her tone of voice and body language shifted somehow, it seemed like she'd dropped our doctor-patient relationship onto another level. She leaned across her desk and lowered her upper body slightly as she did. She became much less authoritative, it felt like she was reaching out for me in a conspiratorial manner, her eyes were full of kindness. "Can I ask you Rachel if you've been under any emotional pressure recently?"

I nodded. "My husband and I have just separated."

She stayed verbally silent but couldn't hide the obvious eureka expression on her face at her accurate diagnosis. "I don't know the details of your separation, and I don't need you to tell me what they were, but I strongly suspect that you have been living under an immense amount of stress for quite some time, am I correct?"

I nodded again, amazed at what she was sharing with me. I'd come to see a neurological consultant not a fortune teller. I was incredulous that she should know all of this from an inside image of my cranial anatomy.

I sat dumbfounded while she described to me my body's response to the stress created by the threat I'd been living with. That the continual pressure my life was inflicting on me had kick-started it into activating its fight or flight response. Because I'd continually ignored the chemicals that coursed through my body preparing me to run for my life and at the same time the disregarded the devastation my relationship with Tim was causing me; my obstinance and unfounded belief in my marriage had overridden any self-protection my body had been trying to enforce. I'd damaged myself because I hadn't listened to it, or to Ivy - my own true self telling me I was in danger, issuing warning after warning. So, in the end my brain did the only thing it could to get my attention: it stopped my body from working.

I hadn't told anyone else about the appointment that evening; I'd gone on my own. I wanted to be sure that whatever the diagnosis was I'd have time to digest it, to work out what my future might look like before anyone else got involved. It was the most grown-up thing I'd ever done, and right now I was glad I'd given myself this chance to absorb my news alone.

The revelation that I'd become so damaged mentally - even to the point where my body had deteriorated to such a degree it couldn't function anymore, horrified me. My pride and my conceited belief that I could make things right for us had only served to allow Tim to continue to be my abuser. The forgiving and forgetting I'd done over the years, the pile of shite I'd continually swept under my imaginary carpet, had all contributed to the destruction of me.

As I sat in the bar trying to come to terms with the unveiling of the reasons for my illness, I wasn't sure who I detested more, Tim or myself. In the habitually unconscious way I had for years, when I was thinking deeply, the thumb of my left hand moved towards my wedding ring finger to fiddle with the jewellery that was sat there. As I touched it, I looked down at the gold band and without any further thought I took it off. That part of my life was over, it was time to put an end to the damage and the cruelty I'd lived with. It was time to stop being the partial perpetrator of my annihilation. I had to start looking after me.

I'd like to say that when I left the bar a couple of hours later, I'd left the wedding ring sitting next to my empty glass in a metaphoric leaving-behind-of-the-past type of scene. But I didn't do that. I took it with me. And in the end, I sold all three rings a few months later for not much money and with the proceeds I got a new tattoo, my nipple pierced and a bank holiday weekend away to a seaside town with a couple of mates where I got outrageously drunk and snogged half a dozen different people.

Naomi was right, I was glad I wasn't a widow.

6

Getting my results from the Consultant was a thought-provoking experience; she didn't quite say I'd brought my ill-health on myself, but it didn't take Einstein to figure out where some of the blame should lie.

The excellent news meant, of course, that rather than my condition being physically incapacitating, or even - as I'd feared in my darkest days - terminal, I would recover fully. The neurologist had insisted, as part of my healing process, I should see a counsellor, explaining to me that it was time to start untangling the web of harm my life had trapped me in. I couldn't possibly expect to cope with my repair alone, she said, as she gave me a business card for someone she knew and trusted.

The last time I'd paid for someone to help me sort my life out hadn't been what you'd call a roaring success. Glenda - 'but you can call me Glen' – had punched a massive indentation in my trust for the entire counselling and psychiatric profession with her misnaming fuck up. I wasn't sure I was up for yet more sessions in the shrink's chair. In my mind's eye the whole episode would once again see me sat in a dreary room on an uncomfortable chair, with a glass of water on my left and a box of tissues on my right, opposite a serious-looking woman, dressed in a corduroy skirt.

It felt like regression rather than the way to move myself forward. Ivy tried to talk to me about it, Nai tried to talk to me about it, but I refused to listen to reason.

****

The reaction of my friends and family to the news that my illness was a form of mental ill health, rather than something physical, was almost jubilant. I heard most of them breathe a sigh of relief; my least favourite sibling was the most straightforward with her opinion of my diagnosis "Oh so after all that it's only your brain that's in pieces, thank fuck for that - we were thinking something really awful was wrong with you." Yeah, thanks for that, sis!

Because I'd chosen to be so stupidly secretive about the slippery slope my marriage had been going down I also hadn't shared the length of my journey from well-rounded rambunctious human-being into the desiccated husk of a woman I was rapidly starting to recognise I'd become. I'd no idea how to explain to my nearest and dearest how much the last few years had stripped away from me because I don't think I truly knew how far down I'd gone. How could I expect anyone else to understand how complete my destruction had been unless I was prepared to face up to it myself?

A couple of days after my revelatory hospital appointment I was spring cleaning the lounge – the last room I had left to do. I was dusting the huge mirror over the fireplace when I caught sight of my reflection. I looked a bit sweaty from the effort of the cleaning, I had a blob of something on my cheek and I leaned into my reflection to try and identify what it was. Being so close to my mirror image gave me a fresh reminder of my passionate promise to meet my own eyes every day and tell myself I was doing a great job at being Rachel. I'd been a bit lackadaisical sticking to it so far, but while I was rubbing the mystery stain off my face, I re-promised myself that I'd start again; immediately. I met my own gaze, gave myself some serious eye contact, I smiled and offered my replica congratulations for not crying today; especially as it was already 2pm.

If I was honest with myself the biggest barrier to shedding any tears was the fact that I had no idea what to do with my grief anymore, I was confused about the direction the sadness should take. Prior to my diagnosis I'd presumed my sense of bereavement had been reserved for the loss of Tim and our marriage, until Inner Voice Ivy pointed out that technically my sorrow should be for me, Rachel, the woman I'd lost in the melee, she was the loss I should mourn.

Ivy was right as usual. I knew this incomparable occurrence in my life had the potential to be the end of me, and for all my brave talk I had no idea how to stop being Rachel Bradbury, the redundant wife, and to start being someone else; my own version of Rachel. Maybe not quite brand new but definitely remodelled.

As I stared at my mirror image the familiar voice of intervention commented.

So let me ask you a question, just for clarification. Do you want the end of your marriage to be the thing that pulls you apart?

The question sent shock waves through me. I knew no matter how many smithereens my old self had been blown into I couldn't even consider continuing to live my life as the shadow of my former self. I realised there should be no question about the direction I was going in. I'd gone as far down as I could, and now it was time for me to work out how to get myself back up again. I owed myself that much and if I was going to maximise my potential as a well-rounded, Tim-less human-being and allow this change in my circumstances to be the making of me, then I was going to need help to un-fuck myself.

I gave myself a wink and a nod in the dust free mirror and appreciated a supplementary compliment from Ivy.

Top quality bit of decision making there my girl!

I left the dusters, polish and vacuum cleaner where they were, found the business card the doctor had given me and made an appointment for the following week. And while I was on a roll, I logged into my laptop and booked a flight to Sardinia to see Jude.

I finished the last of the cleaning that afternoon and as I did, I slowly came to understand that it was the right time for the task to be over, the distraction had been good for me, but I was ready to try moving on now. I felt a fizz of excitement bloom in my body. For the first time in a long time, I felt I wasn't letting things 'happen' to me; I was taking control.

7

My inner circle of friends had rapidly become my new life-line. They lovingly offered me a place to escape to and another home to feel 'at home' in. As I got used to my new life, I bounced from place to place and friend to friend; my overnight bag was my constant companion.

I became a familiar face at a fair few breakfast tables - I stayed with my friend Christine so often I had my own chores to do when I was there. Whenever I arrived her husband Peter would happily go to his den to listen to his AC/DC collection and play on his X-box while his wife and I drank copious amounts of alcohol and smoked the odd joint. She and the rest of my eclectic collection of special people nursed me through the deepest of my heartbreak and insecurities and supported me as I slowly started to come back into myself and look forward to my future.

A week or so before my visit to Jude, I had a text from Lilli, an ex-colleague I'd worked with years ago and had kept in touch with on and off since. She'd heard my news on the grapevine and insisted we have a get together. She lived across the other side of the country now and we agreed to split the journey between us and meet somewhere in the middle. She knew just the place she said, a hotel she'd stayed in before.

We arranged to meet late afternoon on Friday. By the time I arrived at the hotel she'd already checked in and was sitting in the bar waiting for me. Our greeting was rapturous; I was overjoyed to see her. We spent a while discussing what had happened between Tim and I, and as with all the people I'd seen since the separation, when she heard my sorry story, she was shocked at the depth of his disrespect, amazed by the double life I'd lived whilst I'd been protecting the reputation of my marriage, and saddened by my decline.

We had planned to get dressed up and explore what the local area had to offer, but by the time we were on our second bottle of fizz, the bar had started to fill up. There was a nice buzz in the place, lots of happy, relaxed people having fun. It seemed a shame to leave, so once we'd drawn a line under talking about the sad stuff, we started to do what we do best when we're together - make each other laugh.

Lilli is an extraordinary woman; she isn't classically beautiful but she's incredibly attractive, overflowing with self-confidence and ridiculously sexy without even trying. People are drawn to her, men in particular are fascinated by her, so it was no surprise to me when part way through the evening she unintentionally attracted the attention of a party of a dozen or so guys who migrated towards us and settled themselves in and around our space.

While we were surrounded by the testosterone she'd brought to us, she was in complete control of them all. It was mesmerising watching the guys vying for her attention with lots of light-hearted banter and friendly rivalry. It'd been a long time since I'd been in the company of so many strangers and even though my confidence was at rock bottom, I found myself joining in with the banter and laughter. It gave me a sense of freedom and joy I hadn't felt for a long time. I was surprised to find my eyes were constantly drawn to the guy who sat across from me. He lounged comfortably in his chair, his long limbs loose and relaxed. He was self-assured and cool, cute in a boy-ish way, and when he'd stood up to go to the bar, I noticed how tall and slim he was and couldn't help but admire the vision of his delightful denim-clad arse.

I'd brought killer heels and a tit-displaying frock to wear for our evening out, but they were still in our room, unpacked. I'd made a bit of an effort with my appearance in anticipation of meeting my long-time-no-see-friend but the sight of all his sexy youthfulness made me feel old, dumpy and unattractive. I told myself I had absolutely no right to soil this boy's beauty with my middle-aged desire and instead returned my attention to the conversation and threw myself back into to the fun.

No matter how much Y-chromosome entertainment there was going on inside the hotel, Lilli and I were dedicated to our trips outside for a smoke. As we excused ourselves from the group and made our way to the smoking area, the guy I'd been trying not to stare at suddenly appeared behind me. He came close to my ear and said quietly, "Room 2250." I turned my head towards him, I moved so fast with astonishment, my long dangling earring nearly took my left eyeball out of its socket with the force of the backlash.

Seeing him up close, even with only one working eye, I realised he wasn't just cute he was glorious; young, fresh, lean and delicious. I pointed towards Lilli's back as she was leaving the bar, "Do you want me to pass the message on to her?" He looked genuinely amused by the idea. "No of course not, I'm going to my room now and I'm letting you know where I'll be if you want to join me."

I was so confounded by his invitation I was struck dumb. Without a word to him I turned on my heel and followed my friend outside, my eye watering madly from the earring injury.

Lilli passed me a lit Marlboro Light as I approached her. It was late and getting chilly, so we sat close to each other on a bench overlooking the car park. "Are you having fun babe?" I pushed my shoulder into hers and gave her a gentle nudge.

"Hell yeah, are you?" She returned the gesture.

"Hell yeah, they're a great bunch those guys, aren't they?" As casually as I could, I told her. "The youngest one just gave me his room number."

The giggle burst from me then. The ridiculousness of his invitation seemed comical to me, and I expected her to join in with my mirth but instead she turned her body towards me and held my face in her hands, when I was in her direct line of sight and said with conviction, "Rachel, that guy is bloody gorgeous. He's funny and he's sexy and he's given you his room number. If you don't fuck this man, you're off your head."

I started to shake my head in refusal at her suggestion, but it only made her more insistent. "Well, if you won't shag him for your own good, then please do it for me, because if there is one thing I would want to give you to celebrate all the years of our friendship, it would be the courage to take the next step towards enjoying your single life. Let yourself go. You're not anyone's wife any more. It's time to start pleasing yourself, and my god girl, that starts tonight."

My teeth were chattering. "I can't Lil, I'm not ready. I feel awful about myself."

She snorted down her nose with irritation. "Take that Tim-bullshit out of your head babe and go for a jump in a hotel room with a boy who's probably half your age. It's the stuff that dreams are made of!"

The fear of having sex with a new man gripped me so hard I had to jiggle my knees to calm down. "I can't do that; it's been such a long time since I had real sex, never mind sharing my vagina with a much younger total stranger." She didn't look in the slightest bit convinced by my reasoning; I tried a different tack. "Besides I haven't got any condoms."

She snorted in disbelief, stood instantly and broke into a run towards the hotel. I had no intention of helping her with whatever she was doing, I stayed where I was but I couldn't resist turning to look through the huge windows so I could watch her inelegant high-heel trot round the beautifully lit interior of the hotel, I laughed hard as I observed her run in and out of at least three ladies' toilets, until she disappeared completely from my view for a while.

I was calming down from the laughter her manic search had created in me, admitting to myself there was no way I was going to have sex with a man I'd just met in hotel bar, condoms or not, when she ran back towards me, triumphantly waving a pack of three. She dumped them in my lap, and still breathless from her frantic French letter dash, lit herself another cigarette. I saw a glint in her eye when she looked at me and raised her eyebrows "Well? What the fuck are you waiting for?"

It seemed impolite to refuse after she'd gone to all that running-around effort. I nodded in acquiescence, stood, and in a much slower manner than hers had been, made my way inside, towards the lifts.

I could have changed my mind at that point and got off the elevator at the first floor instead of the second, I could have let myself into our connecting rooms and waited for her to get bored of smoking and drinking on her own and come and join me. Sure, she'd be disappointed that I let the opportunity go past, but I knew she'd understand. I kept telling myself I wasn't obliged to accept the stunning boy/man's invitation, but Inner Voice Ivy was very lively this evening and pushed me onwards with encouraging words.

Never in my wildest imagination did I see this momentous occasion happening so soon. It's been years and years since you've had a ride, listen to Lilli, let yourself go! I can't believe you're even thinking about looking this sexy gift horse in the mouth.

The walk from the lift down the corridor to his room felt like the longest one I've ever done. Due to the lateness of the hour the place had a shushed quality, the thickness of the carpet deadened any noise my footsteps might have made but I still felt the need to tiptoe. Like I needed to creep up on him just in case he'd changed his mind. By the time I eventually found room 2250, my nerves were jumping madly around my body. I felt a bit sick with fear, I was completely out of my depth. I nearly turned around to head back the way I'd come, but Ivy made me knock on the door.

There was no response, I counted to ten and then counted again. The door remained firmly closed to me. What was I supposed to do now? Ivy insisted I *knock again, a little bit harder this time, don't be a pussy.*

There was still no answer, and as I waited, I felt the sense of humiliation crawl up my body - what if I'd been mistaken? Maybe he didn't really invite me to his room, why would he after all? I was a useless, undesirable old woman, fat from medication and penchant for beer, I stank of second-hand cigarette smoke, and I hadn't showered for at least 16 hours. What did I think I was doing?

Despite Ivy telling me to try again I turned away from the door and started to make my way back towards the lifts. I was a stupid, stupid woman. As I walked away from the room I put my hands in trouser pockets, my fingers found the square foil packet of the condom I'd taken out of the box in preparation of my expedition back into the world of penetration. The O shape of the shaft end of the sheath and its furled lubricated contents were slippy inside its encasement. I rolled it between my fingers the rawness of the sensuality taunted me: sex, sex, sex, fucking, penetration, lubrication, sex, sex, sex, that's not for you anymore you ridiculous woman.

I was at least halfway to the lift when I heard a door opening and my name being called. I turned to face the noise and there he was, his body halfway out of the door. He was wearing a pair of tight black jocks and a smile, I could make out the definition of his pecs, the smooth hairless skin on his chest was so pale the darkness of his nipples was a stark contrast. I flicked my eyes to his shorts, even from this distance I could see he was hard. He beckoned me to him and despite my fear and doubts I turned round and walked back in his direction.

8

I tried to make my trip back down the corridor appear as sexy as I could whilst my knees were knocking together with terror. As I reached him, he stepped inside the door slightly, his smile welcoming. I went to step into the room, towards him, but for some reason my fingers grabbed the door frame and when I tried to let go, they were frozen in place. He expanded the smile even further and leaned in to kiss me.

I haven't kissed anyone but Tim since Madonna was telling me to strike a pose - that's a very long time to be familiar with just one person's tongue and lips. Now here I was with this glorious creature in front of me - a stranger, who'd laughed at my jokes in an attractive way and dropped his room number into my ear - and I was about to snog him. I'm scared, I'm scared, I'm scared. *Let yourself go woman!* Ivy said at the same time as he said, "Let go of the door frame Rachel, come in please."

His face moved back towards mine and this time I leant into his kiss. His lips were soft, his face cleanly shaved, his tongue was unfamiliar; not unpleasant, just not the one I was used to. He smelled of aftershave and tasted of toothpaste. I must have tasted of cigarettes and pretendy-champagne, I was ashamed of my smelly breath, of my body, of my arrogance to think that I could carry off the seduction of a boy that looked like this; so utterly gorgeous.

As we continued to kiss, he gently unfurled my fingers and once he'd freed me from the woodwork, he walked backwards into the bedroom taking me with him.

He'd been watching the TV. The room was full of the sound of a football match commentator droning loudly and both the bedside lights were on. The light and noise felt like an intruder in my attempt at passion; it was too much for me. I didn't want to be naked and vulnerable in the harshness of the hotel lamps and television glare. I pulled away from his kiss and asked him to turn off the lights. He found the switch quickly and the room fell into semi darkness. He immediately took me back into his embrace and moved me towards the bed, the lower half of his body was pressed against my right thigh, and I could feel his cock pulsing, he was obviously ready for the foreplay to be over but there was still too much light and noise for me to be comfortable. I started to pull away, to ask him to do something about it and he must have sensed my unease, he found the remote and flicked the channels from TV to radio and the room emptied of most of its illumination and filled with the sounds of late night/early morning techno beats.

He was keen to keep going with the amorous mood and so was I, but I think it was for different reasons. His penis was joyfully bouncing against the fabric of his shorts, waiting to be released so it could join in. I was mortified by the whole situation, stunned into unresponsiveness, I wanted to get on with the sex so I could get the fear of it over and done with.

I'm not sure I was much help while he undressed me, and I'd no idea if the sex was any good or not, all I knew was I was in a dark room with a man who wasn't my husband. I needn't have sent Lilli on her wild goose chase to find a condom machine, he already had one and in a very practiced manner put it on himself with one hand while I lay stunned by embarrassment and terror. I didn't ask him to stop, and he didn't seem to sense how far removed I was from embracing his passion. How was he to know I had been so totally disengaged from the sensuality he was trying to create. He had no idea that before my husband had diminished any desire in me, I had been a different woman, not a fearful uptight sex partner but one who would have happily taken all this Adonis in black knickers had to give me and then gone back for seconds and thirds.

To him it must have felt like trying to seduce a plank of wood, he laid me on my back and spread my legs apart with one of his knees. I responded in a Pavlovian way. My body must have been prepared for him because I felt no pain as he started to penetrate me. My insistent need for concealment meant it was so dark in the room now I could just about make out the shape of him above me. Every thrust he made shook my body - he was moving on top of me, and the mattress was moving underneath me, I didn't join in with his efforts and there was no pleasurable sensation coming from my genitals at all. He leaned in towards my face and we started to kiss again. As soon as our tongues touched, I felt his body tense. He came quickly, and as he groaned with the release of his orgasm, he moved his face away from mine, which was probably a very good job because the need to vomit hit me so hard - I could already feel it rising up the back of my throat.

In my panic I threw him off me and commando rolled over the bed with my hands clamped over my mouth trying to stop the flow of sick leaving my body. I managed to get to the bathroom in time but didn't quite make it to the toilet. I did manage to reach the sink and once I was there I had no choice but to let myself go. The stream of vomit started and I thought it would never stop. At one point I came to my senses long enough to worry that the sink would be full before I'd finished puking.

He came to the bathroom door and turned on the light. Suddenly all my surreptitious attempts to cover my nakedness were wasted, my shyness shattered with the flick of a switch and the cruelest light of all flooded the room. Fluorescent tubes from the ceiling and behind the mirror shone bright silver. I caught sight of my reflection - my mascara was resting in an attractive manner on my cheekbones and forehead - I was naked, pale and retching over the sink. There was vomit on my chin, and as I went to wipe it away, I realised it was all over the palms of my hands too. I could see his reflection in the mirror and in amongst the madness, I noticed the sperm-filled condom hanging off the end of his shrinking knob.

In between heaves I asked him to leave me alone and to his credit he draped a towel over my shoulders and stepped out of the room. I looked at my reflection again. I was ashamed of myself, and of the overwhelming emotion and sense of loss for Tim while I'd been trying to have sex with someone else. I was a shambles. I tidied the bathroom as well as I could, I apologised profusely to the kind and concerned man, dressed and left his hotel room as quickly as I could.

****

When I eventually got back into my own room, Lilli was sitting on my bed drinking a miniature vodka from the fridge. I shared the story of my clusterfuck fuck with the boy-with-no-name from room 2250 and she laughed so hard she practically fell on the floor holding her sides and gasping for breath. Her reaction hadn't quite been what I'd expected. I was still feeling nauseous and humiliated and there wasn't one thing in the whole situation I could see to laugh about.

I was in the same frame of mind the day after when I called in to see Christine on my way home. As soon as he saw the look on my face, Pete made us both a cup of tea and then left the room. As I recounted my horrible experience, Christine sat perched on the edge of her chair, her jaw dropped in empathy at my plight. When I finished my tale of woe, I heard Pete guffawing from his eavesdropping spot behind the kitchen door. I felt the sides of my mouth tugged upwards a bit into the tiniest hint of a smile. Christine noticed it and, with what looked like quite a bit of relief, smiled back. "So, will you be seeing him again do you think?"

At which we both collapsed into peals of laughter.

By the time I eventually arrived home I'd realised that the more comical the story became in my mind the less ashamed I felt, and I was full of eager anticipation of being able to share it with Naomi. Unfortunately, today of all days was the time she'd decided to surprise me with an introduction to Sophie.

I was awestruck by the delicacy of Naomi's lover's facial features and fascinated with the surety she had over herself. I was so humbled by her presence I didn't want to look like a bumbling fool in front of this cool-as-a-cucumber character, so I found myself falling into my best behaviour.

I managed to keep the pretence up until after a couple of beers and a glass of red wine and then I couldn't keep back the narrative of the night before and it wasn't long before they were both gasping at the details of the whispered invitation and subsequent wait for an answer to my knock on the door. When I got to the orgasm, vomit, floodlit bathroom part, Nai's shoulders were shaking with the force of her mirth. Sophie looked terrified, trapped in between an appropriate sympathetic response and following her girlfriend's lead. When she eventually gave into herself and dropped her guard, it turned out she had an outrageously raucous chuckle. The three of us laughed so hard I nearly peed my pants.

We spent the rest of the evening bonding over food and wine. I liked Sophie a lot, and I could see Nai did too; there was a completeness about her I'd never witnessed before, like something had fallen into place for her.

At one point during the evening, I went outside for a cigarette. I sat in my favourite spot, the one that looks back towards the kitchen windows, and couldn't help but be drawn to the vision of them both, they were working together; Sophie was setting the table while Naomi finished cooking dinner, there was an ease in the way they moved around each other, a flow to their movements, they looked like they belonged together. Sophie touched Nai's cheek as she passed her, and Naomi responded by resting the side of her face into her hand, her expression was flooded with comfort and love, they both stopped everything else they were doing to enjoy the moment of contact. It was beautiful. I held my breath as I watched them, waiting for the familiar stab of pain that had been a continual feature of my life since the loss of Tim. It didn't come.

I wondered if envy was on its way instead but that didn't come either. I was happy for them, for both of them. And when Ivy asked me, *Is it what you want though Rachel, to be with someone like that again?* I thought about it while I finished my cigarette and I found I no longer knew the answer to that question.

9

My decision to commit to a new counsellor caused a positive shift in my mood and rather than my earlier reluctance I became infused with the determination to make the most of my solo sessions in the shrink's seat and the closer my appointment got, the more I looked forward to meeting Felicity, my new therapist.

I'd already noticed that despite the fact I'd been burning an immense amount of energy cleaning like a demon and being a social butterfly, the bone melting weariness I'd been experiencing pre-separation had lessened considerably.

My brain was no longer exhausted with the continual efforts to warn me of its perceived danger, because the peril was gone. I'd left it behind me along with most of the other accoutrements that had made up my life with Tim. My downward spiral had started because I chose to listen to Tim's lies over my own intuition; despite the continual warnings from Ivy, the inner voice who always had my back, I'd believed in him and ignored myself. By allowing his behaviour to reduce my self-worth to nothing I'd been complicit in his abuse. I'd become his victim and I hated myself for my weakness. What I was starting to appreciate now was my need to call a halt to the angst and heartache. I was ready to find some peace and quiet and allow myself the time and space to work out who I was.

In short, I was sick of Tim's influence on my life. I was ready to learn who I was when I wasn't seeing myself through the lenses of his unappreciative, porn-greedy eyes. Consequently, when Felicity first introduced herself (not a cord skirt in sight - much more Ms Westwood than Miss Marple), I wouldn't say I was ready to throw my arms round her and give her a hug, but I was eager to learn to trust her, and to allow her to lead me to a place where I trusted myself.

She listened carefully, occasionally taking notes on a yellow legal pad with a heavy looking gold and silver pen, while I took her through the details of my torment of the last few years. It was hard to hear myself describe the evaporation of my self-esteem and confidence as a result of my husband's lack of desire for me. Hearing myself tell her how I disliked myself so profoundly that I could no longer bear to look at my own naked body in the mirror, made me feel sad and a tiny bit angry.

In amongst the rest of the probing questions she had for me, she asked me when was the last time I'd enjoyed any physical intimacy.

Well, she had some intimacy last week, but using the word enjoyed would be a bit of an exaggeration. There was no way I was going to bring the presence of Ivy to the attention of this woman so instead I admitted that my fuckless year tally had gone on for nearly half a decade. I looked at her to see if she was shocked by the longevity of my patience/stupidity, but her facial expression remained neutral. I confessed to the re-start of my sex life the week before and its subsequent baptism of vomit. She had a completely different response to the rest of my confidants; she didn't even smile at the bit about the jizz-filled condom sliding down the flaccid dick.

She did point out to me though, that my need to be sick wasn't necessarily caused by the amount of alcohol I'd con-sumed, or even as a result of the motion of the dissatisfactory shag. She explained it was more than likely the fear of the situation and the undercurrent of grief I carried in me that had overloaded my already stressed-out brain with another metric fuck tonne (my words not hers) of emotions, and it had decided to hurl as much of the pain out of me as it could. She warned me that there may be other occasions that were similar, not after sex in particular, but times when the overspill of any heartache I might have lurking within me could well expose itself in the form of puke.

By the time my session was over I was quietly confident that with the help of Felicity, my new, well-attired, head-doctor, the journey into my single woman future may well be a thrill-ing adventure; one I was prepared for and one I was starting to believe I deserved.

When I got home to celebrate the spark of hope fizzing in my belly, I went onto every device I had that needed a pass-word and wiped any reference to Tim and our lives together. As a reminder to myself of who I was to become I changed them all to Joyfulgirl45.

It felt amazing.

****

The following day I flew out to Sardinia to see Jude. As I walked through the arrivals lounge - with my suitcase half full of fruit gums - I saw her before she saw me. She looked incredibly tanned, unstructured and chilled out. I could tell by her face and body language she was searching for me, but she was looking in the wrong direction. I was thrilled to be back in the same space as her, so much water had flowed under both our bridges and the need to feel her, to make her real again was becoming hard to contain.

Suddenly, as if she'd felt my eyes on her, she turned her head to exactly where I was - the beam of recognition lit up her features and we both screamed and ran towards each other. We flew into each other's arms, jumping up and down on the spot, laughing and crying at the same time. We pulled our-selves away every so often but as soon as we did, we returned to our fierce embrace.

It felt unreal that we were together again after all this time. There had been hundreds of text messages, phone calls and video chats between us, which had kept our friendship alive, but the reassurance that came from being in her presence was priceless.

We started talking even before the hugging stopped, we unconsciously fell into the familiar rhythm our conversations had always had; the flow of words and responses, knowing how the other would react to a certain subject or phrase, the snorts of laughter, the teasing, the sentences littered with swear words in place of punctuation. As we drove along the coast road, I kept catching glimpses of white sandy beaches, the sunshine reflected on the clear turquoise sea. There were mountain ranges on my right that spread far into the distance, this place was unknown to me, it was all waiting to be discovered; it filled me to the brim with anticipation.

I found myself fascinated by the confidence Jude had, that she could still talk while driving with uncon scious skill on the wrong side of the road. She seemed so at home in a place that was still so foreign to me, like she'd always been here. It highlighted how much I'd missed the subtle changes that had altered my friend from the person I'd known for most of my life to the version that was here right now; the same but entirely different.

We left the main highway and followed an unmade road for a while - it explained a lot about the dusty 4x4 she was driving. We eventually reached a pair of huge iron gates that opened slowly to let us in. I sensed her excitement, and her grin expanded even wider. "Get ready for this, Rach!"

I thought at the time she meant the first sight of the villa that suddenly sprang into view - a long single-storey stone and white-walled building. There was a riot of archways, curved walls, lush bougainvillea in a riot of colour and a veranda that appeared to go all around the house. Nestled deep inside the veranda was a solid looking, dark wood double door.

As Jude slowed to a stop, the doors flew open, and a riot of noise and action tumbled out of it. Several people came running towards the car, all smiling at me and shouting so their greeting could be heard over the others. From what I could gather in the confusion, there was a mixture of generations all willing to welcome me. I was beautifully overwhelmed.

The car door was opened for me and before I knew it, I was being swept towards the house. My attention was consumed by the smiling children around me, talking and laughing, jumping up to kiss my cheeks. They were on the point of dragging me into the house until, out of the corner of my eye, I saw a smiling figure walking towards me, his arms outstretched. I'd seen a thousand photos of Comitas and spoken to him hundreds of times, but finally facing the man who'd persuaded my best friend to leave her previous glamorous life and plans for corporate world domination, for one that involved living miles away from anywhere and bringing up four stepchildren, was a revelation.

He was shorter than I'd thought, his skin was sun-weathered, he was at least a decade older than Jude and me. As Jude walked past us, she slapped his arse, kissed his cheek and shouted the kids to leave us in peace for a bit. They followed their stepmother Pied Piper style into the house while I came to terms with just how much kindness there was in the dark brown eyes I was staring into.

I'd been a bit worried about meeting Comitas. He'd never really seen me at my best – whatever that was – and I was embarrassed by the number of times he must have overheard me speaking to Jude while I was livid with Tim, or messy with heartbreak, or so drained of my life force I could barely speak at all. I was concerned that by bringing all the bullshit from my life into theirs he would think I was a flaky, wobbly joy-sucker, but as he reached out to kiss my cheeks, he squeezed my shoulders in a way that conveyed such warmth and welcome, I melted into relaxation.

****

That evening we had dinner on the veranda. The photos she'd sent me did nothing to express the sheer beauty of the sweeping views of the vineyard and the ocean beyond. There were so many people sitting round the table, there was no way I could remember them all. I was a bit drunk, a tiny bit awe-struck but so happy to be surrounded by the joyful racket they created.

Jude shone; she emanated contentment. During the dinner I saw her and Comitas catch each other's eye and watched her discreetly flick her thumb towards one of the older women sat on my right — I later found out she was THE auntie - the one in the family that needed watching with the wine! The deeply intimate gesture demonstrated the affection and friendship between the two of them more than words ever could.

I went to bed that evening with a glow of contentment. I'd only half unpacked my suitcase (to share the sweets out), the rest of its contents were scattered across my mattress and the floor. I left it all where it was and climbed into bed and fell asleep immediately.

The next few days followed a pattern. Each morning I luxuri-ated in bed enjoying the smell of Jude's coffee as it permeated the whole house, and once silence had descended, and I knew the kids had gone to school I would go to find her. We would then spend the next few kid-free hours talking, looking at the view, swimming in the pool, eating delicious food, smoking duty-free cigs and drinking wine. Comitas came to join us at some point during the day, he never stayed for long but tried to keep up with our chatter, laughed a lot and then wandered off to do something else - he was great company. I was in para-dise. Jude and I talked over the events of the last few weeks, months, years - my wanking in the toilet after meeting AJ was a firm favourite with Jude – and me if I'm honest! I didn't ask if she was still in touch with Tim, I had a feeling she would be and I didn't want to give Ivy anything to moan about. Jude didn't offer up any insight into what was going on with him either, I had worried it might be a bit awkward, he'd been part of both our lives for so long, it had been him and me, me and her, and her and him, it was hard to remember a time when he wasn't there, and I was relieved and delighted that our friendship was strong enough to evolve beyond him.

Jude got busy again when the kids came home from school, and I used it as an excuse for a siesta. Once homework was finished, they'd insist I get up and play in the pool with them for a while before dinner. I was honoured to be included in everyone's day and so happy to be with Jude. I was sleeping well, enjoying myself, and it was good to be away from all the reminders of my life. I felt free.

The new life Jude had chosen was far removed from what it had been before, and yet she'd embraced it in its entirety. She was incredibly knowledgeable about the business at the vineyard, spoke Italian with confidence, the kids quite clearly adored her and Comitas looked at her with so much love in his eyes it was hard not to stare at him while he stared at her. She was deeply embedded in this family life. Even the auntie that drank too much and was grumpy when she didn't have a glass in her hand cheered up when she was in Jude's presence.

She's changed so much, she's happy and content with her life.

I had to agree with Ivy. From my newfound vantage point as the watcher of my friends' lives, I could sense a completeness in Jude. She was intrinsically still her, but her cockiness and hard edges had been quietly rubbed away, replaced by a calm, gentle self-assurance.

She's filled out, and I don't just mean her body.

It was true, Jude had changed shape in so many ways. She was softer, rounder, her personality and her body. Giving her punishing treadmill workouts a miss suited her as much as this life she was living.

She's become a whole person. She's kinder. I bet this woman wouldn't have ever been on Tim's side, ever - she'd have followed you out of the skanky lap dance club that night, taken you home and tucked you into bed while telling you what a complete twat your husband was. In fact, this version of Jude wouldn't have suggested you go to a lap dance bar in the first place.

I wished with all my heart it had been that way, but I didn't want to think about strippers, hookers and dogging anymore, I needed to learn to leave all the melodrama behind me.

Ivy wasn't quite ready for that yet.

Do you think you had this kind of love with Tim? Did you ever shine with happiness in your partner's presence like you've seen both Naomi and Jude do recently?

The truthful answer was my medical diagnosis had broken my rose-tinted post breakup glasses, I was finally starting to see the truth and I couldn't even recall anymore a time when the love I had for my husband hadn't been tinged with anger, disappointment or mistrust. I had no memory of feeling safe with him. The wholeness that now suffused Jude, the belong-ingness to Comitas and the life they had together, those things had left my marriage a long time ago; I couldn't summon into my mind how it felt to love fearlessly like she was doing now. There was no tenderness left in my heart for Tim. I'd lived with the grief of my relationship for so long I hadn't fallen out of love with him as much as become consumed by hatred for his steady trickle of treachery that had eroded me from the inside out.

I watched Jude in the same way as I had Naomi a few days before, without any envy at all. I was convinced she'd be happy with Comitas; I would have to be blind not to see what this life had already given her. I also knew it was nothing like the existence I'd left behind, and comparing my love, my marriage, to the intimacies of the relationships I was privy to, was the wrong thing to do. There was no comparison.

I'd been fooling myself for years that what I had was worth fighting for and now it was time to let go once and for all.

10

The following day was Friday. As soon as I got the first waft of Jude's kick-ass coffee brewing, I rolled myself out of bed, made my way into the kitchen and began impatiently watching the machine, waiting for it to finish pouring my perfect cuppa. I was on a mission; I'd made up my mind it was time to start cutting some ties and I didn't want to wait until after the weekend to start the process. I was seizing the day.

The kids came into the kitchen one by one, each showing surprise in their own comical way at me being functional before they were on the school bus. I was getting quite fond of this brood - to think I'd wondered where Jude had found her maternal instincts from, and here I was, happy to be everyone's favourite auntie. Note to self, be careful not to be that auntie - the one that has a reputation for getting drunk all the time.

Once I'd got my brew, I settled myself in a shady spot on the veranda overlooking the pool and the view of the ocean which, this morning, was such a stunning blue it was hard to tell where it ended, and the sky began. It felt apt to be surrounded by such incredible beauty whilst beginning to get rid of the ugly past.

The first thing I did was contact the solicitor Naomi's boss had recommended. There really wasn't much for her to do. Tim and I had already sorted our financial situ ation out; I had a brand-new solo-named bank account with a very healthy balance, and I was expecting a couple more payments as the rest of our assets were liquidated. All of which had already been broken down in the finest detail on the business-like spreadsheet of our finances which had accompanied the business-like email Tim had sent me as his proposal for our immediate and un-messy separation; on the very day we were separated. Devious bastard.

I got a swift reply from the lawyer explaining my possible grounds for divorce. Did I think, she said, I could provide enough grounds to establish my husband's unreasonable behaviour?

Hell yes, and then some, Ivy and I said at the same time.

She informed me that if I could, I should let her know the 'nitty gritty' details of my reasons for wanting to disassociate myself from my husband so rapidly and she would move forward with it as quickly as possible.

When I was confident that I had solid legal support I contacted Tim. I tried several times to compose the email until I finally managed to find the right tone; unemotional and straight to the point. I told him I was ready to finish what he'd started; I informed him of my solicitor's details and told him to organise one of his own immediately. I suggested, as it was the last thing to tie us together, he should put the house on the market as soon as possible and sent him the details of a couple of estate agents I'd heard good things about - I even offered to contact them myself to arrange valuations if he wanted. All the time I was typing my hands were shaking slightly and they dithered over the keyboard of Jude's laptop while I worked out how to sign off the email. Ivy came up with a couple of crackers. *Bet you weren't expecting this you recidivist wank-addict,* was one I liked. *See ya cunty,* was another, simpler and more to the point. But in the end, I just typed my name and sent it quickly, before Ivy could tempt me to add a fuck you p.s. to it. "Dignity was your idea, Ivy," I reminded her, sternly.

I hadn't had any contact with him since he'd informed me of my *(optimum)* window of opportunity to get some of my things out of the house so I'd no idea what he'd been up to since we'd split - I could hazard a guess though. I sincerely hoped that when this email dropped in his inbox it might knock him off his stride a bit - maybe even ruin his weekend if I was lucky. I closed the laptop lid with a flourish and, imagining the email making its way through the ether into his inbox, I flicked it the V's and blew a raspberry at the same time.

I'd anticipated feeling sad at this point, but I became distracted by the sight of the swimming pool. There wasn't a breath of wind to disturb its surface, it was so motionless and flat it appeared like glass. I was immediately tempted to be the one to break its tranquility and without any further thought I stripped naked and slid myself gently down the side of the pool wall into the chilly water. As my body responded to the change in temperature, my skin tingled with tiny shocks and goose pimples. I carried on with my slow immersion, my nipples hardened as my breasts and shoulders slid beneath the surface. I resisted the urge to shudder with the cold, I didn't want to disturb the water any more than I already had for now. I rested where I was until the surface recovered from my movement and became still again, I was breathing slowly through my nose enjoying the sensation of my lungs expanding and as my muscles started to melt into relaxation, I began to weep. There wasn't a sound to my tears, no wail escaped me, nor any rib-breaking sobs bursting out of me. It was a delicate release of emotion and as it spilled from me, I felt the warmth of the tears on my face in contrast with the cool of the rest of my skin. I didn't attempt to wipe them away, instead I started to swim with slow deliberate strokes, watching the water part with unhurried serenity as I passed through it, feeling it caress my skin. I watched the ripples extend in front of and around me and continued to weep softly as I swam length after length.

Eventually I rested again. I laid on my back and floated lazily on the surface, and as the heat of the sun began to warm my naked body, my breath caught at the back of my throat a couple of times and my tears stopped; a sense of relief flowed through me followed by a deep sense of peace.

When I was ready to leave my haven, I pulled myself out of the pool closest to the cabana and found a fresh towel. I loved this little space, it was painted pale blue and white with floor to ceiling muslin curtains draped across its many windows, providing privacy. A couple of long, low comfy chairs were positioned in the double doorway, the optimum place to enjoy the view. Behind the chairs was a wall of mirrors, they were cleverly placed to catch the reflection of everything on the outside, to give the sense of being surrounded by the light dappling on the pool that was in the process of repairing itself after my disturbance, the gardens, the vineyards and the ever-present ocean beyond.

The early afternoon light was flattering. I looked at my reflection; my body and hair were still dripping wet; I had the towel clutched to my chest protecting my modesty.

Who are you hiding yourself from? There's no one here to see you.

"Me. I'm hiding myself from me."

Don't do that to yourself. Felicity set you some homework - maybe this is the time to do it. Drop the towel, be brave, look at yourself, find your favourite bits of you.

I'd spent so long being ashamed of my form and its inability to stop my husband spending money on images of bald pussies and fake tits, I felt almost embarrassed to reveal myself to myself.

But Ivy was right. I needed to do this.

I dropped my towel, and for the first time in years I looked directly at myself. I had a light tan from the few days lolling about in the spring sunshine, the light shining behind me was complimentary. I was relieved about that.

My pre-holiday bush tidy-up had created a neat triangle of trimmed pubes, the shaved side bits were already starting to grow back leaving me with the groin equivalent of an 8 o'clock shadow. I studied my thighs - they'd always a bit too chubby for my liking — no thigh gap - but they were reasonably toned from my years at the gym, my calves were shapely, my ankles were slim and as I looked at my feet, I appreciated them even more because they weren't squashed into high heel shoes. I liked the look of them when I was bare-footed, I supposed they were a bit cute really.

I knew I'd been carrying more weight as a side-effect of my anti-depressants, but I was still well proportioned. My belly was a bit rotund, and I definitely had some back fat, but I had a classic hourglass shape to me, it was actually quite lovely. With huge thanks to my mum's genes, my tits were ample and still quite firm. After years spent with other women as lovers, sisters, friends and changing room partners, I'd come to realise that my nipples were unusually large, they were sensitive too and responded to the gentle stroke I gave them now by in-stantly hardening and sending a rush of pleasure into the core of my body.

I'd never quite managed to achieve Madge's sculptured arms but my shoulders were broad and strong, my neck was long, and my face was the same one I'd been looking at for over forty years. I was definitely starting to show my age, but in a strange way it suited me. And now I came to think about it, my smile had once been described as a 9.5 on the Richter scale. I remembered I was very fond of grinning once upon a time. I had a crack at it now and watched as my crows feet became laughter lines that crinkled attractively. I liked it, and I really liked the freckles that had come out to celebrate the Sardinian sunshine.

The homework Felicity had set me had been for me to decide which parts of my body I loved the most, I was still trying to decide which bits of me I could admit to being my favourite, when a long low wolf whistle brought me back from my tunnel vision. I knew without looking it was Jude. In our mid-teens during one of our six-week holidays from school, we'd been together almost constantly, and she'd decided she wanted to learn to whistle between her fingers; it nearly broke us up once over. She drove me bonkers with it, until one day completely out of the blue it happened. I was relieved and she was delighted, and spent the next few years blasting out saucy whistles at any given opportunity.

She came into the cabana and threw herself onto one of the chairs. "What you up to, you sexy bitch?"

I was mortified that she'd caught me out, studying myself like this. "My homework. Felicity says I've to find two things I like about my body before my next session."

Jude turned to study me. "How are you supposed to choose just two things from all of that gloriousness you carry round with you?"

I snorted. "Fuck off Jude, I'm serious here; I'm swaying towards my nipples and my feet, I'm thinking they're my best features."

I watched the lob-sided reflection of her face pull a puzzled grimace. "Rachel, you are one of the most gorgeous women I've ever met, you're beautiful and funny and sexy. I'm so sad you can't see that. I understand why you feel down on yourself right now, but it won't be long before all the confidence that's been stolen from you comes back, and when it does a magic little light will come on inside you and you'll be irresistible. You'll love yourself and you'll have lovers beating your door down. I promise."

The idea sounded quite tempting to me. "Well, if I'm going to be as sex busy as you say I am, I hope I don't puke up after every time otherwise I'll have no energy for the next one."

"That's more like the attitude you need! Now - I have come to propose something to you. The kids are due back in an hour or so and it's the weekend." I picked my towel up from the floor and covered myself up, that was enough exhibitionism for one day. I sat in the other chair. "If we get a move on, we can be gone by the time they get home - I think it's time for us to go and have some Jude and Rach time, don't you?"

I sat to attention. "What, a night out?"

Jude frowned. "Nah we've got some celebrating to do, let's go away for the weekend. I know just the place."

11

We'd had many weekends away together in a surplus of places. On one occasion in Ibiza in our mid-twenties we'd spent so much on hotels, drink and Class As we could have bought a decent second-hand car with the money. Another time we went to London for the day but we were having so much fun we missed our last train home and had the most outrageous time with two gay guys in a flat in Paddington – some of the details of that weekend are still lost to me nearly three decades later. I could go on; we have a hundred stories that start with each other in the mood to party, involves some kind of mischief, that leads to an adventure and more often than not results in a massive hangover at the end of it.

But it felt different this time, as Ivy had pointed out, Jude didn't seem like the same woman who'd taken us to a lap dance bar in order to explore her bi-sexuality, she was calmer, more settled than I'd ever known her.

She wasn't the only one who was morphing into another person, this time last week I would have told you that I had no idea who I was anymore but my decision to start the divorce ball rolling had started a shift in me, I was still infused with the afterglow of my naked swim and cathartic weep and I was beginning to feel a change coming on, I was ready to become a work in progress. The thought of my unknown future created a thrilling under current in my belly that pulled the corners of my mouth into a soft smile.

****

We were only an hour or so away from Jude's home but slap bang in the middle of a tourist town that boasted bars, restaurants, markets and shops. Jude had booked us a two-bedroom apartment with a balcony overlooking a busy street. After the isolation of the vineyard, it felt wonderful to be in such a bustling place.

The first evening we went to a seafood restaurant, it was one of her and Comitas' favourite places she told me. They loved it here and came often, Jude was greeted like a long-lost friend, and we were shown to a table with the best people-watching spot in the whole place. We sat side by side looking out onto the street as people promenaded past us. Happily, we reverted to our familiar game of trying to guess the relationship between the couples we saw, making each other laugh as our stories became more bizarre as we went along.

The restaurant was busy in a relaxed, no real rush kind of way, we drank, and we talked. We'd always been able to fill any available space between us with words, they didn't always mean a great deal but talking was what we loved to do with each other. Our mirth was endless, we laughed constantly, infused with a couple of beers and the fact that there was no one else (children) to hear us I told Jude the story of the night with Lilli again and the man/boy with the scrummy arse and a hotel sink full of sick. "Course you know I've had a lot of time to think about why he came to me with his room number rather than Lilli."

Jude frowned at me "Why do you think he did that?"

"Well Lil is a top-notch chick; she has something of the scattered rose petals on silk sheets about her, she looks too much like hard work for a one-night stand, but I was easy pickings, probably came across as grateful for any old shag. I was the low hanging fruit, wasn't I?" Jude plonked her drink down in a way that indicated she was a bit exasperated. "No, Rachel you weren't, you are every bit as attractive as Lilli, you're even more so than she is because you don't have her aloofness, he more than likely thought you were an attractive woman who had made him laugh and looked like a right filthy ride." She paused for breath, and to light a smoke. "It's time to take your knobhead husband's eyeballs out of your head, see yourself through your own for a change, it's time to appreciate how beautiful you looked this afternoon when you were having your little re-acquaintance with your naked self." Two more beers appeared magically in front of us. "Besides, from what I can gather the pre-sick sex wasn't up to much, maybe he needed someone to practice with - maybe he's the one who's grateful you turned up at his door, did you ever think of that?"

"Oh god Jude, I hope I wasn't his first time, the poor lad will be traumatised for the rest of his life." We burst into laughter again, the seriousness of the conversation dropped in favour of something more suitable for a Friday night in a Sardinian tourist town.

The following day we went for a wander and an explore. After a browse through a lively market we hit a rich seam of boutiques, shoe shops, artisan jewellers and an art gallery. We mooched in and out of the shops for a good part of the day, we roamed along winding alleys as one lead into another until, like magic, we found ourselves in the middle of a huge square full of bars, cafes and restaurants. Even though it was late afternoon the atmosphere was vibrant, with lots of people eating and drinking. Jude and I smiled at each other as if we'd won the jackpot, we made our way to the place closest to us and found a quality spot right in the eyeline of the guy behind the bar.

We eventually left there five hours later; and made our way for a meal from the restaurant next door. By the time we'd devoured suckling pig and a bottle of red we were drunk and full of food, the only thing on my mind was getting back to our apartment so I could unfasten my pants, take my bra off, scratch under my tits and lie down.

That had been the plan, until we turned into one of the alleyways we thought would take us in the direction of home and what had been a quiet, quaint little street that afternoon was now crammed with people having a party, it was so busy we had to turn our bodies sideways to get through the crowds, the rhythmic dance music was coming from a variety of bars creating a celebratory energy, accompanied by the undeniable, irresistible smell of weed.

All thoughts of going home were gone and within half an hour we were dancing to some amazing tunes, we had beer and scored a spliff. Maybe neither of us had changed as much as I thought.

****

When I woke up the next morning, with a well-deserved hangover, I found myself having to concentrate hard to find the memories from the night before. I had the vaguest notion that we'd had a brilliant time, but the details were proving hard to find just for the moment.

I sniffed the air searching for an olfactory clue that Jude was awake, but the absence of the smell of coffee forced me to get myself out of bed to see where she was; there she lay, uncovered and face down on her bed sprawled out in a very un-step-motherly fashion – at least she'd managed to take most her clothes off. I took the responsibility for making the coffee I knew she'd need and as I stood waiting for it to brew, I had a couple of vivid flashbacks. A bar, the spliff, fantastic music and some gorgeous people.

And the guy, you forgot the guy.

Oh my god, the guy.

The recollections came then, thick and fast. I'd been stood at the bar in a packed-out club, two cold bottles of beer in my hand. I was waiting for my change from the waitress with a pair of arse cheek revealing shorts when I noticed the guy stood opposite was staring at me with undisguised admiration. He was wiry but his muscles stopped him being too skinny, he had long unruly sun-bleached hair and deeply tanned skin. It was obvious he was a lot younger than me, but my confidence was boosted by my recent hedonistic indulgences and Jude's continual insistence that I was worthy of some attention and instead of turning away from his stare as I would have done nearly every day for the last twenty-odd years, I met his gaze full on and pulled out my best 'come and get me' smile.

My next memory was of being stood in a street full of people having fun, surrounded by music with heavy bass and throbbing beats, the feel of a wall against my back and the front of the flirty blondie's body up against mine, his hands in my hair as he pulled my face into his space, into a kiss, into many, many kisses; they were good ones too. Wow, check me out, I'd pulled!

"Coffee, I can smell coffee" she came to me holding her hand out for the cup and headed straight outside to sit on the balcony, "So" she called over her shoulder "Blonde, skinny, kite surfer dudes hey?" She laughed. "He was cute, babe. I think your light might be on." I was delighted at myself and my stranger-snogging skills, it was fun to let my hair down. It made me feel a bit wild.

I liked it, a lot.

****

I've never known Jude not have a hair of the dog the day after a big session and today was no different, we went out for brunch and ordered a bloody Mary each. We had planned to stay another night, but I could sense she was unsettled "Do you want to go home, Jude?" she turned to look at me "Oh, Rach I was just thinking that, I want to go home to Comitas and the kids! I haven't been away from them for this long before. I never expected to miss them so much, they drive me up the wall most of the time but being away from the little buggers has made me realise I love them to bits." She bit her bottom lip and raised her eyebrows in surprise as she said, "I want to go home and make sure they're all ok and get them ready for school tomorrow, oh shit Rachel I'm some small people's mum, I think this feeling I'm having might be responsibility." We both laughed at the comic timing of the waiter bringing us two more drinks immediately after her shocked disclosure.

"Do you mind if we go home today babe? I know we have the apartment another night but..." I was eager to support her and her new found sense of duty, to encourage her to go into the family life that obviously suited her so much, but I knew absolutely I didn't want to go with her. "Of course not Jude, if you need to go then go, but if it's ok with you I'm going to stay." I watched as a grin spread across her face "Wow, that's a great idea, I'll come and get you tomorrow then shall I?"

Noooooooooo, that's too soon.

I said, "I'm thinking I might stay on here a bit longer and have a few days on my own." I couldn't wait to spend some time alone.

She left an hour or so later and I went to explore the parts of the town we'd missed yesterday. I wandered the streets for a while and found my way to the beach, it wasn't bikini weather, but it was warm enough for a girl from the UK to hire a sunbed to chill out on and I passed a happy couple of hours people watching and having a natter with Ivy.

We decided that despite what I'd said to Jude I wouldn't stay here for a few more nights, if we were going to have an adventure, we were going to have a proper one. On my way back from the beach I called in at a car hire place I'd spotted the day before, I could see the guy behind the counter suss me out and mentally start rubbing his hands together as he moved towards the top-end, more expensive cars, the ones with air-con and leather seats, but I am the queen of negotiation and

I left twenty minutes later with a totally bashed-up red jeep with holes in the canvas roof and an ashtray that hadn't been emptied since it came off the production line about ten years ago. It suited me just fine.

12

I set off on my road trip in my shagged-out red jeep and not much of a plan apart from a plotted route for the day and my accommodation booked for that evening. I had no idea if I would find my feet and enjoy my little taste of solo travelling or be back on Jude's doorstep the following day, but I knew for sure I had to give it a go. The other side of the road thing was uncomfortable for a while but with the help of Ivy the driving instructor combined with closing my eyes and putting my foot down at a couple of roundabouts, I didn't make too many mistakes and by the time I arrived at my first destination I was confident with my adapted driving skills.

I was so distracted with the challenge and adventure of my road trip it was a couple of days before I realised that I hadn't logged on to my emails since I'd contacted Tim the week before. When I eventually got round to it – thanks to the free Wi-Fi in the restaurant I was sat in - my inbox was full of the usual spam of special offers for all kinds of things I didn't really want or need - no thanks, I don't want to be hypnotised into eating less, where's the fun in that? - so it took me a while to scroll through them until I found Tim's familiar email address, the one we'd set up together donkeys years ago when we got ourselves connected to the latest must-have thing called the internet and bought our first PC - you know the computer I mean, the one that eventually ended up being Tim's pornography playmate. Seeing an unread email from him didn't create the aerobic zone heart rate I was expecting nor the dread that would usually cause my fingers to shake as I opened it, I'm not saying there was of that at all, that would be a lie - but its intensity was dialled down considerably.

His email was brief, he agreed to selling the house. "But I will sort the agents, there's no need for you to get involved at all, I will ensure you are appraised of the valuations when I get them."

Appraised of the valuations? Seriously? What a knobhead. I suppose they'll be optimum negotiations, will they?

"I will find a solicitor as soon as I can after the weekend. I agree to you divorcing me on the grounds of unreasonable be-haviour, but please may I ask that you don't vilify me with your reasons for wanting to formalise our separation so quickly."

Because I was sat in a public place, hugely chilled out from what I was beginning to consider my magical getaway, and just about to eat a meal I was very much looking forward to, I didn't react immediately to his reply, instead I logged out of my email account and put my phone firmly on its screen as if that would prevent the words in the message from affecting me any further; and tried to forget about it.

That night I slept badly, I tossed and turned for ages and when I did finally succumb to sleep my dreams were full of tales involving a massive injustice, one that I couldn't put right no matter how hard I tried. In my dreams I was frustrated to the point of anger and sadness. The next morning, despite the glorious weather and my thrill at carrying on with my travels, my energy levels were at rock bottom, my legs were heavy and ached badly, gravity was not my friend that day, every-thing weighed me down and I hadn't felt so fatigued for quite some time.

An hour or so into my drive I was assailed by a view so breath-taking I pulled over to the side of the road and sat for a while, taking time to soak up the spectacular vision of the inland mountains and the coastline beaches and ocean. From my vantage point there wasn't another soul in sight as far as my eye could see, no cars, no people, just peaceful sounds of birds singing and insects having a chat to each other, the sun was warm enough now to create a faint heat haze that gave everything an otherworldly, misty hue. I was completely alone on this piece of the planet, just me, my red Jeep and the memory of the request from Tim not to tell the truth, the whole truth and nothing but the truth to the divorce court. All for appearance's sake - so he didn't come across as a heartless bastard to the strangers that would officiate over the end of our marriage. His words were drip, drip, dripping into my brain and melting my peace and contentment.

Ivy said, *I know he's not quite asking you to lie about his behaviour, but he might as well be, you know that don't you?*

I didn't want to think about this stuff now, this was the brain equivalent of breaking the calm surface of the swimming pool, I knew once I'd started the ripples of mental torture they would go on for a very long time, but she carried on neverthe-less. She was merciless.

He's asking you to be complicit in his self-deception, he wants to keep pretending that he's a nice guy and he's asking you to support his idea of himself, so he can still look himself in the eye. He's asking you for a favour, the cheeky prick.

In an effort to get away from my inner voice I started the engine again and set off with such ferocity I left a dust cloud behind me, I tried to drive the anger away, but the winding roads were slowing me down. I needed a release. I needed to let go of the fury his arrogance had infused in me, the force of it created a shudder that shook my whole body, I felt physically sick, I had no choice but to let it all release out of me with a scream that came from every cell in my body, the louder I screamed the better the release felt. I shouted and swore, I banged my hands against the body of the car, I grabbed the steering wheel tight and rocked backwards and forwards. A long roar left me almost like I was exorcising the memory of his careless, selfish words, and following swiftly behind it was a maniacal laugh that took me so long to get control of I was back down the other side of the mountain and heading towards the coast before it stopped.

When I eventually got to my accommodation, I parked the car, dumped my bags in my room at the B & B I'd booked and quickly found a bar by the beach and decided to get completely smashed.

By the time I was on my third beer I was mellowing out a bit and starting to appreciate the beauty of the place I'd just driven to. I breathed deeply and tried to concentrate on the sights that were in front of me right now rather than the torment of my past. I was due to go back to Jude's tomorrow and I didn't want to ruin my last night alone by allowing Tim to spoil what had been a truly life changing experience.

I asked for my bill but before the waiter could bring it for me, I found myself with unexpected company, my table for one had suddenly become a table for two. The seat across from me had a bum on it. I turned to look at whoever it was that had invaded my space so rudely with my best hard stare. A deep voice with heavily accented English spoke. "Hello, I hope you are well today?"

Oh here we go, he's going to try and sell you a watch, or a rip off designer handbag or timeshare or something equally dodgy.

I allowed Ivy's suspicion to flood into my tone of voice as I said, "Can I help you?" He smiled, a truly dazzling smile that lit up his face, he had gorgeous white teeth, he was olive skinned, tanned, late 40's, a bit of salt and pepper in his hair and goatee, fit but not buff and well-dressed but not flashy - it's amazing what one glance can reveal. As I was taking in the sight of him, he carried on talking. "It's so strange we should run into each other again. I have found myself thinking of you and wishing

I had spoken to you last weekend." His accent was so smooth, so sexy, and I was intrigued by his comment; I decided to give him a few more minutes of my time. I raised my eyebrows and nodded sharply, giving him permission to carry on.

"On Friday evening, in the seafood restaurant I was with my sister at the next table to you, I saw you with your friend and you interested me straight away. I'm sorry to admit that I found myself so fascinated by you I eavesdropped into your conversation" He had my complete interest now! I'd no idea he was ever in my vicinity, but he'd seen me, not only had he seen me, he'd remembered me, and couldn't get me off his mind...

Dingfuckingdong.

"I feel I have to tell you that, in my opinion, you are not the low hanging fruit as you described yourself. You are a very attractive and sexy woman, and any man should be lucky to have your attentions."

I began to reappraise my original thoughts about this man's intentions and accepted his offer of another drink, and when that one was finished, I bought him one back, we talked about nothing in particular, no heavy subjects at all. I told him about my trip, the places I'd visited and the fun I'd had, he was suitably impressed with my determination and courage to travel alone and laughed at my funny stories. He told me about his work (architect) his sister and her kids, and his renovation project on a property nearby. The sincerity of our flirting was obvious, his eye contact was almost hypnotic and when he leaned in towards me to light my cigarette and stroked the back of my hand at the same time, my nipples hardened instantly.

We talked for hours, the people walking past us changed from towel carrying sunbathers into freshly showered, cleanly dressed bodies in search of cocktails and dinner. We shared a plate of food and a bottle of wine and when we were done, we split the bill (at my insistence) and he offered to walk me back to my B & B.

Even without the distraction of the restaurant our chat was still easy and friendly, the playful tease between us was obvious so I don't know why I was so surprised when he moved towards me for a kiss. I was unprepared for such a display of affection, but I quickly remembered I'd recently discovered how much I liked kissing someone I fancied, and I found myself willing to join in the fun. Our mouths met with a passion that filled my entire body with heat.

His tongue was forceful and insistent, my response was equally so; I was so overwhelmed by it all, I couldn't catch my breath. I pulled back, moving away out of the intoxicating sexy space between us and said "Stop." He did as I asked and drew away without hesitation. "I'm so sorry Rachel, I think I must have misread you. I apologise if I overstepped the mark." He held his hands up palm forwards in supplication, I considered his attractive earnest face for less than half a minute. "That's ok, you didn't misread me I just wanted to be sure you'd stop if I asked you to," I smiled. "You can carry on now if you like."

When we returned our concentration back to the kiss there wasn't any doubt about what we both wanted. My tear-jerking grief, my scream-inducing anger were all washed away, I had no room for any of that. I was so filled with the thought of sex, there was no space left in my mind for anything other than this stranger who was treating me like a desirable woman; and my need to feel him all over my body.

By the time we arrived at the quirky white building with the flower filled window boxes that was my accommodation I was full to the brim with desire for this man, there was no discussion about whether or not he should come to my room it was a given that we were going to lie down together without our clothes on and once we'd closed the door of my spacious bedroom we went about the process of taking them off ourselves and each other as quickly as we could. Our kissing only halted briefly so he could pull my t-shirt over my head and his bra removing skills were so adept I almost stopped to ask him where he'd learned that one-handed trick from, but there was no way I was going to interrupt the flow of this foreplay, it was nothing short of magnificent. My suitcase and bag were still in the middle of the bed where I'd thrown them in my Tim temper tantrum hours ago, we worked round them. The first time.

The second time – less than half an hour later - we had sex in the shower, my soon to be ex-husband had never been up for sex in the shower - he preferred it in the back of a car apparently. I on the other hand, loved the mixture of soap, water and genitals, they are the perfect combination providing warm, wet and bubbly lubrication, what's not to love? It was at this point in the proceedings I appreciated how useful my years of yoga classes were, fucking with abandon in small spaces requires an immense amount of flexibility.

I was so deep into the throes of passion I nearly missed Ivy as she brought my attention to the position I was in; *Pssst Rach, I know you're a bit busy babe but check yourself out, you're in the shower, slippy with shower gel and water, bending forward, stood on one leg with the other one wrapped round your lovers waist, who happens to be fucking you from behind, if you lean forward a tiny bit more and look between your legs you can see his cock sliding into you, and while you're there...*

I didn't hear the rest, the suggested glance towards the erect penis thrusting into me was enough, my orgasm was multi-sensory, the sight of the sex someone was enjoying having with me, the sound of his wet body slapping against mine, the feel of the warm water running over our conjoined bodies, the taste of Tea Tree oil and mint shower gel and then another sound; his groan as he started to come, I was overwhelmed by my own senses. I've never been a quiet woman, my orgasms have always been welcomed and celebrated with gusto, and this evening was no different; the release of the need and desire for this passionate, uncomplicated physical connection was honoured with a moan that seemed to start deep inside my vagina and force its way through my body and was eventually expressed as the most glorious sound I'd ever heard; the sound of me reaching a climax that signified the end of years and years of uninvited, enforced chastity; it was the sound of finding my freedom, my own-self, my much missed sexuality.

And I was in the shower.

13

A couple of days after I got back from my holidays I ran into Alison. If I had a list of people I never wanted to see again she would have been very close to the top of it. Still, the fickle finger of fate had evidently decided we were going to be in the supermarket at the same time and nothing I could do now could prevent it. I tried to dodge her. As soon as I clapped my eyes on her I skidded myself and my heavy trolley round the corner to the next aisle as quickly as I could. For a brief, giddy moment I thought I'd got away with it, until I heard her call my name. I could have pretended that her voice, like fingernails down a blackboard, hadn't got my attention and carried on regardless but I knew deep down there was no getting away from her, at least not without giving her the satisfaction of knowing how trapped I felt by her proximity. Once she had me cornered, she approached me quickly, she didn't even try to disguise the evil delight on her face, I was sure I saw her lick her lips.

"Rachel, how wonderful to see you!"

Fuck off you vulture.

"You look absolutely gorgeous."

She did that thing that disingenuous people do when they pay you a compliment and then realise there's some truth to what they've just said, she stopped speaking her next sentence and stepped back a bit so she could see me in my entirety and said "Actually Rachel, you really do look gorgeous."

Don't sound so suprised you evil bitch.

I continued to keep myself from showing her how nervous she was making me. My tongue was stuck to the roof of my mouth it was so dry. "You have a tan too! You look so different. What is it about you?" She put her right hand on her hip and waved the red nail varnished forefinger of her left hand at me in a figure eight and wobbled her head from side to side.

If she calls you girlfreind now, please bite her stupid wiggly finger off.

I smiled slightly at the thought of carrying out Ivy's wishes, unfortunatley Alison took it as a friendly gesture and an invitation to carry on her babble. "I must say Rach, love, you're obviously doing a lot better than we've all been imagining you would be."

SHUT UP YOU HORRIBLE GOSSIPY SKANK.

I imagined her and all those other vitriolic nonentites I used to call 'friends' picking over the bones of my marriage.

I was about to tell her I'd been to see Jude but Alison was on transmit now, there was no way she was interested in hearing how well or otherwise I was getting on, all she wanted wanted to do was cause me harm, and she was going in for the kill. I could smell it coming off her, see her relishing every second of our accidental meeting, waiting for the moment she could deliver the fatal blow: and then she did it. The start of her next sentence had enough shock revelation to knock me off my feet and flat on my arse in the middle of Tesco.

"I was only saying to Tim's girlfriend the other day that you'd been quiet, that we hadn't seen you for ages. We were wondering if maybe you'd gone into hiding to lick your wounds. But," there went the finger waft again, and a fake tinkly laugh. "Judging by that tan you've been away somewhere! You lucky thing."

Why was she still talking? She'd done her harm, the least she could do now was flee the scene of her crime. Didn't she know it was time for her to leave me alone, so I could absorb the bullshit bombshell she'd just dropped on me? I could feel myself on the edge of a faint, my vision was blurry, my ears were ringing, bizarrely now my mouth kept filling with water that I couldn't swallow fast enough; it felt very much like pre-vomit juice.

I'd expected her to have something vile up her sleeve, but it wasn't that piece of news that she'd just thrown into her monologue so casually. Tim's girlfriend? What bloody girlfriend? Why was he parading a new woman around our social circle already? I wanted to cry, I wanted to scream at her, slap her, be sick, shake her so hard her hair extensions fell out, but Ivy's insistent voice came to me.

Take control Rach, breathe deep and remember dignity at all times, don't let her see what she's done to you, say something, wipe that self-satisfied look off her face, this might be your only chance. Do it now!

To my huge surprise I found a smile combined with a faint hint of battery acid, and with a voice that sounded very cool and not a bit fainty I said "Tim's girlfriend? Which one do you mean?"

It was Alison's turn to be on the back foot now and she looked suitably crushed, it was so delightful it motivated me to carry on. "Are you talking about the cute one with short dark hair? Do you mean that one?" She shook her head in the negative, wordless at last. "Oh, right, in that case you must mean the blonde!" Still speechless, she nodded. "I get so confused between them all, which is understandable I suppose because he has had so many of them, but I realise now, if it's the blonde one I'm thinking of, you're talking about the girlfriend he takes with him when he goes dogging." Ivy and I were high fiving each other while I watched her jaw drop. "Anyway, Alison, this has been fun, but I really must get on." I turned and walked away, leaving her where she was in the pet food section which was hugely appropriate because her mouth was opening and closing like a goldfish.

I had a bubble of laughter in my chest that under any other circumstances would have been a pleasure to let go of but the news that Tim had another woman burst it before it could be released. I knew logically it shouldn't have come as a shock that he had a girlfriend; he'd had at least one while we were still married so now we were officially separated then he was free to fill his boots with fresh female flesh, but the brevity between the end of our marriage and his introduction of my replacement to our shared acquaintances was positively indecent. By the time I'd got back to the safety of my car I could feel my bottom lip start to tremble. I had been living under the misapprehension that he'd done all the damage he could, that I was starting to see a faint glimmer of hope for my pride and self-respect, but this latest news was evidence of yet another way he'd chosen to dishonour me and our lives together, this was the ultimate 'fuck you' gift from him to me. He had moved on so quickly, it was yet more evidence that the email-plus-spreadsheet bombshell he had exploded on me had been a long time in the making. It had obviously been brewing during all my desperate, futile, but pathetically sincere attempts to rescue us; to administer mouth-to-mouth to our dying marriage. I had clearly been in a minority of one.

****

Naomi listened to me – once again – for as long as it took me to blow my stack, shout, scream and slam her kitchen cupboard doors closed as I put the groceries away at the same time as losing my shit – multi-tasking - I'm nothing if not efficient!

Then she did that thing she does so well, she took the whole situation and started to make it comical. I always enjoy this habit so much I joined in and before long we created different scenarios of my meeting with Alison and our subsequent upsetting conversation until it was so funny, I was doubled over holding my stomach and crying tears of laughter. When we'd eventually finished taking the sting out of it all, we had a beer and as we chinked our bottles together, we used our usual toast. "At least he's not dead."

I would be lying if I said I hadn't thought about Tim constantly since we'd separated, but I was working hard to come to terms with my life, and his, as single people, as two people learning to live without each other. I hadn't expected him to have moved on so quickly, Ivy was a bit puzzled as to why I still managed to be surprised by his disloyalty but I couldn't help myself, it hurt and I openly admit the news created a few more sleepless nights for me, or I would sleep and then when I woke my first thought was of them both. Tim and the blonde girl, sharing the intimacies that transcended sex; that's what hurt me most. Where he put his cock wasn't really that important, I'd watched him shagging her after all, I knew he was a slave to his penis, I'd got used to thinking like that, it was the thought of another woman seeing the bit of hair behind his left ear that stuck out at a weird angle or watching his naked arse when he walked to the bathroom, the two of them dancing round the kitchen while they were making dinner together. Those were the images that cut me to the quick.

It was my experience in Sardinia that kept me going through my darkest days, the entire trip had left me with an afterglow that was almost radioactive. I'm not surprised Alison thought I looked different, because I was, and it wasn't just the sex that had started the revolution of my feelings about myself.

While we're on the subject – the night of my coincidental meeting with the Sardinian branch of my fan club, I'd had more sex than I'd had with Tim for the last ten years of my marriage.

But who's counting?

"Well, you, were Ivy. You kept the score."

Oh, yeah. True. Ok, carry on.

After the shower yoga fuck, there was another quick and dirty one on the bed. After a beer and shared ciggie on my balcony I insisted he show me the one-handed bra removal trick again and he did it with such flair it would have appeared churlish not to reward his skills with a BJ. After that I lost count of the glorious ways I orgasmed there were so many. We did fall asleep at some point, but I seemed only to have closed my eyes for a few seconds before I felt my nipples being teased with dampened fingertips of one hand while the fingers of the other caressed my clit, both parts of my body responded immediately to the attention and I lay on my back with complete abandon while my lover used his fingers to make my nerve endings explode into the most delightful moan-making pleasure.

Our post-post-post-post-post-post coital chat the following morning turned to his plans for us that day, but I had no time for the walks on the beach and long lunches he was suggesting, my itinerary was already set, and it involved a four to five hour drive to get back to Jude's in time to surprise the kids when they got home from school.

When we realised we only had a couple of hours left together before we needed to go our separate ways the mood changed completely. The dirty tease and gymnastic sex stopped, replaced with tender, gentle kisses, delicate slow movements that made my body tingle with a different kind of anticipation, and when our foreplay came to its natural conclusion we automatically chose the face-to-face missionary position, our eyes never leaving each other's so we could witness the depth of our lust and our need to be connected.

After a huge, post coital breakfast and a kiss that nearly had me booking back into the hotel, I drove away from the kerb where he was stood with only one backward glance and a long-armed wave out of the broken soft top, my lips were swollen from kissing, my body ached from our karma sutra sex marathon, but the smile on my face was a mile wide. I'd no regrets about leaving, I'd run out of condoms for one thing and for another it felt like the right time to abscond with a wank bank full of fond memories and an injection of euphoria that beat any drug high I'd ever had.

14

May 2012

I'd been off for work for nearly five months by the time I went back. It was decided as part of my phased return I would spend the first couple of weeks breaking myself in gently with the help of Laura my (ex) trainee. It was a wise decision. I loved Laura, she was full of youthful energy and enthusiasm and despite her almost anarchic attitude to the corporate world she was a natural at her job.

Observing her work with passion and drive was like watching a flash back of myself pre-poorliness, once upon a time I would have seen her as a professional rival, my natural competitive instinct (thanks, Dad!) would have kicked in and no matter how much I cherished our friendship I would have been compelled to find a way to be better than her. However, I was amazed to discover I didn't mind that she was such a roaring success with the clients I'd spent nearly a decade developing relationships with; in theory she'd stepped in for me on a temporary basis, but the reality was she'd taken over my territory and made it her own.

I had taught her well.

I tried to settle back into my role, to reacquaint myself with my previous enthusiasm for the world of medical sales, networking and monthly targets but it seemed someone had removed my overachieving chip. I found myself not really caring about the barely disguised fierce competitiveness the rest of my colleagues were demonstrating. I realised how much of a shift I'd had in my mindset when the national sales league tables were published at the end of the quarter and I wasn't fraught with professional angst because I wasn't in the top five, my status and reputation at work simply didn't motivate me anymore. It wasn't just my attitude to work that was changing, I was on a steep learning curve about what was and what wasn't important to me now. The revelatory nature of my continued counselling sessions with Felicity provided me with enough to keep my mind busy, so that I didn't have much room for anything else. I was in the process of rethinking almost everything I thought I knew about myself.

Her consulting room had become my safe place, she'd become my safe place. Time would fly by during our meetings, and we left no stone unturned with our discussions and frank exchanges about my psyche. It was often an excruciating experience facing up to what had happened over the last few years of my life and my toil didn't stop when my hour was up. There would be some meetings when the aftereffects of our discussions lasted for days afterwards. My emotions were battered and bruised from the brutality of the honesty she demanded from me when I was working out the answers to her probing questions. Other days I would skip out of her building full of hope and excitement. I never had any idea what was coming my way when I sat in the olive-green chair opposite her at the start of our meetings; but I did know whatever it was it would turn out to be exactly what I needed.

During our more intense discussions I'd observed Felicity's habit of leaning forward in her chair and resting her arms on her thighs, I learned very quickly that this unconscious move from her was a precursor to a deeply profound, thought-provoking question. Without exception they had me digging deep to search for the right way to answer her, a way that would pay respect to her efforts and skill that were enabling me to separate myself from the damage my marriage had caused me, from the mental abuse I'd suffered at the hands of Tim.

Her guidance helped me to begin to understand why and how I'd allowed myself to get to the very edge of disintegration for the sake of something that wasn't worthy of me, and why I'd thought myself unworthy of it rather than the other way around. With her encouragement I began working through the torturous thoughts, that my most abusive relationship was with myself. She helped me navigate my way through the disgust I had for my own weakness.

My trip to Sardinia had been a huge turning point for me and we constantly referred to it. She left me in no doubt about how much courage it had taken for me to stand in front of the mirror in Jude's cabana and finally look at my damp, naked body with appreciation rather than shame. We talked about the delight kissing the boy in the bar had brought me and the sense of liberation I'd carried with me ever since I'd had sex with a stranger I'd met in a restaurant, but most of all we talked about my solo trip in my knackered 4x4, the sights I'd seen, the laughs I'd had, and the undoubted gift I'd given myself the day I decided to travel on my own.

There had never been a formal agreement about the number of sessions I should have with her but within a few weeks after my holiday there seemed to be a finality to our conversations and I could sense we were coming to the end of our relationship, that it was almost time to cut the shrink/patient umbilical cord. At our penultimate meeting - I didn't know at the time that's what it was, but it was - I watched as she did the sitting forward thing and as she leaned into me I leaned away with mild terror of what she was going to make me face up to this time. I thought I was done with the tough stuff; I watched her warily but instead of the serious professional face

I was expecting she gave me a beaming smile. "How do you feel about yourself now Rachel?"

For the first time in the history of her leaning forward inquisitions I didn't need to think about my reply, I felt my back and shoulders straighten and I matched her grin. "Proud. I'm really, really proud of myself." As soon as I spoke her whole body snapped to attention, she patted her open palm on her chest several times.

"And I'm proud of you too, I truly am. You are on your way to a most remarkable recovery." she stood up from her shrink's chair and came straight to me, we threw our arms around each other and hugged tightly as we both cried jubilant tears.

I sold my rings the week after.

15

July 2012

With some of the funds from the sale of my engagement ring, I had my left nipple pierced - an experience that left me in total shock with pain and delight at my bad ass self in equal measure. I'd spent the money I got for the sale of my wedding ring – quite fitting really – on the fees my solicitor charged me to change my name. This was something I'd been thinking about since I'd last seen it written in full - Rachel Penelope Bradbury. The sight of it pissed me off, and for once it wasn't my middle name that did it, this time it was my surname; not even really mine. It was Tim's name. The one I'd taken to show my commitment to him, and the one, as it turned out, to be on loan temporarily until he didn't desire me anymore. Why would I want to associate myself with it now? With him now?

It didn't take me long to decide I was going to revert to my maiden name, and, with permission from my mum – oddly enough called Penelope – I dropped my middle name too. I rebranded myself. It was another giant leap towards becoming my own woman, Ms Rachel Stone.

Right now, though I was still Mrs R P Bradbury, and in an effort to stop the constant friction between the lacy D-cup and my new nickel titty-ring I was spending most of my time with my hand shoved down the front of my bra. Which is exactly what I was doing when I arrived home from work on a random Thursday evening and straight into an impromptu garden party.

It was exactly this moment the course of my life shifted completely.

As I walked in the house, I could hear music, voices and laughter. Intrigued, I made my way towards the sound of it and spied Nai and Petra through the kitchen window. They were sat together on the bench by the water feature, giggling a lot while cracking open what looked like a very costly bottle of champagne. Sophie was deep in conversation too. She was leaning her shoulders against the wall in her usual insouciant stance, one leg bent at the knee so she could rest her foot behind her, talking animatedly to a handful of people I didn't recognise; she was gesticulating wildly with one hand while dangling a bottle of beer between her index and middle finger of the other.

I stepped outside into the warmth and glow of the evening sun. Petra saw me first; the volume of her voice when she shouted my name alerted me to the fact that she was a bit pissed. "Rachel, bloody hell, where've you been? You nearly missed this bottle too!" She held it in the air and waved it in my general direction. "Come on Nai, get Rach a glass, she's gonna need a drink.... we're celebrating!"

Naomi handed me a freshly poured flute and a ciggie at the same time. I liked the look of both offerings so much I had no choice but to take my five-finger nipple shield away from my poorly bosom.

"I've had the most amazing week, Rach!" Petra took a swig from her glass. "Hope you're ready for this...I'm going back to New York!" She raised her hands in celebration spilling what looked like at least a tenner's worth of champagne. "I've been promoted!" Her voice rose again, excitement radiating from her. She chinked my glass again, then took another long swig. "I've got it, I've been offered Director of Sales!" I was delighted for her. Petra had dedicated herself to her career, and the promise of a directorship had been the deciding factor when her company had asked her to come back to work in the UK. It had been a big sacrifice for her - she'd missed her Manhattan lifestyle madly - but in the end it had paid off.

I chinked glasses with her and Nai. "I'm so happy for you babe, but I'm going to miss you badly; I've got used to you being around."

"Yeah well about that...as part of the expansion of the department I'll be looking for new sales execs and I'm going to need a second-in-command, someone I can rely on and trust implicitly, someone I know will have my back completely... some award-winning kick-ass sales chick who's free to move to New York in about three months' time..."

I was nodding at her, encouraging her to carry on with her story, excited for her. Petra continued, "I've been thinking this through for the last forty-eight hours. If I'm going to do this right, I need someone by my side who has your skills and experience, I need someone like you. Last night I came to the conclusion, that it's not someone like you I need, it is you. You are the woman for the job."

I stared at her in disbelief, then looked at Nai to make sure I wasn't imagining what she'd just said to me. Nai was beaming at me. Petra carried on, "The salary's off the scale. You can come live with me if you want, until you find your feet, and you'll be away from here - away from the memories and the fear of bumping into Alison again or seeing twatty-Tim and his blow-up girlfriend."

This time it was my turn to take a huge slug of my drink, and as I swallowed the champagne bubbles down, excited ones came the other way to meet them. Tim's voice came into my head - I hate it when he does that. I heard him snort and tut and ask me in a voice full of derision if it could really be that simple? Ivy answered the specter of his voice for me.

Why shouldn't it be that simple?

And she was right. I definitely needed a change. I had no responsibility for anyone or anything anymore and the thought of moving away from the vicinity of my previous life wasn't an unattractive one either.

And if we're going to go anywhere, it might as well be New York because, come on, how cool is that?! Tell her you'll think about it.

I grabbed the bottle and filled our flutes again and said, "Why the fuck not!"

My attention was stolen away from any further celebration when I heard Sophie shout, "She's just called! She's in a cab from the station, she'll only be a couple of minutes." She ran past me back into the house and as I turned to look, I saw the others in Sophie's party almost stand to attention.

I looked at Nai over the top of Petra's head and mouthed, "Who's here?" She mouthed back to me, "Olivia's coming for the weekend."

That explained so much to me; the reason for so many unfamiliar faces in the garden, the atmosphere of pent-up excitement I'd sensed from Sophie and her group of friends, and her reaction to the news her friend was on her way.

Olivia was here.

From what I'd gathered during the many times her name had come into conversations, Olivia was a much-loved and revered friend of Sophie's, and, I presumed, the others that were here this evening. She was a well-respected Art Historian who spent most of her time living in the middle of nowhere on an island off the coast of Scotland on her own in a place with no Wi-Fi (I mean come on!). She was a heroine to Sophie. She'd talked about her often and it was obvious from the way she described Olivia she was a force to be reckoned with, someone she admired greatly and who in her own words, "has saved my arse in so many ways I've lost count!". And then she'd tell us a story about how she'd got herself into some kind of trouble, and Olivia had come to the rescue, how wise her advice had been at the time, how insightful and knowledgeable she was, she was the woman so many people trusted with their deepest secrets because she never, ever let them slip. She was a protector, a saviour; she'd helped Sophie deal with the heartbreak of her parents cutting her off from the rest of the family when she'd come out to them.

From her many tales about this legendary woman, I'd built a picture in my head of how she looked. I'd gathered she was older than me by at least a decade, and in my mind, she was a wiry, braless goddess with arse length wavy grey hair. She wore a multitude of fascinating bracelets and rings; she was beautiful and elegant - the kind of woman who could get away with wearing cowboy boots and a gypsy skirt. I've no idea where I got all these ideas from, because in all the descriptions of Olivia's amazingness, I hadn't heard anyone ever mention her looks; these were the blanks I'd had to fill in for myself. As thrilling as my conversation with Petra was about the life we would have in NYC - the places we would go, where we would shop and eat and drink - when I heard Sophie's excited voice peal out from the kitchen announcing the arrival of her much-loved friend, I was compelled to turn and watch as she made her way into the garden via the dimly lit kitchen. I actually held my breath as I waited for her to step outside into the softening evening light. I had no idea why, but for the longest time I'd wanted to meet this woman and now she was close by my heart beat a bit faster while I waited for her to reveal herself.

Sophie was glowing with pride as she stepped to one side to let Olivia into the garden. My eyes were transfixed on the person in front of me. She was absolutely nothing like my mental pictures of her. She wasn't at all slight or wiry, she was tall, and she carried some extra weight, but it suited her. She looked statuesque. She was wearing a black Led Zeppelin t-shirt, black jeans and an ancient leather jacket with zips and studs. Her hair was buzz-cut short and pure white. She didn't seem to be wearing any jewellery at all and as much as I didn't want to be seen to be making assumptions, Ivy took the words right out of my mouth.

She wouldn't be seen dead in a gypsy skirt Rach, but you were right about the cowboy boots.

The only word I had in my vocabulary to describe this woman in front of me, was "butch"; but she was the sexiest thing I'd ever seen. The personification of sex. It oozed out of her. I'd never seen anyone like her in my life. Even though she was across the garden from me and completely unaware of my presence, I could feel the pull of my attraction to her. I wanted to touch her, to feel her skin and I was convinced that when I did my fingers would be left dripping with some kind of sweet sticky liquid. She captivated me; I couldn't take my eyes off her. She must have felt the weight of my stare because eventually she turned to look at me and smiled a warm gentle smile.

I melted.

I watched greedily as Sophie took her straight to Naomi; she proudly introduced them to each other, and I saw both women scan each other quickly. Within a split second they decided they were on safe ground and fell into a genuine, heartfelt greeting.

I couldn't tear my eyes away from the scene. I could sense Petra had lost interest in our new arrival and was keen to go back to our previous conversation, but my head wouldn't turn away; I was hungry for the sight of our new guest.

By the time Sophie eventually came to me and introduced us, I'd studied Olivia's face so intently I'd worked out she'd had chicken pox when she was younger because she had the faintest trace of a scar on her forehead that could only have been from picking off a scab – and I should know, I've got loads of them. I'd also figured out she'd had lots of piercings at some point in her life, but they'd all been taken out now leaving behind the scars and tiny indentations in her ears, nose and eyebrows that gave her game away.

When Olivia moved towards me, I clumsily held out my right hand to shake hers. I had absolutely no idea why I'd done that. *What are you up to Rach, shaking hands? Why don't you just curtsey and get it over with!* I felt myself blush at Inner Voice Ivy's taunt and my own gawkiness.

In response to my formal greeting, Olivia held out her hand; at the same time as I withdrew mine. As soon as I realised what she was doing I brought my hand into the shake again, just as she was about to pull hers back. I was mortified by my behaviour and even more so when the Hokey Cokey dance our hands were performing meant, when they eventually met, instead of the polite shake I'd intended for my greeting, our fingers were forcefully intertwined. To make matters worse, as soon as I felt her contact, I gasped and squeezed my fingers tightly, trapping hers into our digit embrace.

Oddly enough my pelvic floor muscles spasmed at the same time.

I met her eyes to see if she was as embarrassed by it all as I was and that's when she started to laugh. I felt the deep chuckle come from the very centre of her, it reverberated through her entire body and when it eventually burst out it was the dirtiest laugh I'd ever heard. The vibration of it ran up my spine and as I shuddered from its force and effect, I felt my nipples harden and my newly placed ring got caught on the lace of my bra again. The pain was so sudden it made me wince in such a way that she stopped her laughter instantly and replaced it with a deep rumble of a voice expressing concern, "You ok, love?"

"Yeah, I'm fine thanks, new nipple piercing giving me a bit of trouble, you know how it is." As soon as I said the word nipple her eyes dropped to my tits, which made them go even harder. She said, "But I wasn't anywhere near your nipples!"

Wanna bet! shouted Ivy, as Oliva slowly moved her gaze from my throbbing bosoms and back to my eyes. It felt like a very deliberate move, as did the filthy, flirty smile she gave me.

****

The next morning, it being a Friday, I was off work, which was fortunate because I had a rabid and very unexpected hangover. I was used to having the house to myself on my extra day off, and while I wasn't quite yawning and scratching my arse when I went to the kitchen to make myself a cup of tea, I wasn't far off.

I got the fright of my life when I realised I wasn't alone. Olivia was sat at the table reading a broadsheet newspaper. She was looking at me over the top of it, interest written all over her face. She didn't smile but said huskily, "Good morning you."

I felt like her voice had invaded my body. I had to catch my breath as every nerve ending responded to it. I wanted this woman so badly, the deepest, darkest parts of me throbbed and the aftershock of that created a flush of tingling under my skin, like an itch, one that my entire body wanted to scratch.

I distracted myself by making tea (how frightfully British of me). When I asked if she wanted one, she shook her head and held up her nearly full cup. Thankfully she didn't speak which was a huge relief because I wasn't sure my nerves could stand it. While I was waiting for the kettle to boil, I felt myself blush with embarrassment at the thought of being watched and probably doing something stupidly clumsy. My back was aching with the effort of keeping my posture upright and my stomach muscles were sore from all the sucking in I was doing, for some reason beyond my comprehension I desperately wanted this woman to like me.

Talk to her.

"And say what?"

Ivy sighed. *You're never usually lost for words Rachel, come on get on with it, break the silence.*

"I can't, I'm shy...."

You're a shit fibber, you are NOT shy, say something. SAY SOMETHING!

Ivy was really starting to get on my nerves now, she was making me even more nervous. I was trying hard to appear casually engrossed with the mug and teaspoon I was using to squeeze the tea bag dry but when I turned to throw it in the bin, out of the corner of my eye I saw that Olivia was in exactly the same position as she'd been when I'd turned my back on her – her hand was still raised to show me the contents of her cup, her head dipped forward slightly and her eyes peering over her silver framed specs.

In the harshness of the morning light, she looked older than she had last night. Her jowls were heavy and the lines around her mouth told their own story of her years of commitment to smoking the roll ups I'd watched her so skillfully build the evening before, fascinated by the movement of her fingers. Her skin was pale and, without the leather jacket to disguise her shape, she was a bit chubbier than I'd first thought. Her forearms were exposed now, and she had a mismatch of tattoos on her left arm but on her right was an intricate abstract design with vibrant colours that went from the knuckle of her middle finger and wound its way around her hand to her wrist and then up her arm as far as my eye could see inside of the short sleeve of her button-down collar green and white check shirt.

I was still on the other side of the kitchen, but the current of attraction I felt between us was so fierce it was almost visible. When I opened my mouth to speak to her it was with the intention of complimenting her on her ink but instead, I said, "Please will you come to bed with me?"

16

She watched herself as she slid her hands inside the waist-band of my knickers, she never took her eyes off my body as it became more naked. I hadn't trimmed my bush for weeks. I hadn't shaved either. My usual reticence for anyone other than me to see my fuzzy, springy pubes dissipated when I studied the concentration on her face as she pulled my cotton pants down.

Her hand movements were deliberate, confident; every piece of her skin that touched mine set my body on fire as she pulled the fabric far enough down my hips and beyond to reveal the lips of my vagina. She brushed her trailing thumbs deliberately over my protruding, blood-congested clitoris and I pushed my hips towards her, desperate for more, but she dragged them away from my demanding movement and slid them deeper into the folds of my labia.

My whole body was tense with anticipation, I held my breath as she slid her thumbs away from my genitals, I could feel how wet they still were from their brief but breath-taking visit to my cunt as she expertly found nerve endings I didn't even know I had in the deepest inners of my inner thighs.

She moved her concentrated gaze away from her task and dipped her head to the place she'd just touched, and replaced her thumb with the tip of her tongue. It wasn't a lick, it was a short, sharp flick. Almost like a slap across the face, only sexier. And then she pulled away from me. I thought I was going to explode, if I'd been in bed, I would have grabbed my pillow or my sheets in my fists in an effort to contain myself, but I was half sat, half laid on the broadsheet paper that was still resting on the dining table. There was nothing to grab hold of, nowhere for all the pent-up frustration to be dispersed to. Instead I wrapped my fingers in my hair and pulled my head forward; my complete focus now was her and her green eyes looking at me, an unspoken question in them.

My stomach muscles quivered with the effort of keeping my upper body taught and upright, my thigh muscles trembled, my eyes were locked into hers - I was captivated by her. She raised her eyebrows, another enquiry, a subtle tease. Surely, she couldn't be asking me if I wanted her to carry on, couldn't she feel my desire pulsing from me?

I was about to beg her not to stop but the feel and sight of her right-hand gliding along the curve of my waist silenced me, she let her fingers trail around the shape of my breast, my nipples hardened even more with her touch. Deliberately, slowly, she took her middle finger, the one wrapped in tattoo ink, and placed her thumb, still slippy from my juices on its nail. I instinctively knew there would be pain. "No, no, please don't!" I whimpered, helpless to stop her as she released the finger from the grip of her thumb directly onto my new piercing.

The pain was unbearable. It brought me right to the edge of a scream. I grabbed my hair tighter, pulled myself up higher, even as they filled with tears my eyes didn't leave hers; I wanted to make sure she would see the shock response to her cruelty in my face. I waited for her to apologise for her brutality but instead she gave me a slow, lazy wink, drew her nipple trigger-finger down my breastbone, spreading the rest of her fingers alongside it to drag the skin of my stomach, as they joined in and moved towards my vagina. I could feel the afterburn of the torture to my nipple and then the burst of erotic sensation as her abusive finger became my pleasure giver. She gave me one last lopsided smile and took her mouth back to my cunt.

The orgasm Olivia gifted me was, without a doubt, unlike any I'd ever had; the pleasure so extreme it teetered on the edge of agony. I couldn't stand the intensity any longer and she was ignoring my pleas for her to stop, in a desperate attempt to calm her insistent tongue I wrapped my legs around her head and pulled her into me, trapping her face and fingers, into my throbbing vagina. At the same split second, she slid fingers – I wasn't sure how many – inside me and hit my G spot in a precise, perceptive move. I'm sure if her voice wasn't muffled by my labia, I would have heard her shout "Check Mate".

This orgasm was less of a come and more of a sonic boom that blasted around my entire body - it left me fighting to catch my breath and caused my inner thighs to contract around her head with every aftershock that followed. I was worried that if I released her, she might carry on with her tongue on my enflamed clit, so I kept her face locked by my legs into stillness where it was until she pinched my arse cheek hard leaving me no choice but to let her go.

(I think it's worth mentioning here that I genuinely had no idea I had a G spot, I thought they were like the Loch Ness monster- a thing of fable.)

Olivia was still fully clothed; I was quite relieved to see at least she'd taken her specs off. After I'd released her from my wrestling thigh grip, she sat back into her chair and smiled at me, I slid myself off the table, pausing for a second to unpeel the newspaper from my bum cheeks, and straddled her lap, she opened her arms to welcome me, her face was still slightly damp and smelled of me. I held it in my hands and kissed her deeply, her lips were soft and full, her skin was smooth underneath my fingertips as I ran them down her neck and released the first button on her shirt. She grabbed my wrist and put a halt to the opening of anymore.

We were still kissing, and desperate to show her who was boss I trapped her bottom lip in between mine and sucked it deeper inside my mouth. Once it was my captive, I ran my tongue gently across its folds and creases. I dipped the tip of my tongue into the delicate flesh, I felt the rumble of her desirous groan vibrate through us both, she tried to pull away from me, but I wasn't ready to let her go. I bit into her flesh lightly with the intention of preventing her withdrawal but she carried on pulling away from me. I bit harder, I was worried I might be being a bit too forceful, but I bluffed it out, convinced that the pain would be too much for her and she'd stop the tug of war. She didn't.

She still had a forceful grip on my right wrist while I had her bottom lip held violently between my teeth, we were locked in a battle of wills. I took the opportunity of her distraction and slid my left hand quickly between our bodies. I lifted my still naked form out of my own way and popped the top button on her black jeans and with an artful move I didn't know I had in me, guided my hand flat against her belly and down through to her underwear and pubic hairs and plunged my fingers into the wet, warm folds of flesh they grew to protect. My lust for her was immense. Once I'd reached my goal, I was eager to feel as much of her as I could. I had to force myself to slow down, to remember this was no longer about my satiation. I'd had my go; it was her turn now.

I was so concentrated on familiarising my fingers with the most sensitive spots of her most private parts my ruse to keep her still failed, I released my teeth from her bottom lip and she pulled her head back away from me. I could sense she was about to tell me to stop but before she could our eyes met, the power of the moment carried the same passion as the sex. I witnessed the split second she allowed herself to be drawn into me, to join in with my emotions. The expression of reluctance on her face melted and she transmogrified from being someone fucking a stranger because she'd had the cheek to ask, to becoming a lover, someone who was sharing the experience as both a giver and a taker. In that instance her body relaxed and instead of rigid resistance, my fingers found acquiescence as they sank into her. My rush to prove myself her sexual equal was no longer necessary. It was time for us both to enjoy ourselves.

We still hadn't relocated to anywhere soft; I didn't want to break the spell I'd managed to weave her into, all I wanted to do was give her as much as she was prepared to take. I knew instinctively she was showing me a part of her she kept secret and as much as I wanted her physically, I wanted to love her too, to treat her to the intimacy she deserved. I stood up from her lap, the force of my action pushed the table away from us both. I'd love to say that her clothes dissolved into nothing-ness and there were no awkward minutes while I attempted to make pulling off her cowboy boots a thing of sensuality, or that her odd socks didn't distract me slightly, but this was real life after all and it's nothing like the movies. I got through that challenge – as seductively as possible – I pulled her jeans over her hips and they fell to her ankles, I was on the home run. I went for the last layer, her knickers; but she wouldn't let me in. Instead of me ripping the last vestige of barrier from between us she shouted, "No." It was the first word she'd spoken to me since her 'Hello you' a fair few orgasms ago. It shocked me so much, I stopped immediately.

"Don't. I can't. I don't do this bit." Olivia began to reach for her discarded clothes but there was no way I was stopping now - I had this woman in my sights and wasn't getting up from my knees until I'd had a taste of her. The desire to feel her nerve-filled silky skin against my tongue was a compulsion. I held my covetous hands back, moved them away from the elastic that hugged the fabric to her waist.

"Please, Olivia, let me. Please." My plead paused the grab she was making for her jeans. She hesitated, I took the opportunity of her stillness and ran my thumb slowly down the outside of the fabric of her pants I dug into her covered crack and I felt her shift towards it, her mouth was saying one thing but her body wanted something else. I couldn't wait any longer, I pulled her pants to one side, the previously hidden coarse dark brown and grey hairs of her pubes were wet from the stimulation our sex had created. This was the final confirmation I needed, I knew she wanted this as much as I did, using both hands, I slid the tips of my fingers inside the lips of her vagina and drew them apart; her pink skin sprang into my vision.

17

And the next thing I knew, I was all alone, stark naked, on my knees on the rock-hard flags of the kitchen floor while I watched her walk away from me still hitching her jeans up over her hips as she left the room.

There was no illicit taste of Olivia's much yearned-for pussy on my lips, my fingers were as dry as the bones they were. I was stunned. I had been so close to the object of my desire I'm sure if there was a slow-motion action replay to run it would have shown the tip of my tongue less than a millimetre away from her clit. And then she said, "No. No. No. I really don't do this bit. We must stop. This doesn't happen to me. I'm going now." She pushed me out of her way and stood up, determinedly taking her vagina and her clitoris with her, regardless of how moist they were, how they begged for attention, and left me to stare at her kneecaps in complete shock while she pulled up her jeans and walked out of the room.

My vagina was still twitching from the multiple orgasms, my pierced nipple was still throbbing from the flick of her finger, and I was alone. Pins and needles were just starting little fires in my feet where they were trapped under my arse cheeks, but I was rooted to the spot with the confusion and hurt of her rejection.

I eventually uncurled my poor, stiff, legs, gathered up my clothes, made another cup of tea and spent the rest of the morning in my room dithering between a delightful warm afterglow and a stunned turmoil of shame. On the whole it wasn't the most pleasant post coital state I'd ever been in.

****

Sophie had invited half a dozen of her and Olivia's friends' round for a dinner party that evening and as she started preparations, she insisted Nai and I left her to it, so without much more need for persuasion we went to the pub.

Once I'd left the house, the tension of being in the same space as Olivia began to melt and with that came relief. With my second beer loosening my otherwise redundant tongue, I unfolded the whole sorry story to Nai - the sex, the orgasms, the rejection, my poor achy knees. I half expected her to be able to give me some illuminating insight into Olivia's behaviour, but she was as baffled as I was. She was sympathetic of course but she still managed to tip her glass in my direction and give me a lascivious wink and a lick of the lips. Fortunately, by the time we got home, Nai had, as usual taken discomfort and shame and turned it on its head, and we'd laughed most of it away. Any residual angst I might have been feeling was hidden by the bottles of Peroni I'd polished off.

Sophie had cooked a delicious dinner accompanied by copious amounts of wine, and a 'think of it as a sorbet' spliff between courses. Even though Nai and I had only just met most of the guests, the conversation around the table was relaxed and unguarded. It turned out that Olivia, when she wasn't rejecting desperate-for-a-shag bi-subsexual women, was full of warmth and comic humour, and despite my discomfort and determination not to let my libido be influenced by her again, I couldn't take my eyes off her. She still didn't respond to me in any way at all.

There was a definite similarity between the rest of the party, they were all women and all younger than Olivia, they each had a sparky confidence and their own brand of raw sexiness. As the evening wore on, they began to swap stories about how they'd met Liv and how at some point during their early friendship, they'd all, without exception, attempted to seduce her. They each took it in turns to regale us with their stories, everyone different but with the same outcome, rejection.

Nai and I kept catching each other's eye across the candle-lit table, her eyebrows raised, and eyes opened wide on more than one occasion. Despite the intimacy of the topic being discussed and the fact that the subject of their disclosures was sat within earshot, there was a joyful camaraderie between the women, like they all belonged to an exclusive club, and they were delighted to be wearing a badge of honour. Olivia was laughing heartily, she seemed to be enjoying the teasing and the attention she was getting, and why not, there was no re-crimination or hard feelings in the room, that much was clear. All these women adored her.

Meanwhile the only thing left for me to do was laugh along and pretend that her propensity to knock back her lovers was brand-new news to me, despite the fact that less than 12 hours ago I'd been laid across the table, just about where the cheese board and port bottle were now, with her head trapped in the vice like grip of my thighs and her fingers on my G spot.

I didn't see her again after that evening, she and Sophie left early the next morning on a weeklong road trip to catch up with more friends. I lay in bed listening to their muffled, semi whispers and exaggerated quietness as they got ready to go. I couldn't help thinking that wherever it was they were heading for, there would be several more candle lit dinner tables popu-lated by Olivia's discards.

That set me off once again trying to work out what had happened between us and why she'd been so definite with her refusal for what would have been cunnilingus laced with an immense amount of effort and lust. Ivy came to my rescue in the end and reminded me that it wasn't as if everyone around the table last night had been bragging about the orgasms they'd been allowed to give the enigmatic lesbian; they'd all been vetoed by her vagina at some point or another.

I dropped the abject horror of my sexual advances being rebuffed for the length of time it took me to wank myself half to death with the memories of the sex I'd had with a lesbian that lived in the Scottish islands.

****

Nai and I made the most of the absence of her girlfriend and for the first time for ages we got to hang out together. It couldn't have come at a better time for me to have my confidant's full attention. I had a lot on my mind, since I'd accepted Petra's champagne-fueled job offer and committed myself to moving to New York; the only thing I'd really been thinking about was Olivia, and it was time for me to change the subject.

We Skyped Jude and had a few hours long distance drinking, smoking spliffs and over-analysing everything – it was very productive. In the end it was agreed I would be crazy not to move to New York, and as a result of my definite decision, Naomi confessed that she'd been feeling it was time to officially ask Sophie to move in with her, so now I was leaving, her final excuse was gone too. Of course, no conversation would have been complete without one of us sharing our recent sexual exploits. Since the other two were in long term relationships, and the unspoken rule was that it was just too weird to talk about shagging our full-time, long-term partners but that casual sex with near strangers was an essential item on the agenda, I got to relive my story.

Starting with my fanatical attraction to her, asking her if I could take her to bed with me and the subsequent nipple flicking, G spot hitting, mortifyingly rejected fuck. I couldn't tell them about the sexy bits without a discussion about my subsequent thought patterns; how much I'd wanted to try and reciprocate and why, despite the fact she'd rejected me and left me without so much as a 'thanks for letting me taste your pussy, Rach,' I wanted to see her again so badly it was almost the only thing I could think about.

Once she'd got over her long-standing disappointment that she was now 'fully committed to heterosexuality' and she would never get to 'shag a lezzie on Nai's dining table' followed by the congratulatory 'ding-dong you filthy bitch,' Jude pointed out to me, and Nai was very quick to agree, that my experience with Olivia was yet another rite of passage of single womanhood.

At this point I have to confess that when either of them has been dating unenthusiastic dickheads and I've been ensconced in my smug life with my fabulous job, weekends away, holidays to exotic destinations and a husband that pretended to be faithful to me, I never really understood what these women were going through. I had always listened to their woes while they'd been dating weak, unavailable men but I tended to make glib suggestions about how they should just forget the person who was creating them such heartache and move on.

Over the years they brought names into my life: Jonathan, Junior, Ally, Rick, and they repeated them obsessively for weeks and months on end, to the point – in my previous opinion - of eye-rolling boredom. I was desperately unqualified to understand their pain, I was without empathy; until now. Now I was on the verge of tearing my hair out with frustration at my failure to engage the unlikely goddess into wanting to be with me, or at the very least, commit to receiving an orgasm from me. Jude's voice came over loud and clear: "Ahh Rach, Olivia is your Jonathan." Oh shit no, I really didn't want a Jonathan, Jonathan had consistently treated Jude with complete disdain and yet she had been obsessed with him.

For a very long year and a half Jonathan had been the only subject matter on our agenda while Jude worked out inventive ways to get to see him, devising plausible reasons she could give him so she could accidentally-on-purpose bump into him, or on one memorable occasion, when he hadn't replied to her texts for over a week, she'd turned up on his doorstep dressed in sexy lingerie and stockings.

We'd extended plenty of invitations to him to join us with our partying, but he'd either turned us down or said he might think about it, and then didn't attend, always without explanation. It was safe to say they weren't on the same page relationship-wise, and he wasn't interested in her at all, unless they were bumping uglies. She had wanted him badly and he'd abused her. Surely, I wasn't the kind of woman that got involved with a 'Jonathan' or a 'Richard'? Richard had been the guy who had eventually caused Nai to give up all hope on romance, he was incapable of kindness, honesty or faithfulness and I'd witnessed her torture herself waiting for a text or a call, or even just the tiniest indication of him wanting to see her. These men had treated my friends in appallingly arrogant and careless ways, and now here I was finally walking a mile in their high-heeled shoes, and it was shit! It made me ashamed I hadn't been more sympathetic before.

By the time we left Jude to see to her four boisterous but charming step-kids and the delightful Comitas, I was coming to terms with the reality of my situation. I'd stepped into the trap of getting hooked into an unrewarding imaginary relationship with someone incapable of commitment. Ivy and I said to Nai at the same time, "I've been single for less than six months, I can't believe I've fallen for this already!"

To help soften the blow of this new revelation Nai broke out a packet of magic mushrooms that she'd smuggled home in her bra the last time we'd been to Amsterdam, and we spent the rest of Saturday in a delightful mellow state laughing at everything, booing and hissing every time I tried to bring the conversation back to Olivia, and eventually imagining what our new and much altered lives were going to look like a few months into the future.

The rest of the time, when we weren't bickering about who's turn it was to go to the fridge for wine, we spent a lot of our energy expressing our love for each other.

18

I resigned the following Monday with the intention of working out my full notice but after conversations with HR it was agreed I would tie up my loose ends, use my accrued holidays, and finish much earlier than the three months I'd expected. I leapt at the chance for some down time that didn't include the guilt that was wrapped around a doctor's 'refrain from work' note. After all, it was still summer, I had my meagre belongings to pack up before I skipped across the Pond, and lots of people to see before I waded arse deep into a new job and another life in another country. It was a relief not to have to do all of that and pretend to work at the same time.

Despite the excitement of my unexpected life changes and the distinct rosy glow my future had surrounding it, I couldn't get Olivia off my mind. The thoughts of her now transcended the flash back images of our sex and fixated on the attraction I'd felt towards her. I tried hard to keep hold of my insider knowledge of the infamy she had for her lack of reciprocity, but it didn't stop her rejection hitting me hard. The harshest thing for me to accept was the glaringly obvious fact that I was still a lot more fragile than I'd imagined myself to be. She'd shone a light on my vulnerability and that distressed me.

My bravado had taken a kicking. I felt delicate and unsettled, my determined giant strides towards becoming a divorcee as quickly as possible lost their impetus. It wasn't lost on me that I'd attached my desires to an emotionally and sexually unavailable woman, and I was in danger of falling back into my own trap, only this time instead of a master of destruction, I'd chosen a mistress to damage myself with. I was sad and cross with myself.

I took another emotional battering a few days later when my Deed Poll arrived. Seeing my new moniker in black and white gave my already hollow heart another carving-out. I was desperately sad that I'd lost Tim and let our marriage slip through my fingers. Everything else paled into insignificance and I fell back into mourning my previous life, I was tormented by the thought of Tim with a new woman in his life, I tortured myself constantly with images from the video I'd seen of him fucking his dogging partner who, according to Schadenfreude Alison, was now his girlfriend. My mental health deteriorated and began to affect my physical health, all I wanted to do was sleep.

Ivy had other ideas though. I was laid with the duvet over my head attempting to block out the glorious sunny day I was making myself miss by being miserable, when Ivy shouted at me.

Stop it now, you're better than this. Take a deep breath Rach, put your shoulders back, and push yourself onwards, this is all part of your learning curve. If you fall at the first hurdle we're screwed.

Her words were irritating more than motivational, but she did have a point. There were things for me to be getting on with and lying in bed wasn't going to get them done. I only had a couple of months before I was heading off to my new life, now was not the time to lose sight of the previous ferocity of my determination. I needed to remember that I hadn't let my marriage slip through my fingers at all, Tim had ripped everything that was good about it to pieces, me included, and there was no way I was going into my future enslaved by his surname. Mrs Bradbury was a non-requisite in my life now, I was Ms Rachel

Stone and I had the paperwork to prove it. With reignited resolve I drove 150 miles to the nearest passport office to Fast Track through the process of officially rebranding myself for my new adventure.

****

On my way home, I called at Christine and Pete's for a coffee. They were the in middle of decorating the kitchen, and as I walked through the door Pete gave me a tin of paint and a brush and a four-finger wave as he left the room – and Christine and I to finish the glossing. I enjoyed the distraction of the labour, the cups of tea supplied by Pete, using the state of the kitchen as an excuse to eat takeaway food and the general mood of making the most of our time together before I went away. It was the fun I needed. I realised the company of my friends had completely distracted me from my damaging thoughts, the aches and pains and lethargy had left me again and my body had coped well with the work it had done.

When I eventually left on Sunday afternoon, I decided to make the most of the wonderful July weather and rather than take the motorway I drove the scenic route home instead. I lowered my car windows and hummed to the tunes on my favourite CD. I was full of joyful energy.

Even Ivy's voice was buoyant when she came to me.

I think it's time for you to start counting your blessings, my love. I'll start if that helps. Tim always hated having the car windows open, didn't he? If he was here now, he would be moaning about the draught while fiddling with the controls on your stereo, fucking about with the buttons, messing up your settings.

She had my attention; I was nodding at her comments.

It's a great feeling to be able to do what you want when you want, isn't it? To be able to drop in to see your friends for a cup of tea and stay for days on end without having to feel guilty or explain yourself to anyone because you have no one to answer to. This is how your life is now Rachel, you are in control, you can please yourself what you do and when you do it. You are free.

I listened to her words, I appreciated her point and as she told me I was free I felt a swell of excitement fill my body, it was joyful, I was joyful. To celebrate I turned the music up full blast and sang at the top of my lungs all the way home.

****

It was late Sunday afternoon when I eventually made my way back to Nai's. The spring in my step had returned and my optimism level was back at 10. Sophie was home from her trip – without Olivia I was relieved to see - and she and Nai were loved up and celebrating their decision to live together.

Over dinner Naomi casually asked Sophie about the multitude of rejected women Olivia had left in her wake. Sophie was very open as she explained Olivia's reasons for being so unwilling to accept the love others wanted to give her. She told us how, in her early forties, Olivia had been through her own emotional battles. She'd had a much-loved, long-term partner that had been unfaithful to her with a colleague and it had hurt her so intensely, she hadn't had a long-term relationship since. Despite her magnetic ability to attract a multitude of women she'd lost the capacity to release herself into the hands of another lover, no matter how willing they were to try.

It made me desperately sad to think that the woman I revered had been so broken, and worse still was the thought that she'd never been able to repair the harm someone else had inflicted on her. Sophie told us that Olivia admitted she got immense pleasure out of her orgasm entourage telling almost apocryphal tales of the time they'd been rejected by Olivia. She loved the attention and the notoriety; she said it helped to dull the pain she still felt. I hoped one day I'd be in her presence again, sat round a dining table with her other conquests and be able to let her enjoy the story of the broadsheet newspaper, dining table, inner thigh suffocation sex session I knew I'd never forget.

****

The following week I had my last day at work, which was almost as surreal as seeing my new name on my shiny, un-battered passport when it had arrived. My job had been a huge part of my life, my successful career was my pride and joy and now here I was sat at the top of the table in an Italian restaurant taking part in my leaving party. It was akin to an out of body ex**perience as I sat and listened to my (ex) boss, who was more than a bit drunk, as he expressed sincere feelings about losing me from his team and told the story once again about my second interview when he'd asked me what I expected from the company in return for my hard work and dedication and I'd told him a decent car. He still thought I'd been joking – I hadn't. My colleagues had clubbed together and bought me a fabulous pair of Manolo Blahnik's – Laura's influence I was sure - and a packet of condoms for when I had 'sex in the city'. We all got pissed, went to a karaoke bar, Laura cried, so did I and my boss told me he'd always found me incredibly sexy.

All in all, a good night out.

During the next day, while I was watching back-to-back Big Bang Theory on DVD, eating junk food and drinking full fat coke I had a vague recollection of Loz asking me if it would be ok for her to give AJ my new mobile number. Several cocktails in I'd waved her question away and said "Of course, it would be great to have a catch up with him before I go." I hadn't seen him since he'd instigated my toilet cubicle wank and the effect he'd had on my libido had been filed in my mind as a massive overreaction from a rabidly horny, neglected wife. I wasn't that woman anymore. I was the kind of gal who had sex in showers with almost strangers with an excellent repartee in chat up lines, one who had recently discovered her G spot. There was no way one man's pheromones could have that effect on me now I was all orgasmed up.

Silly me.

I was waiting for Nai to bring me my takeaway from the chip shop, hoping that maybe a strong dose of beef dripping might be the thing that finally soaked up the last remnants of the tequila slammers I'd thought were such a good idea at 3am in the morning, when his text arrived. It was a brief one but full of implication. "I need to see you."A thrill shot through my body. My reply text belied my butterflies, "That would be nice."

AJ's reply was instantaneous "I realise you're probably very busy, but do you have time for a couple of nights away before you leave?"

I was encouraged by Ivy's *Woofuckinghoo Rach, you're going to shag the splendiferous guy of your dreams,* and I hoped the subtext of 'nights away' meant just that. Now I'd finished work I did have time before I left, I had loads of it, and I could think of a lot worse ways to spend it.

I could hear Jude's voice telling me to be cool and wait until much later to reply but I didn't want to be someone's tormentor, especially not his. "That would be lovely, when do you have in mind?"

We arranged for the following weekend, I calculated it would give me time to get my 'personal' care sorted at the waxing salon – I'd recently decided shaving was no longer good enough for me now I was a single woman – and give myself time to build up some fizzy excitement about seeing him. He asked me if I had a preference for location or accommodation or would I be ok to leave it to him? As thrilling as I was finding my independence it would have been churlish to refuse, so I let him get on with it.

By the time Naomi had brought my food he'd texted me the address of a hotel in the Lake District. He'd arranged an early check in for me so I could enjoy the spa facilities if I chose and he'd get there as soon as he could on Friday evening after work.

I was delighted at the thought of a couple of nights away, and even though our instantaneous attraction felt like an imaginary event, I was even more delighted at the chance to see AJ again.

I had surrendered my company car to Laura who, with much glee, had told me she was going to remove all traces of Radio 2 from the preset buttons. I had the use of my dad's old banger out of his garage in the meantime and I had nearly bitten her hand off when Nai offered to lend me her car for the trip. I've got to say there was a huge part of my shallow self that was delighted to be arriving at such a spectacular setting with the roof of her brand new shiny red Merc down, it kind of set the tone of the weekend for me.

The extravagant undercurrent of the trip kept up when I checked in and the receptionist told me there were two suites booked in my name, they had been instructed to let me choose which one I wanted. I followed a very reverent guy carrying my bag to the first room, it had floor to ceiling windows, the huge bed was in the middle of the room facing the view of the hotel's gardens and lake, the bathroom had a roll top bath, again positioned facing the window and big enough for a rugby team. It had decadence written all over it, and while I tried my hardest not to burst out laughing at the outstanding course of events that were unfolding before me, Ivy was having a field day.

Holyfuckola Rachel, check this place out, you can do some serious rolling about sex on that bed without worrying about falling off. Let's go and see the other suite!

I chose the second room in the end. The set up was similar but the bedding was a beautiful rose pink, and as soon as I saw it, I had a vision in my mind of the contrast between mine and AJ's skin highlighted by the blush of the sheets and lust melted me from the inside out.

I'd done as he'd suggested and given myself the afternoon to have a loll in the spa, a swim, a hot stones massage and a pedicure for good measure. When I tried to pay for my treatment, I was told not to worry about it that everything was taken care of. I smiled graciously but I heard Ivy guffaw with delight.

It was getting on for 6pm by the time I'd finished. I got dressed in my 'Friday evening' outfit, the one Nai and I had spent the last three days talking about, rummaging through my wardrobe for, and eventually deciding on, soft jersey, navy palazzo pants and a white halter neck that showed off my shoulders, I felt elegant and sexy. I sat outside on the terrace with a glass of wine enjoying the sunshine and studiously ignoring my nicotine monster demanding his fix.

I was jingling with anticipation and in my heightened state I felt his presence before I saw him. I've no idea how I knew he was close by, but I did. I turned to look for him just as he came into view walking towards me. He was wearing a crisp, white cotton shirt that fit his slim body where it touched, and a suit in the same navy as the pants I was wearing, he had his jacket thrown over his shoulder and as he came closer to me his face was wreathed in a smile.

Ivy guffawed again. *He's like Mr Darcy Rachel, look at him, he just needs a wet shirt and we've cracked it! Wow mate shit like this doesn't happen to us very often.*

I felt shy, almost embarrassed by his beauty - he was out of this world. He plonked himself on the seat next to me, for some reason I couldn't look at him. He didn't turn to me either. Instead, he broke my tension by saying, "All week I have been trying to work out how to greet you this evening, a peck on the cheek would probably be the most appropriate gesture, but you see, after the effect you had on me when we last shook hands, I'm not sure it's safe to touch you again in a public place."

As I let my filthiest, most delighted laugh rip out of me our heads turned towards each other. He was laughing too, his eyes shone warmth into mine and my shyness evaporated, replaced by a connection I'd never really believed existed.

19

We stayed sat on the terrace and shared a bottle of wine. Apart from the quality of the sex in my dreams and the voltage of his touch I knew so little about this man I was sat next to. And yet it felt like I'd known him all my life. I was certainly familiar with which side he dressed himself on because I'd seen it for myself the last time we met, and I could see it again now.

We flirted outrageously but without any sexual references. When he talked, I couldn't take my focus away from his lips, when I talked, I couldn't tear myself away from his eyes. I lost track of everything apart from him until the Maître'D came to find us to let us know our table was ready. I didn't even know we were waiting for a table, but the thought of food made me hungry. As we stood to allow him to guide us into the dining room, AJ stepped aside to let me pass. I almost reached out to touch him but pulled myself back at the last second and instead, I gloried in my best 'check-out-how-sexy-I-am' walk that I hadn't done since I was a teenager walking past a building site.

Dinner was delicious, as was the chat - our banter was easy and fun. He was great company, and I could feel the friendship flourish between us. When he mentioned he'd had a very early start, a busy day and long drive and he was ready to turn in for the night, my whole body burst into life. Maybe now we'd get to be close to each other, maybe now we'd touch. But we didn't, he pulled my chair out for me, he opened every door for me, he leaned in towards me temptingly close when he pushed the button to call the lift. My mouth was watering with the anticipation of us finally being in a private space together and as we arrived at the first floor, he asked me which room I'd chosen for myself, and it occurred to me that he wasn't taking me back to our place for sex, he was walking me home.

As the penny dropped, I stopped in the middle of the wide, thickly carpeted corridor. He'd been walking alongside me, and he turned to see where I was. I couldn't keep the shock, disappointment, and bemusement out of my voice, "Are we in separate rooms AJ? Did I have one of the suites and you have the other?"

He walked back to me and came into my personal space; electricity shot through me again and I felt the hairs on the back of my neck stand up. "I wasn't sure what was going on between us Rachel. I booked two rooms as insurance. I had myself convinced that the connection we have was in my imagination and that I'd built you up too far in my mind. But being with you again I realise now that wasn't the case there is a breathtaking amount of chemistry and potential between us. The last thing I want to do is ruin it by coming on to you too soon, by being impatient for you. I think we both need time to do this justice."

I nodded and smiled, and as much as I wanted to feel him closer than he was already, preferably inside me, I kept my hands by my sides and resisted the urge to reach for him. I tried to calm my leaping libido down a notch and restarted my walk. For the first time ever, the key card worked, unlocking the door the first time, I quickly stepped into my room. I didn't instigate the longed-for kiss because I didn't trust myself not to rugby tackle him to the floor and ride him right where he was. "Thank you for a wonderful evening AJ, I've had a fabulous time and as much as I want to be with you tonight I agree there is something incredibly special between us and I'm content to wait to explore all the possibilities of it. I'm looking forward to tomorrow already."

✳✳✳✳✳✳✳✳✳✳

I was so full of anticipation and sexual tension I didn't think I'd be able to get any sleep. I stripped naked, climbed onto the huge bed and slid between the rose-pink sheets, the pulsing sensation coming from my newly waxed vagina was begging me to play with it, but I resisted the temptation. I didn't want anything to spoil my first time with AJ, I wanted to save myself. Ivy and me had a bit of a giggle about me being Elizabeth Bennet to AJ's Fitzwilliam Darcy Esquire and I eventually fell asleep to the sound of her voice discussing the finer points of the works of Jane Austen.

20

Now

I wake up early the next morning to the sound of the birds singing and lie for a while surrounded in luxurious bed linen, captivated by the view through the windows at the bottom of my bed. The need to pee eventually overtakes me and as I make my way to the bathroom, I notice a piece of hotel stationary that had been slid under the door. It's a funny and very sweet invitation for our second date. Starting with breakfast and ending with dinner, AJ has provided lots of options for the hours in between – not one of them is sex in the bath.

In the end we mostly ignore the entertainment AJ has suggested. After breakfast we have a walk in the hotel gardens and find a seat in a sweet-smelling shady spot underneath a rose pergola. Surrounded by cushions we settle ourselves at either end of the long deep bench. We lounge opposite each other, and we talk. The air between us is thick with sensuality, but we both do a very good job of ignoring it. The more we deny it the more our attraction entices me, it is so palpable it feels like foreplay.

Ivy has taken the day off. She knows I am deeply content.

I find out he'd often thought about having kids, but he'd never met the right woman. He has never been married for the same reason. He has a massive family, that is mostly dys-functional and, apart from his much younger sister, loving and supportive. He has never smoked a cigarette. He admits to some drug use in his early student years, but he'd become bored by it and hasn't touched any since. He drinks, but only socially, and he runs ten miles a day, rain or shine.

In the face of his almost abstemious confession, I want him to know more about me than my fantastic one-handed spliff rolling skills, or mine and Jude's coke scoring competition. I don't want the shallowness of the drugs and booze lifestyle to sully his opinion of me. Instead, when I answer his questions about the things that make me, me I dig deep into the places I'd discovered existed when I'd been with Felicity, and I let him see the real Rachel.

I try to keep away from the subject of my unfaithful husband and my general devastation but how can I when it makes up so much of my recent past? He is an excellent listener and because of that I reveal a lot more than I should, considering I am supposed to be on my best seduction behaviour and driving him mad with desire. I drop my guard completely and allow myself to trust AJ enough to know that Tim's opinion of me will not influence his obvious appreciation of who I am working hard to become.

We are apart for less than an hour while we both dress for dinner. I am so determined to live in the moment, to bask in the warm glow the day has left me with, and to enjoy the giddy expectancy of the evening ahead, I sing in the shower and even dry between my toes.

Wearing just my newly acquired bra and knickers I stand in front of the full-length mirror. This time I don't need Ivy to help me come to terms with how I look. I can see for myself I am a beautiful, curvaceous woman, full of confidence and a light that shines from the inside out.

AJ is waiting in the bar for me when I arrive, a bottle of my favourite champagne sat on ice waiting to be opened. I can't remember the last time I've felt so spectacularly special.

We talk and laugh through most of our dinner but immediately after the waiter takes our main course plates away I feel the atmosphere between us change. I hear AJ take a deep breath, "I have something I need to speak to you about Rachel."

He looks and sounds so serious my heart sinks with fear at what's coming next. I feel the blood drain from my face as I nod my head slightly to encourage him to carry on.

"I think about you all the time, I find myself fantasising about you."

I can feel the colour come back into my cheeks and my eyebrows shoot up in a comical suggestive way.

His laugh is genuine. "Not like that, well not all the time." He looks at me and gives me a bashful grin, "My fantasies aren't all about taking your clothes off and exploring every inch of your body. More often than not I find my imagination puts you firmly into my future, living with you, being with you, you being with me."

I stare at his face. I have nothing to say to that, I hear Ivy clock in for her evening shift and shout gleefully, *fuuuuuuuuuccckkkkk I wasn't expecting that!*

He fills the chasm of my silence. "I know what you've been through Rachel and how much that has hurt you, but I promise you this, if you and I are together I will never let you down. I'll buy you a shot gun and if I ever so much as look at another woman you can shoot my bollocks off."

The sincerity in his voice makes my heart burst open. I feel a rush of love for him that is so strong I stand up and lean over the table; I put my hands either side of his face and kiss his forehead. It's the first physical contact we've had since we met more than twenty four hours before.

He grabs my hand and pulls me to him, he is strong, and he has taken me by surprise. I stumble towards him knocking the table with my hip and I hear glasses and bottles chime as they ricochet off each other with the force. By the time I am in his space he is standing too, waiting for me to join him, he mirrors my face-cupping action but instead of coming in for a kiss as I expect, he holds me away from him, he runs both this thumbs along my cheekbones, around the shape of my face and under my chin.

Everything that I have stored in me that is solid, hard, fossilised by pain, rejection and grief instantly liquefies. In one simple action he's expressed his emotions and I feel treasured, adored, worshipped - and it feels wonderful; it feels like I am home. Then he kisses me, and that is perfect too.

I want him so badly. I want to feel him all over me, inside me; I want the sensation of his skin on mine, I want to bring my dream from all those years ago to life, to look down at our conjoined bodies moving with the same rhythm as we seal each other's fate. I want him. He still has my face in his hands and the moan that comes from the back of my throat is a combination of lust and contentment. I realise he's felt it escape from me when he moves his hips slightly and I feel his erection graze my lower belly.

I hear someone say politely, but pointedly, "Well I never..." and I drop back to earth with a bump. We draw ourselves apart, he is still holding my face, tipping it towards his, our eyes find each other's, and we start to laugh. Without looking for the interrupter of our passion we separate again and sit delicately in our own chairs. The waiter appears instantly and asks me if I've decided on my dessert.

AJ's cock please, and if it's at all possible can she have it for breakfast too?

I discover how hard it is to swallow Deconstructed Lemon Meringue when you are chock-a-block full of lust. Apparently red wine's ok though, as is brandy, because I get through plenty of that.

After AJ's declaration and our public display of passion our conversation changes; we stop talking about our past and our dysfunctional families and start to talk about the things we've always wanted. I listen to him explaining how ambitious he is for his career; he has the next five years mapped out and the five after that are in his sights. He wants to be the best he can be, and I completely understand that. His drive is impressive. He's a skillful man with an excellent reputation, and I don't doubt he'll achieve everything he wants. He turns the attention to me again and asks me about my job in New York, what had it been that had made me want it so badly, that I was prepared to emigrate for it?

The only answer that comes into my head is, "Because it's in New York." I deflect his question by suggesting that we go and sit outside and get some air. Someone brings us blankets and we sit next to each other on the stone steps that lead down to the water's edge. We are wrapped in our own red and black tartan cocoons, two deeply connected individuals keeping their distance from each other.

His question about my new job gets lost in the midst of our relocation and once we get ourselves settled again his enthusiasm to express his vision to me cranks up a notch. He is painting a picture that looks like every girl's dream; a life with a man who promises me faithfulness and security, a man who I have literally dreamt about, who fills me with so much desire I can imagine making love to him for the rest of my life and still not being able to get enough of him. And I can see that he feels the same way.

During the day I'd told him a story about my childhood when my dad had made a regular joke about 'going to see a man about a dog' when he'd been going to the pub. How I'd always woken up the next day hoping he'd finally brought one home, how disappointed I'd been when there never was one. AJ refers to it again now, "We could get that dog you always wanted. Maybe we could get your dad to get it." I laugh with him.

The nearly autumn chill starts to soak into my bones, and I shiver violently. AJ moves up a step to sit behind me, his thighs hug into my waist, his chin rests on the top of my head, and he wraps his blanketed arms around me. I lean back into his body. I can feel his ten-miles-a-day healthy heartbeat bounce against the back of my ribs, and we sit there for the longest time in comfortable silence, listening to the night creatures, watching the breeze ruffle the surface of the lake. Suddenly the outside lights of the hotel are turned off plunging us into darkness and, like a magic trick, the sky is unexpectedly full of stars.

He squeezes me tighter into a hug. "I'd love to take credit for arranging that, but it was just a happy accident." When he talks, the movement of his jaw rustles my hair, and I feel his voice reverberate from him and through me at the same time as I hear his words. Being here with him feels like love, and safety.

We both lie back slightly to look at the vastness of the sky and the intensity of the stars against its darkness. We fall back into our silence. There is no need for words for a while. I let the warmth of his body and the depth of his feelings sink into me. I am looking for the words I can use to paint him a picture of my vision for the future, a way that I can join in with his dreams and ambitions for our future together; but there are none. As I stare at the enormity of the sky I realise why I am finding it so hard to describe how I see my life unfolding. It's because I don't know. I've spent so long trying to keep my body and soul from falling apart that I genuinely don't know what it is I want my future to look like. I've lost sight of me and of it.

It is a blank canvas.

And I tell him so.

21

I ask him to come and sit next to me so I can see him. We sit facing each other with our knees touching and I grasp his hands into mine and pull them as close to my heart as I can. I know he'll feel the sincerity of my words as I say them.

The concept of the life AJ is sharing with me is a wonderful one and part of me yearns to be with him. I feel strongly our life together would be happy, but I also know without doubt there would be a cost for me. I am too early into my self-discovery, still too raw from Tim's influence to be the woman AJ deserves me to be, to be the woman I deserve to be. If I join in with this dream, I will be giving up on the chance to truly discover the woman I have the potential to be. I don't quite know who that is yet, but I know I need to find out, and I need to do it alone.

My intrinsic reaction to Olivia's rejection had been to blame myself. No matter how much work I'd done to repair my spirit with Felicity, at the first sign of rejection I'd automatically fallen back into mental self-harm. Tim's detrimental influence, like it or not, is still a lingering powerful force. I am still branded by him and the stubborn groove on my finger from my wedding ring is a constant reminder of that. The friendship AJ and I have developed in the last couple of days is an irrevocable one, and as much as I know I am hurting him, it is my deep respect for him that brings out the truth. I don't believe I could speak with another person the way I do with him tonight, because I know primarily, more than anything else, he wants what's best for me, and I for him.

As far as I am concerned AJ is too good a man to let Tim ruin him too.

To add some light to the shade, I tell him about my dream, seeing myself sat on top of him, riding him. I describe the shock I'd had when I saw him again, and eventually without any timidity at all I tell him about my furtive, interminable-dry-spell-breaking wank in the toilets at the hotel.

He throws his head back and laughs delightedly and then confesses he'd done exactly the same thing after I'd driven away from him.

At some point just before dawn one of the staff comes to check on us to make sure we're ok. We aren't really, we are both dismayed by my decision, but, because I believe that it makes everything feel just a little bit better, I order tea, and he orders several slices of toast.

The daylight is taking over from the stars when the food arrives. I pour the tea while he butters the toast, and just to prove how perfect he is for me, he gives me just the right amount of Marmite. I study him while he is concentrating on his task, he looks beautiful in the morning light, he looks beautiful all the time. My heart aches.

I think in the end it's the food that finishes me off; the mixture of carbs and sugar turn my yawning muscles up to full, and despite my will to keep this magical day alive, I find myself drooping.

Our fingers are interlaced as we walk back into reception. There are a couple of indulgent smiles from the receptionist and the night porter who is just finishing for the day. We step into the lift away from anyone else that might see us and sink back into the kiss we'd started hours and hours ago after his heartfelt declaration. This time we are gentle with each other. He is so tender it nourishes me; it is the easiest thing in the world to return his unforced passion. Without discussion we both make our way to my room, the crisp clean turned down sheets are still the perfect colour of dusky roses, the pillows look irresistible. I have a desperate urge to lie down, to feel the welcoming comfort and warmth the bed promises my tired body. I kick off my shoes and surrender myself into it. AJ comes into the bed behind me, he curls himself into my back and encloses my entirety with his body, he kisses my shoulder and pulls the duvet over us both and we fall asleep.

He leaves the hotel – and me - a few hours later. I can't ignore the huge regret I feel as I watch him go, but I also take time to appreciate the amount of courage it has taken me to say no to the world on a plate that he represents; it even came with a Jack Russell, and I've always wanted one of those.

I don't check out that day or the day after, I stay where I am until I've worked through my regret and finally I feel ready to leave. When I do, instead of going home, I go in the opposite direction and I drive aimlessly for a while until I see another place I fancy staying in. I am embracing the experience of the freedom Ivy and I had talked about. I have Nai's car but apart from that I have no reason to go home. I offer her the use of my Dad's Ford Mondeo to tide her over, but her text back is something along the lines of not being seen dead in it even when it was brand new twenty years ago and to expect a very large bill for the taxis she is going to be taking.

❋❋❋❋❋❋❋❋❋❋❋

If I'd learned anything at all in Sardinia - apart from how flexible my body is - it is the healing powers of time spent on my own.

I need to explore my inability to see myself with a future, my lack of vision has kicked me up the arse and I need time to contemplate some things - well, an overabundance of things if I am being completely frank. I have an immense amount of thoughts to think, and a persistent inner voice called Ivy that will not shut the fuck up.

I am been deeply disappointed that I haven't been able to see myself in AJ's plan for his life. Equally it seems melodramatic to mourn over the end of a relationship that had never really started.

But as Inner Voice Ivy points out, *It's the loss of the potential that's a fucker Rach. You didn't just say no to him, did you? If you were going to do that long term relationship thing with anyone then he's your man. What you really said no to is being with anyone at all. You've acknowledged your need to be on your own, and that's a big step.*

I find it hard to argue with that irrefutable logic.

I am still in the hotel with pink sheets when I get a brief text from Petra saying she's sorry she hasn't been in contact for a while. She says she's been balls deep in the restructure of her department, but she really wants to touch base with me as soon as she can find the time in her hectic schedule.

I haven't even finished reading it before I feel Ivy wind herself up to the occasion. There is nothing she loves more than to deride any saying that needs inverted commas.

Oh please, 'touch base.' Promise me you're not going to start saying shit like that when you 'commence your new career' - I think I might have to stop speaking to you again if you do. And if there's one hint of blue sky thinking or running anything up a flagpole, I'm off. I can't stand all that corporate blah blah.

I know I don't know much about my future, that much is pretty obvious. The blank canvas I'd been faced with when I was trying to share my dreams with the best-lover-I-never-had is testament to that, but Ivy's jocular piss-take on corporate life starts to unwrap another layer of subjects for my consideration.

When AJ had been talking about his ambition for his career and asked me what attracted me to my new job, the only thing I'd been able to come up with was its location.

My initial reluctance to share that in the light of his fierce ambition confirmed to me I didn't really want to be 'balls deep' into work or have a 'hectic schedule' - it all sounds too much like Mrs R P Bradbury to me. I am Ms R Stone now and the only thing I really wanted out of the deal Petra had offered me was to go to New York; because I haven't been yet.

As soon as that thought comes to me my body responds in its own way; my ribs feel less constricting, and I am able to breathe deeper. I hear Ivy slap her thigh in delight.

About bloody time. I thought you'd never come round to my way of thinking. I know how much of yourself you've invested into your professional life but why does it really matter? You've got nothing to prove to anyone. Why keep punishing yourself for the sake of ambition? Use all that energy on something that makes you well in your head and gives you your health back, something that brings you happiness and peace with who you are.

"I can't let Petra down; I've already accepted the job."

Bullshit Rachel, she'll understand; under all that power dressing and air kissing she's still your friend and she wants you to be happy. There's probably a queue of eager overachievers gagging for that position. Let one of them have it. I dare you to text her back now tell her you've changed your mind; you don't want that job.

As soon as she says it, I know with all my heart she's right. I don't want the job. I don't want to go back to fifty-hour weeks, chasing targets and measuring my self-worth by how high up a league table I am. I might be a bit rudderless in terms of the general direction of my life but maybe it's time for me to embrace that. And rather than strive for something I think I should be doing, take some time to learn what I want to do. Who I want to be.

Now you're getting it.

After that comment Ivy leaves me in peace for a day or so, and I immerse myself in the game-changing decisions I've just made. Trying them on for size. I am beginning to like the sound of my life being about me and who I want to be.

She comes back to me again as I am sat under the shade of an oak tree, eating a Mr Whippy ice cream with my feet in the clear but cold water of a river. I am engrossed watching teenagers, and some grownups who should know better, jump off a high bridge into the deeper, faster-running water further upstream.

Do you fancy a go?

Her voice makes me jump slightly. "No of course not, I like life far too much to start throwing myself off bridges."

That's the best news I've had for ages. I wasn't sure I'd ever hear you say that again, that you like life, I must confess you had me worried for a while back there. I thought we were done for.

To all intents and purposes my ice cream is nearly finished, but I've done the thing my brother had taught me, I've shoved the flake down through the ice cream to the bottom of the cone, so even if it looks to the outside world as though all I have left is the empty boring bit, I know I've saved the best till last. I raise it up in front of my face, a salutation to the fitting metaphor and before I push it in my mouth I say, "I'm not done for, Ivy, not by any stretch of the imagination. It feels to me like I'm just about to start. Here's to leaving the best till last."

I watch another teenager drop feet first into the depths below him, a scream of terror quickly followed by a yell of triumph when he survives the experience and discovers he's alive enough to bob back to the surface again. It reminds me of something from way back, something only the two of us would know about. "Do you remember that documentary we once saw about New Zealand and the footage of the oldest bungee jump in the world? That kind of jumping off a bridge I'd definitely do. I've wanted to do it ever since I watched that programme."

I bet if you were there you wouldn't do it. I bet you'd chicken out.

"Now how would you know that, smart arse? We don't know what I'm capable of yet do we?" She isn't always gracious in her defeats isn't Ivy, so I presume she's changing the subject when she speaks again after a slight pause.

Do you remember talking to Tim about your 20th wedding anniversary?

I'm not expecting that, she never lets me talk about Tim, why is she bringing him up now? He has no place here with me on a sunny Thursday afternoon eating ice cream. But she's started so there's no way to mute her. I let her carry on.

He wanted a show-off party and a fortnight getting pissed on cocktails in an adults-only resort in the Maldives. You wanted to take a couple of months off work and go to Australia, didn't you? You wanted to travel. You could do that now, take a trip, to wherever you feel like.

I feel the grip of possibility suddenly seize me. The most alive I'd felt in the last few years was when I'd trusted myself and dropped feet first into the unknown, why shouldn't I do that again? And just like that; my pieces fall into place. Ivy doesn't say much to me after that. She doesn't have to.

The next day I buy a backpack and then drive home to collect my passport.

THE BEGINNING

I'd like to express my gratitude to you the reader, for investing your time and money on this novel.

I sincerely hope you enjoyed it.

If so, please will you take a moment to post a review on your social media and/or the platform you bought The Redundant Wife from.

You can also find me on Instagram and TikTok @kay_green_author come and say 'Hello' it would be great to meet you.

Thank you

Kay x

Acknowledgement

Thank you everyone who has encouraged me to realise my dreams of becoming an author. You are many and I am grateful for all of you.

Mum, my heart beats for us both.

Dad, David and Aunty Joan I love you. Thank you so much for never, ever reading this book. Trust me it's the best for everyone concerned.

Erica, you have always been the biggest supporter of my writing - and so much more - your encouragement and belief in me are part of the foundations of this book and all the others I will write.

Fiona, your 'I want to go to sleep but I can't put this book down' texts to me while you were test reading TRW has been the light at the end of my tunnel many times. You have never questioned my ability or my ambition.

Nadine, you confessed you'd been terrified to test read for me (in case it was shit!) and told me you began to read the first page with one eye closed and your fingers crossed. Your delight, enthusiasm and editing skills have completed this process for me.

Last but not least. My boy Salty Phil, you have the patience of a saint, I can't wait to test it again with my next novel. I love you.

www.ingramcontent.com/pod-product-compliance
Lightning Source LLC
Chambersburg PA
CBHW021228190726
48289CB00005B/1224